P9-EMP-844

THEMINEFIELDS

THEMINEFIELDS

A NOVEL BY **STEVEN C. EISNER**

Cindy,

With Affection,

When Words Count Press
Baltimore, Maryland

Copyright © 2012 by Steven C. Eisner

All rights reserved. No part of this book may be reproduced in any form or by any electronic or mechanical means, including information in writing from the publisher, except by a reviewer and the like who may quote brief passages in a review.

First Edition

When Words Count Press
P.O. Box 26900
Baltimore, MD 21212
www.whenwordscountpress.com

The characters and events in this book are fictitious. Any similarity to real persons, living or dead, is coincidental and not intended by the author.

First printing 2012

Library of Congress Cataloging-in-Publication Data

Eisner, Steven C.
THE MINEFIELDS / Steven C. Eisner 1st ed.

ISBN 978-19378360-2-3
LCCN: 2011941963

Book design by Asha Hossain

Printed in the United States of America

For Harriet & Henry Eisner

THEMINEFIELDS

CHAPTER 1

I drew open the curtain to my eighty-three-year old dad's emergency room cubicle at Mt. Zion Hospital. It was 6:30 a.m., a half-hour after I had received his summons: "Sam, come right away." I arrived well before my mother and brother. Our Harry Spiegel was dying. He lay there still and silent, a thermometer in his mouth, his eyes closed. At least five tubes ran from his arms, legs, and groin. The ribbons of his hospital gown were untied and the flaps spread over him like a second top sheet. These were the least of his problems.

A heavy, soiled sandbag had been draped over his right leg up to his hip. I wondered whether the patchwork of stains had come only from his insides or was left over from other soldiers in decay? The sandbag had a purpose—to stop the bleeding after a routine injection poke. I understood this pattern. My dad was on the blood thinner Coumadin. With such patients, simple needle pricks could erupt into small geysers. So there he was, my poor, sweet Old Faithful.

Despite the respirator tube delivering oxygen, Dad's face remained a sickly, asphyxiated shade of yellowish gray. In addition, just about every body part where a needle-wielding nurse could find a vein to tap was now purple, blue, or black. In some places the patterns formed a rainbow. He was war torn by the months of blood taken and blood given and the constant stream of antibiotics that had been infused into him to try to counter the shutdowns of successive organs. It had gotten to where only a pump and a hose could void his urine, collecting it in a clear bag at the foot of his bed. Everything on Harry was hanging out. I mean everything.

When I walked up to Harry's bedside, he slowly lifted his hand, palm toward me in a simulated Indian-chief greeting. Then, he drew in his fingers, turned his wrist, and gave me a quick thumbs-down, as if to say, "My dear son, it's over." That day he looked at me with such tenderness. That day I was not the brute, as he once called me. I seemed only to be his beloved Sam.

His eyes, when open, remained fixed on mine. I took his left hand and started rubbing the back of his battered paw as if he were one of my children.

It was at this point that Harry's nurse chose to swing around the curtain long enough to bark her report over the TV playing in the background. "Your dad had a very shitty night." Fortunately, she left quickly, ducking back out into the hall. I'm sure she hoped both Harry and his needs would be long gone by the time she returned for her next rotation.

"What time is it?" my dad whispered in an agitated voice. He looked quite fragile, much the way I remembered his mother, Omie, looking when I sat with her the night she died twenty years earlier. "There is no clock here. I…um…need a clock," Harry said. "Penn Medicine always had a clock I could see. Not in this…um…*farkakt* hospital!"

While still rubbing his hand with the tips of my fingers, I said, "It's 6:30 in the morning, Dad. You can tell by what's on TV. That's George Foreman, trying to sell us a chicken rotisserie oven. Only three payments of $29."

"You know, I don't…um…really like chicken, Sam. Now if …um… the 'heavyweight' had one that cooks a goose, that would be an entirely different story." He gave me a weak smile for which I grinned broadly.

Harry leaned up from his angled bed that I had notched to about forty degrees to try to make him more comfortable. Was the bed in an

2

incline, recline, or decline position? Wherever it was, it didn't bring his head close enough to mine for what he was about to say. Determined, he heaved himself forward, as if he were on his ninth chin-up when his body could only withstand two.

"Sam…um…I'm drowning here. I can't get comfortable." He pulled himself even closer to me. "Get me opium. Or put a pillow over my head. One or the other will do."

Dad had always kept busy. It was then that I realized Harry was at work orchestrating his death. There may have been no clock handy to watch the seconds tick down, but he knew what time it was.

I held my dad's hand more firmly. I shifted his pillows. Fed him ice chips with my fingers. I asked his surly nurse three times for some Sprite, which had become my father's drink of choice since his health failed. Would 'Mother Teresa' actually bring it?

"Here's your Coke," she said at last, spilling some of it as she handed it to me. I sighed. Harry seemed not to notice. I bent the straw and slipped it into the cup and watched him drink. I excused myself to go to the bathroom, making it very clear to him that I would be right back. I had turned on *Sunday Morning*. "There's your friend Charles Osgood." Dad looked scared. His eyes followed mine, much as a dog would fix on its master after being tied to a parking meter. He continued to stare at me as I slipped beyond the curtain.

My real goal was to find the overseeing emergency room doctor to get a report on Dad's condition and to figure out a plan. As I suspected, many of Harry's vitals had shut down. His lungs were filling with water. He was indeed drowning, although the doctor called it "great discomfort." He said, "At a time like this, we give patients in your dad's condition a powerful shot of morphine."

"And if he were your dad, doctor?"

He said with great empathy, "I'd give him one right now. There may be a few radical procedures left to preserve his life for another week or two. If you're asking me, I'd apply a heavier dose an hour after the first."

I said, "I appreciate the options. Let's go for the two rounds of opium, as my dad calls it. I'd like to respect his wishes. He's very uncomfortable."

"I'm heading to see him right now. By the way, your dad's on his game. Morphine is an opiate derivative."

"Right, and Doctor, I need to call my mother and brother to see what's taking them so long to get here. How long's our window?"

"A pair of hours, max." Together we walked back, and when we got to Dad's bed, the doctor spoke kindly. "Mr. Spiegel, I know you're very uncomfortable. I'm going to give you some morphine that will help you sleep. Within a few minutes, I promise you, sir, you'll feel better. Scout's honor."

Dad patted the doctor's hand. Then he patted mine as he shot me a blink that approximated a wink. I kissed him on his forehead and turned away as tears ran down my face and the morphine seeped into his vein. Then he asked, "Where's Elizabeth?" I was working so hard to be his finest possible concertmaster, and I felt badly that I hadn't as yet delivered his first violinist—the love of his life—to bid him farewell.

The farewell business had always seemed like a lot of theatrics for the 'big screen,' the tearjerker ending with musical swells, sadness on steroids. Until I experienced the pain of goodbye for myself, I had no idea how excruciating it was to lose a loved one. Only as Dad's life was on the verge of ending did I realize that, in addition to the sadness, we have a need, as feeling beings, to bring closure to the lives of those we love. We seek our rightful place in the proceedings. And my role, at that moment, was to ease him into the next.

I said, "Mom will be arriving with Mikey in a few minutes." This time he didn't bother to approximate a wink or a blink. He was a maestro until the finale, when his first violinist failed to show. My mother and my brother, Mikey—down from New York—didn't or couldn't understand the urgency of the moment. Harry's eyes were closed and his breathing was pronounced. He looked peaceful. The trumpet that had started playing the finale to *Sunday Morning* seemed prophetic under Dad's staccato snore. "Nurse Ratched" never returned. A chipper young blonde took over instead. The second injection was administered. Occasionally, my father opened his eyes to see if my mother had arrived—which she had, along with my brother—and perhaps he also opened them to discern if he was, indeed, still alive. I kissed his forehead again and now made room for Mikey and Mom to hold his hand. We three watched Harry W. Spiegel, calm and inexorably still. I sat by the curtain. Twenty minutes later his breathing stopped. *Sunday Morning* came to its end. The trumpet cleared and the kettledrum was left to solo out with a light patter, fading to quiet.

CHAPTER 2

I glanced under the wing of the plane and saw, emerging in a cloud, my dad's face: his hooked nose, his large eyes, his broad smile, and his kinky hair. My comment was muffled by the noise of the engines, "So you decided to visit me on a cloud. Our lives become storybooks, eh?" That's how I saw Harry Spiegel again for the first time, six months after his funeral, as I was en route home to Philadelphia. I was flying Star Spangled Air, of course. Every paid seat helped keep our client in the sky to see another day. It was the least I could do.

With the LA pitch behind me, and two local international advertising agencies competing against us, to win we needed a solid A, maybe it had to be an A+. I gave our performance a B+. Still looking out the window, I said, "So, Harry, there goes $150,000 in out-of-pocket new business expenses. Not to mention the six weeks of agency time to prepare. You should have paid me a visit sooner and perhaps that 150 would still be hugging our bottom line." Harry always swallowed hard when we took this kind of risk.

I knew my dad's conflicted sense about spending money. It stemmed from his Holocaust experience. In his late youth, Harry lived in so much uncertainty, it became hard for him to be anything but miserly; he was haunted by the constant fear of losing it all again. His desire to sell the ad agency out from under me on two occasions taught me as much over our years together in business. I learned he didn't want to topple my dreams, but that in his mind, he always had fears about life and security. Just like a squirrel living in October every month of the year, Harry was busy amassing his acorns, always hoarding as many as he could find. He just wouldn't, couldn't relax, even when his bank account contained the fully retained $1.2 million I had paid him to buy Spiegel & Associates. And once he put it to work, over time it compounded to three.

I remember him holding out on buying that silver Mercedes he wanted so badly. It was only after he survived his second heart valve replacement that he finally convinced himself. "Since I'm not a goner, I've run out of excuses to procrastinate further on my Mercedes purchase." But who prompted him so? Elizabeth, my mom who he adored. She was the one who finally convinced him to buy out the founder of his advertising agency, which became Spiegel & Associates, and then on my watch I named it Spiegel Communications.

My mom was the one who urged Dad to join the country club. "Harry, it will be good for business." To move to the larger house. "We need it for entertaining." To buy the condominium overlooking the ocean. "It will be good for client crab feasts." Then there was the Mary Cassatt painting, where she said, "Harry, I just want it. It will be the best investment we ever make." My folks loved American Impressionist artists and had fine art shipped to them on loan from New York galleries, mainly because my father knew he could ship them back COD, which is precisely what he did most often.

That is, until Elizabeth stomped, "Harry, you are not sending this beautiful Mary Cassatt *Mother and Child* back to Chapallia Galleries or you can send me right along with it." I remember Dad scratching his head, pondering the ultimatum. But he knew that once Elizabeth had spoken, the Cassatt was staying. And in the end, she said, "For Christ's sake, Harry, buy that goddamn car you want so much and spite Hitler already."

Oh, Harry, I thought, as I looked at his image on his cloud, *I could use some of you now.* This all-night flight would get me home for the

STEVEN C. EISNER

lunch meeting with the Pennsylvania State Lottery. Our agency would present the new ad campaign and the results of our most recent research, which showed our theme (*Just imagine what you could do!*) had achieved unaided recall of 52 percent and that when just a few words of the line were prompted, its awareness level jumped to 73 percent. This was the best pair of numbers we'd seen since we had won the account a decade earlier.

I had finished reading *The Human Stain* and planned to take an Ambien to help me sleep. But I forgot to take my Dopp kit from my suitcase before checking it curbside. My cell phone and laptop were in the suitcase too. I wondered when I'd last sat by myself in the dark, unable to sleep without any of my communication gizmos?

As we flew over the Rockies I closed my eyes, but my mind raced everywhere except to sleep. The next pitch was for Bermuda Tourism. I had this stirring notion of starting the commercial with passengers in line to board a plane chucking all their communication tools into a trash bin and leaving their worries and connectivity behind. *Bermuda... The Best Way to Really Get Away.* And as I mouthed this beaut out the window to Dad, he made a farting sound back at me. I smiled and retorted, "I know it stinks. I'm desperate for a vacation."

I looked at the young man across the aisle...the other poor *schlub* still awake. And what was he doing with such purpose? Probably texting his girlfriend all the news and stories he had to offer, so over coffee at her apartment there would be nothing left to say. I reminded myself to check *Webster's* to see if the verb "text" was now listed before the noun.

I had an operating officer at Spiegel Communications named Bud Ashley who, at age fifty-six, proudly reported that he could text faster than anyone else in his age bracket. He had recently mentioned this to me when he said, "I'm all thumbs, Sammy, just like the kiddies." One day from our offices, Bud texted Lance, an associate creative director who was leading a presentation in London for our online blackjack client, a large, new account for which we were creating and placing international advertising. Ten minutes into the presentation, Bud sent a text to Lance to see how things were going.

Lance returned the text by saying, "We're bombing here." We learned later that, twenty minutes in, he had recovered. By the end of the meeting, he had received a standing ovation. But due to this modern-day communication device, Bud had decided to take action on the first text bulletin and barged into my office with his newsflash. We were in the midst of updating our projections, and he subtracted out all anticipated income from this client for the remainder of the year.

I asked, "What the fuck are you doing, Bud?"

He replied with pure glee, "Modern technology. Don't you love it?" This was a $100 thousand-a-month retainer client that Bud, on a text, decided to trash. Had he not figured out how many bodies this impulse would put on the street?

Bud had become head of operations—my number two guy at Spiegel. He was the consultant I brought in to help better retain earnings after we won the Star Spangled Air account and to build Spiegel Communications to heights where we could sell our company for a high price. Bud knew the selling game, how to massage the balance sheet as he put it, "so it no longer looks like an aged hooker wearing too much makeup to camouflage her wrinkles." Instead, he promised to "turn our lovely lady into an American beauty on the order of Angelina Jolie." Was he still thinking? Or simply futzing with his hi-tech toys?

My wife, Amy, was also my business partner. She and I had made the sale of Spiegel Communications within the coming five years our major strategic objective. And there was Bud wrapped up with his gizmos instead of putting his head into real idea generating. Were we all becoming connectivity crazy? Was it more important to learn about the intricacies of the newest device instead of developing something worthy of communicating?

Just then the plane plunged. Every sleeping head popped forward as rows of pillows fell to the aisle like Frisbees to the grass. I felt as if I had just swallowed my stomach. Were we going down? Was this how I'd close my life? By myself, in a plane without Ambien, and feeling every second of the crash? Would I see all the carnage, and then become part of it? As more than just the fasten-your-seatbelt light flashed on, I panicked—I didn't have my cell to say good-bye to my wife and kids.

The pilot broke the silence to reassure us, "Ladies and gentlemen, what we just experienced was a little dip." Dip, my ass. The plane felt like the elevator broke loose from its harness. The pilot moved on to discuss the weather and our projected arrival time in Philadelphia. Now, had we been flying Southwest Airlines instead of Star Spangled Air, the pilot would have continued chatting about the clogged highways on the ground below.

Southwest had learned how to skew bad news so that it felt pretty darned good, whether it was about rough takeoffs, bumps, or delays. Spin-doctor pilots weren't a major annoyance for me. What I really disliked about Southwest were its attempts to knock my client, Star Spangled Air, out of their biggest hub: Philadelphia. Since late 2001 when Spiegel Communications had won this prized account, saving this hub had become by far our most critical assignment. Losing PHL to Southwest would certainly stop much of the fluttering of our flagship account, crippling their efforts to emerge from the bankruptcy courts. As for Spiegel, we could lose our largest piece of business. Such a loss would have a devastating effect on us.

Although our victories for Star Spangled Air were energizing me, all the turmoil, with its life-and-death implications for Spiegel, terrified my wife. With my father no longer around to do the grousing, had Amy taken up his slack as world-class worrier? Was Amy becoming my new Harry Spiegel?

Despite some of my own nervous jolts at the moment, as I looked out the window to watch the red blinking lights on the wing before we landed, I thought things on the ground were looking pretty good overall. Bud was successfully retaining earnings. Our creative product was getting attention and plaudits from the marketing press. We actually thought we were close to winning the coveted O'Toole Award for creative excellence.

A healthier, more stable SSA on our accounts roster would greatly increase our purchase price when the time came. On the other hand, the loss of this account would make us far less attractive. In fact, it might ground us as well.

And so I rode the roller coaster that was my life. SSA might go up, but my relationship with my wife of twenty-eight years was plunging downward. No wonder I had become so dependent on Ambien. Our superior marketing was winning the battles in Philadelphia. But how was the war going? Exactly what was the war? Who started it and why did it rage on so? And how might it all come out in the end? I fastened my seat belt and looked out my window as we circled PHL. I saw dozens of planes slowing into gates or starting their race down runways. First, I smiled. Then I shook my head. Finally, I clenched the two arms of my seat with all I had as I prepared (*Geronimo!*) for landing.

CHAPTER 3

My wife Amy would, on occasion, proclaim at cocktail and dinner parties or when out at a restaurant with friends, "Sam here was born thirty-five years old and came out of the womb attached to his briefcase. He simply bypassed being a kid, but that didn't exclude him from becoming the prodigal son—just as we were settling in New York, Sam sprinted back to Philadelphia to save his dad's business. Built it up tenfold. Then bought it from him for $1.2 million. It was like giving all the money he had made back to his father. Who gets a son like that? And get this—he kept Harry on his payroll for an additional seven years. Paid his country club dues and healthcare premiums."

I often wondered…was anyone ever asking Amy for this often volunteered dissertation? Then I questioned if she was saying it because she admired me. Or was it because she thought I was a first-class *schnook*?

My first turn at the cash register was with Monopoly money, and it came about with Ben G. Selborn while "working on the railroad." Our train, built in our first-grade classroom, started with cardboard boxes gathered from the grocery store. With purpose we dragged them out of my mom's Rambler and his mom's Impala and assembled and decorated them to make our very own SEPTA railway for all of our fellow students to enjoy. When we had completed our first full train, we got to work on our next. After successful brainstorming on the jungle gym, Ben and I planned our upgrades. They would be cardboard boxes that were sturdy enough to sit on, not in. We were becoming moguls! Titans! Innovators!

By this time, I was also making tickets and distributing play money for buying seats. I went around hole-punching the tickets. Ben planted himself in the first car. He was a stringy, freckled, blonde-haired kid with a cowlick that never stopped waving around when he talked. He had strong vocal cords and a great ear for imitation. Ben could reenact railroad sounds with clarity. And when everyone had bought a ticket and had settled into their seats, he would shout, "All aboard!"

The problem with Ben was that he was also a bully. He pushed, scratched, and had temper tantrums complete with every exaggerated action: the pounding of fists, kicking and screaming, all with his head facedown to the floor. He was programmed to overtake people who seemed weaker. Most kids were scared of Ben. I wasn't. I knew he was a bully, but thought that just made him a tighter-fisted businessman. And with his demeanor, no one dared get on the train without paying.

Our skills seemed complementary as we achieved, at least in our minds, greater purpose in the classroom…the building of our own Reading Railroad. Our plan was not complete until we upgraded customers to first class. That's when we added folding chairs to our string of train boxes. These chairs provided straight-back seating and required our patrons to put up additional Monopoly money.

Our boxes with connected chairs became so popular that soon we crossed boundaries into the second first-grade classroom. These rooms were becoming one long track across America. It was 1960 and Ben and I seemed to be riding some special wave, the wave that carried John Kennedy, Alan Shepard, and the Beatles into America's enthusiastic embrace.

Later, when everyone had purchased tickets and we were all seated in our train cars, the teachers took turns reading *The Little Engine That Could*. Looking back, I understand life doesn't get a whole lot better than that.

Ben and I met Billy Gottlieb in fourth grade Sunday school. We called him Billy G. He laughed at our jokes. We laughed at his. Asking to be excused from class to visit the bathroom in close succession made us a conspicuous trio. We'd beeline to Wagner's Drugstore in our khakis or navy pressed pants. We'd buy innocent stuff like Pez candies, Red Hot Dollars, and Marvel comics. On occasion, we'd get a pack of Rolos and slip them into our pockets, until Billy G. observed, "We all look like we're bringing back boners."

Mind you, we weren't getting away with anything. Our teacher, Mr. Bernstein, knew exactly what we were up to. And we actually wanted to get back to his class because he was a funny dude who was as amused with us as we were with him. Bernstein had a great sense of humor, and he was one of those teachers who was a chum. I remember once when we walked in from Wagner's, Bernstein stopped us at the door and said, "You three have to pay a toll to enter. That will be one Red Hot Dollar from each of you." Then in front of the class, before saying another word, he slowly chewed and savored each one of them before getting back to a Bible story.

As our friendships further solidified and Ben, Billy G., and I turned thirteen, we entered the Bar Mitzvah circuit. We thought we understood the difference between party gems and junky parties. The bad ones had a commonality about them: unlikable disc jockeys who stood behind their tables vacantly staring out toward the floor. Most of them were mainly vapid outcasts, early adopters of leisure suits and Nehru jackets, which they continued to wear past their fashion moments. When we looked at them as a group, we just knew they'd much rather be home in their bedrooms beating off. They stank at spinning records, and they knew it.

The best Bar Mitzvahs were the ones where there were real bands, especially those inspired by the Temptations. Soul groups with ten to twelve musicians backing up four singers in brightly colored costumes. These guys rocked and were usually imported from New York or DC. Ben, Billy G., and I got transfixed and inspired by these band extravaganzas. But most of our friends' parents couldn't or wouldn't splurge for such excess. *Tada!* Our business idea was born.

Since the days when Ben and I had gotten to know each other on the railroad, we had broadened our management skills to create magic shows for kiddie parties and neighborhood carnivals. We charged real money, which we donated to charities. There seemed to be some Barnum & Bailey in each of us. "Suppose we imitate Mick Jagger? How 'bout we put together a cool light show? Crank up the music real loud and get the kids moving like in an arena? Suppose we dress like rockers? What if we put Billy G. on the drums to accentuate our records? We could deliver the illusion of a band but at a fraction of the cost. Would this not be cool?"

If we could string these ideas together effectively, we thought we'd have something big. That Christmas, Ben and I asked our parents for two turntables and microphones. They came through with an entire PA system, and our business was born. We called it "Party Circus."

It definitely started with *chutzpah*, belief, and little self-censoring. We wanted to pitch our vision of monthly parties to the Jewish Community Center. I worked the phone for an appointment with the program manager, Ken Teitelbaum. We walked tall to the JCC lobby and were immediately greeted by Mr. Teitelbaum, a dwarf measuring no more than four feet. He was a ringer for Dr. Loveless from the TV show *The Wild, Wild West*. As we towered over him, we felt a sudden surge of empowerment.

Best friends since age four, Ben and I knew one thing at this moment: We dared not exchange glances or we'd burst out laughing. As we greeted Teitelbaum, we made sure to look straight ahead as we followed him to his office. If we cracked up, all we were working to achieve would end in an instant. We sat in the two metal folding chairs in front of his desk. Looking at him when he sat down, he reminded me of a little bird attached to his perch. And for Mr. Teitelbaum to get into his chair, he had acquired a well-practiced "spring into action" hand movement to the middle of his throne as if to pole vault his way to his seat of power. Oh my God, my entire body was about to break down and double over as I watched him get situated. Then Teitelbaum leaned forward as if chomping on a cigar, but he had no cigar. "So what do you boys have for me?"

15

Ben and I agreed that I'd start us off. "Mr. Teitelbaum, we have twelve themed nights that will appeal to the high school students who will now have a place to go on Saturday nights. We'll flip records but we'll also bring a drummer and a light show so it feels like they're watching a band. We'll keep it fun and contained." I said it just as I had practiced the night before in bed.

"Fellas, it's the kind of thing our members have been asking for, a structured fun evening where the kids get dropped off."

I continued, "Unlike others who do what we do, our themes keep the nights varied, organized, and the interest high." I felt confident, but still nervous that at any moment laughter might explode from deep inside me.

"Like what kind of themes are you talking about, fellas?" His forefinger stump went whirling around his face, tempting greater laughter, still.

"Take our *Gilligan's Island* theme. We bring hula dancers, leis, cutouts of island trees, pineapple drinks, coconut contests, beach dancing with Beach Boys music and the limbo stick."

As if still working on his cigar, Teitelbaum's lips barely parted when he spoke. "I like that idea. It's not the same old same old."

Ben chimed in, "Topical."

I trumped him, "Tropical." We felt we were hitting all the right notes that would bring Teitelbaum to a negotiation. It was this feeling— of Mr. Teitelbaum following my trawler out there at sea—that sustained me so many years in the advertising business. I'd watch many like him: And now he's coming up to the hook. Yes, sir, *he's nibbling. Now he's biting and the hook is in his mouth. Yes, sir, we've got liftoff.*

"Well, boys, how much do you charge for these nights?"

I was all set with a crisp answer. "Our basic package is $300 a night. But for a package of twelve nights, we'll reduce our fee to $250."

Teitelbaum said, "You say basic package. What are the add-ons, boys? We're a nonprofit."

Ben spoke next. "The $250 gets you the DJs, the two of us, the colored lights, and our drummer. The hula dancers, prizes, and props are all itemized in our outline here. Figure another 100 for the add-ons."

"Well, I'd want you fellas for the themes. (*Score. Double score.*) So we'd have to budget you, say 350 for...what's your name again?"

"Party Circus," I added as I handed over our business card, fresh from the printer that morning, hoping the ink hadn't smeared.

Teitelbaum continued, "We'll have food costs of, say, a hundred dollars—sodas, chips, and such." The cigar-chomping action continued between sentences, still absent a stogie. "Say we base it on a hundred kids. We want to keep the cost low for members. So the J's entertainment budget would put up a little more than half. It will just cost the kids, say two bucks. I think that could work. How 'bout references?"

Ben said, "It's all in the proposal, as well as our contract."

Looking down at our card he said, "Very good, fellas. Let's say I get back to you on Friday and see if we can afford Party Circus."

As we reached our ride, who was Ben's mom, we both doubled over in laughter. The kind where you stop making sounds and think you might never breathe again. We got the call the next day for twelve bookings. For years after, Ben and I remarked, "We owe everything to Dr. Loveless."

Ben and I didn't play any instruments. Instead we danced, strutted, and jumped about, flipping through a pretty good selection of forty-fives. We could always count on Ike and Tina Turner's "Proud Mary" to pull an evening out of a hole. And that was after we had already exhausted "Satisfaction" and "Honky Tonk Women," my personal favorites.

The Jewish Exponent pronounced Ben and me "Two Terrific Teen Tycoons." Our competitors stood behind their sound systems. We stood in front. Mikes in hand, our quick quips seemed to stick, as did our audacity to sing. We shouted along with Jagger, Young, McCartney, and Sly, albeit often off-key, but somehow it worked.

CHAPTER 4

Despite my early business ventures, I still did what other normal kids do growing up. Most summer nights after dinner, we played baseball in the neighborhood. Timmy Barr's father was the leader of our ball games. When we were younger, Mr. Barr pitched for both our Phillies versus Mets teams and was our umpire. Timmy, because he was born in New York, was the only kid who wanted to captain the Mets, and most often I managed the Phillies.

As we got older and got better, we retired Mr. Barr as teammate, but we kept him on as ump. He took this demotion hard, but as the season moved closer to fall, we'd get underway with football. Here too, at the start, Mr. Barr quarterbacked both teams—until our own throwing arms grew more powerful, and once again, Mr. Barr was barred.

During this period, bonding time with my own dad came in other ways. Unlike Mr. Barr's classic baseball swing, Dad's looked more like Arnold Palmer's. So instead of counting earned runs, we talked shop: advertising and Party Circus. He always took my business as seriously as I did his. From an early age, I knew he really believed in me.

Dad often brought the Wollensak reel-to-reel tape recorder home from his office to play me his latest radio jingles. I was always happy to haul it in from his trunk and looked forward to those moments as I parked the sound machine on the kitchen table. Dad would hand me his fresh-from-the-studio recorded spool. I'd thread it and hit "play." I still remember so many of the tunes and lyrics he shared with me then. There's a reason for jingles; they never leave your mind.

For Gleem Paints, it went like this: *Things are really looking up today, so much so that some folks say, "What's going on, what's going on around here?"*

Or, the one for Goetze's Meats: *Make each meal a big success, try a little tenderness; Goetze's Meats are tenderly yours.*

And my favorite for Cloverland Milk: *If you don't own a cow, call Cloverland now, North 9-2222, North 9-2222.*

After Dad left the kitchen, I was supposed to start practicing my French with those horrid repeat-after-me ALM records. Instead, with delight, I'd keep playing Dad's jingles over and over again until I had every last word planted in my head. In forty minutes or so Dad would return to the kitchen to spoon out ice cream straight from the tub, freezer door wide open as he adoringly looked over at me listening intently, and I could see his great tenderness and excitement at my enthusiasm for his business.

I knew exactly where my career was heading: straight to his office, to help build Spiegel into a household brand. Dad's pride in me was apparent and I worked hard to keep up his admiration, so my next stop on the success train was running for president of the student government. I gave it all I had, and it turned out to be one of those experiences I'd flash back to throughout my life.

Vince Michaels was a science teacher at Germantown Friends, a progressive private school in Greater Philadelphia. Vince had this sing-song way of speaking tinged with a Southern drawl. Born in Rogers, Arkansas, he would tell everyone who cared to listen, and that wasn't many of us (he wasn't one of the big draw teachers), "I'm not a Southerner nor am I a Midwesterner. I'm afraid I'm a man from no man's land." *Who the hell cares?* I'd ask myself each time he repeated this riff. He'd go on to say to our class, "I bought my first gun and fishing rod from the store there in Rogers from the nicest man you'd ever want to meet, who I knew would be famous one day, Sam Walton, and sure enough!" He often brought his students his opinions and much trivia. On Walton, he got it right. Vince wore lots of plaid. And drove a rusted-out navy blue pick-up truck, its drooping bumper held up by a rope.

I think Vince spent some time in the National Guard, but he was a vocal Vietnam protester, probably much to his daddy's dismay. By the time he got to us, he'd become a fine enough teacher. But where he most enjoyed spending his time was in advising a few handpicked students whose sensibility he most closely shared. By far, I was not one of them. Matter of fact, when I saw him coming down the hall, I wanted to dart the other way.

His favorite disciple was a girl named Linda Wong. I think he liked her wide shoulders. She defied some of those Asian stereotypes, as she was tall and quite broad. I think Mr. Michaels tagged Linda Wong as someone he could comfortably go hunting with. In the spring of my junior year when I ran for president, Linda Wong also entered the race. She was quite bright, having skipped her sophomore year to join our class. I didn't know her well. Linda Wong's dad was a dean at the University of Pennsylvania, where Linda was taking advanced math classes. Aside from being tall and big boned, she had straight black hair. She often wiped her oily face into her palms. I imagined that her palms gave back more than they received.

Linda Wong and Vince Michaels walked the halls together, just short of holding hands, with lots of head nods and far too much eye contact. Their movements suggested they were discussing very important business and if you were oncoming traffic, you had best get out of their way.

In those days, before middle schools had become grades six through eight, running for President of the Upper School spanned seven through twelve. So when I decided to enter, I wrote my speeches, prepared posters, and did so by customizing my messages to a wide range of ages and interests. I was turned on by politics and had a considerable amount of exposure to the upper school because I had been the weekly assembly chairman for two years. This was more a plus than a liability, but I worried maybe I had too much limelight.

The seniors didn't vote because the election would no longer affect them. It looked like I had the juniors sewn up. Linda Wong had the sophomores in her camp. I was very fortunate to have a close friend in Beth Ehrenberg, a freshman who acted as my campaign manager. She was well respected, wise for her age, influential in her class, and beyond exceedingly cute. She had it all. I felt very comfortable with Beth, a natural in the world of politics. I could see her as senator one day, becoming the kind of leader people would describe as "too sexy for the job."

When we were down to the final week, Beth laser-focused. Her instincts were keen. She felt the majority of the freshmen were on board so we turned our attention to the seventh and eighth graders. Here, too, I had lots more exposure than the other candidates because most of these kids had recently been to my parties, but we thought that knowing me in this context might be a hindrance. Linda Wong (or Vince Michaels) was onto this same idea and decided to make a lot out of it.

Like any good candidate, I was keeping an eye on what my competition was up to. At the weekly assembly before the Tuesday election, we delivered our speeches. I, along with the four other candidates, marched to the podium. By this time, both Linda Wong and I knew it was down to the two of us. Linda's and my themes were aimed to pick up seventh and eighth grade votes. When we finished and stepped off the risers in the gymnasium, Vince Michaels unabashedly ran over to Linda Wong with a big grin and said, "Girl, you nailed it!" At which point, he lightly wrapped his arm around her shoulders pulling her into his chest. He didn't even look at me as I came down the steps. Their connection was feeling an awful lot like trouble.

On the day of the election, I learned Linda Wong and Mr. Michaels had sneakily papered the seventh and eighth grade homerooms with Linda Wong signs. These posters were stunningly negative: *What Can He Do For You? He's All Business. He May Know How to Flip a Record, But Can He Lead the School?* Lastly, Linda Wong (or was it actually Mr. Michaels?) arranged to address these two homerooms right before the voting began. Totally losing sight of his role, not to mention electoral decorum and fairness, Mr. Michaels joined Linda Wong as she announced what she would do and what she thought I wouldn't. There was no time to call foul.

The votes were cast two hours later and the winner was to be announced before the end of the school day. I was in shock. How had my science teacher turned out to be my nemesis? As Beth learned, while soliciting last-minute votes for me, the kids were all asking, "Why does Mr. Michaels hate Sam so much?" Michaels turned out to be Wong's Trojan horse. And Beth and I wondered was there something else Trojan going on here?

At 2:00 Linda Wong and I were called into the office of the head of the math department, Mr. Radcliff, where the outgoing officers had gathered to tally the results.

Matt Hart, the outgoing Student Council President, said, "We've counted the ballots several times over and there is no question, we have an absolute tie." In the case of a tie, the protocol was for the outgoing president to cast the tie-breaking vote. Matt and I were friends and I believed I had his. But then he followed up by saying, "I have refused to follow this procedure. There is a clear contradiction, as no seniors cast ballots. I'm a senior and I'm not breaking the tie. As I told Doc, if I'm forced to vote, I'll flip a coin for next president." Doc was our principal.

I spoke up. "But, Matt, you're supposed to break the tie."

"Sam, I'm not. I'm firm on that. Instead, there will be another vote on Thursday. Tomorrow we'll hold a special half-hour question-and-answer assembly. All posters are down. Good luck to both of you. I will be making this announcement straightaway."

I was growing glum about my predicament. Beth was pissed. Tuesday night was film forum and I was planning to miss it, until Beth got wind of my decision. "Sam, you're doing what? You're not showing up to film forum? And letting that bitch and that snake of a man sneak around and take what's ours? The hell you are!"

Wow. What had gotten into her?

"Sam Spiegel, you're going to pick me up and we're going to get to school a half-hour before the movie starts and shake every damn last hand at the door and ask for each and every vote. No one's pushing us around. You hear me?"

It wasn't me any longer. We were us. I never forgot her passion, belief, and fire that day.

On Thursday I ended up getting substantially more votes. The poster attack backfired. I could tell this from the students' line of questioning before the revote, which, bless her heart, Beth framed beautifully. She knew not to be first up. But when her time came, slow and deliberate prior to the revote, so that no one could miss a word and I didn't know it was coming, she looked Linda Wong straight in the eye and asked, "When a candidate resorts to negative posters, what does that say about the candidate?" Barbara Walters couldn't have framed it up better.

I was becoming very practiced in holding back my laughter but not so my tears. Two flicked to the floor after she asked the question.

Linda Wong answered, "It was a bad mistake," trying to push her shame away with Beth's eyes locked on hers. "I think I got myself snookered into one big negative smear campaign." It was as if Beth had planted a passionate kiss on my lips. And that was what I hoped might be coming next; I was falling in love.

These determined attempts to dream big and then rack up successes, like chasing the presidency, appeared to be constructed for Dad. His Holocaust pains were always present, until yours truly hit one long for him. And in so doing, on these occasions, Dad's steady doubts about maintaining optimism for a sustainable life would minimally subside. It was at these moments that I seemed to restore hope for him. So, early on, it appeared to me that Dad depended on my triumphs as some sort of fix to help him win at his own coping game.

Thus, at a very young age, collecting wins became my mission. It made Dad feel better, and that, in turn pleased me, but it was not the only impetus for my tugs toward achievement. I also knew I had to compensate for the other tragedy that had struck our family. As my father called it, "Spiegel's second holocaust," the one that came when I was six and my brother was twelve. That's when Mikey caught on fire.

While unspoken but keenly implicit, I understood that the two holocausts required me to work overtime to make a *mensch* of myself. And it was this second holocaust that we all experienced together, where my mother instructed us to bottle up the memories and place this nightmare behind us.

I dutifully obeyed her command until shortly after winning the election. That's when I decided to force myself to relive this tragedy—I think more than anything, to gain a better understanding of why Mikey's connection to me appeared so hostile and how this event was affecting our entire family. It was through an assignment for Mr. Groth's writing class that I defied my mother's wishes and wrote about Mikey's accident as "my most profound life-altering experience to date."

If I had followed my mother's orders not to revisit the Halloween accident, it might well have been the student government election I'd have written about instead. Then three days after my win, during Mikey's weekly call home from grad school at Syracuse, he asked Mom to put me on the line. Expecting some kind congratulatory comments from my big brother, instead I got stung. And this stinging triggered my need to relive his tragedy.

When I put the phone to my ear, Mikey sputtered into it, "Samuel," (he always called me the name my parents used when they were mad at me) "when you tied in your election, I told Mom and Dad, 'Sam will win.' I had no doubt about that because the Golden Boy never loses."

I was stunned, and didn't know how to address my disappointment because his congratulations never came. It seemed that his mantra was, "Life's never fair for me with you in the picture, Samuel." It had become my well-trained response to take Mikey's quips and to hide my real feelings. That's what my mother wanted me to do when it came to Mikey, so I just said, "Well, it was a rough race, Mikey, and the win didn't come easily." What I really wanted to say was, "Why can't you ever be proud of me?"

He concluded the conversation with, "I'm sure, Samuel, however the win came, that you feel pretty darned good about yourself."

Mikey got away with his mean actions with no consequences whatsoever when he decided to dish out barbs to our parents or especially to me. His belief, so it seemed, was that our parents hadn't protected him from getting burned and that I was the chosen one as a result, spared all the consequences and scars and getting all the glory. Mikey seemed to live for this song and played it loud and often. And my mother let him rant as if she needed him to do it to punish her.

Mikey just couldn't be a brother, or certainly not the brother I wanted him to be. Therefore for him I became the recipient of his constant resentment until that phone call, when I snapped. I had had it with his behavior. That night I quit playing my passive prescribed role of taking it and defied my mother's wishes. That's when I went to work on my final paper for Groth's class: *My Memories and Feelings Surrounding Mikey's Accident.* It got me an A+, but more importantly, it was the start of my understanding of how such a trauma can affect the inner workings of an entire family. And I learned that Mikey's scars would always be mine to share as well, in ways he'd never fully understand.

It happened on Halloween night in 1961. I was six, and my brother was twelve. Halloween was a big deal in our neighborhood. We started planning our costumes and candy selections weeks in advance. My father, our family food shopper, had designated that year as the one in which the Heath Bar would replace the Tootsie Roll. "No more little turds," my brother and I happily recited as we giddily danced together in a circle.

As for our costumes: I would transform myself into a pirate, aided by a black vest, eye patch, mustache, colorful gold sash, and a frilly white shirt. Most of my outfit had come from my mother's ballet recital storage closet in our basement. Except for the cool, thin leather boots, which Mom had rooted out at the Goodwill Store.

Mikey, who had been making recent requests for bagpipe lessons, I thought because he wanted to wear a kilt, spent entirely too much time in Mom's closet trying on girlie things. And that year he had it in his mind to trick-or-treat as an exotic Hawaiian dancer. I remember my father saying with disdain, "Mikey, you're going as what?" I thought it was weird, too. But there was no dissuading him. His outfit featured an authentic grass skirt, a shiny greenish-blue blouse, and three leis, also culled from Mom's ballet closet. I remember my mother saying, "Mikey, you make such a good-looking girl. Would you like some dangling earrings?" Everyone laughed uncomfortably. Dad's chuckle came with an eye roll. But, hey, it was Halloween. If not then, when?

Seven of us neighborhood kids, ages three to twelve, had decided to go trick-or-treating together: Timmy Barr; his sister Paula; the three Feinbergs; Mikey; me; and Timmy Barr's mother, Maureen, the so-called grown-up who would accompany us. She didn't seem like a real grown-up. There was something very wrong with Maureen Barr. She was a diabetic, but that was only for starters. She was probably very depressed, as she slept a good bit during the day. We'd catch her after school slumped over on her living room sofa, heavily snoring with her eyeglasses smashed sideways into the cushion.

We all ate dinner early that Halloween evening so that we could push off at 6:00. My mother wanted my dad to accompany us, but his disdain for Maureen, maybe even his embarrassment at Mikey's costume made his decision final. He didn't join us.

The weather was mild that night. All the kids wore costumes and no coats, except for Mrs. Barr, who wore a thick seal overcoat. All she was missing were some sardines spilling from her pockets. When we had completed the two blocks on both sides of our street, Hillside Avenue, with bags half-filled we turned up Willow Glen where newer split-levels had recently been built.

The second house on the left was the Olivers', where Brian, who was my age, and his sister, Erica, who was about Mikey's age, lived. We rang the doorbell and all seven of us lined up roughly by age with our bags poised in our hands. Mikey, being the eldest, patiently waited at the back of the line near where the Olivers' lidless jack-o'-lantern sat with its single flickering candle. As we stood in the dark waiting our turns for candy, the area around us suddenly flashed brightly.

We heard this rapid fluttering of combustion like when a lit match meets the lighter-fluid soaked coals in a grill. We turned and followed the flash to its source and watched in horror as the bottom of Mikey's grass skirt burst into flames. He grimaced, screamed, and ran to escape the searing heat. But there was no escape; his clothes were fuel driving the fire, and the blaze was consuming him. The faster Mikey ran, the more voracious the fire. With each frantic step, the burning climbed higher.

Next Mikey's shiny green blue blouse caught fire as he darted to the edge of the Olivers' yard and then ran across the street onto another front yard. We all screamed as Mikey reached a neighbor's white picket fence and began to turn back toward us. The size and ferocity of the fireball that engulfed him grew. As he made the turn, I blacked out.

The next thing I remember seeing was Mr. and Mrs. Oliver using a floor rug to pat down poor Mikey's charred and smoldering body as he lay facedown on a neighbor's lawn. Moments earlier, a guest at the Olivers' house had tackled my brother and rolled him around several times in the grass to extinguish the fire.

Mikey didn't look human. Parts of him were brown, others as black and crinkly as a roasted marshmallow that had slipped off a stick and fallen into a campfire. Burned swatches of my brother's clothes were seared to his skin to the point where you couldn't distinguish burned body from burned clothing. Smoke rose everywhere and the odd smell of his charred flesh permeated the air.

Just imagine the scene that followed as we came back to our house to knock on our door. My father approached with a fistful of Heath Bars while my mother peered from behind, eager to catch a glimpse of the next group of trick-or-treaters. But instead, the door opened to their son and his charred body, still smoldering like a freshly doused campfire. From there on, all I can remember came at me in a slow motion sequence of events capturing raw panic and the absolute horror of the night.

My father dashed for the phone and struggled with the knotted cord to get it to his ear. He dialed frantically, but the phone's circular dial was exasperatingly slow. Dad was calling Uncle Irv, our family doctor, who lived a block up the street. "A horrible thing's happened. Oh, my God, Irv. Come quickly."

My mother's palms were planted against her face and her elbows stuck out like antlers. They wouldn't or couldn't leave that position. She was screaming, shivering, staring at her Mikey, and shrieking to Harry, "Call Irv! Call Irv! Harry, call Irv!" Which he had already done. When your child is in such shock and obvious pain, you want so badly to hold him, but my mother didn't know what to do next. If she tried to touch Mikey, would her fingers stick to his skin? Would she hurt him more? Nobody could figure out what to do with their hands, Mikey included. It was like deciding whether to embrace a hornet's nest.

Finally, my mother composed herself enough to step forward and held Mikey delicately by the tip of his right elbow, which seemed unburned, and led my brother to the bathroom at the top of the stairs. Gently, she cupped Mikey's hands into her own, placed them under the faucet, and turned the cold water on full blast. She had to do something and this was the best she could figure. Cold water for burns.

Uncle Irv flew up the stairs, waving his black doctor's bag. With great concern, he examined Mikey. Then, this mild-mannered man began barking strict orders in quick succession while bending down to inspect my brother more closely. "There's no time for an ambulance. Harry, grab your car keys."

Mikey, just beginning to understand the severity of his situation, started to shriek uncontrollably. With bold strides, Irv and my dad carried him to the car. Irv got in the backseat with my brother. I saw my mother standing at the door of our house trying to decide where to be. Should she accompany her seriously injured son to the hospital, or hang back with her terrified six-year-old? I wanted Mom with me. I was scared. The next instant she dashed down the sidewalk, shouting "Oh, my God; oh, my God!" Her hands pressed against her cheeks again.

When she reached the car, she dove into the front seat as the family Rambler took off, tires screeching. I'll never forget the sound of those tires as I stood there stunned, eyes fixed on the empty spot where the car had been. I was bewildered and alone. Everyone had left me. Our neighbors looked on from both sides of our front yard. Mrs. Feinberg, from next door, pulled me to her house as I continued to stare at the empty space where the Rambler had been. Would I see my brother again? Would he die? Why did this happen? Where was God hiding?

Mikey's survival remained unclear for more than a month. His crazy, but highly competent, plastic surgeon shocked my parents that Halloween night, when he abruptly blurted out to them, "I don't know why I get these shit burn cases—they always die anyway." Over the following weeks, the surgeon's bedside manner improved little. Whenever my parents asked him about Mikey's condition, he would simply repeat, "Nip and tuck. So very nip and tuck." It became our family mantra.

Then one day shortly after Thanksgiving, when my parents returned from the hospital, my dad took me aside and said, "Sammy, tuck has overtaken nip." By the way he said it, I knew they had gotten good news from the grouchy doctor. Because of my tender age, I was not allowed to visit Mikey in the hospital. I didn't see him for three months and I rarely saw my parents during this period either. My grandmother, Omie, had come to stay with me. As a way for Mikey to see me, my father arranged for me to be on television, on the Bozo the Clown show. Following my appearance, three thousand get-well letters poured into Mikey's hospital room. Some came with gum. A couple dozen came with dollar bills.

I remember being very scared one particular night when my parents were unusually late in returning from the hospital. My grandmother was sound asleep, but I was still anxiously awake in my bed. I sat up and peered out my bedroom window overlooking the addition to our house where my mother gave ballet lessons, only to find two large raccoons staring at me. I was terrified. Where were Mom and Dad? I wanted to run to their room to take cover…slip under their sheets. Be with them. But Omie was the only one home, sound asleep in Mikey's bed, so I hid under my own sheets and blankets and shivered as I cried myself to sleep.

When I was told Mikey was finally coming home, after three months of round-the-clock medical care, I was so excited. He'd be my big brother again. And we'd play hide-and-seek, Shoots and Ladders, and Chinese checkers. All the games we'd enjoyed before "The Accident" would come off the shelves. We'd resume our regular Saturday evening rituals—dining on chicken potpies or TV dinners while watching the latest episode of *Leave It to Beaver*.

I was all set to pick up on my childhood precisely where we had left off. But the moment I saw Mikey, I couldn't believe how sickly and awful he appeared. When you came out of the hospital, you were supposed to be better. Mikey looked worse than when he had left. He arrived walking slowly with two nurses at either side, and with a large bald spot in the back of his head. Mikey's skin, where I could see it, looked like cottage cheese mixed with apple butter.

His nurses immediately placed him in a specially configured hospital bed, which had a large metal hoop covering him in a half circle. It held his blankets so they wouldn't make direct contact with his raw skin. Everything about him and the special equipment in his room was severe and so sad to see. Interacting with Mikey was a lot like connecting with The Thing, a monster in a movie I should have never experienced at such a young age.

My brother convalesced for nine months. We weren't a home any longer; we were a MASH unit. All the action in our house revolved around the comings and goings of Mikey's medical, educational, and emotional support teams: tutors, doctors, nurses—even our rabbi. A constant stream of visitors came bearing gifts: stuffed animals, games, books, cookie trays, brownies, and seemingly endless balloons. I was distracted at school and having trouble learning to read. During this time, I took a backseat to everything Mikey.

At a key point in Mikey's recuperation, probably sometime in mid-March, the metal hoop was lifted. Was he finally coming back? That evening I looked in one of our basement closets. These closets had become very spooky to me because Mikey's burned costume came from one. I wondered what other horrors lurked inside. But the closet across from that was where we kept all the Christmas decorations. And I was on a mission.

I dug around under the strings of multi-colored tree lights to find the book. Once spotted, I brought it upstairs to Mikey's room, and hid it behind my back until I approached his bed and asked, "Can we read and snuggle?" That's when I handed him *The Night Before Christmas* and said, "You didn't read this to me yet this year." He smiled. "Well, climb in, Sammy." And with my many trepidations suppressed at that moment (or maybe only barely), I did.

The following September Mikey returned to school. He had to bring a fluffy pillow to sit on and carried it with him from class to class. He still looked rather freakish, but friends and teachers worked hard to make him feel more comfortable in his new skin.

My parents shared their awful guilt of exposing Mikey to great harm. Mom had allowed him to wear the grass skirt. But who would have suspected it would catch fire? Dad had refused to chaperone us because he couldn't abide Maureen. But who would have guessed he'd be so sorely needed? Fortunately, after some therapy, the finger-pointing subsided and my parents reached a stalemate, but the shadow of guilt and disappointment never fully lifted from the Spiegel household.

What happened to Mikey? Although no number of surgeries ever erased his new bumps, lumps, and designs on his back and buttocks, thankfully his front side and his face escaped permanent injury and scarring. Mikey remained a very handsome young man. But after the accident, he struggled with chronic weight gain and low self-esteem. His significant inner strength, which had helped him survive the accident, never fully returned. And although our parents, especially my mother, strove tirelessly to ensure Mikey's survival, neither parent seemed capable of finding a way to help him restore his sense of self-worth.

My brother's deformities, and the terrible guilt they engendered in my parents, seemed to cause emotional withdrawal within all of us. In a misguided effort to overcompensate for what they saw as their "tragic moment of parental neglect," Mom and Dad embarked on a new, seemingly realistic course of action that would have unintended consequences for my brother and me. In the spirit of "honesty" (more like brutal honesty), my parents' new, self-proclaimed virtue brought them to the place of preparing Mikey, in advance, for the harsh new realities he'd face for the rest of his life.

Out of "kindness," and a desire to inoculate Mikey against future disappointments, they sat him down and told him that his scars had made him imperfect. He needed to get on with his life, of course, but they said he also needed to realize his "damaged" condition would compromise most, if not all, of his future life experiences and that many hopes would be dashed. Mikey, at age thirteen was told that he was damaged goods. And the resolve that once shined so brightly within him for self-betterment and self-fulfillment gradually diminished. In its place grew a seemingly compulsive need to assign guilt and extract compensation for his suffering.

When I was seven my survival instincts kicked in, and I resolved that my stock would always sell at a premium. My merchandise would never tarnish, become damaged, or be discounted. I was determined that I would achieve enough success for two.

I would get the prized wife, the revered career, and enjoy wealth and abundance that might allow me (the unscarred one) to hand some of my riches to Mikey. I would become the unlimited recipient of parental pride. I would compensate for the tragedy and disappointment Mikey's accident had brought them. This would be my role in the family. I wouldn't waver or dillydally. Not then. Not for a moment. Like a sprinter, I was off.

CHAPTER 5

Beth Ehrenberg became my high school girlfriend. She was incredibly and lovingly precocious, and at ease with herself whether whipping down a steep mountain on skis or deftly analyzing a novel. She was the kind of girl for whom clichés like "lit up the room" and "turned heads" were coined. Her insights would always go to places beyond the obvious. What I liked most about her was her sense of adventure, her forward ho, her ability to experience joy and stay with it for a while. Her emotions were deep. Beth never suppressed what she felt in her gut. She could be a drama queen, but it was not just for effect. It was because feelings stayed with her.

When she had been my campaign manager, I figured I couldn't mix business with pleasure. The weird thing is I really believed this, so our romance started after I won the election at the end of my junior year. One spring evening, at a party I was attending instead of working, I caught sight of Beth. Party Circus had a rare night off. Later, when my father did our books, he remarked, "Samuel...um...what happened this weekend? Business is off."

I told him, "Dad, just this once...I went to this party and instead of making money, I fell in love."

He responded with a big smile and said, "Samuel, you can't build a business with such distractions."

Fortuitously, Beth lived in the same neighborhood as the Party Circus lighting and sound technicians, Lester and Greg. Lester stored the equipment with a sense of pride. But knowing that Beth lived next door to Greg, this led me to send out an executive order to start storing all the equipment at Greg's house with the statement, "In the spirit of fairness, it's Greg's turn now to store the equipment." When packing up, I'd come early in the afternoon to be with Beth and then help Greg and Lester bring the amps and speakers to the car. After the party was over and equipment was put back, I'd be with Beth well into the morning.

During that time I penned one of those awestruck teenage love letters, something I had never written to anyone before or since, filled with phrases like: "A magnetic attraction is so special; it's exhilarating. It's like running out of your house during the first winter snow. And each day for me still represents breathing in and living with that first snow. We are like magnets because we are able to cling together and communicate a feeling." And: "The Fiords we sailed on that night will linger because what we experienced was love. And the heavens can open up. And the Red Sea can part. And the demons can say, 'Leave her alone.' But I won't because I can't."

My powerful pen zoomed our romance forward. Beth and I were in love and loved each other's bodies. Our intimacy was very fulfilling and was expressed just about everywhere: off hours at my mother's ballet studio, on the beach, under the stars, in Beth's pool. Once, very embarrassingly, we left some spots of Beth's menstrual blood on Greg's den sofa, discovered by his mother the next day. What a sport that Greg was. He not only was storing the equipment, he was covering my ass and called the stain carelessness on his part. "Mom, it was a small McDonald's ketchup packet that squirted out too far."

It seemed my best friend and partner, Ben Selborn, loved Beth too. Was it because I did, or was he sincere? It was clear, though, she had the ability to spin multiple boys at once, like plates on the end of poles. Beth's flirting with Ben put a strain on everyone's relationship including the partners in commerce. I brought this competition to a head and made Beth pick her suitor. In the end, it was my plate that never quite toppled.

We got each other. The rest, as they say, is history. But not exactly the sort of history anyone could follow that easily as our love fest ended because of our three-year age difference, which hadn't seemed to matter before. The summer after my sophomore year at Wesleyan University in Middletown, Connecticut, when Beth was finishing high school in Philadelphia (by the way, she sailed into the student council presidency without a revote), we thought we should be pragmatic and not put each other's lives on hold, so we agreed to part. Amicably.

In the fall of my junior year of college, within moments of my arrival at my dorm, I saw an attractive coed standing on the steps between the second and the first floors. She was blonde and had a striking resemblance to Liv Ullmann—every Jewish boy's fantasy. And here was mine on the stairs of my new home! Amy Reinhart's smile, delightful blue eyes, and puffy lips immediately enamored me.

I found myself seated next to her at dinner that night as we dug into Carlie's casserole. Carlie was the resident assistant in our fourteen-person mini-dorm. Her casserole was more like a potpie, which made it even more enjoyable. Carbs weren't the enemy then.

What seemed to charm Amy was Carlie's comment about how I had arrived. "Did you see Sam Spiegel come in...in a puff of smoke?" And she said it in such a way, when I heard it at the time, to be quite flattering. But by dinnertime, and after I'd thought about it further, I found it more perplexing, and perhaps not necessarily complimentary at all. What did Carlie mean by it? Why was Amy so intrigued? Did I come off as some sort of zany magician?

Returning to the apartment most nights proved quite anchoring, even though our quarters were too tight and not all of our housemates meshed. But for our small group that did, there was something quite comforting about our simulation of a family dinner. I loved when it was my cooking night. I bought the food and wine. The wine was my little addition that stuck. Bistro cooking had become my passion, inspired by eating in Paris during a trip my parents gave to me after high school graduation. Early on, my crispy duck, lentils, and artichokes set a high standard. At first, my meals were thought of as too gourmet, until the five of us got down to tasting them.

When it wasn't my turn to prepare dinner, I would try to take a seat in the living room area with a bird's-eye view of my other pal-chefs creating their dinners. This had become my own personal early evening ritual complete with a Dewar's, soda, and a twist of lemon in hand, as I watched our own in-house "Julia Child Show" unfold before me. Of course, what made it all the more fun was determining the varying levels of cooking skills, as the tone of the show could go from instructive to calamitous on any given evening. I'll never forget watching Amy's maiden voyage in the kitchen.

I don't think Amy had cooked chicken pieces before and seemed perplexed by their shapes and thicknesses. Frankly, she wore an overwhelmed *I Love Lucy* face throughout her preparation. First, the breasts, wings, thighs, and drumsticks were squeezed together on the baking tray. Then she removed the wings and drumsticks, and then reluctantly put them back on the tray.

With a deep sigh signaling serious trepidation, Amy shoved everything together into the oven, which she kept opening and closing. Maybe she was thinking, *If I'm cooking, I better be looking.* I was struck by the difficulty she had with her baking mitt. She was wearing the glove on her left hand but used it as if it were covering her right…four fingers shoved into the thumbhole.

With her mitt in such a jumble, I learned where the term "all thumbs" may have gotten its start. I so badly wanted to say to Amy, "Flip your glove around." And I promise, not one of us would have admonished her one iota if she had brought her right hand into the mix. The chaos in the kitchen mounted; watching her was like watching Curious George make dinner.

When her dish arrived at the table, Amy warned us that something might not have worked out so well. She was very cute and had an endearing way of completing her sentences with some stammering, taking the certainty out of her statements. It seemed she had learned if something is supposed to be good, and if some steadfast stuttering was brought in for good measure prior to presenting the end result, and if the final result was bad, everyone will have been forwarned. On the other hand, if, by chance, things worked out fine in the end despite everyone expecting something disastrous, then "*Tada!*" it was her charming modesty that got her through.

We all cut into our chicken pretty much at the same time. (We may have been college students but this group had table manners.) The meat was shockingly rare, and each person pushed away their plate at about the same time, exclaiming almost in unison, "Oh, no!"

This is where Carlie proved herself to be such a pro. She leaned over to Amy nicely but authoritatively, and said, "Honey, this needs to go back in the oven for at least another half-hour at four hundred degrees." And like no one else I ever knew at age twenty-one, Carlie could get away with starting a sentence with "Honey."

When it came her turn to make dinner again, Amy promised us her grandmother's brisket. I took bets with my dinner mates on "whether there would be blood or no blood running from the brisket." And our mod-mate Mitchell brought five Pepto-Bismol tablets to the table with the pronouncement, "Here are tonight's dinner mints." Amy had a good sense of humor and laughed right along with us.

My conversations with Amy picked up speed and began to get more personal, tender, and trusting. We loved an Italian restaurant in New Haven called Consiglio's. We took off to movies and lectures together. We got caught up in each other's lives. Amy seemed to like that I was a self-starter and she followed my lead. At the time, I was co-hosting a college television show, making a documentary film, and trying to secure a coveted internship at Doyle Dane Bernbach advertising agency in New York. Amy seemed captivated with me, or was it my ability to make things happen?

In the spring of that year, Amy would comfortably slip down to my room most nights while I was acutely aware that, although Beth and I had officially called it quits, I was still fielding or making the occasional call. Okay, maybe it was more than occasional. I remember those early confusing nights when I got off the phone with Beth at around 11:30 to greet Amy at my door at 11:31. I worried about blurting out Beth's name while on top of Amy.

I got the offer from DDB and with happy anticipation accepted my internship for the summer and first half of my senior year. This experience would be integral to my senior thesis, "The Workings of the Creative Process." Amy, a year behind me, planned to intern at Ethical Culture Fieldston School, also in New York City, where she would teach drama to sixth graders. Amy was majoring in education, and the Ethical Culture experience would be the centerpiece of her applied studies.

Since we would both be in Manhattan, we decided to live together, subletting a one-bedroom apartment on the Upper West Side. With a U-Haul hitched to my Torino, we moved our stuff out of our college apartment and began our future together in the Big Apple.

On our first night in the "City That Never Sleeps," something came over Amy. Maybe it was the out-of-season pomegranates we had eaten earlier that night...something you can only find in New York in May. Maybe it was just the excitement of having our own place together. Whatever it was, it led her to slide down my body and venture a blow-job. This was a brand-new move, and it took me by surprise. She was figuring it all out as she went along, and I, too, was happily connecting on instinct. Then, suddenly, mid-motion, Amy stopped herself from all she was going for.

It was as if an alarm had gone off in her head. She lurched upright, her whole body seized up as if in a trance. Then she sneezed. Not one of those quick mousy squeaks that end and leave you thinking, *What the hell was that?* This was a fully developed, rain-down-on-me sneeze. Then, she sneezed again. Six or seven times. It was like one of those awkward scenes in a Woody Allen movie when all we could do was laugh, which we both did without restraint.

I enjoyed talking about my dreams with Amy. She was excited because I was so excited. I fantasized aloud about someday building the next DDB in downtown Philadelphia. I was no stranger to audacity. The New York kinetic energy had become infectious. We were caught up in a whirlwind of optimism. We saw the possibilities. Amy joined in supporting my aspirations with great vitality. That's what I loved so much about her. She was my greatest cheerleader, and I became enamored with her enthusiasm for my ideas and me.

CHAPTER 6

On my way to work, I'd get off the subway each morning at 47th Street and walk through the Diamond District. There was a determined pace at this time of day, especially on the blocks where the men wore *payos* underneath their tall hats as they cranked open the grates covering their storefronts to greet the morning. It was as if these Orthodox Jews, cloaked in black overcoats and starch-less white shirts, slept outside their establishments only to wake for this moment. Saks Fifth Avenue, which I passed paces later, remained quiet at this hour. These blocks were where the old world met the new. Hermès greeted *schmatte*. Commuters passed merchants and nodded as if to communicate, "I'll be back."

As I looked at these shopkeepers, I thought I saw a glint in their eyes as they wondered who might make their day. Maybe a sheik staying at the Waldorf? A pharmaceutical rep looking to celebrate her nice commission with a new bracelet? Or would it be the NYU graduate who knew it was time to hook his girlfriend for keeps? Even the Hebrew National Cafeteria seemed alive at 8:30 in the morning. In my first week of work I thought, *Only in New York could hot dogs sell in the morning.* I learned later as I strolled on the Hebrew National side of the street, by way of a tall sandwich board outside their doors: "You Don't Have to be a Millionaire to Enjoy Heavenly Coffee, Chock full o' Nuts."

This was an early incarnation of co-branding as formalized years later when Baskin-Robbins first shared a roof with Dunkin' Donuts, and Taco Bell saddled up along-side KFC. At Hebrew National the smell of java wafted its way to blend in with three other prominent aromas: sauerkraut, Gulden's mustard, and kosher dogs, calling to mind a bouquet found at the circus. I left Hebrew National with coffee in one hand and a bounce-back coupon for $1.59 in the other. This would get me a foot long dog, a Dr. Brown's soda, and a bag of Lays for lunch. It went on to read, "The sauerkraut's on us." Smart dogs!

At DDB, I anticipated my mostly active days with excitement. I was now a "casting" cameraman, which meant I operated the video camera and helped direct the actors auditioning for commercials. This had become my job after Barb, the casting director, pronounced I had a feel for guiding talent. She began deliberately leaving the room with longer gaps between reappearances. What started as the duration of a bathroom break turned into the length of a coffee break, which advanced to, "Take over the session, Sam." After a month or so, art directors, copywriters, and creative directors were directed my way with their requests.

And they were learning my name: "Sam, could you please get me a close-up?"

"You bet."

What was so satisfying about my job was that it brought me in touch with all disciplines within the agency. Our department was the place that started the process of turning storyboards into finished commercials. Associates ended up with me after they sold their creative ideas to the client, with the happiest anticipation of what was about to emerge—their visions on celluloid. My suite often felt like the triumph zone, where the actors tried out for parts to bring storyboards to life, to be seen on televisions across America. I remember a giddy copywriter, Hank Aaronson, leaning toward me as I ushered one actor out of the room to bring in a new one in.

"Sam, I ended last week with loose ideas plastered all over my walls. I didn't think I had a Chinaman's chance of my spots seeing the light of day. This had to be one of our superstars, Strone or Beinhauser. Certainly some much bigger deal around here than 'little me.' Then, who's the man, Sammy? They're putting almost a million into this production. Shit, it seems like just yesterday that I was delivering papers for a buck in the morning. Sammy, give me five," as he twisted himself around in a complete circle on his right toe, his back heel taking off from the ground; and I was now, "Sammy, give me five."

Everyone had a deep crush on Sandra Maulborn. She was the hot DDB producer. She bunched her long blonde hair into a sexy tortoise shell clip that every guy who fantasized doing her imagined removing first to unleash her golden locks. Sandra had recently married the executive creative director, Harley Ross, of Wells Rich, Green—a rival powerhouse agency that had created the *I Love New York* campaign.

Word had it at DDB that Sandra moonlighted for Harley, an infraction, according to the personnel handbook. Ross was smart, marrying Sandra before he started shooting *I Love New York*. He'd consult with her every night until he got the creative where it needed to be. Sandra was production magic and Harley was her lucky dog.

Everyone, in fact, wanted to work with Sandra. She could convince those directors who could afford to pass on the best projects never to pass on hers. They'd hear her voice and start accepting. She was Polaroid's wonder woman and Polaroid was the darling of our agency. Her success in orchestrating the Mariette Hartley and James Garner commercials made her indispensable as her team knocked up to the heavens one killer spot after the other. Bill Meyers, chief marketing officer at Polaroid, said, "We're never comfortable at a shoot until Sandra says 'action!'"

Not only did Sandra look like Candice Bergen, but Candice Bergen was one of Sandra's closest friends. Talent who carried the big voices, like Herschel Bernardi of Charlie the Tuna fame and Mason Adams, who made Smuckers "Smuckers" dropped everything when Sandra came a-calling.

Now Sandra needed to find the right voice for a new campaign but had no idea where Joseph Beinhauser, the overseer of the new VW initiative, was taking it. Joseph had been working on concepts for the Volkswagen Project Trio campaign, and after months in Northeast Harbor, Maine, had just finished shooting photographs to bring his ideas to life. Aside from being the creative director on this project, Joseph assigned himself the role of art director, writer, and photographer. No one got in his way when he was on such a tear.

Although Joseph had many other names besides the one given to him at birth, and some were indeed pretty brutal, he was most often called "Houdini." Apparently anytime the agency was in a real fix, Beinhauser was brought in to work his magic.

After spending a year behind the casting camera I graduated from college. Then when my internship turned into a permanent job, I summoned up the nerve to ask Sandra if I could shadow her in the final weeks of Project Trio. It would be a great learning opportunity and early triumph for me, as the VW account bankrolled a large chunk of our agency's payroll. Without any hesitation, Sandra said, "Absolutely, you'd be a godsend, Sam. I'll clear it with Barb." As soon as she got the OK, Sandra filled me in on what was really up. "Until now, Sam, Volkswagen was a quirky little economy car. Out of nowhere they became our biggest client and also our biggest champion. Their sales were booming in the States, but they've flat lined. Asian imports are getting hot."

I asked, "Are they selling fewer cars because the appeal for Volkswagens has waned or have they sagged because of the other imports?"

"Good question, Sammy. I think it's a bit of both. So to counter the decline, VW is introducing three different cars besides the Bug: the Scirocco, the Rabbit, and the Jetta. They planned to test market these babies in Europe. But with falling sales here, we're getting them first. Everything has moved up on us. They're suddenly trying to become a stylish carmaker. As Joseph is so fond of saying, "VW will no longer be going to bed wearing a sleeping cap."

Trio was a big, big deal for Volkswagen, but even a bigger deal for DDB. Word in the halls had it there was "unrest" on the account. I learned this phrase was a euphemism for "big trouble." Joseph Beinhauser had teamed up with Sandra to save it. The project was down to March Madness as we approached August, weeks before we were due to pitch our work to VW on September 1st. The meeting was actually being talked about as a "face-off." I remember thinking, *if you refer to your actions as an offensive, could we still actually be allies?*

Joseph had just returned from Maine and was ready to brief Sandra on the campaign. I was invited to this meeting and was introduced as "one of the new hotshots in production." I hadn't really ever met Joseph. I had only passed him in the elevator. His entrance, though, was legendary. He sauntered into every room as if taking center stage and always smelling of vanilla.

Looking at Sandra he greeted us in mid-sentence saying, "Every fucking muckety-muck will be there all at once…Günter wants no pre-sell of this work. And this is no agency review? The fuck, it isn't. And another fuck goes to Günter!" (Günter was VW's Marketing Czar.) I thought it was Joseph's mouth that could use another one of our products, Coast Deodorant Soap.

"You mean we pitch our ideas on the 1st and hear if we're still their agency on the 2nd?" Sandra questioned.

"Something like that, honey. There will be six of them peering down on us as if we're their little chimps." Looking over at me as his note taker and using his fingers to count as if I were deaf, "*eins*, Günter, *zwei*, the President, *drei*, Chairman, CFO *vier*, *fünf*, Exec VP of Sales and the President of the dealer's association, *sechs*." By this point our room smelled like a Twinkies factory.

Sandra eyeballed Joseph hard. "Why have you kept me out of the loop, Joe? I have no idea where we're heading."

"Because I think we're nose-diving off a cliff."

"Well, save us some time and aggravation and just drive us off the Brooklyn Bridge."

"Sorry, Sandra. I don't have detailed boards yet. I came here straight from the airport. I've got the pictures shot, pacing figured out, rhythm straight in my head. And a line. No, not a line...the line! I hear the music. And I've got Henderson calling me five or six times a day, "How's it going, doctor?"

"When he asks me for a report," Sandra said, "he shortens the *doc* and elongates the *torrrrr*. So how's our *doc-torrrr* doing? And he's always muttering, 'Our doc-torrrr must need more teams.' All of account management have their panties in a wad over this pitch."

Beinhauser snapped back, "More teams...this is when you know the panic has set in. Throw more people at it. Like life preservers on the Titanic...so that everyone remaining can bob around in the water to freeze to death. No thank you, Sandra. Sometimes the stakes get so high I break out in hives. Want a nice treat? Come to my side of the table and peek under my shirt."

"No thanks. You can keep your welts to yourself."

Here I was on the tenth floor overlooking lined-up cabs on Madison and 49th in a meeting at Doyle Dane Bernbach. The expressed purpose of this confernce, one in a series, at the most creative agency in the world with two of the industry's finest talents...was to save the VW account. The revolutionary "Lemon" ad, created by Bernbach, still hung on the wall by my bed at my parents' house in Philadelphia. And now, here I was charting history with the best of them. I called Dad that night with my news. And when he heard of my doings, he gave me his best, "Holy mackerel, Andy!" I loved pleasing Dad.

"Sandy, it is what it is! It's still a fucking Nazi car. It was Hitler's 'chicken in every pot.' What do you think these sons of bitches know about style? If they focused on Beemers and collapsed them down, I would say, they'd have something. Mini Mercedes—okay then. But this is a carmaker that makes cars to look like insects? Come on, now."

"Joseph, I get it! Get past it."

"No. Stick with me here. Cars from high, marching, high-boot types who spent hours spit-shining these shoes and they weren't doing this to make them beautiful, mind you. What we're doing here is gussying up Volkswagens with some lipstick on the grill. It's like a *New Yorker* cartoon that doesn't need words. That, my darlings, is our campaign."

"So how am I supposed to help you, Joseph? What do you want from us?"

Beinhauser looked my way again. "And who the hell are you?"

"Sam."

"Well, Sam-I-Am, welcome to our three-ring circus! Sandy, years back, out of nowhere, VW called Bernbach on the phone. 'Zeece is Volkswagen calling.' It was the most politically motivated incoming communiqué in advertising history. Bernbach lucked into one of the greatest branding jobs of all time. As Nixon would say, "He was the Jew boy they decided to ride in on."

It just came out of my mouth, "To help counter negativity of German cars coming to America. Smart. Hire a Jew to handle it."

"Precisely, scholar boy. And what did we do? We did our magic. In no time flat, we made economizing and Volkswagen as fucking American as Colonel Sanders. How about them green eggs and ham, Sam-I-Am? Now, we're going to throw all the equity we built into these unsightly cars right out the window and make them fry on the sidewalk? When you get right down to it, our bugs look like fried eggs on wheels. Better yet, Sam-I-Am…how do you youngsters say it? We'll 'catch you on the flip side' and turn these ugly forms of metal into things of beauty. Then we'll call them stylish."

"So, you're saying we're throwing what we built out the window?"

"Not exactly, Sandy. I'm just saying we're turning our funny-looking chubby boys into *gesund* girls. Actually we're turning our pot-bellied boys into 'girlie' triplets. But these girls will keep wearing high boots. We'll make each of them a pair Jane Fonda might be fond of wearing, with suede to soften them up, and voila!"

"So, doc-torrrr…our assignment is to make cover girls but never lose sight they all were once boys."

"You got it. That about sums it up. And we've got one shot, kiddos. The McCann agency is circling us like a goddamn helicopter." He fixed his eyes on the ceiling. "But somehow they've found a way to muffle the noise of their propeller. We shoot first. They shoot second." Now cocking his fingers like a gun, "Or, maybe they've already shot their load and everyone is now waiting for me to shoot myself in the foot."

"Joseph, that's one shot you don't know how to make," Sandra countered.

"Honey, I've got the campaign. We just need to load the gun right. Sam-I-Am...you're sitting ringside at the best bout going in the biz today. I'll meet you both at 10.00 tomorrow. We'll be soaring by 10:30, I promise you that, kiddos."

Joseph and his vanilla essence stood up and walked out the door. I was beginning to understand that wearing vanilla might be his idea of a hoax on his world, because he was any flavor but.

CHAPTER 7

The commute home felt very different from the one to work, especially during the summer. My walk back to 47th Street had but one purpose—getting to the subway without interruptions from panhandlers or pickpockets. At that time of day, in the July heat, New York seemed depressing as well as unsafe. All the uplifting morning activities moved in reverse when the sun was fading. There was a lot of sweeping, cleaning of tables, and washing down windows. Streets overflowed with trash. New York stank all summer long.

Going home was like anticipating a trip down a funnel. The underground offered little olfactory relief, as commuter perspiration mixed with the pervasive smell of urine. Most nights, no matter how long I tried to hold my breath, I'd catch a whiff. I didn't inhale until, in my head, I had counted to 200. It had become a game to break my record before gasping for air. My all-time high was 238 seconds.

Another annoyance was the occasional open guitar case next to the feverishly strumming guitarist. But that bothered me less than the hawkers of overly priced carnations. As much as I love flowers, I hate carnations, and buying them underground was a double negative. And a triple negative, for me, was a pink carnation. To this day, I find myself avoiding anything pink.

It was Friday. I left work early to catch Amy's final Ethical Culture Summer Camp Drama performance prior to the kids dispersing like swarms of privileged bees to the Hamptons. By this point Amy had graduated from Wesleyan and she was back with me in our sublet. She was well liked by the principal at Ethical Culture and had been offered a position teaching fifth grade in the fall, but she was holding out to hear if she'd be offered a job at the Dalton School, which was her first choice.

I was coming that day to watch the play *I Am Anything But Plain*, directed by Amy and written by an eleven-year-old camper. The camper was not just any Upper West Side Jewish kid exercising her creative expression and right to get ahead. No, this child, Randy, was the offspring of a celebrated author, and the day before, I learned from Amy that many of the parents attending the show worked in New York's arts and media. It would be a well-heeled audience, to say the least. As Amy commented that morning, "Here's the first play I've ever directed and wouldn't you know I'll have Walter Kerr with his spiral notepad and fountain pen in my audience!" Amy gave me her wonderful cheeky smile with her parted thick lips that connected well to her trademark indented chin dimple. She made me laugh. Sometimes very hard.

I sat six rows back in the center, and two seats to my left was Tom Wolfe's dead ringer. Strike that, it was Tom Wolfe. Neil Simon didn't get a more distinguished audience than my girlfriend for opening night. I spotted Amy as her left hand rose as if connected to Leonard Bernstein's, so ready she was to conduct her first play. She pointed her forefinger at Randy, now center stage. With much poise and what appeared to be an equal measure of determination, this tiny Ethel Merman, Randy the Deliverer, cranked up her voice and started to belt out her lyrics. "I'm not plain. 'Unusual' is my name. I'm not plain, just filled with fame. I'm not plain…but unusual brings much pain." I could imagine my Amy, directing Randy to elongate the word "pain," so as to give out her diva best.

The musical blended humor and pathos. And delivered a bellowing showstopper at the end from…who best? Randy, of course, who put on her Annie's finest Tomorrow to send the audience to their feet with a vigorous ovation. I spotted her parents beaming as if giving birth all over again. Randy signaled to Amy at the curtain call to join the ensemble onstage to receive her dozen roses. The Hamptons' entitlement of it all made me really wonder about New York and raising kids there. Then came the hugs.

It was Amy who, with her full-of-fun approach to this musical, guided her students with tongue-in-cheek throughout the show to enchant the audience and to launch another great aspiring writer's career. Randy's mom led the parade of grateful parents. When she came up to Amy to shake her hand, she quickly pulled her in for a kiss on both cheeks (as if to reinforce, "Honey, I've been to Paris many times and you deserve both. And you over there,"…meaning me…"snap the damn picture already," as if to say, "we've got a six o' clock at Lutèce to toast our star's début.").

I was very proud of my girlfriend as we hailed a cab to our pick of the night, PJ Clarke's, on Third and 55th, for Amy's favorite drink and dinner. I gave her a kiss in the cab. "You really did it, girl! Those kids love you."

In 1978, New Yorkers were still tempting fate with steak tartar and Clarke's made it a nightly ritual, along with their famous burgers, which were served at about the same temperature. Our overly impressed-with-himself waiter sang his usual refrain, "Shall we serve your burgers, 'room?'" It was time for some new material. In addition to reliving her rave reviews, Amy and I had much to catch up on that night in late July.

Amy pulled from her purse a gushing handwritten note from the lower school principal of the Dalton School. She'd gotten the job she wanted! I was so pleased by her success. And truth be known, I was also impressed that the letter I helped her construct to accompany her résumé got a callback and an interview within only a few days. "I'm so happy for you. Dalton's such a class act."

We ordered Amy's favorite champagne cocktail and clinked glasses. "I'm thrilled! It's where I want to be, knock wood….So, how are things at work, Sam? Did you get the lowdown on Project Trio?"

"I met the Vanilla Wonder. He certainly smells the way they said he would."

"What's he like?"

"Arrogant, determined, smart as a whip, and consumed with worry. I'm pretty taken with the way Sandra handles him."

"You like that Sandra."

"I do. She's teaching me a lot. Volkswagen's in trouble, and so is the agency. It seems that Beinhauser and Maulborn were put on this assignment to save this account."

"You're kidding me. Doyle Dane Bernbach losing Volkswagen? C'mon!"

"That's what's so scary about this biz. Agency people are never really in the driver's seat. Hey," I said, changing the subject, "I made a reservation next weekend at the Newfane Inn to celebrate your birthday and Saturday night we're heading to the Four Columns."

"How cool!"

"You only turn twenty-one once."

"And then I need to stay twenty-one at least for another five years. That's so nice, Sam. Thank you."

What I didn't tell her was that coming out of the Four Columns kitchen, on top of the pâté we both love (Amy said it was like her grandmother's chopped liver), would be her engagement ring. I was planning to get down on bended knee at her birthday dinner with a ring atop the chopped liver. Could there be a more fitting proposal for my Jewish princess? I could see Beinhauser, were he at the next table, applauding my creative stunt.

I smiled. "Cheers," I said. Our glasses clinked again. But then I told her about a call I had gotten from my father. "Amy, Dad's cardiologist informed him that he's got to replace one of his heart valves and it's not a 'maybe' proposition. It's a serious operation with a long recovery period. It's planned for January sixth in Birmingham, which is like a factory for this kind of surgery. They're going to replace his valve with a pig's."

"Oink. I'm sorry, Sam, you know I love your dad," as she sucked up a big laugh that was about to follow.

"So, Dad started up about the company. He's always been a planner. He tells me, 'I'll be out of commission for several months so I've got about five months here to figure out, um, what to do about watching the store, if there'll be one left while I'm recovering.' He was hinting all over this conversation for me to come home to run things at the agency. Amy, how's Philadelphia sound to you?"

"What's he saying, Sam? We should leave New York now? What about Dalton?"

"I don't know what he's saying, Amy. For starters, he's going to have a serious operation. I think we need to investigate things there a bit. I want you with me."

"So my celebration dinner is about going home to Philadelphia? Why, of course, master!" She snapped, "You know best, Sam!" Amy was aggravated with even the notion of exploring this further, which pissed me off and prompted me to get the check, leave the restaurant, and hail a cab. Each of us claimed our side of the backseat, looking not at each other, just out our own windows.

Amy and I put this discussion on hold. After a while I think Amy saw it as something that had passed and gone away. I, of course, didn't. Dad needed me and I liked being wanted…and the notion of being there to build up the company was very appealing. And although this issue remained dormant for a while (maybe it was more like simmering somewhere out of Amy's direct scope), for me it remained very much on my mind and not as a weight, mind you. More like a star for which to reach.

The next morning, as I waited for the Vanilla Wonder to join Sandra and me in the conference room, my mind wandered. Thinking like a marketer, I imagined Joseph, depending on how he felt each morning, choosing among a variety of flavors he could splash on his face. For instance, he might be in a snappier mood and come in with more of a punch. And if so, I envisioned him wearing pure cinnamon. Tomorrow, he might be more playful and wish to smell like bubblegum. When he wanted to sting the room with his entrance, more than he already did, he could do it with Tabasco. You get the picture. The products were easy enough to find and to package. I thought about scents from all parts of the spice and sundry sections of the grocery store being assembled into a single kit to cover the gamut of a person's moods. I imagined the first floor of Saks Fifth Avenue, with its sprawling cosmetics and perfume counters, awash in spices. I liked my idea and brightened thinking about it.

"So, Sam-I-Am, you seem cheery today. I think I must have made a good impression on you."

I said, "You did and a most fragrant one."

He laughed. "I like you, Sam-I-Am. And Sandra? I know I've been an asshole. This pressure has been eating me up inside. Harder on you, I know. And when I'm up against it, I hole myself up. I apologize."

"Someone woke up on a better side of his bed this morning," Sandra said.

"I walk a lot in Northeast Harbor. I love Acadia. There is something so alive with the waves hitting the rocks, and you're close enough to feel the spray. Worries, for me, diminish when I'm by the sea. Yesterday, you heard me philosophize enough to make you want to puke. But I did so for a reason. Everything about this project rubs me all wrong. Don't quote me here, but in certain ways our client would be better off starting with a new agency."

"Bite your tongue, Joe."

"No, really, humor me, Sandy. It's just us here." He looked around the room and under the table. "No bugs. No moles. And yes, I'm talking about McCann. It would be easier for me to win this campaign if I were working at McCann Ericson. Working here at DDB, I've had to fall out of love with a lot of what we've done so right all these years for these guys. And we love our shit. Who more than we? We're proud of it. There are lots of traps if we stay in the realm of what we know. And if that's where we had decided to head, we'd be dead. That much I know for sure."

"So how far have you strayed?"

"Far. Sandra and I got lost for a while. Over time, after all our preaching to stay on point, to be true to the brand, which I've repeated to Volkswagen more times than I wish to remember, 'Let us not wander.' Then whom did I need to break in during this process of change? Myself. Like a goddamn wild and overly sexed horse, and I assure you it wasn't easy."

"I can hardly imagine Joseph, our broken man."

"So I baked on all of this at our summer home in Northeast Harbor. Acadia was therapeutic because I was reminded every day that waves break in new configurations before the others sweep in. Until you really watch a wave crash, they all look just about the same. You think a wave is a wave. But in reality, each one is quite different. The wind and weather cut them in different shapes."

"Joey, you certainly didn't sleepwalk your days away up there." And then Sandra took a big gulp of her coffee as a way to punctuate her point.

"Placid has a short life span. Clouds rush in. Not a lot of bunk when you see it day to day. Ask the lobstermen or fishermen; they know exactly what to watch for. When your livelihood is at stake, the waves are the only real thing that tells you what's what."

As I listened to him, I realized what a captivating storyteller he was, and what a gift it is to be riveting so much of the time. We all like good tales. Stories sustain us.

I also thought that Joseph's scent that day should have been sea salts. He was so good at describing Acadia that you could smell the ocean off his back.

Suddenly out of nowhere, like the mouse that roared, I asked, "Joseph, what is VW's voice and how are we going to change it come September?"

And at that moment I knew, as did he, I was no longer Sam-I-Am.

"Sam, Volkswagen ads are certainly some of the finest ever made. Since I haven't created the best of them, I'm able to say so unabashedly. In Northeast Harbor lingo, they hit the rocks in a formation that's consistent, which has made the brand personality clear-cut. We landed on the right-size wave and then pounded away at it for a good long while. Good insights, metaphors, and parables. I'd call what we've done 'a very defined type of day,' not overly sunny. But not absent of sun either. The kind of day you don a sweater, but only a cotton one."

"A streak of days when there's a nip in the air but not a cold front," Sandra inserted.

"Absolutely. Brisk but not cold. Confident, but never brash. Self-effacing, yet never timid. See him, Sam? See Volkswagen run? How does the guy who drives the snowplow get to the plow? The billionaire who rewards his VW-owner nephew with all his money because that nephew's a successful cheapskate. We've had the guts, the smarts to tell these stories. And if we break commercials with these new cars in that voice, the consumer...who is smarter than we ever give them credit... will think nothing has really changed. Samuel, then what?"

I said, "I guess we'd have to pack it in."

"Right you are, smarty-pants."

Sandra stopped him. "So this campaign will feel like a new car company?"

"Not exactly. But it will feel like a car company reflecting a different mood in the country. This campaign won't tell people how they should feel or signal how smart we are. And there's the difference. Instead, we'll hold a mirror up to everyone and reflect the thinking of Americans today. A car for today. Not yesterday's car."

Sandra inched out to the edge of her seat, "So what you're saying, Joe, is that America repurposed Volkswagen?"

"Exactisimo, my darling. Americans made this car company think more...see more...act differently."

"So it's the car that is following the people. Not the Germanic other way around."

"Now we're talking, Sandra. We're not leading people to a new calling. We're listening to their call. And because we've built a ton of equity, in our case, self-improvement is credible."

"Bravo, Joe."

"Now we've got to make it stick. Get our client to buy in. That's the trick here. It's going to take every piece of cunning we've got."

"Joseph, you'll work up your setup, which already feels like a winner. Sam here, and I, will load the gun. What are the deliverables?"

Knowing a bit about rah-rah, I said, "And what do we do with the damn circling helicopter?" I was feeling my oats by then.

Joseph fired back, "We'll shoot them out of the sky and make them go bye-bye. The line is simply, 'It's a New Generation of Volkswagens for a New Generation of Americans.' We've come out of Watergate. We're licking our wounds from Vietnam. We hired ourselves a president who's a smart peanut-farmer preacher from Bum Fuck, Georgia. Our country is healing." Miming a cat taking broad licks to his front arm, "We're redirecting ourselves back to what's important. Hope. Values. Believing again. Feeling good."

What a sharp thinker, I thought. *This could be me someday.*

"What's wrong with this picture, cuties?"

"Not much. What about the music?" asked Sandra.

"It's an anthem. No lyrics to speak of. Until the end. And the words are spoken. But the music is lyrical. It's riddled with optimism and free-dom. And lots of emotional crescendos. It's Chopin meets Gershwin with strong punches of Bernstein. And it's sixty seconds of soft dissolves of people getting back to what's really important in their lives. It's a travelogue. It's America getting back on its feet, getting high on some natural buzz. Life's highs, my friends, nothing artificial. Are you vomit-ing yet or eating this up, Sam-I-Am?"

I picked up the wastebasket under the table and opened my mouth wide into it.

"Ah, Sam's getting bolder by the day. And it's all shot in Maine."

"Whoa, cowboy!" Sandra cut in. "Sounds beautiful. But all North-east Harbor scenes? Joseph, that's way too upscale."

"I'm a step ahead of you, my darling. Most everything I shot could be anywhere. Caucasians, Blacks, Hispanics, Asians. I've got mixed na-tionalities and ages in the same scenes, in the same cars. People and cars within wonderful settings. Sunrises, sunsets, fathers fishing with daugh-ters. Mothers throwing baseballs to their sons with that girlie kind of throw. Sorry, Sandy. Face it, girls throw funny." His hand cut through the air in slow motion until his wrist snapped limply at the end.

"Then there are young couples in fields with flowers and picnic bas-kets and wine. A baker and his assistant putting a wedding cake in the back of a Rabbit. And in all these pictures are our cars: romanticized, shiny, sleek, alive." He swept his right hand into the shape of a camera's lens, peering through. "It's a new generation of Volkswagens for a new generation of Americans."

Sandra chimed in, "Lovely, Joseph, really lovely. Nice having you back with us! Tell me about the voice you hear?"

"He's fresh, but a bit brash. Like he owns the world but he doesn't really know that yet. He's experienced, yet still optimistic. He's enterprising but open-minded...classically trained," as he looked my way, "from, say, Wesleyan. Exuberant. Longing. Wanting his part of the dream."

"I've got a ton of photo selects here," he continued, placing boxes of slide carousels onto the conference room table from the stacks on the floor. "Sandy...find the shots. Make the dissolves as stunning as you are. Seductive. Sweet. Sexy. The music, with the pictures, has to move all hands across America out of their Frito bowls and onto their hearts. *N'est-ce pas?* Or let's just forget about all this, and as Sam said, 'pack it in.'"

Joseph stood up, staring at attention, saluting in that impish John-John Kennedy way as he inched himself closer to the door. Then, he turned to us again and advanced himself forward as if he dissolved into Charlie Chaplin toddling an imaginary cane, still with sea salts lingering in the air he left the room.

CHAPTER 8

The ring that topped Amy's pâté had not only been a surprise, but also, was happily accepted, the first big step on the way to our nuptials. Next up was our "parents meet parents" engagement dinner in Philly.

When the big night arrived, Amy's mom and dad, Jack and Jeannie arriving from Boca Raton, were delayed, having flown in from Fort Lauderdale to Newark instead of Philadelphia. They were aware that the dinner was planned for 7:30 at my parents' house in Elkins Park, and hopefully the wrong airport was an honest mistake. This is how I imagined their conversation as they drove their rented Olds from New Jersey, normally an hour and a half ride that turned into three:

"Jack, do you know where you're going?"

"We'll sniff them out, Jeannie. The Jews in Philadelphia are all clustered in a row and right about now they're all roasting their briskets. We'll just sniff them out."

He figured our housekeeper was preparing brisket and had decided to use his nose instead of a road map to find our house. "What'll be the difference if we're a half-hour or even an hour late? The longer they cook that meat the easier it will be on the knife."

Jack was always ready with an off-color comment that amused Jeannie and kept their dysfunctional marriage alive enough. Jeannie was usually passively angry with her totally self-absorbed husband whose uniform manufacturing business had gone bust. Her disenchantment with Jack lay just below the surface and had simmered that way for years, but she remained loyal through it all. She loved when Jack made her laugh. Laughter seemed to be the way he earned his supper. Amy, I had figured, had picked up on building our relationship on humor. In many respects, her wise cracks sustained us as well. However, Amy and Jeannie's laughs were not the same. Amy's were more full blown. Jeannie's were more like snickers that farted out of her as punctuation marks to Jack's wisecracks almost as if Jeannie was playing a snare drum, hitting the metal as well as the skin.

Jeannie always said that at moments like this she wondered what her deceased father might be thinking from above as he stood, we all joked, next to his main man, Moses. Randolph Shendler, Jeannie's dad, was a rabbinical student who hailed from Russia, and became a *schmatte* merchant in America. Eventually, he ran a moderately priced clothing empire that carried his name. When he amassed enough wealth to really be called wealthy, he answered to a higher calling. He became chairman of the Anti-Defamation League, right at the end of World War II. No small feat in a lifetime, or even three.

As a result, he became for all of eternity, in his daughter's eyes, the man who could do no wrong. So what did that make Jack by comparison? A *schlimazel*. For Jeannie, her dad's compass was hers, too. Her father had also taken care of his own people, setting up million dollar trusts for each grandchild that would mature when each turned twenty-one. But that money evaporated when Jack used it to try to save his business. Enough said. You get the picture.

Fortunately, Jeannie liked to laugh, and Jack, we heard, was Henny Youngman that night in the car.

Jack and Jeannie Reinhart finally arrived at our engagement dinner two hours late. Amy was pacing by the door as they entered to the smell, not of brisket, but of rib roast. Jeannie knew the distinction. Rib roasts are cooked without carrots, onions, and celery and much more fat wafts into the air than with either brisket or tenderloin. Jeannie apologized profusely exclaiming, "I know we've now doomed our kids' marriage."

Jack chimed in, in a Johnny Carson sort of way, "We were conscientiously following the smell of your brisket until this pungent skunk got in our way."

My parents laughed a bit uncomfortably but welcomed their guests into the den of their spacious home. Jack was right; we were in the heart of brisket country where many had been eaten hours earlier. My folks were hospitable people. Elizabeth and Harry loved parties and knew how to throw them. The food they prepared was always good and quite plentiful. Their joy for such events showed on their faces. Their cups runneth over…until we hit my engagement dinner. As Amy and I glanced at each other, we knew the evening was rapidly sinking.

Things got worse. While the roast was being reheated, Jack, who'd gulped down a few shots of Jack Daniels prior to being served matzo ball soup, now had difficulty negotiating his spoon's short journey to his mouth. Elizabeth, who prided herself in being direct, pointed her finger at Jack and observed, "You can't eat matzo ball soup? What kind of Jew are you?"

Jack attempted to make conversation while he unsteadily maneuvered a matzo ball onto his spoon. Jewish geography, he knew, was always a successful icebreaker. "So, Harry, what camp did you go to?"

Harry, the Holocaust survivor, never missing a quick comeback, gave Jack his answer, "Buchenwald."

By the time the gathering broke apart, Amy was in tears. Harry muttered his closing line of the night, "If only Jack can find the hotel without killing the bride."

Amy left with them.

What came next will sound odd. But it's a confession, or perhaps an omen. As soon as the Reinharts departed, I called Beth Ehrenberg. Despite our breakup, she was my closest confidante and the one person in the world who understood me best. "Could I pick you up and go for a ride?" I asked her, "I'd like to talk." By then, Beth was a sophomore at Brown and back home for the summer. I think she had always thought she'd be the one on her way to this engagement dinner. But she also knew she was three years my junior and still slogging through college, and I was on my restless tear. I learned Beth, too, had had a rough night; it was Sabbath dinner and she had overdosed on too much of her folks and family.

Lucky for Beth's family, a year prior, her father, Marshall Ehren-berg, sold his potato chip business that had real prominence in the mid-Atlantic region, winning the country's "best chip" award in early 1976. While his kettle was hot, Marshall turned over his keys to Frito-Lay, and cashed in his chips, so to speak, receiving a handsome payout. The income enabled them to purchase a new home, the former Burn's Hill Estate, which had a prestigious Philadelphia pedigree with its elaborate topiary gardens, six swan fountains, and grass tennis court.

Certainly, my call stirred Beth's curiosity, especially after I had shared some of the details. We had always helped solve each other's problems as we deeply respected the other's opinion. We hadn't seen each other in a year and a half, but she was my first, as I had been hers, and although that fact should have been the last thing on my mind that night, I suppose it vanquished other loyalties. When I turned the cor-ner and pulled to a stop, there she was, as confident and as beautiful as always. I leaned over to open the door and she swung her lavish curves into the front seat. We kissed hello and I began to drive.

In the depths of the Brandywine Country, I found an obscure new place for us to park. We pulled off the road, windshield wipers squeaking as the rain poured down on the car and I recounted the details of the evening's horror show. "What a holy disaster. Everything that could go wrong did go wrong. The Reinharts were two hours late. Amy's father got drunk. He couldn't get the matzo ball onto his spoon, much less to his mouth. Everyone was distraught and embarrassed. Biting comments flew around all night long. It got so painful, all I wanted to do was to see you."

My head flopped into Beth's lap. She stroked my hair. Then, with-out hesitation, we climbed into the backseat and embraced. We always understood where to touch. We hugged and ran our fingers ever so lightly over each other's bodies. That night, as the patter of rain intensified, I enjoyed her lovely shoulders. The windows developed their familiar steam. As I hiked up Beth's denim skirt, I knew it could never be this good again. Two hours passed in record time. Our hold on each other was tight. We didn't say much and we didn't want to let go. And—don't judge me—all I wanted was to say, "This engagement is off because it's you I want to be with," but I couldn't get those words out.

Instead, we climbed into the front seat, a decision I would live and relive over thousands of nights in the years to come. But at the time, I knew we had to get back to our separate paths. It was the right call, what I really wanted. I started up the car and moved forward, but the wheels spun furiously in the mud. The tires kept digging deeper and deeper into the ground. We were there together in some hidden part of Brandy-wine Country at 2:30 in the morning on my engagement night, squarely stuck. I thought of AAA but had no idea where we were or how to find a phone. Our friends were fast asleep. Call our parents? *Right.*

Fate intervened. A man wearing a Stetson hat pulled up in an old Lincoln Continental. I wondered if he could help us and if it was appropriate to risk flagging him down. I had very little money on me. Clearly, he saw the steamed windows and the predicament we were in. I had only one choice. I popped out of the car and reported on our situation. At this moment I could only hope he could be trusted. "Sir, we're stuck."

"No shit, Sherlock." And this man with the Stetson hat took over like a guardian angel. He told us he'd bring around his truck. "I'll get you out of there."

And he did. Beth and I believed this was how our love story ended—driving off together for the last time before I married the other gal.

CHAPTER 9

That's what we grow up to think. That it's all basically cut and dried. Until we learn it's not that way at all. Yes, I was back in New York. Back with Amy. Back at Doyle Dane Bernbach helping save its biggest and most coveted account from going off to a competitor. But to say leaving Beth the day prior would be forgotten...that would be an inaccurate statement. Because the simple truth about Beth was that she never quite left my heart, my mind, or my spirit.

In advertising there are rituals for big pitch days. Everyone does his or her superstitious best to bring around the right outcome. A week before each major contest, not a day earlier or a day later, Beinhauser put his white pitch socks on and wore them until the pitch was over.

At the point he took his white socks off, in whatever midtown or out-of-town conference room he had just played, he hoped they'd be washed and returned with a love note and accompanied by champagne, meaning the account had been won. His white socks trick had become legendary on Madison Avenue. Even clients knew of his antics. Sandra said he was currently on a roll with six straight wins, so we all silently prayed his socks would come through a seventh time.

Before we left in separate cars to go to our client in New Jersey, Beinhauser recited his litany of white socks wins: "Two triple crowns," he said, "an Avis save, a Seagram's win, an American Tourister win, a GTE win, an American Airlines save, a Chivas Regal win, and now Volkswagen, my highest purse contest to date. Which brings me back to another Kentucky Derby." He asked Sandra to predict what account he'd be saving next.

She answered, "Ponderosa."

Beinhauser snapped back, "I'll not be wasting my fraying white socks on those clowns. That one can go to McCann." He waved his car keys and I spotted a VW logo dangling from them, as he said, "Most of the VIPs in Kentucky wear wonderful hats at the Derby, for when their horse comes in. I'm sporting my brand-new derby for this stellar win." He walked out of the room with his smart new brown cap with VW embroidered on the front, and in small lettering on the back bottom rim were the words: Scirocco, Rabbit, Jetta. This man didn't miss a trick.

I asked Sandra, "So what's your lady luck?"

She said, "You really don't want to know."

"Trust me. I do."

"Well, I don't wear a bra."

"You don't say. Does Joseph know this little ditty?"

Sandra said, "He won it off me on a dare."

I wondered how long her streak had been going. As long as Beinhauser's? And he had everyone thinking the wins were about his socks. From then on I looked everywhere but at her chest.

The account guys traveled in Henderson's car, a Porsche that was politically okay because Porsche, I was told, was a cousin of sorts to VW. Sandra and I rode with Alvin in his VW bus carrying the slide carousels, projectors, and the sound system. Sandra insisted on two stacks of four projectors. One we'd use. The other, we'd have ready in reserve, if, "heaven forbid," the first stack got fucked up. Everyone at the agency was big on "heaven forbid." I wondered if this was another superstition to keep a pitch on track. As it turned out, heaven forbid was a Bill Bernbachism. Alvin would run the projectors. I would help him get the machinery to the conference room. Sandra would conduct traffic and work hard to keep Henderson away from Beinhauser.

Joseph's vintage Karmann Ghia, which he normally left up in Northeast Harbor through Thanksgiving, had been returned for this pitch. Sandra said, "Joseph had to have this car to drive to the pitch in order, as he told me, 'To have my socks work right.' He'd had his favorite lobsterman, Guy LaSalle, deliver it to Joseph's place in Chappaqua for a couple hundred dollars and a steak dinner with all of us. Joseph's grilled steak dinners before pitch days are legendary. As he put it, 'I must make us strapping lions.'"

And it was the night before this pitch that I learned that Guy LaSalle was no regular lobsterman. He had a Ph.D. in political science and for ten years had headed up the history department at Bates College until, as he put it, "I got a call from the sea." He bought a house on Little Cranberry Island and became a full-time lobsterman. He proudly pointed out to us over dinner, "I've delivered the entire Little Cranberry electorate since I've been living there. Now the whole island votes."

I said, "That's mighty impressive."

"I fill a fourteen-by-fourteen taxi-boat and take the islanders to the mainland," he told me. "I bring beer for before and after all levers get pulled. Last year we islanders sent Carter's brother, Billy, a case of Acadia Beer. Billy's note back to us now hangs above the Captain's wheel and his letterhead says, 'From Jimmy's often burping brother, Thanks for the beer up 'ere. Each bottle got better as the day moved on.' Twelve caps were enclosed in the envelope with his note. Joseph's header simply read, 'Vote. For Beer, Before and After.' And Beinhauser used the bottle caps to frame the note." LaSalle looked at me and said, "You know, Sam, you work for a genius."

"You mean the one who smells like a quart of Breyers?"

"Let me tell you this about your Mr. Vanilla here. He sees the world as no one else I've ever met. You may ask why a smart man like Beinhauser is making commercials for a living? I think he really believes in the profound power of the message, and he's convinced this old cynic here that there's something to your game. His spot for Lyndon Johnson made the point. It ran once but it may well have saved the world from the A-bomb. Just think, had Joseph been old enough to have served Churchill, that war could have been over in six weeks."

"Now kids, you understand why I do my best work up 'ere, because I've got old Guy so snookered."

And it was that night, when Beinhauser bulked us up to be lions for the next day's pitch, that Sandra drove us back into the city and we talked about that quintessential and brilliant 1964 anti-Goldwater spot, "Daisy Girl," as it counted-down to the A-bomb. She told me, as we reached the FDR, "On one of my early Polaroid shoots, Bill Bernbach was on the set and as he leaned into my ear, he said, 'Sweetie, my name's on the door, but let's never forget, we're all working for Beinhauser. Watching him always makes me feel like a pisher.'"

The hour before a pitch in the client's conference room is about as high stress as it gets in the business. Sandra, Alvin, and I first set up some very heavy-duty scaffolding made of steel piping, which, Alvin told Sandra, "Can hold the eight projectors and a gorilla." The projectors sat in two stacks, with one on standby in case the main one went on the fritz. Sandra had a thing about hiding the wiring behind skirting. Alvin was charged with painstakingly pinning fabric to the scaffolding and muttered, "Now I can tell everyone I've been promoted to wedding seamstress."

Sandra said, "Alvin, I heard that. Should I get one of the other 'chipmunks' to help me out here?"

That was a nasty shot and seemed out of character from Sandra. I was glad she wasn't taking whacks at me.

The air conditioner was cranked up high. "Beinhauser," Sandra said, "won't play in a warm room. He likes it at 60 degrees." As I looked around, Sandra's unmistakably pert nipples attested to this fact, and again I was reminded why Joseph was called Houdini.

Alvin and I finished the skirting and moved on to wiring up the sound system. I placed two speakers on either side of the screen and brought the wires to the amp sitting on the fortress built for Godzilla.

Then I used gaffers tape to hold down the wires, as Sandra had instruct-ed. We had brought two screens. One was gray, that we'd set up if the projectors worked in the rear of the screen, in that case we'd have to flip the slides the other way around. The other was a white one for front projection, that, earlier in the week, we had made the decision to use.

There were two reasons for choosing the white screen: Beinhauser and Beinhauser. Joseph told Alvin, "I hate rear screens because every shot looks like it was taken in Seattle. Yes, Alvin, the gray screen can hide the wires and the projectors, but who the fuck cares if they're ex-posed? This is theater, son."

All week long, Joseph kept harping about this until Sandra finally shrieked, "We're fucking on board, Joe! Now, please go home and tor-ment your wife and kids instead."

Alvin, as it turned out, was everybody's punching bag. People's be-havior before pitches was rude and often bordered on outrageous. But the stakes were so high and the lack of sleep was apparent. Sandra had managed to keep Henderson away from Beinhauser, which I understood was a major blessing. On the patio outside the conference room, Bein-hauser paced back and forth with scripts rolled up in his hand, rehears-ing his opening. Was he nervous, too?

At precisely 11:00 all six Titans walked in. Precision was their thing. And we were prepared and ready to go. At this moment, Sandra was everyone's mom. She signaled to Henderson to kick off the presen-tation with a short introduction about Beinhauser, the rock star, whom, by the way, he referred to as "Doc-torrrr" Beinhauser, even to the client. Then Beinhauser gave Henderson the hook to take center stage.

Wearing his VW derby, Joseph talked about Northeast Harbor and the waves and the difficulties of taking a fresh look at what Volkswagen was becoming. He talked about how much goodwill and equity had been built up over time, and masterfully explained Volkswagen's credibility and its deeper understanding of the American mindset. His lead-in was stunning. Nothing short of it. He went on to say, "Men, our spots aren't commercials. They're sixty second anthems that talk to Americans as we shoot them in their hearts." And he announced in his own beautiful delivery, "It's a new generation of Volkswagens for a new generation of Americans." He let the line seep in for a good six seconds before talking further. He had such a beautiful sense of timing and knew the effectiveness of the pause and how to use it.

Then he repeated the line. He went on to speak about the spirit of what he had shot. "The healing of America. The hope we wish to inspire with our cars and our message." Then he thanked Sandra for doing all the heavy lifting and thanked me as the newest DDB 'star buck' and he even made room for some Alvin plaudits before he commanded, "Hit it, Alvin."

The music, as envisioned weeks ago, came alive in Joseph's concert hall...a rhapsody of America. The shots, with the beautifully timed dissolves, were poignant. And Sandra nailed the voice. In the end it was an actor full of optimism, but who still understood the letdowns of the world. It was the voice of, none other than, James Earl Jones.

My eyes were tearing up as the three sixty-second spots were presented in rapid succession. Then there was some applause. Not the "on their feet screaming bravo" applause like after an aria. But certainly polite enough. Henderson came back to the center of the room and clapped his hands toward Joseph and then toward Sandra. He took on the role of Mr. RaRa, "Here is to our future and here's to selling boatloads of new cars." He raised his Coke glass. "To our success." The glass was then lowered to the table. "Now, men, let's open the floor for Q and A."

At this point Günter took control of the room. "On behalf of all of us at Volkswagen of America, I want to thank you for this impressive effort. As you all know, this is a very important moment in our history, and I presume, yours as well. So to stay focused and on point, my associates here have asked me to orchestrate this Q and A session. Joseph, I'd like to start with you and ask—as forgetful as I can be from time to time—how long have we been working together?"

"I think you had your third-born when we got started, and Kimberly is now a young twelve-year-old beauty, right?"

"Twelve she is, and that's very kind of you to say. And, Joseph, in the space of these twelve years, can you imagine how often you've said,

68

'My friend, we've got a persona to protect. Let us all stay loyal to our brand.' Do you know how often I've repeated this command to my comrades? Even my kids play this phrase back to me."

The Titans chuckled in unison.

"I'm sure, a gazillion times. And Günter, I think that's been solid advice."

"Precisely. I quote it all the time. You built this persona with us and have helped keep our train on the tracks. I remember not long ago, you looked me square in the eyes and said, 'Persona, Günter, remain loyal to the brand...to deviate will tempt a train wreck. You remember saying these words?"

Joseph goaded Günter gently with his response, "That must have been something that came out of Henderson's mouth."

Mild laughter from the Titans.

"Could it be, Beinhauser, my friend, that what you brought us today is, in fact, a train wreck?"

Without a beat, Joseph shot back, "Günter, I'm not a 'trust me' kind of guy. And I've never known you not to speak your mind. There must be a good reason you've turned to me to say what we presented today is a train wreck."

"No, Joseph, I said, '*Could* this be a train wreck?'"

"Günter, I want to be clear on what you are saying so that I'm able to respond appropriately."

"I think you changed our persona instead of building on what we've previously done."

"I think, *mon frère*, you changed your cars on us, as you should have, and we've had to communicate something brand–new, and I just reached into our built-up equity pile and said, 'We hear you, America, and thanks for helping us repurpose and reshape the future of Volkswagen America with these new cars.' That's what we're saying in our work, Günter."

"Then, my darling friend, those wonderful stories you and your guys tell so well in our past car commercials now need to take a backseat, ja, to something brand-new, a slide show? It wasn't more than a week ago I was listening to Mel Brooks interviewed by Barbara Walters and some-how he got onto what he detests most: slides in someone's basement. He said, 'I'll take a dentist's drill before going to a basement to hear click, click, click.'"

Everyone could see that Beinhauser had lost his cool on that sharp shot. Fully sarcastic in tone, he said, "Günter, aside from a tweak here or there, you seem to really love what I've brought you." The room re-mained silent and everyone's eyes followed Joseph as he walked over to the patio door, opened it, and stuck his head outside to take in a breath.

Then Henderson piped up over the silence: "There is more passion for this work in Beinhauser's pinky than any other professional I've ever seen in my career for any other campaign he's believed in."

Even I knew then that Henderson was flapping his mouth to fill space, to buy time for Beinhauser to compose himself.

Joseph, now quiet, tiptoed around on the wide stage in front of the projectors as if he were a mime. He took off his specially made handsome brown VW derby. He brushed down his silver hair with his hands. Was this some sort of meditation, as a way for him to regain his composure? Or was this a presentation trick? I was eager to see what would come next.

Although I was not experienced in pitches, much less "save the ac-count" presentations, this felt like the showdown moment. It was as if Beinhauser was balancing ever so delicately on a tightrope, figuring out his words, as if he had just turned Churchill to say, "We will fight them on the beaches. We shall fight in the fields and in the streets."

Staring directly at each Titan, one by one he said, "America has been aching for many years now. Longing to trust again, to have hope restored. This campaign, men, is all about reflecting our customers' feel-ings and desires for what we cherish most of all, hope...and to share why your company created these three new cars. What we have here is restoration of faith, faith again in America...maybe not quite the over-haul that Germany faced decades ago. But after Vietnam and Watergate and a shaky economy, America wants badly to believe in itself again. To have the heart we're known for. That's what we brought to you today, gentlemen."

"We brought Volkswagen's heart. And who has built up the best equity bank in car-making history? Volkswagen. You created three new cars to be a part of America's new beginning. I was just fortunate enough to write the anthems to reflect your courage." Joseph put his cap back on. Then he took it off as if he were Mickey Mantle waving his goodbyes to his fans.

Was he in fact saying farewell to these Titans and our lifeline? I think right about then, everyone on our side was worried that was precisely what was happening.

"Thank you for your great work, gentlemen, on these three wonderful new cars."

To me, Beinhauser was God, and we in the room his disciples. Joseph went back to tiptoeing, hat dangling a bit in his hand, and then he stopped hard by the slide projectors. Everyone could see that his performance was not quite over. He put his cap back on and turned to the Titans and stared them down one last time. There was quite the practiced pause. What the hell was he up to?

Finally, he spoke. "Want to see what your train wreck might look like?" And he stepped back and found his way behind the projectors.

At this point, he positioned himself to face his audience, and in one swift move, reached down with both hands and grabbed the side of the scaffolding and completely sent everything crashing hard to the floor in front of him. The projectors and amp tumbled, with a huge rumble as glass shattered everywhere.

I happened to be in eyeshot of Alvin. His mouth opened wide enough to bite into a whole cantaloupe. No, make it a watermelon.

Joseph ended his soliloquy with, "Gentlemen, here's what your train wreck will look like if we don't proceed. I'm that confident in this direction." He stepped out of his loafers, slipped off his socks, and gently tossed them into the middle of the mess he had just made. Then he put his shoes back on and walked out of the conference room.

Two days later, Günter arrived at our building on 49th and Madison and immediately rode the elevator to the tenth floor. He was a man

71

on a mission as he headed toward Beinhauser's corner office. As I heard it told, the door was wide open. Joseph was sitting on a stool, drawing peacefully on a sketchpad. Günter walked in with an open note in his hand and something hidden behind his back. He proceeded to read the note.

"There is far too little passion left in this world. You, our darling boy, have a lock on a mighty sum of it. This is our firm green light on 'New Generation.'" Günter produced two-dozen roses from behind his back. "Please share these with the troops." Then Günter stuck his hand into his front pocket to pull out the balled-up pair of white socks. He stared Beinhauser down and started his windup. "By the way, my boy, they really stink." Then he released the socks with a broad curve of his arm, a pitcher to his catcher.

CHAPTER 10

Although my dad seemed to love Amy and the fact that his sonny boy, as he referred to me from time to time, was getting married to a "beautiful gal," the engagement dinner fiasco and the energy it consumed had almost seemed a distraction from his quest. He wanted me to join him in business and was cooking up ways to get this accomplished.

It had become his personal political campaign, this wooing me back to Philadelphia—to the point he started calling me at work. It's true, Mikey never expressed interest in working at the company or in advertising in general. ("I'm a reporter," he'd often announce to me. "I've learned how to have my own life, Sam. You can play up to Dad all you want.") The fact of the matter is, for as long as I could remember I wanted to join the family business. But at this moment of intensive courting of me by my Dad, I wondered how Mikey felt about being passed over. Did he take it as another in a line of rejections?

Prior to that, Dad's phone calls had always been to my apartment and in tandem with my mother. He would pick up the other extension, thinking that nobody knew, but of course we all knew. He would say nothing until he had something to say. But his rather heavy breathing in the background was always a give-away. I'd wait a few minutes before greeting him with a "Hello, Dad." And since this was routine, he'd say "Hello" back. There was never an ounce of embarrassment when I busted him for eavesdropping. My mother would then say, "Oh, Harry, get off the phone." But he wouldn't. I think he couldn't. He seemed to never want to miss a word.

So these calls to my office, without Mom, were a little alarming. After he'd caught up on my news, what interested him most was going down his checklist. Dad always made lists. And he wasn't satisfied until he'd spit out every last point he had penciled on his sheet of paper. Also, he'd stammer with "ums" between his words. His halting speech became more frequent when he was nervous about what he had to say.

"Um...Sam, you know about this operation I need to have. It's no... um...simple procedure and I'll be out of commission for some time."

Wishing I could move his words along, I asked him, "Isn't Harvey Lodenberg your number-two guy?"

He said, "Well...um...there's a debate on that subject. Sol Katz is doing a lot of the client contact work with the bigger accounts. And Harvey Lodenberg is technically Executive Vice President, but he's a rather peculiar fellow with the clients. Smart enough guy, but Harvey's a bit weird and his wife is weirder. And then there's that young writer, Jesse, who's been writing for the National Horse Racing Association account. But...um...I've been told he's been looking around."

He always answered simple questions with dissertations. I had interned for Dad over the course of three summers before going to DDB and knew all thirteen associates well. But he always felt compelled to list everyone, and to editorialize about his or her present position in the company. I said, "It would be a shame to lose Jesse. He's part of the future."

"Um...you know these young guys...they're always looking for more money, and there's a limit." He often warned me about the impending doom of able young personnel leaving or accounts pitched that would go to another agency. As smart and discerning as Dad was at home and around friends, some of whom were German refugees as well and in whose company he was a leader, I learned over the summers that Dad's confidence shriveled at the office. And there, he must have felt more like an American outsider. He often remarked about his pleasure in having me as a son, "Sam, you're a natural winner." He liked my confidence and how it reflected on him. The truth was that Harvey Lodenberg was smothering this buck, Jesse, by over editing his copy and showing him who was boss at every turn.

I said, "Dad, I'm in a hurry to get back to the Polaroid casting session."

"If it's not Volkswagen, it's Polaroid. If it's not...um...Polaroid, it's Avis. Sorry to bother such an important man."

"Come on, Dad, I report to people. I've got responsibilities here. Tell me quickly what else is going on." Harry Spiegel seemed to have little awareness of the fact that I couldn't talk long or very freely. And then he popped his surprise. What this call was all about.

"You know the hot agency that's winning all the awards, BRC?"

I told him, "Yeah, I'm quite familiar with them. That's where Jesse came from."

"Um...right. Well, I met with them about a potential merger and they're interested."

"How long has this been going on?"

"This is...um...a recent development and that's why I'm calling you. I would appreciate you meeting with them. The oldest might be ten years your senior. The youngest is about your age, a creative rock star from Canada, Loren...um...Rucker. I made a date a week from tonight for you to have dinner with just the three of them at Cuzzin's, and you and Amy are more than welcome to stay the weekend."

"How serious is this?"

"Serious enough for me to want to get your opinion about them. We would bring them some stability and they're all award-winning creative guys."

"If it's serious, I'll make plans to be there. I'll check with Amy about staying over."

"That would be great, Sam. I set it up for seven. Give my love to Amy. Your mom and I would be delighted...um...if you can spend the weekend with us. We'll all go down to the beach house and spend a night or two. And we'll get crabs. They're big and plentiful this year." Click. Dad's recruitment campaign was full throttle and his busy scheming was working on me.

The next week, I drove my trusty Torino down to Philadelphia and arrived at Cuzzin's at 7:00. Amy planned to follow by train the next day. Cuzzin's was a mainstay mid-quality Philadelphia restaurant and was right near Lux, the largest agency in the city. Whenever Spiegel & Associates was in a pitch with Lux, my father would mentally fold and write off the chances of winning. The BRC partners had all come from Lux, and so a merger with them might be a strategic coup. I was the first to arrive at the restaurant and announced I was part of the party of four under the name Tony Braumberg. The BRC guys, their office also nearby, evidently often ate at Cuzzin's.

"Oh, you's with the boys tonight. They're usually late but I'll seat you anyways. What to drink?"

"A Dewar's and soda with a twist, please."

The hostess sat me at the table under a signed picture of Tony Orlando and Dawn from when they played the Philadelphia Spectrum circa 1974. I wondered how many other smoky, dark restaurant walls this group might have been gracing that night. All of the artwork looked as if it had been arranged by a drunk at the bar flinging framed pictures like darts around the room.

Hanging by the front door was a framed photo of Dick Clark with the caption, "Philadelphia's Oldest Teenager." And next to him was our towering Pope himself, Pope Sylvester Stallone, who must have devoured many a thick steak from Cuzzin's...that is, between bouts of beating whole sides of beef with his boxing gloves.

In between the celebrity photos were several sizable shiny oil paintings of Spanish dancers and bullfighters. In another corner was a large autographed poster featuring the animated Hamm's Beer bear. The Hamm's campaign was one of Lux's success stories. Under the visual was a caption that promised, "The Beer Refreshing."

The "boys" were late but I was rather glad. I spent an interesting, reflective time alone with my scotch. What was I doing there? Although I had only a bit part up in New York, I was in on saving one of the biggest, most prestigious, car accounts from sliding blocks down Midtown. I had a first name relationship with some of America's most notable advertising living legends. And here I was staring up at Dick Clark.

Amy was not happy about having to postpone her final decision about teaching at Dalton as a result of what was brewing for me in Philadelphia. My father, at fifty-eight, a man I had always believed to be invincible, seemed all at once vulnerable, as if he had slipped and broken his hip and was on the floor calling up for help.

The truth was, that in my mind, I saw a beat-up racetrack in need of much fixing, but it was a track nonetheless. And I felt ready to take on the challenges of my family's business. A big part of me looked forward to moving back to Philadelphia to start kicking this agency forward. I had some hints, thanks to a call I'd had with Jesse before coming down, that the old dudes were chasing out whatever youth existed. But that didn't deter me. Actually it spurred me on.

I wanted to build Spiegel & Associates' reputation on great work and to compete on the same playing field as Lux. To become an advertising force as opposed to getting by on lucky breaks. I wanted to supplant them. I wanted us to become the leading creative shop in Philadelphia and then in the mid-Atlantic region. From there, going on to be recognized as a top-tier independent national player, where our value earned from all our great work would someday fetch us a tidy sum when we'd sell.

I looked up at the signed Hamm's bear poster. As Beinhauser would say at a moment like this, "Bring on those bears and let's see how they dance." If the Hamm's Beer bear was any indicator, if you asked me he looked too blitzed to dance. But I thought, if this BRC offer could leapfrog things forward for Spiegel, so be it. I'm certain they wanted to turn me around and see my hokey-pokey, too…"that's what its all about."

When they entered Cuzzin's I recognized Tony Braumberg from the local awards show Dad and I had attended several summers back. He had a scraggly beard and droopy eyes, but wore a pair of tinted black-rimmed glasses, perhaps to make himself look more serious or hip. What I noticed most was that he was far too hunched over for a man in his early thirties. His partner, Loren Rucker, was tall and lean and came into the room like a war hero. Then there was Tim Cloud, stocky, with dark hair, wearing a plaid shirt. He appeared as I'd imagine Fred Flintstone might if he weren't a cartoon. Our waitress trailed them with three Pabsts.

I had gotten the scoop on these guys from Jesse, who had, indeed, begun shopping other agencies and suggested, "Get your ass back to Philadelphia and save your dad's agency." He had told me the BRC boys enjoyed cocaine a tad too much, and the first client check to arrive each month was earmarked for their habit.

As I watched these three bright young things shuffle over to my table, I wondered how my fifty-eight-year-old dad would feel about turning his first monthly client check, usually from Brookstone into vials of coke for the conference room table.

The founder and CEO of Brookstone was Dad's first-year roommate at Penn and became his lifelong friend. When Dad arrived in the States, he applied to Central Scholarship, a Jewish Federation "do good" organization that helped Holocaust survivors continue with their education. When accepted at Penn, with the support of Central Scholarship, Dad had secured the funds to pay for his degree. When the founder of Brookstone, Dad's roommate, started his business out of his farmhouse in New Hampshire, he asked Dad to handle his account. But first Dad would have to spring for a conference room table, because the closest thing his agency had to one was the partner's desk in his office.

I stood up and shook hands with Tony who seemed nervous and suspicious. Then I leaned in to greet Loren, who seemed very tuned in and full of enthusiasm. He and I immediately connected. Then there was Tim. He was warm. Someone I'd feel comfortable with fishing in a rowboat or enjoying a beer at the ballpark.

Tony spoke first. "When we split from Lux we stopped drinking Hamm's since it was no longer mandatory. Thank God. Cause each one of us thought that it tasted like piss in a can. Shit, it was free in the agency, but everyone snuck in Coronas. Actually poured them into the Hamm's bottles. Then we expensed them back to Hamm's. But testing other beers and malt liquors was part of our job at Lux. And shit, we did a lot of Corona tastings. Now that we're on our own, we can't afford Coronas."

"Sorry to hold you up; we got caught on a conference call," said Loren. "We got the local Wendy's business recently and when they call they want us to drop our jeans."

Tim added, "I drop my pants just to moon them. They just like junk."

Tony then said to me, "Maybe you can bring something down from New York to replace 'em with. They really blow. What do you do up there anyways? Is there really a Bernbach or does he just live in Oz?"

Tim reacted to his partners. "So your dad says you want to come back and start at the top."

Loren said, "Maybe your first move will be to fire Tony. Then the rest of us will consider working with you."

Chuckles all around, but Tony's weren't genuine. He started working to take the levity out of this encounter and control things. "What will you bring to the party? Aren't you right out of school?"

"Last I heard I'm working for the most consistently creative shop in the world."

He retorted, "But aren't you in the mailroom?"

"If you own a business now, I bet you're in the mailroom much more often than I am—like hounds sniffing for checks." Then I just about snorted as Loren and Tim looked at each other as if to say, "He comes back quick."

Tony chuckled. "I guess you got that right." He sipped some more beer.

I took the pause in the discussion to turn the attention away from me. It felt a bit like an inquisition.

I asked, "How do you guys like the work you're doing in Philadelphia?"

Dodging the question some, Loren said, "It sure beats the game of bumper cars we've been playing of late. Tony put a nice gash in my vintage Mustang backing out last night."

Everyone was on this smart-aleck track. I wondered, would we ever cover real stuff? Or was this as real as this night would ever get? Sniffing everyone's butt?

Tony was suddenly distracted by something at the front of the restaurant. My back was to the action, so all I could do was follow his eyes, which were getting wider and wider around the table until they bulged like a bull's.

Tim and Loren spotted what Tony was looking at. Tim said, "Oh... my...God," and brought his hand to his face to cover his eyes. He opened two fingers to peep through the blinds he had made with his hand. I swung my head around to see what was going on. There was a drugged-up black hooker sauntering our way. Her shirt totally unbuttoned and jeans unzipped. She directed her comments toward Tony. Mind you, she was not selling roses or pink carnations.

"Roxanne's here, Tony-love. Hotter and wetter than ever. She's here to lick your ass and make you come in your whiskey glass."

Of course, I was the only person drinking whiskey. Tony's suds were coming from Pabst.

Roxanne's hand had moved down to her underwear as she sat on Tony's lap, dancing and seemingly oblivious to others' presence. "Feels real nice down there, don't it, sugar?"

Tony said, "We're having a meeting here. You need to go."

"Go where, sugar?"

"Out of the restaurant."

She reached for Tony's right hand and said, "Put it deep into my crab soup before I suck it off." Then Roxanne reached for Tony's left hand, smeared it on the butter plate and then brought it to her chest saying, "Here's where the butter belong, sugar."

Loren became enraged. "Tony, get her the fuck out of here."

Tony practically dragged the woman out of the restaurant in a head-lock. He was gone for a good twenty minutes, long enough, I guessed, for her to suck him off.

The evening never recovered. Tim laughed the whole time. As soon as he tried to contain himself, he'd burst into another uproarious round of chuckles.

Embarrassed beyond words, Loren just shook his head again, and again. I focused on him as the three of us worked our way through our drinks. "Sorry, Sam. Tony's been having marital problems."

And after that all of us laughed so hard, the beer spurted from Tim's mouth and onto his pants. I wondered if this was Tony's wicked sense of humor unleashed on me for the first time or was it a bona fide holy-shit moment that could only happen at Cuzzin's?

Our burgers finally came. *Oh yes, Dad, this was some high-stakes merger discussion.*

CHAPTER 11

The day after the Cuzzin's adventure, Dad invited me to join him for lunch at the Union League. This is a private business club in the heart of Philadelphia that got its start in 1862 honoring the policies of Abraham Lincoln. As we arrived in the main dining room, Dad and I spotted Lawrence Lux and followed the maître d' toward him. Lux was eating lunch with two associates. "Hey, Harry, trying to lure Sam back to Philadelphia? He's the right one to start your youth movement. You better scoop him up before I do." He laughed. I did, too. So did Harry, but uncomfortably. Lux shook my hand. I shot him a smile. Dad nodded but continued walking to our table as if shrinking away from the big man on campus.

Harry Spiegel was his own breed of ad man whereas Lawrence Lux was the stereotype. Lawrence was suave—an out-front people person with real star quality. He was the kind of guy you'd see cast in movies about the industry. Harry, on the other hand, was a backroom plodder—a numbers guy, a detail man. Not glamorous.

Each morning, per Harry's instructions, Harlot, the "girl" from the mailroom/kitchenette, sorted the mail. She'd open any envelope that appeared to carry a check. Sometimes, she'd pull out a coupon and keep it for herself. By noon she gave my dad a report on the accounts receiv-ables. Fifteen minutes later, she would return with his lunch, delivering it to him at his desk in front of his fireplace.

On most days, Harry Spiegel ate at his desk. He'd have Harlot make him rye toast spread with 2 percent Breakstone's Cottage Cheese. He was as faithful to his preferred brands as he was to his family. Harlot made the sandwich open-faced, "Just how Mr. Spiegel likes it."

Along with the sandwich came a paper towel and a cup of Earl Grey tea. Never Lipton. Out of respect for Harlot, Harry would always toss his used paper towel into his own wastebasket. He'd never leave it balled up or placed on top of the plate or stuffed into his tea mug.

Harry spent his lunch hour updating his monthly income projec-tions, which he tracked by day, week, and month. He kept these numbers on a folded sheet of paper in his wallet along with a list of the thirteen employees' salaries and past raises. Heaven forbid Harry lost his wallet! Then, all his secrets and calculations would have to be reconstructed; maybe over two open-faced super-sized cottage cheese sandwiches.

At 12:30, the end of Harry's allotted lunch hour, Joanna, the agency comptroller, would bring him a small stack of checks to sign, each care-fully assembled with the supporting invoices attached. Harry scrutinized them as though reading the Torah scrolls. If he'd had a good cash day, he would sign checks and send them out early, taking a discount as com-pensation for making the payments faster than required.

Harry always deducted 5 percent. Never more. Never less. I learned, some years later, that the 5 percent discount was his own special policy, created by him and never approved by his vendors, but most quietly went along with it nonetheless. It was Harry's way of driving up a little extra cash to the bottom line. Some suppliers eventually began jacking up their bills to Spiegel by 10 percent. Still, Harry Spiegel would im-mediately subtract 5 percent, so if you're following the math here, the supplier would wind up 5 percent ahead.

While Harry ate his Spartan lunch, Lawrence Lux played golf with a client or associate, further bronzing his very tanned face and flashing his brilliant white smile wherever he went. Afterward, Lux and his guests enjoyed a massage, a steam bath, a shower, and their second shave of the day. They'd comb their hair neatly with Vitalis or Brylcreem, returning their combs back to the cylindrical tubes of blue sanitizing solution.

Lux would drive his guests downtown in his navy Jag for lunch at the business club. This was at about the time Harry would be opening his wallet to enter the day's cash total onto that large, folded, tattered sheet of paper, and then mandate the 5 percent discounts for the checks he'd sign. From what I understood, Lux frequently joined his mistress post lunch for an afternoon tryst at the apartment he had set up for her. Word had it that Lux had a monogamous relationship with his mistress, which is to say, she was the only woman with whom he cheated on his wife.

So here we were, father and son, looking down on the city that he wanted to stay a part of and I wanted to conquer. When I got through all his machinations and ums and had given my report on the Cuzzin's fiasco, I saw my dad in a very new light.

He was more endearing than ever before. He was not one to compliment those he loved. But that day, in the late summer of 1978, he handed me a truly beautiful bouquet, one without carnations. "Sam, I'm so proud of you and all you've, ah, done in your young life. I feel privileged to be your dad." I looked out the window, mainly to hold back my tears. "What an experience you're having in New York, at the top of our industry." He spoke with admiration, and maybe even wistful envy.

I thanked him for his kind words and encouragement. And I really was touched. He seemed so vulnerable as I asked, "What's really going on, Dad? What's on your mind?"

"I tell you, ah, Samuel, I'm a very fortunate man. I love my family. America's been good to me. You're on the cusp with an exciting job, a lovely gal. But I'm worried sick about the future of our agency. None of us is getting any younger, and I feel everyone's nipping at our heels for any account we have that has a pulse. Our friend over there has a whole team trying…um…to snag the racetrack business out from under us."

"Who? Lux?"

Dad pointed his way and continued, "I haven't been sleeping well, and when I saw him in the locker room the other day I went up to him and said, 'Pick on someone your own size.'"

"You didn't."

"I did."

"What did he say?"

"He said, 'Look here, Harry, the advertising game is on one big Monopoly board. I figure you have your car, iron, or thimble skipping around it…um…just like I do. You can always hand your properties over to another player if you want out. Or simply let me take my shot at 'em. Frankly, Harry, it's not more complicated than that.'"

"Wow."

My father paused and stared at me intently. He didn't often make direct eye contact. "I got to be honest here, Sam, he half-scared me to death with those words. Maybe it's…um…this pending operation. Shaky accounts. I don't know. I sure could use some help down here." At which point a phlegm ball got caught in his throat. "But I worry every day that we could go down. And…um…I couldn't live with myself, after the path you've cut for yourself in the Big Apple, if I brought you back home permanently and it all came to a close. How could I live with myself?"

"Dad, I'm learning it's all one big crapshoot. I watched DDB defend their biggest account. But it could have gone either way. And here you are alone, with all your chips on this one table, worried that they'll all be swept up. How is there really a choice here?"

He ended the discussion by looking out the window as if he too was about to cry. And then we drifted to small talk, knowing the real topics had been covered, for now.

Eventually Dad grew restless; maybe because he didn't know what checks Harlot had deposited that day. Or did he miss his toast with the cottage cheese on top? Perhaps it was Lawrence Lux delicately raising a napkin to his thin lips as if the inevitable had already happened—he had won our Horse Racing Association account, and he knew it signaled that the Man in the Gray Flannel Suit's punch would have Harry out for the count.

After the waiter cleared the remainder of my Cobb salad and my father's mainly untouched petite filet mignon, we stood up. I motioned for Dad to walk ahead of me. He navigated the white linen–covered tables filled with Philadelphia's business elite, hunched over and looking shorter than I ever remembered him, as though a piece of his spine had been chopped out.

CHAPTER 12

Leaving the dining experience at the Union League for the one that was to take place on the patio overlooking the ocean was like being airlifted from a polo match and parachuting into a rodeo to ride a bull. Despite the three years we'd been together, during which Amy had made the obligatory pilgrimages to Philadelphia and then occasionally to my parent's beach house in Bethany Beach, Delaware, she had a surprisingly light grasp of the institutions and customs of "going to the shore." We had been remiss in introducing her to the Eastern Shore crab dining experience. Being nonreligious Jews we often made the finale of the weekend all about beating the daylights out of steamed crabs.

The closest thing Amy had ever eaten in the crab family were stone crabs on special occasions with her grandparents in Boca Raton. These were broken open with a nutcracker and served cold, pristine, and accompanied by dainty forks and a cool mustard sauce. In Bethany, we used wooden mallets and some diehards sported bibs to protect themselves from errant squirts, but my family believed bibs were for ninnies.

I told Amy, "Darling, you ain't seen nothing yet."

Our crab feasts were held on the patio of the condo. There is real irony to steamed crab dining, because this local ritual, even though it's as barbaric as eating ever gets, comes with serious etiquette.

My mother was Amy's self-appointed professor for her maiden crab voyage. "Amy, first you must find week-old newspapers and know for sure you've completely finished reading them. They go under the crabs. The newspapers need to be fully opened to cover the table. I've used this multilayered procedure for years. The stack must be ten entire open pages deep. Trust me on this. Never less. Because crabs make a big, mucky mess, and in order to cover our table we use up all of Sunday's *Philadelphia Inquirer* or half of the *Sunday New York Times*. The daily papers alone, Monday through Saturday, never quite cut it."

Amy shot me a look as if to say, "You've got to be kidding."

Then Mom passed around a huge amount of paper towels for our hands, mainly hers, and explained, "Amy, the reason this meal is eaten on the porch has to do with the fact that crabs are seasonal, caught in the spring and summer. So crab eating is good for the outdoors. Secondly, and most of all, it's a very messy proposition.

"And it's no sport for ninnies!" Dad interjected from the kitchen. "So, Amy, are you crabbing with us or crab-walking sideways to get out of here?"

"I think your persuasive powers have convinced me to stay."

"In that case, here's the drill..." Mom continued, in her matter-of-fact manner, as if our decision to return to Philadelphia had already been made. "Since Samuel's planning to take over the family business, you need to know all about crabs. For the National Horse Racing Association, Harry's biggest client, their board members from around the country meet in Washington so they can zip up to Bethany to have crabs with us here. It's a great way for you to keep clients happy, and there's a lot of that in this business, you hear?"

"When exactly is Sam coming back to take over the business?" Amy shot me quite the face.

"As soon as he can get down here, I hear, with Harry's heart matters and such." At which point Amy's face made an "Oh, my God." And that's when Elizabeth picked up a mallet, banged it twice on the table, and then was out with her charge, "Let the crab eating begin. Sam, could you please do us the honor of getting the crabs from your father's car?"

I said, "*Ja, Frau Commandant!*" And it felt like the very right moment to sneak away from Amy.

My mother had this dinner completely timed out. I immediately went down the elevator to retrieve the double-bagged crabs from the trunk where they had been resting ever so briefly in peace. At purchase, the crabs were carefully folded shut to hold in the warmth and steam. The unwritten rule was that the crabs never stay in the bag for more than a half-hour or, as my mother would say, "We might as well throw 'em out."

"Amy, we 'liiike' jumbos," Mom's Philadelphia accent came charging through. "But jumbos need to be claimed before 5:00 p.m. or they're gone. So dinner with jumbos must start no later than 5:30. Real crab eaters will settle for extra-larges. For us, larges are a maybe proposition. And mediums and females, we leave for the once-a-year crowd."

"Or the *goyim*," my father chimed in from the kitchen.

Trying to be dutiful, or sarcastic, I wasn't sure which, Amy asked, "Elizabeth, should I be writing all this down?"

"No need. You'll get the hang of it." The other wooden mallets were distributed. "We call them bangers or hammers. And we need steak knives, too. You need to understand your crab utensils. 'What is the knife for?' you may ask."

Of course, Amy had questioned nothing. This was an Elizabeth discourse through and through and her domicile-turned-lecture hall for Amy. "Are you quizzing me, Elizabeth?"

Mom kept talking as she answered her own questions. "We put out knives. No forks. No spoons, unless we are having crab soup."

I chimed in and recited, "So, Amy, why is this night different from all other nights?"

Mom continued, "Oh, Samuel, you're so silly. Let's face it. It's laborious, dirty work, this crab eating business. But it's so tasty and worth it. But be warned, honey…it's work!"

I put out wastebaskets for the debris. I knew the drill, as my mom continued, "And the knives carry out two functions. First is to circumcise the crabs. No, actually if you get right dowwnn to it, you're cutting what approximates the penis right off these things."

Dowwnn is another one of those Philadelphia pronunciations.

"Mother, Amy can't really visualize all that you're saying unless you allow yourself to be a little more graphic." I joked.

"Sam, it's all part of the food chain. The second function for the knife is to remove the devil, which actually are the lungs. Of course some dainty eaters also use the knife as a polite bridge between the hammer and the claw. I think that's just a lot of hooey! If you're eating like a Spiegel, just bang the damn claw, no buffers. And finally, beer is the drink of choice, nothing else. If you get yourself a glass of wine, eyebrows go up. Sam's last girlfriend drank wine with her crabs."

"And just look around; she's certainly not here," I said.

My father walked onto the patio. "So Amy hasn't bolted. She's either very brave or exceedingly deaf."

"Crazy is more like it, Harry," she said as everyone laughed.

I confidently lifted the crab bag. If the crabs don't slip through the steam-laden bottom first, chances are good they will tumble out onto the table in an orderly fashion to the oohs and ahs of the veterans. But at that moment, Amy's eyes and mouth opened wide in amazement (or was it more like disgust?) at the sight of all those muddy, gunk-covered crabs hitting the table.

As my mother demonstrated the finer points of extracting the succulent white meat from the shell, Amy's eyes met mine in a look that telegraphed: *I wish I could wash my hands right now, please God, and get the hell out of Bethany.*

My mother continued poking around the insides of the crab as she pulled a plump lump of meat out with her fingers. The sounds of cracking shells and spurting juices competed with the waves breaking below us. It was hard for a beginner to tell whether this eating was a delicacy or carnage.

My mother nudged Amy. "Don't be shy. Pick up your hammer and beat the living daylights out of those claws. This is where the meat is a tad darker, and some say, even more delectable." Amy survived the crab-eating marathon, but it was the car ride home I wasn't sure I'd survive.

After our feast, at about 8:00, Amy and I pushed off for New York. We had both washed up thoroughly but it didn't matter—in a confined space like a car you just had to wait out the stink of crabs on your skin, kind of like dog doo on your shoes or gasoline on your fingers.

"Sam, why are we driving back to New York when you've decided to stay with your mommy and daddy? Does it matter at all, my soon-to-be husband, what I might think? Or is it all about you?"

"I think we should listen to the George Carlin tape I picked up in Society Hill yesterday."

Amy ignored my comment. "We're just getting underway in New York and you want to pull that knotted rug we just bought at Alexander's right out from under us. Be my guest. I think we're doing pretty well in Manhattan. I like where we live and that we're building something for ourselves. Sam, we can keep your Philadelphia/Bethany package as an option down the road, but come on…not now! And Sam, when does this goddamn stink get off my hands?"

"Honey, you need turpentine!"

This was a very tough ride back. The two of us had been getting along well in New York and seemed to be on the same wavelength, until the thought of leaving for Philadelphia moved our cheese. Up to now, Amy had admired my sense of purpose and determination, and I had enjoyed seeing her become more defined, but this conversation was beginning to feel antagonistic and mean spirited. Then too, she hadn't witnessed my father's emotional breakdown at Union League or heard him say, "I'm not sure there will be a business for you to come back to if you don't come now." Or had the pleasure of watching Lux taunt Harry with his glances and cutting remarks.

I asked Amy, "Do you think what my dad said over lunch was all an act?"

"I didn't say that. I'm just saying, whose life is it anyway? Theirs or ours?"

"I think there is something at stake here that's bigger than just the business. It's our future. It's about creating a life we can build on. You know, roots and grounding—a place to bring up kids. We'd have family around, a lifestyle we can afford. Trees, a house, and cars, which, by the way, we wouldn't need to lock away at $200 a month. I think life could be, excuse the expression, pretty damn good in Philadelphia."

"Oh yes, storybook. So all of a sudden you've fallen out of love with New York?"

"I love New York. But I think we're staring at a decision. I understood this wasn't a trip home to meet the merger partners. I think my dad knew that part was a lark. He set up this weekend to invite me and you into the family business. Maybe to save it."

"One thing's for sure, Samuel J. Spiegel. There's no person in the entire universe that's more cut out for a career in persuasion...you can sell yourself out of a paper bag. And you do it every goddamn day!"

"Should I consider that a compliment?"

She didn't answer.

During the ride back to the Big Apple, we decided that, considering it was probably too late for a private school teaching slot, and she didn't have a teacher's certificate for Philadelphia, and having minored in political science, she would look for a job in Mayor Rizzo's administration. And due to a Carter federal grant, there were great job opportunities to help kids who needed work to stay in school. We'd find a large brownstone apartment to rent. And as planned, we'd be married the weekend before Thanksgiving in Florida and start our Philadelphia story in December.

As we traveled alongside the Hudson River, Amy asked, "So, Sam, when's it my turn to deal the next hand?"

I never forgot her question or the way she delivered it.

CHAPTER 13

"The Golden Boy must be married where the Kennedys go off to get entertained. For my wedding, my in-laws pitched a tent in their backyard and we had a barbeque while it rained."

It was right before my wedding and Mikey struck again, spewing forth his thoughts about my position in the family. My folks had invited him and wife Sylvia to join us in New York to purchase my wedding suit and outfits for them, my parents treat. Amy's mother had come in to help shop for Amy's trousseau.

Mikey started in: "I'll need a custom-made suit for Golden Boy's coronation or I might as well not show." And mind you, we were in Manhattan, not Elmira, New York. My guess was there were plenty of husky outfit stores to choose from, which Mikey wouldn't be caught dead in. Instead he chose to be his indignant self. He always got his way after a big outburst.

And what, exactly, did all this ranting get him? It was my wedding, but he felt the need to hijack my moment and make it his own.

Despite Mikey's outburst, everything was falling into place. Amy's grandmother set a generous enough, but modest, Boca Raton budget of $5,000 as the ceiling for our 1978 wedding to be held at the Boca Raton

Resort and Club. Thanks to Jack Reinhart's skills of persuasion, when he could get his shit together, he got the hotel to start their season a weekend earlier than usual as a way for us and our guests to have the place to ourselves.

Due to my previous party planning experience, I became the designated point person and worked with the general manager, Derek Danyeski. He had been arranging black tie events for the Boca Raton/ Palm Beach elite, including the Kennedys, for a pair of decades, and during our planning sessions he often lovingly referred to Jackie. As Mr. Danyeski said when finalizing the entree, "There is no one in the country Mrs. Kennedy—pardon me, Mrs. Onassis now—likes planning affairs with more than me. 'Darling,' she is always calling me 'darling' and letting me do my job, 'you have the liberty of breaking all ties.'"

"Go ahead. Please," I said to return his focus to our decision between duck and rack of lamb.

He nodded. "So, Sam, my boy, let's make it rack of lamb with wild rice, pine nuts, and pomegranates, which are in tip-top shape in November. We'll key everything off the pomegranates. And Sam, word has it, they're good for what follows on such nights," he said with an exaggerated wink. He told me that he had planned a special gift for us but would keep it a secret until the night of the wedding. Somehow mixed in the final menu lineup and cost sheet sent to me was a copy of a handwritten card Danyeski sent to a Marshall Grant.

My Dear Marshall,

Would you kindly consider your group performing in lieu of our house trio on 11/20, when we open up our hotel for these swell newlyweds who can only afford our trio? This would be a personal favor to me, and sweet of you.

Best Regards,
Derek

I learned that Marshall Grant was in Doc Severinsen's league and it was quite a "swell" gift. I had never before seen the word "swell" written out. It's a word that seemed to duck into the English language ever so briefly and tiptoe out with the Eisenhower administration. My folks were to host a cocktail party, also at the Boca Raton Resort and Club, to be held after the Reinhart's rehearsal dinner. All this before Amy and I would take off on Sunday morning for our honeymoon. But nothing further could commence until my old friend and Party Circus associate Billy G. and I had a pre-wedding outing, which he had carefully planned.

Billy G. was a veteran Boca Raton vacationer. His grandparents owned a beautiful sprawling apartment in Old Floresta. Billy G. would spend winter and spring breaks in Boca. "Sammy, today I'm buying you an Hermès tie to go with that suit. You're not walking down the aisle wearing a generic necktie. The tie shopping should take us forty-five minutes max, and then we'll have a nice lunch at the Griddle."

I was always impressed by Billy G.'s generosity and planning. With the abundance of French-made neckties at Neiman Marcus, I had my eye out for one that I could wear over the years, in all seasons. I thought it could well become my good luck charm for pitches, as Beinhauser taught me was a "must" for big wins in this business.

I spotted a rather traditional Hermès pattern with its primary color an out-of-the-ordinary purple mixed with blue. It was elegant and the clerk wrapped it in simple crinkly tissue paper, then placed it in a tie box with a ribbon, so that when fully assembled it made me feel Mikey might have been right. I had my special tie for my coronation, and during lunch at the Griddle I told Billy G., "I'll always remember this day with you."

Before I walked down the aisle to accept Jack's daughter's hand in marriage, I had my first special moment with my soon-to-be father-in-law. He gave me a gift that was given to him by his father-in-law at his wedding on December 8, 1942, his engraved Patek Philippe wristwatch. He took the watch off his own wrist, and then with hands shaking from too much imbibing the night before, he wrapped it around mine. It was a lovely gesture. He said, "I've been warming up this watch for thirty-six years. Now it's in the hands of a true champ. Take care of my girl…now on *your* watch."

It seemed like a moment he'd anticipated ever since our engagement dinner fiasco months before. Engraved on the underbelly of the watch, below Jack's wedding date, was Amy's and mine: November 20, 1978. I wondered if I would ever pass this same watch down to my son-in-law. Would I have a daughter? What would that be like? And how would I get along with my girl? Then I wondered…would the watch still run?

I told Jack, "I'm honored to wear your watch and will cherish it along with Amy." I thanked him with a kiss on his cheek. He returned one on mine. Little did I know, until some months later, how temperamental this watch would be. It would stop and start at whim. Two different jewelers attempted to fix it over the first decade of my marriage, with no success. The second jeweler announced when I came to pick it up, unfixed, "This watch can't be repaired. It needs to be resurrected. Then born again."

What struck me, twenty minutes before the ceremony started, was the way our wedding party nervously gathered behind the chapel. First, I saw my two grandmothers, who were in their late eighties and so happy to be a part of this celebration. They were proud of their new dresses, both from Strawbridge and Clothier in downtown Philadelphia, where they always bought important outfits. Their hairdos were prepared one elevator stop below the hotel's lobby, as were their faces, both worn with dignity. They looked as gratified as I had ever seen them.

They met Amy's only living grandmother, Betty Shendler, whose dark-dyed hair was placed lovingly in a bun. She distinguished herself with her own look and wore an exquisite dress purchased from Neiman Marcus, which she anguished over for several days because of the price. We got reports on the status of this dress via phone conversations with Amy's mom. "Grandma has it on hold. But she should go ahead and buy it. It's lovely." And bless Betty's heart—she was not often wrong about a lot. Although later, I felt the family's balance and good judgment had come unhinged when its matriarch, Betty dear of blessed memory, was cranked into the ground months later dressed, I had heard, in that beautiful gown.

Jack showed up physically for all the events, but emotionally he was a no-show. Aside from the successful removal and presentation of his watch, and managing to walk his daughter down the aisle, we all let out a sigh of relief when he reached the chuppah. So much of him must have shut down when his business closed.

And Ben, my best man, and the other three ushers, Mikey, Billy G., and my new brother-in-law, Alan, all seemed out of sorts. Ben was laboring on his legal pad every free moment with what I understood to be his best man's speech. Billy G. seemed to be gravitating between being very stoned and chatting it up with Amy's older, unwed sisters, and Mikey, who fell asleep on the beach and wouldn't you know, had a face like a beet.

The Hermès tie notwithstanding, Billy G. seemed bewildered by a real-life wedding for his friend. He repeated throughout the weekend, "What's it all mean, man?" Or maybe it was his weed talking. As for my new brother-in-law, he showed up wearing a white suit, though he was instructed, along with the other ushers, to wear blue. And I knew from that day forward, "I'd say pot-a-to and he'd say po-tah-to."

Ben raised himself out of his chair and took a spot behind the band mike with his yellow legal pad in hand. With a commanding Party Circus voice (I flashed back even further to his famous "All aboard" train conductor commands in first grade) he started in, "What few words do you use on a day like this when you lift your glass and release your best friend to his bride? How about, annulment? Could you please hurry up on that annulment, guys?"

Polite laughter.

"Anyone else for it? Please raise your hand?"

More laughter.

"Samuel J. Spiegel has been my chum since we were knee-high to grasshoppers. I've never laughed harder than with this guy. I've never taken in more life than in the presence of Sam. And I've never learned more from anyone in my life than from my now-married pal." He shook his head. "Amy, what am I going to do with myself? Is there room left in your bed?"

Laughter again.

Ben cupped his fingers around an invisible cigar and gestured to shake off some ashes. "I don't think Sam's quite in the sharing mood at the moment and I can understand why...Amy, you look marvelous!"

More laughter and as he gestured with his pretend cigar, "Let me wish for you, Mrs. Samuel J. Spiegel...all and more than what I've gotten from our fellow. L'chaim."

I smiled broadly. What a good friend and charming best man I had in Ben. Amy seemed enchanted. I hugged him hard as I caught my dad with his head cocked back, eyes closed, my mother's hand in his, beaming toward heaven, as if he had it all in place.

We spent several nice days in the Bahamas on our honeymoon, which, I must confess, we passed in a drunken haze. Between shooters, the locals plied us with congratulatory drinks of every imaginable tropical fruit and rum variety. By the end of each evening, we could not be sure who was paying for the entertainment of watching Amy and me get plastered.

The morning of our departure, Amy dragged me out of bed, dressed me, and somehow got me to the Boston Whaler that would take us to Eleuthra airport. It was a short ride, but felt like forever. I couldn't remember ever having had as big a headache or a more sour stomach, and I barfed over the bow many times, right down to my bile. The captain who ferried us to the airport, as I stumbled off his boat, said, "Son, here are a few words to take witcha. Never go cold turkey. That's what wusses do. You got to ease yourself back to sober. Keep sipping Bloody Marys, son, Bloody Marys."

By the time we switched planes in Charlotte to head back to Philadelphia, Amy had nodded off and the captain's advice had worked. I was sober and wide-awake until I focused on what I was getting myself into with my father in Philadelphia. That's when I rang the attendant's bell for another Bloody Mary and drank it in a hurry.

CHAPTER 14

So what exactly had I gotten myself into…leaving New York to join my father's shop in Philadelphia? In retail terms it was like transitioning from spending my days at Bergdorf Goodman to a Goodwill store. In fact, if ad agencies had cash registers (which ours actually did, in a live person, my dad), Spiegel's would have had a crank. And while there were still customers that were loyal to the notion of a local shop, which was a good thing for us at the moment, loyalty wasn't enough of a business plan for profitability, sustainability, or any real recognition.

I had visited Spiegel & Associates growing up and while interning, but I had never stared it down as a potential owner. As a child, I remembered enjoying going downtown with Dad on the occasional Saturday. While he was getting something done in his office, pipe in mouth, I would roam through the other offices in the brownstone and often settle in the art studio. I'd hop up on a stool, sit over an easel, and start drawing with various shades of pastels until my hands, arms, and pants were covered in chalk.

On my first day on the job I realized nothing had really changed about this place, physically or culturally, in the eighteen years since my childhood visits. The furniture was the same. The number of desks, the same. The lack of light in the building—same. The reception desk—same. It was 1979, and the whole place seemed to be stuck in the days of radios and telegrams. If all of this wasn't an immediate indication that my family business was in a time warp, the incessant smell of smoldering pipe tobacco stoked these embers of worry. Although everything about Spiegel & Associates indicated that the gas lamp was low on kerosene. I recalled my most inspiring high school teacher, Kevin Groth, saying to his class as our school got its first auditorium to replace the gymnasium for plays, "It's all about the people. Give me a log hut with only two simple benches, Mark Hopkins on one and me on the other, and the rest will take care of itself."

I wondered if Mr. Groth's philosophy could hold true in the context of a business built on image. Could our talent compensate for a lack of sexy trappings, like an office that looked like it was lost in *Our Town*. That, of course, assumed that the comrades at Spiegel & Associates were, indeed, talented. No one at Spiegel was anything close to being a rain-maker, and most of the existing accounts were hangovers from the past.

Of the thirteen employees, I interacted primarily with Harvey Lodenberg—our utility player, and outside office hours, weekend cantor. He was awkward, but he had a great marketing mind. I learned a lot from Harvey. We began working together on saving Spiegel's oldest account, Cat's Paw Heels and Soles. Around this time, the country was still recovering from a deep economic downturn. Harvey said, "Let's get out of the office and crack this one, Sam." So we spent several afternoons together hanging out at a number of shoe repair shops. We took turns interviewing and recording customers. And we found a common theme—people were bringing in forgotten shoes they had found jammed in the backs of their closets as money was now needed for basic necessities.

On our ride back to the office Harvey said, "We're all pack rats. We just don't appreciate it until we need something we can't afford. Sam, to save an account, you've got to leave the office and look into the eyes of the customers." And before the end of our drive, Harvey had his insight crystallized down to the one line Cat's Paw adopted and that saved the account: *Shop the shoe store in your closet.* On reflection it was as razor-sharp a line as I've ever heard in my career.

Then there was Sol Katz, who handled most of the large accounts. Sol knew the secret to his survival. "Get under the skin of your most important clients and don't ever stop sucking." He was a small man, although he had a lot in common with a tick. That was how he became a member of our lifer's club—he always found his way under our clients' skin.

Next there was Harold Mach, who primarily oversaw the smallest, barely ticking accounts in the shop. Harold was marked for dismissal. And then there was Roy Bormen, the so-called "young buck," who was twenty-two years my senior. Roy held the title of Creative Director, but in reality, it was Harvey who was our finest concept player. I knew very early on, Roy had to go.

My dad counted the money. He kept the costs down and oversaw the Horse Racing Association's Co-op business, which he had developed into a decent account, with advertising running for multiple tracks in various parts of the country. That account had been protected for a while because the head honcho and industry visionary was also my mother's uncle, Stanley Carlsberg, who ran several courses including Keystone Park in Philadelphia, Pimlico Race Track in Baltimore, and Saratoga in upstate New York. He also partnered with a prominent businessman from Kentucky to operate Churchill Downs, the home of the Kentucky Derby. It was my mother's Uncle Stan who had helped Harry get his job at Louis T. Jacobs Advertising, the precursor to Spiegel & Associates.

But because of Stan's progressing years and the fact that he was busy selling off many of his assets to Magna Entertainment Corp., in Canada, his influence had waned considerably within the association. He rarely attended meetings any longer and when he did, he seemed to defer to others. This caused my father to sleep less and worry more about losing this business, as I had learned the day he took me to the fateful Union League lunch and announced Lawrence Lux was circling the tracks we always believed belonged to us.

Besides Cat's Paw and racetracks, we had the Klaff account—a scrap steel gatherer that, after melding bits and pieces of steel together, would sell their wares to GM, and transform them into a fleet of Cadillacs. And that client was a close cousin to the Baylin Brothers, whose business was remnant *schmattes*. Newer *schmattes* that got stitched to older *schmattes* that made one long swatch of *schmattes*. Then they were turned, miraculously, into Burlington coats.

I always wondered how the Baylin brothers got the musty smell out of these soon-to-become overcoats, because, when I first took a tour of their facility with my dad, I leaned in close to Harry and said, "Are you sure the Baylins don't manufacture cheese?" Although I always could get a laugh out of my dad and he from me, on this occasion his very being erupted into a noise that sounded an awful lot like a tidal wave breaking hard on the beach. That day his laugh was as bountiful as I ever remembered it.

Also on our roster was Eastern Venetian Blinds, a product that seemed at the time to exist primarily to collect dust as it was decades out of fashion, yet still found in many neighborhoods—not adorning windows, mind you, but on curbs awaiting bulk trash pick-up. This left the Horse Racing Association and the poorer man's version of Sharper Image—Brookstone—as our sexiest accounts. I knew we had only one direction to go…up. Or out, as Lawrence Lux intimated to Harry when he said, "Either stay in the game, Harry, or kindly take your thimble off the Monopoly board and give us what's left of your properties."

We were caught up in some backward decade of the media age where we still had a reception desk that sported thick rubber cords that plugged into round pegs to connect calls. Our through-the-airwaves media buys were still primarily traveling without pictures, while we churned out lots of print ads, including daily classifieds for "Apartment Czar" John H. Newsenhoff, a very successful apartment developer.

Although the ad-making on this account was like taking out the trash—because what we prepared for them were no more than glorified classifieds that would soon end up lining bird cages or starting fires in fireplaces—these mundane assignments came with a bit of cachet, because the entrepreneur who ran the company was a major Philadelphia philanthropist.

In my early days at Spiegel, on my way to work from the apartment Amy and I shared on Rittenhouse Square, I'd pass our respected seventy-eight-year-old client John Newsenhoff in his pink Lincoln Continental parked beside a building site, soon to be Philadelphia's new symphony hall, which when completed would carry his name. Each morning he would be in the same spot, sitting directly behind his driver, smoking, I assumed, cigars from Castro's Cuba.

Some days I'd actually bring my car to a stop to observe old Mr. Newsenhoff as he watched his very own monument to himself grow. I was touched by this small but powerful man peering out his window as his legacy evolved brick by painstaking brick. I was also impressed that my dad had snagged his account. Although it wasn't sexy, Harry Spiegel was the man Newsenhoff picked and when he did, old Newsenhoff proclaimed, "Hey, Harry! This certainly is a feather in your cap!"

He wanted my dad to understand exactly what had just happened to him. As a third-generation wealthy Jew, John Newsenhoff thought enough of my father to hire him, even though Harry had only recently been dropped off a boat at Ellis Island and hadn't as yet developed the American pedigree and time-honored respect a Newsenhoff would be accustomed to, which is what he meant when he said, "But, Harry, you, my friend, have a *Yiddishacup*."

When Spiegel was given the honor to promote this monument to John H. Newsenhoff, to be called the Newsenhoff Symphony Hall, for all of Philadelphia to come experience, we prepared an elegant two-word call to action, written by Harvey Lodenberg, "Listen, Philadelphia!"

Now what did the Spiegel associates think about me? The young buck who came back to Philadelphia from only a short stint in advertising in New York and with the privileges of a son? Like dogs, each employee had his territory marked. "I own this account, therefore I rule here." Flag in the ground. Until territories started to blur and no one was quite sure who might service the new account that the young buck (me) had recently slaughtered.

And what did this mean exactly? Ad agencies are divided, or so it seems, into parcels of land...plots one owns or thinks one owns. That is until the young Spiegel started to rearrange things. That is when I began to garner business that was primarily of my making. And with each new account I brought in, each served as an opportunity for potential: raises, promotions, and new account assignments. That's when the new and unchartered schematic at Spiegel started to take hold and when the jockeying to connect with the prince began to unfold. And it came fast.

Another point of note here was that, as a business in 1979, we had no photocopier in our office. DDB had a whole bullpen of copiers in a dedicated wing and satellite copiers everywhere else. Spiegel's two secretaries were instructed to use three carbon sheets for each letter or memorandum. This lack of a copier, as it turned out, became my first new business opportunity.

Harold Mach, the B-level copywriter/contact guy in our shop, which made him, at best, a hack by anyone's standards, was busy trying to save his job. Harold had become our self-appointed office manager and purchasing agent for the scant equipment Spiegel had invested in over the prior decade. Though for years he had inhabited the second largest office next to Dad's, they rarely talked. For three months going, Harold had been researching and ruminating over a copier purchase, accepting bids and getting to know every dealer in town over free lunches. This had become his day job.

I wondered why Harold would ever want to make up his mind on a copier? As a potential customer, he was finding his way into his favorite restaurants without picking up a single tab. And through his endless search, enabled by my father's natural inclination to part with as little money as possible, Harold was literally stalling his way to survival.

And frankly, what would Harold be doing for the company if he didn't have this big copier decision to make? Most of his little accounts had checked out. Writing small apartment classifieds for Sunday's real estate pages was a one-day-a-week job, even though he spread it out

STEVEN C. EISNER

over three. Harold lived for Thursdays, the day his overworked classifieds got picked up by the newspapers. Or did he?

Finally, after much prodding from me, my father asked Harold, "So
what kind of copier are we getting and from whom?"

Harold replied triumphantly, "I've picked our winner—Samson
Duplication." The head of this company, Eddie Samson and his wife,
Elaine, had twice taken Harold to his favorite restaurant, known for its
Crab Imperial. Harold had a kosher household and by going to Book-
binder's for lunch every so often, he got his fix of treyf without his moth-
er-in-law or wife ever catching on.

The Samsons were an endearing Jewish couple. And after their
schlepped-out courtship with Spiegel & Associates, when delivery day
finally came, they decided to celebrate the arrival of our new copier as if
our company was hosting a bris. All thirteen associates surrounded the
Sharp machine. The Samsons granted me, the baby of our organization,
the privilege of making the first copy. I did as they instructed. Our troops
applauded politely.

When the copy came out I said, "Look at it! It's whole. No deformities. I'd say it's time for cake!" To a Jewish person, everyone laughed,
including the Samsons, who thought my comment was a riot. The non-
Jews scanned the room looking for the cake.

I immediately connected with this "Ma and Pa" team, and before
they exited, I asked if I could take them to Bookbinder's for lunch and
talk about their marketing needs. They readily agreed and it became my
turn to sell them on us. I won their hearts, and shortly thereafter, their
account.

It was a beginning, because with the exception of a few middle-of-
the-road horse racing TV commercials—with a host of visual clichés like
jockeys bouncing up and down and gently whipping their horses—we had
no demo reel to speak of and no rainmaker to facilitate any real change.
This double punch became my job: to build a TV reel by convincing existing clients that Arthur Godfrey might actually be dead and to get some
new business in the shop fast. The other option was just to euthanize
Spiegel and head back to New York and make Amy and Lux happy.

104

With my goals clearly defined, I stalked business as if the food in my pantry couldn't/wouldn't be restocked until I first got some fresh kills. Soon after I landed the Samson account, it hit me one sleepless night as I was trying to figure out my role versus my dad's—how many other, much larger mom-and-pop retailers in the region were going through the same family business transitions as Harry and me? A bunch! I pursued a large appliance chain in the region—Luskin's—and a large carpet retailer—Carpet Fair—both based in Baltimore. I learned that Baltimore accounts were easy prey, because Philadelphia agencies were considered a nearby trade-up, closer to New York but without the snob factor or high rent expense further up the coast.

My firsthand understanding of the father-and-son transitional dynamic became a lubricant for making these sales close quickly. Working with a father and all that came with it was my honey that helped me amass bees, and suddenly our local reputation as "the horse racing agency" broadened to that of a budding Mid-Atlantic "retail shop."

After literally calling Spa World's head of marketing each day for about a year, I altered my game and called for a lunch date with its chairman, Rod Seff, whose 40th birthday celebration Party Circus had facilitated some years back, and I got through to him. I learned, on this dogged mission, that the secretary is often the linchpin or killer of the "connect." Penny Parks, Rod's assistant, had done me one better. She set up a dinner date at Villa di Roma. "You'll get a lot further with Rod at night," she told me.

At dinner, Seff shared that he'd dropped out of school in tenth grade. Not because he was a bad student, quite to the contrary. He was just "plain bored of school and ready to get on with life." At age sixteen, he worked on and around Broad Street, Philadelphia's equivalent to 42nd Street, where Rod's dad had an interest in a strip club and gave his firstborn his first break…to work the bathrooms.

An entrepreneur from the beginning, Rod asked himself what patrons needed more than anything else from such a room? Anyone? Quick now, don't blink. Accessible condoms, of course. And so, with four quarters and a twist, you could access Rod's Trojans from wall-mounted dispensers, and soon thereafter, his small, booming business was born.

Rod bought condoms in bulk so that each rubber cost him about a dime. He made ten times that amount on each and in short order, Rod stalked then stocked ten clubs. On average, he moved fifty condoms per bathroom per day, making it a total of five hundred a day. Business was steady. It was 1953. There were constant takers on hand. And Rod's condom concession turned monopoly.

That meant, as a sole proprietor, Rod made $3,500 a week against costs of $350. Over the year and a half he stayed in this business, Rod amassed $246,000 before taxes. By age eighteen, he had bought two failing health spas for $25,000 apiece and paid cash for a home, as well as a black Jaguar in which to carry his "babes." This left him with $81,000, part of which he used to pay his taxes while putting the remainder into a savings account.

In my career, I had never met a person quite like Rod. He was my personal Walt Disney. Between meetings in his boardroom, he read Plato and Dostoyevsky. He had gotten involved early on in the Libertarian movement, but his life's ambition, as he was a contemporary of Jack LaLanne, was to take the fitness business out of the sweaty doldrums of society and make health spas mainstream, as McDonald's had accomplished for the hamburger, as Dannon yogurt overtook pudding, and as personal computers were soon to bury the electric typewriter.

Rod told me this over and over again until his notion became my notion. Boy, could he sell a vision. For him, persuasion was a science. He'd lean forward in his chair, "Before I check out, everyone in this country will have a place where they can go for a low monthly fee to get in shape, no excuses. Strong bodies make for strong minds. It's the path to excelling in your job, having energy for the kids, and it doesn't hurt in making the girls swoon...." (There was another word like swell.) I certainly was sold, and in turn, was given the chance to handle Spa World's advertising. Never more motivated than by Rod, I worked hard for him every day.

And damn if he didn't achieve his dream, with Spiegel as his marketing team. The industry became a stock market darling in the eighties as *Time*, *Newsweek*, and *U.S. News & World Report* harkened "The Age of the Fitness Boom."

A new and improved Spiegel & Associates had been born. As announcements of our new accounts began to appear in the newspapers, the business community started shaking their heads and asking, "How on God's earth is Spiegel getting all this new business?"

CHAPTER 15

Amy and I were two years into our marriage, and I had been laboring until very late most nights to ramp up our first television campaign for Spa World. The agency had already finished the Samson Duplication television spot and we were finalizing storyboards for the Matz's Crabmeat pitch coming up in eight days, announcing the arrival of a crab cake product "fit for the grill."

I had been building a good relationship with Mendel Matz for years. He and his family had a summer place next to ours in Bethany. Being neighbors in our Sea Colony community, I knew Mendel Matz regularly used television to promote his products. He liked me and always said, "Sam, you're such a go-getter." So when contemplating freshening up his advertising for his crab packaging plant in Salisbury, Maryland, he called me in and said he might be ready to make a change.

Amy and I had planned a long romantic weekend in quaint Oxford, Maryland, on the Eastern Shore. We vowed to catch up with each other's lives, and each other, during this three-day break. It was a very hot Thursday in the middle of August. We'd push off around 3:00 to arrive in time for dinner. Amy had taken the day off to run errands.

When she returned to our rented brownstone apartment, carrying the dry cleaning, she turned the key to our front door, but it wouldn't open. The nighttime chain latch was attached. Since we always went in and out the front door each morning, Amy realized something was amiss. She hung the dry cleaning on the tiger doorknocker outside our apartment and darted up the stairs. Marvin, the "manservant," as our landlord referred to him (Amy and I knew better; he was our landlord's main squeeze), was home, listening to Barbra Streisand records and dusting. Amy's knocking prompted him to the door. "I think someone broke into our apartment," she screamed.

"Oh, my Lord dear Jesus," he said as he dropped his fluffy duster to the floor. Amy dove toward their phone and called 911. The police arrived in less than five minutes, as our neighborhood was often heavily patrolled. They were already convinced that our apartment had experienced a break-in because, on the way, they had noticed a dangling receiver at the payphone on the corner. The pair of cops said it was "a telltale sign. The robbers call your number and if the phone is still ringing when they enter, they know they have the place to themselves." The police asked Amy to stay with Marvin as they went around to the back. Sure enough, the basement sliding glass door was smashed in. Amy tracked me down at Spa World, where I was in a marketing meeting with Rod Seff. I didn't mind the interruption…it was almost a blessing because the meeting I was having with Rod and his team was tanking.

The news of the break-in engendered some sympathy, which was good because what I was hearing in Spa World's boardroom was that our first two weeks of new television commercials had not generated the needed telephone leads to make the month's projected numbers. Decisions were leading to alter course by aborting our spots and replacing them with an older, surer bet, one that tied into Labor Day Weekend. This is a critical sign-up time in the spa business. I excused myself and high-tailed home, sick to my stomach about the news in the boardroom and the break-in.

Our apartment was a complete wreck. Every bedroom drawer was pulled out and thrown to the floor. All our clothes looked sifted through and were heaped in piles. Couch cushions had been yanked off. Cabinets, in which we kept our new wedding gifts, were left open, emptied, including two generations of silverware and English China from Amy's mother's family—every last piece was gone.

Also gone was Amy's diamond engagement ring, given to me by my grandmother. Amy kept it in the apartment, as wearing it on her CETA job where she was assistant director of the local chapter of the Carter administration's stay-in-school program, was not appropriate. Everything of any value that we had recently covered on our insurance floater had been taken. Gone were $35,000 worth of, primarily, family heirlooms. We were completely unnerved as a result and felt vulnerable.

I called our insurance agent and shared the police report outlining everything that appeared missing, which was basically everything of any value. The police suspected the thieves were looking for whatever they could convert to cash to buy drugs and promised to check with fences and pawnshops in the greater neighborhood. Amy and I started to put some of the strewn chaos back into the drawers and then decided to take our three-day getaway anyway. We needed it.

The part of the ordeal that I couldn't get out of my mind was the nearby payphone receiver found dangling and our phone ringing. I said to Amy, "If the police were so sure that the robbers called ahead to our house, how did they know our number?" There were crisscross directories for real estate agents but for small-time crooks? Please.

Another thing that jarred me some during the two-and-a-half hour drive to Oxford was, after such a trauma, where was the tender hand of my wife? Throughout this entire ordeal, now several hours old, where was her touch? And where was mine? It was beginning to feel to me like we never seemed to physically connect in any substantive fashion. For the first time in a year, I thought about Beth, who, I was sure, would have been eagerly saddled beside me comforting and stroking me, and I her. With Amy there was zero, nada, zilch. I wondered if she was thinking the same about me. Do married couples stop touching each other and just hold out for those fewer and fewer screws? Or was something just wrong here?

CHAPTER 16

The romantic weekend came and went, and although it failed to turn into Casablanca, "Here's looking at you kid," by the end of it, I had figured out how to save Spa World. Tuesday at 4:00, I placed a call to Rod to make a dinner date for that night. He had some strange habits, including eating dinner at 11:00 p.m. And he kept his associates around the office until then. He paid his men well, and when they signed up to work for him they knew they were owned. These long evenings and control issues drove one of his senior staffers to a cocaine addiction. Each of his top five guys was either separated or divorced, and Rod was on his second marriage, too. Since I was not residing on his plantation, meaning I was not directly on his payroll, my relationship with Rod was one of much greater independence.

There were eighteen years between us. We valued each other's brains. He knew he was my mentor. But in certain ways, I was his, too. He trusted my opinions, my marketing instincts, and my eye. And although he was perceived as a tyrant, under all his bravado, this was a man with a warm heart. I always told him what I believed. He liked my passion and my convictions. We connected well.

When I made the call to Rod I knew two things. First, our new creative director and I had nailed a solution for Spa World's Labor Day special. And second, I decided to bypass the marketing manager go-between, Stan, who was the one with the cocaine habit. His drug use wasn't the reason though; I really liked Stan. I just needed to go to the top with our idea and not risk the dilution that often occurs with a go-between. I knew Rod would appreciate my direct approach. And I had a plan as to how to play the dynamics with Stan the next day. I'd just tell him the truth. It usually worked.

Rod had a special table at Villa di Roma and his favorite Chianti had been uncorked. I poured a glass for both of us while I waited for him, and started sipping and wondering how Beinhauser might handle this encounter.

Rod always had Villa di Roma's owner, Charlie, personally chill his reds before his arrival. Many years back, Rod blew his top after his first sip of the night. "Charlie, where do you keep your wine cellar, in the fucking oven?" Every time I joined Rod at Villa di Roma, and I was always seated first, Charlie told me the same story. Tonight was no exception. And yes, Charlie got the temperature down to a delightful autumn day.

Arriving ten minutes later, Rod was right on time and dressed in one of his signature black suits. All his suits were handmade by an Italian tailor, Bruno Pascaller, who fit him at his office. I always thought his tapered pants were far too reminiscent of what Mary Martin wore in Peter Pan, but I assure you, I never conveyed this tidbit to him.

Clearly his black hair had been styled that day, also at his office. Fluffed, swirled, and sprayed down. I learned he was super-conscientious about hiding any balding spots. I was confident that not even his wife knew for sure how much of his hair was real and what had been woven in. When Rod wanted something, it was done—and done right.

As usual, when Rod walked into the dining room, all the guests got a heavy blast of his Skin Bracer, which temporarily overtook the garlic-infused restaurant. Before he'd come to the table, he always puffed up his hair, both palms to the head. And as soon as he sat, he grabbed the rims of his glasses and pushed his lenses as far back on his nose as they could possibly go.

He gave me a warm handshake and asked, as if when I last left him I had been rushing off to see a Phillies game, "So how was your break-in?"

I said, "Everything that had any value whatsoever is gone."

"Is everything insured?"

I nodded.

He shook his right hand limply, which was a common gesture for Rod but really so unlikely for a man who possessed so much machismo. But in time I understood this hand movement was some merged Italian/Jewish signal he had concocted that summed up "Thank the Lord." Then he said, "Now you can take the money, Sam, and buy something you really want."

I told him, "Amy and I got out of town for a three-day weekend, but all I could really think about…"

"Was?" he interrupted, and I'm pretty sure he thought I was going to say the break-in. Beinhauser would have been so proud of my pause. It gave an extra punch to everything that was coming next that night.

"The Labor Day sale."

He said, "Boy, that's a good thing because those numbers you're getting us are a disaster."

I took another slug of Chianti to turbo charge my "save the account" soliloquy. "Rod, I think the messages in our commercials are motivational, but not urgent enough. I now understand that your very lifeblood depends on the phones ringing…now!"

"Sam, what do you want me to do with these spots? Throw them in the gutter?" He said, "That would be another disaster." Punch two. My second big ouch of the night.

"Rod, we found a way to make these spots work a lot harder." At that moment I wanted two things not to happen. First off, for him to ask, "How much more is this going to cost me?" And second to rehash my flop. Rod Seff was always very direct and when something he needed wasn't happening, he had no mercy. So I continued, blocking another incoming uppercut. "We're going to take some of the footage in the two commercials and rework it in such a way that people will want to get up out of their comfy chairs and make a call."

"What have you got?"

I was encouraged. He hadn't gone to "cost" or "flop." So far only "disaster."

"Here's what kept me up at night, and then it came to me. What are we really trying to get done here? To have people reach for their phones and call." And I knew to just go for it, no more building this up or fiddle-fucking around. I had to throw it all at him and let him bite or flee. "Picture this, Rod, think Hitchcock."

Hitchcock intrigued him…yes…good! Nice head nod.

I repeated my personal connection again. "Picture this, Rodney." (The name Rodney just came out of my mouth. The only person I thought maybe called him that was his dad. His mother had been dead for some years.) "The telephone is off the hook and it's swinging before your eyes, like a hypnotist's watch." (Maybe in the end, it was those robbers that gave me a return gift—that image of the telephone they left dangling in the phone booth.) "The sound effect is like a metronome tick, tick, tick, tick."

As I leaned far forward in my chair I looked at my watch, which one should never do when having dinner with a client, but on that night it was part of the effect. I even tapped on its glass. "Tick-tock…as if time is running out. And the voiceover comes in to say urgently, as if someone's going to die, Rod, 'You only have until Monday at 10:00 p.m. to call Spa World for their $3.98 a week sale. Only $3.98 a week.'"

"Sam, the call center isn't open past 6:00."

"Rod, on this Labor Day, the fuck it'll close. We've got some call making-up to do and we're keeping it open until 10:00."

He looked at me, a bit stunned but then his face warmed to give me a huge grin.

I continued. "At $3.98 a week? That's less than the cost of an over-stuffed sandwich," which I delivered dramatically as if to say, "Get out of your chairs, you dumb potato sack fucks, and make the goddamn call already." I could hear Clint Eastwood in every syllable I uttered from that point on. "And then we intercut all the workout scenes we so pains-takingly shot for the spots that are running now. And with urgency, the announcer comes in again while you see the phone swinging."

I was almost across the table drinking Rod's wine as I continued. "And get this, Rod, the big closer here: 'Most Labor Day sales can only save you money; this one can save your life. For $3.98 a week, grab it before it's gone.' And Rod, every time you see the dangling phone, you see…," as brazen as I could deliver it…,"your big-ass phone number. The number is up four times longer than in any spot you've ever run." I rested my case and took another swig of his favorite Chianti; I felt deserving of the rest of the bottle and maybe a second as a bonus. The grin from Rod could have spread across two mountaintops as I read his mind. I'm sure he was thinking, *This is why I bought this kid.* End of story.

This TV spot ended up breaking every call record in the history of Spa World, two times over. And throughout the span of this ac-count, which lasted for over a decade until Rod sold out to Bally Fitness, "Swinging Telephone" never retired. It was like a great relief pitcher. It could always be counted on to get the job done. It would be used to save a month, make a quarter, exponentially grow annual sales. And those times when Rod pushed his glasses back into his head with both hands, looked me straight in the eye as if his staff had turned invisible, and said, "Sam, we better use Swinging Telephone," God almighty, I never felt so good!

CHAPTER 17

Although Spa World was a publicly traded company, Samson Duplication, Inc., was a fledgling Ma and Pa Sharp dealership with aspirations and a "can do" attitude. When we, "the agency," turned into being good listeners, beyond consumer research, what I learned was that the most distinguished work we produced was as a result of back-and-forth discussions about their business, at the ownership level. In so doing, we often revealed a brand's DNA, and once we unearthed that code, we'd be prepared to give them great work. One of the best examples was with that quirky pair of retailers, Eddie and Elaine Samson of Samson Duplication.

I would meet them about a mile from their offices at a dark generic Chinese Restaurant called China Wu. This was a long way from Harold Mach's system of sneaking in some expensive crab while being wined and dined as a "customer" at Bookbinder's restaurant. I met the Samsons outside their offices so as to have uninterrupted conversations, because Eddie, in order to save or gain a copier sale, would answer every call he received, no matter who was in his office and whose time he might be burning up.

And he'd answer in the same smarmy way: "This is Eddie Samson. How may I help you?" He'd go sweeter still once he discerned he had a possible customer on the line. He'd put his finger to his lips to keep Elaine and me quiet in the background and he'd sometimes say to the caller, "I've got five or six ad men here." (Although usually it was only me.) And he'd hear on the other end something like, "You can get back to me."

"No. No. No," he'd say. "There is no one more important than you at this moment." His spiel always seemed lifted straight from a Dale Carnegie motivational speech.

When the Samsons and I arrived at China Wu, the staff of three servers and their greeter fawned over us with bows and broad waves of their hands. They also knew to immediately bring Mr. Samson and whoever was dining with him a serving of brown rice, as prescribed some years back by Elaine for Eddie's always acting-up ulcer. She contended that the solution to a lot of life's problems was quick food intake. I was accustomed to the drill here, what drinks and food would subsequently be ordered. But this was a special lunch because this was the day the Samsons were reviewing their final media plan for their first-ever television buy.

Immediately following the meal, they'd get to see their finished TV commercial. The spot was called "They Need Me." I got one of our paste-up artists, using tweezers, to replace the messages in two fortune cookies with two custom-written ones that I planned to have Eddie and Elaine open separately at lunch. My artist bubble-wrapped them for easy transport so that they could be presented at about the same time their brown rice would reach the table.

The fortune in Elaine's cookie read, "It takes courage to go the distance." Samson Duplication was the first copier dealership to dare use television to sell their wares. And the cookie for Eddie, who starred in the commercial, mimicked Billy Crystal's iconic line, "You Look Marvelous." They greeted the cookies with great glee and actually ate them before their rice. Later, when the check came, Eddie insisted on picking up the tab and said, "This way I won't have to pay the 17.65 percent on top of the check." (Which was the standard commission for ad agencies on top of production costs.) I politely chuckled and graciously thanked them for lunch.

I was gradually gaining an understanding with clients of when to turn on the proverbial tape recorder in my head. Usually it was over a meal, and I'd snap immediately into being "on duty" even with a drink in my hand. I'd learned that, with a drink, it's actually better for all concerned. That's often when the inner stuff flows more easily. People let their guard down, but only after trust overtakes suspicion, which often is present in the formative months of a client-agency relationship. That is why the greatest work often comes after the first year.

I will always remember what Beinhauser told me about a lunch he had with his VW client. They were on their third Manhattan when Günter said, "Let's face it right here and now, Joseph, we're never going to win any beauty contests with our child." (He was talking about the Bug.) He leaned into Beinhauser and said under his breath, "We make the ugliest car on earth." That VW verbiage is pretty much what ran in an ad in the *New Yorker* three months after those words were uttered—inside cover, with a headline, "Ugly Is Only Skin Deep!" And the truth is, one slightly drunk client who got a little too comfortable with his ad guy turned out to be that day's copywriter. Active listening is the most powerful weapon in the business and leads to the ad man's survival, and the client's growth, if we just practice it well and often enough.

There's an art to this active listening as, simultaneously, you must carefully pounce and finesse without the client really knowing what you're up to. It requires agility. And when working at its best, in visual terms, it's like the moment a spider spots a fly in the air and madly starts spinning her web.

Eddie often spoke about his passion—first for the mimeograph business, earlier in his career, and then for copiers. He told of what he liked about what he did, but had trouble getting to the nugget. "Purple-colored hands...the smell of the ink...the machine's design...the cranking motion with the mimeo...the sliding action of the glass moving back and forth in a copier." In all these moments of trying to be real, to enlighten me about what turned him on, I heard nothing, nothing, and more nothing. He really wanted to see his hands turn purple?

And then during one lunch of enlightenment, I asked him, "To date, what has been the happiest moment in your professional life, Eddie? The moment you knew, 'I like doing this thing that I do better than anything else in the world.'"

He bit.

He said, "It was five years back on the fourteenth of April, late in the night and this accountant in a small firm was in his office, maybe it was the morning of the fifteenth already I don't know. And he had done all the hard work leading up to tax day. There were dozens and dozens of tax returns. But you know what he was looking forward to most of all? The part that would come next, the mindless job...that of making copies of all his months' toil. He didn't want to hand this job over to his secretary. He wanted the pleasure of doing this minutia himself. Maybe it was his quirk. We all have them, Lord knows."

My internal tape was rolling.

On "Lord knows," I knew. I sat up and said, "He wanted the satisfaction of completing his work and probably putting the returns in the envelopes for his customers himself."

Eddie continued, "He did. He even had handwritten notes ready to paperclip to these copies." He put down his chopsticks to pick up a fork. "It's crazy, Sam, after all these years you'd think I'd get the hang of these things."

"Eddie, you're a good American, so I'll cut you some slack."

"Thanks. So where were we?"

I said, "At handwritten notes."

"Right. The originals had already been signed and sent to the IRS. The fact of the matter is legally he had days, maybe weeks to send the copies to his customers. But he had his system. He wanted to get everything out before the end of tax day. And late in the night, in the middle of his labor, his copier, that is to say my copier, stopped working and his goal was put to a stop. But he remembered what I had told him when I made the sale. I told him what I do is like a doctor. Maybe better than a doctor. You can always get me out of bed to fix the problem, day or night, no matter what. Well maybe not on the High Holy days...then

Before pitches, we try to understand the people behind their brands. In this instance, through field intelligence via television station managers, store buyers, and other suppliers, we were able to gain key insights into the likes and dislikes of the Matzes. How they spent their free time, the charities that had meaning for them—right down to their quirks and even a few of their family secrets. For instance, Maxi Matz was Matz's television persona. We learned he feared that if Spiegel won the account his days as pitchman for the family business would be over. From the beginning of developing our campaign ideas I pondered, "What do we do with Maxi?" This was ever present in my mind right through to pitch day. Why? Because if we retired him…we'd be out.

We picked up some other stray facts through a few close insiders. Maxi was a dutiful hobbyist drummer and would play along with Brubeck tapes most nights before turning in. We learned Florine was constantly on the prowl for a role for herself in the family business and husband, Mendel, routinely got her involved in marketing. Oh joy! But clearly Mendel ran the show, and up to pitch day, the two of us had been bonding famously.

For this meeting, on a Friday before Labor Day, they came to our offices, car packed to go on to Sea Colony after the pitch. We had turned our conference room table (Yes, we had one by then!) into what looked like a middle class Labor Day picnic table with a red, white, and blue tablecloth, blue and red plates, and matching utensils. The room was patriotic and festive. In the center was a platter of beautifully cooked crab cakes made without an ounce of filler, breadcrumbs, or the like—cooked to the exacting specifications of the recipe found on the Matz's Crab Cake Grill package.

On the label was also a "call to action" to send for other Matz family recipes for crab cake side dishes, that we also prepared—their Eastern Shore style coleslaw, which used a fair amount of Old Bay seasoning, and potato salad with tricolored chopped peppers. As it turned out, I would be beholden to these pitch luncheon sides for bailing me out of trouble late in the meeting.

On the far side of the conference room, we placed an outdoor grill on top of teak flooring. We set up a small glass table with prepared crab cakes waiting to be grilled. Grilling crab cakes was the Matz's hot new calling, to join steaks, hot dogs, hamburgers, and chicken on big summer holidays—days that were becoming critical in growing Matz's sales. Our spec assignment was to introduce their new crab cake process for grilling.

We used a caterer friend of mine who was a guy you'd only find in Philadelphia. His company, Charles Levine, operated two kitchens: an upscale one for all segments of Philadelphia's more affluent population, and another that was kosher and required the presence of a rabbi to make sure all food and food preparations were carried out within the strictest parameters of kosher code. As the Hebrew National commercials of the day put it, "We answer to a higher authority." It seemed, so did Charles's kosher kitchen.

You may ask why on earth we brought in a kosher caterer for our crabmeat packers.

Well, in our due diligence, we uncovered the biggest Matz family secret of them all. While everyone who knew them well knew they were Jewish crab providers, already a nearly unfathomable concept, worse yet, two insiders we reached out to reported that the Matzes kept kosher. And what did that mean, exactly? To consumers, it meant that the makers of their crabmeat never taste-tested a single can. What if their competitors had received this information? They'd shell the Matzes and eat them for supper.

The meeting got underway at noon in our conference room as they broke bread with our team. "Break bread" was what I called it on the phone when I invited Mendel and his family for our lunch pitch—it connected well with our kosher inside info. As the Matzes took their seats, they were impressed to see their crab cakes.

We placed the recipe cards in front of the well-arranged trays. The slaw and potato salad flanked the crab cakes. Seamlessly orchestrated was the arrival of Charles Levine with a platter of smoked salmon and sable, referred to in our parts as "revelation fish," and that morning, freshly inspected and blessed in Charles's kitchen by his hired rabbi. The Matzes were duly impressed, and it didn't hurt that Matz's Crabmeat was Charles's preferred crabmeat supplier, acknowledged by Mendel as he shot me a wink that suggested, "You really get it, Sam." Everything was lining up nicely.

As Levine put the fish down on the table, he made one quick comment while gesturing with his left hand, "Here's the lovely kosher tray." And then, with his right hand, "And here are the Matzes' beautiful crab cakes. *Bon appétit.*" Mendel beamed, looking at the way we were fussing over his cakes and family. Soon thereafter, he had his eye on some revelation fish. He then shook hands enthusiastically with Charles who left with a bow.

"Thanks, Charles. Everyone, please dig in." Maxi also focused on that fish and heaped four big chunks onto his plate. But more importantly, he peered at my team as the enemy. I knew that I had to find a better plan to warm up this man.

Although I rarely eat during pitches, I felt obliged to do so in this instance. It was important for me to have a few bites of their crab cake and rave a bit. I scooped a small amount of that overly peppered potato salad onto my plate. After I tasted it, using my fork, I hid the small mound under the remaining crab cake. There was friendly conversation going on between our two teams.

I was also conscious when we had new business lunch meetings that while we were providing nice eats, our prospects weren't there for the food. I learned that "meet and greet" lunches should last ten minutes, not longer, before the show begins. Although eating continued, of course. I stood up and took my place in the front of the table closest to where the Matzes sat, as I gave them the official welcome, introduction, and setup. I let them know that our research had clearly indicated their family name was treated with great reverence.

I felt particularly nimble, as I looked Maxi Matz directly in the eye and said, "Great brands are built first and foremost because the product is consistently a better product. Then the communications must set you apart. Maxi, in all your commercials, you've done a fine job bringing home your competitive advantage of being the 'shell-less crabmeat packer.' Fifty percent of shoppers who buy crabmeat at least twice a year can recall this fact. Well done, Maxi! And although Phillips Seafood has good recall as well, they don't have your unique selling position. Maxi, we want to keep you and this fact front burner."

Of course, I knew this thinking all came from his papa, but on that day it was Maxi's to own.

I continued. "And for our introduction of grilling crab cakes, we thought, who better an endorser than the innovator for decades—and that would be, precisely…? Anyone? Maxi Matz, as brand personality! You will introduce this new product over the grill itself, and the coals will be nice and hot when we shoot them for real. And using your spatula as if it were your baton, in just a moment, we'll have you conducting crab cake perfection to the *William Tell Overture*."

I asked Maxi to come over to the Weber grill in the corner of the room. I put a huge chef's hat on his head. He looked like an absolute idiot, but I just smiled adoringly. Then I gave him a chef's jacket and a humongous grilling spatula. Perhaps he'd no longer feel like nailing my head with it. I stepped back and said, "Take it away, Maxi." We started up the music, and for thirty seconds Maxi was both engaged and engaging, pretending to grill the crab cakes to their proper doneness. He even flipped each one over without sticking to the grill as we had the foresight of brushing lots of olive oil over the grates.

You never know how audience participation will play. In my experience when it plays, it plays extremely well, as it had with Maxi, the ham! (And that, my friends, would be *treyf* of a different flavor…) Next Mendel said in his best Southern sounding twang (We learned he grew up in Newport News.), "Very nice, y'all! But that's not the end of the show for today, folks. As a matter of fact, Florine and Maxi have been working on a theme song for the Matz brand, which we'd like to share with you now."

This was a new-business presentation twist I had never witnessed before. Maxi took a drum pad from his leather briefcase and two drumsticks and started beating out a rhythm. Florine pulled a sheet of paper from her pocketbook and announced, "Mendel is trying to get the rights for this music. I have changed the lyrics to work for our crab cakes. The song is something on the order of Match Maker from *Fiddler on the Roof*. Florine began to belt out her jingle as though she were playing Carnegie Hall.

Matz maker, Matz maker, make me a cake.

A crab cake divine.

Tender and fine....

I was dying. I couldn't look at anyone's face. It was like that moment Ben and I had with Dr. Loveless at the JCC, when I knew we had won the pitch but couldn't believe what I was seeing. My laughter was ready to spill out all over that room. All I could do at the moment was to excuse myself to the nearby lavatory. There, I flushed the toilet twice to muffle my explosion of laughter. I needed a handkerchief to stuff into my mouth to quiet down...Kosher Jews who process crabs and wish to own this Jewish melody to sell their treyf products...not even Mel Brooks could have come up with such a sketch.

As I gained control of myself and returned, I used an excuse that came to me earlier in the meeting, "As much as I like peppers in the potato salad," I said, "they have never quite agreed with me. But that new jingle, my friends, is really something." Then I bit down on my tongue so hard it started to bleed.

CHAPTER 19

It had been a terrific surprise for Amy and me to learn that all of our stolen possessions had reappeared at an antique store on Pine Street, where a sting called Operation Bear Trap was being run.

As it turned out, our insurance agent was a work-at-home mom and made her clients' files, knowingly or unknowingly, accessible to her twenty-three-year-old son. The son actively reviewed these files and planned robberies based on the information within. The stories in the newspaper suggested this robber broke into each house with a clear plan, an inventoried checklist prepared by his insurance-agent mom. In fact, he regarded her customers as ones they shared. I guess in a perverse sort of way, he was right.

It was reported that he worked quite methodically, house by house, for over a year. I guess the fortunate fact was that he had the decency to rob people who were well insured. He looked at his burglary enterprise as a tightly run business. And I had my answer to the question that had bugged me all weekend long when Amy and I were in Oxford: How did the burglar know our phone number?

All the stolen goods that were sold to the front were taken to a vault at police headquarters for safekeeping until the sting ran its course.

What did this mean to us? We had used the insurance money to put 40 percent down on our first house in the lovely Mt. Airy neighborhood of Philadelphia and had become bona fide Americans with our first mortgage and a baby baking in the oven. But then we had $35,000 worth of merchandise, mostly family heirlooms, that we were expected to buy back. When we got this "happy news" from the police sergeant, that every last item stolen from us had been recovered, it was all too good to be true. Or was it?

There was a moment of silence when I got off the phone with the officer and wondered aloud, "Could I just feign amnesia? What call? What sergeant? They recovered something?" Where was the money coming from to buy everything back? What else could we do but to buy it back? Most of what was stolen had been in our families for at least two generations. And with a mortgage and a baby on the way, we did what every other baby boomer did at a time like this: We got ourselves deeper into debt by way of a home equity loan. Then we bought back all the important stuff.

Those wedding gifts we never really liked stayed at the police station. We thought none of the gift givers would ever be the wiser. After all, we had been brutally burglarized. "What happens now if it rains on your parade, Samuel?" I could hear my dad saying. "Will you be knocking on my door like brother Mikey, constantly looking for a handout?" It was a troubling and haunting thought, but with my ability to grow business, I thought there would always be another reserve to build.

Our son, Adam Spiegel, was born exactly on his due date, which we thought was very considerate and brilliant of him. Amy and I had just finished a few renovations to make the nursery ready for our prince and had ratcheted our borrowing power up to the max. Then what did this already stretched dual family income household do? Well, of course, we got ourselves a nanny. Much to my chagrin, we decided not to go the route of a nanny from France or Sweden. Instead, our nanny was hand-picked from Spiegel's nightly janitorial service. Her name was Amanda Booker. She wore a pair of very obvious upper and lower dentures that would shift around when she talked. In our case, we combined a nanny and a housekeeper, making our arrangement a sensible twofer. Amanda Booker became our first in a series.

Amanda could have easily been a character from Flip Wilson's playbook. Looking back twenty years later, we realized with horror that, for all we knew, considering we hadn't run a background check, Amanda could have been an ex-con. Amanda was an expert at talking loudly to Adam, especially when she was trying to put him to sleep. His eyes would drift shut, and then, moments later, they would jar open. Why? Because all the "sweet nothings" she spoke to him and songs Amanda screamed into his poor little ear drums blared like a buzz saw.

She was very conscientious and troubled by the fact that "her baby" had difficulty nodding off. So she went to work on a solution. She felt that gently rocking him in her arms while talking him to sleep might be the proper counterbalance. In reality, and understand me here, although Amanda was a good soul, she just wasn't a gentle rocker. Frankly, she had the tenderness of Gorilla Monsoon and she shook our baby as if her motions were coming from a stagecoach riding over stones, rocks, and the occasional small boulder.

There was a day when Amy said to me after one of Amanda's rocking fests, "Adam's got to be brain-dead by now." In retrospect, it was a miracle he wasn't. Thinking back on it, it was no wonder Amy felt compelled to soothe Adam at night to make up for the tumult Amanda brought about during the day. Amy assumed the role of Adam's cuddly, teddy-bear Mom. And Adam made it clear that he hated his crib. That was because he understood that his mother was too big to climb in beside him. So Amy made him a nice nest of blankets and quilts on the floor in his room, and she and Adam shared this nest and most often nodded off together. But that was only after Adam was lovingly breastfed. Does this all sound as if there's some jealousy or disdain in my voice? Nah!

And until he was actually in dreamland, Amy dared not move. That is, if she actually wanted to move. Unless he was out cold, Adam was a human radar detector who could detect any motion. So, it seemed to me at the time that Adam had become Amy's captor. In retrospect, I wonder was it really the other way around? Had Amy made Adam's nursery her Camp David? The difference here is that when you stay at Camp David, you eventually return to the White House. Amy never did.

Most nights my wife would nod off even before Adam. When I knew they were both sound asleep, ever so gently I would tiptoe in to perhaps nudge Amy to a state of semi consciousness, so perhaps she might consider sharing a bed with me. Once in a while, I would successfully help her maneuver back to our bedroom. But for the most part, over the seven years following Adam's birth, Amy and he slept pretty much uninterrupted together in their nest, until Adam, and therefore Amy, had graduated to a bed that replaced the unused crib. When our daughter joined the family some years later, Amy's pattern was transferred over to Audrey, making my solitary confinement last for about fourteen years. Maybe that's what drove me to get a dog. I needed company.

CHAPTER 20

Amy and I loved Vermont. For seven straight years we made it our primary summer vacation spot. We worked it out to be able to get away for two consecutive weeks and rented a home in the mountains with Adam in tow. One summer, my brother Mikey, his wife Sylvia, and their daughter Karla joined us for the second week of our trip, renting a house nearby.

These homes were part of a community called Moose Mountain. We had previously vacationed there with Mikey's family. My brother made sure to phone and pounce on the concierge service at Moose Mountain weeks before we called, to reserve a house. To me, it seemed his plan was to outflank Amy and me in pursuit of the most desirable house in the resort.

All the homes had great views of the mountains, with the same well-equipped kitchens and basically the same floor plans, plus or minus a bedroom or two. You couldn't exactly go wrong with any…but not according to Mikey. One thing Amy and I learned early in our marriage was not to share a house with any of our siblings. (Years later, we expanded our rule: We stopped sharing a house with each other.)

This particular summer we vacationed in June because Amy was pregnant with Adam's baby sister, Audrey, who was due in August. By way of a scenic route through Pennsylvania and then upstate New York to break up the drive, we stayed a night at an inn in the Catskills. When we arrived, Amy wanted to take a bath and a nap before dinner. Adam and I followed one of the inn's nature maps into a densely wooded section nearby. If Adam hadn't had an eye twitch at that time, indicative of some kind of stress he was experiencing, as we entered the woods I would have said, "Lions and tigers and bears, oh my."

What was happening on Adam's cute face was more than an occasional spasm from our otherwise, relatively stable boy. Clued into his obvious discomfort, I asked, "Adam, buddy, what's going on? You seem worried about something." I gave it a shot. Adam usually didn't hold back on what was going on in his head. As it turned out, he had a strong premonition from a dream he'd had. He told me, "Mommy's going to die in labor."

Wow, I thought, as we entered the dense forest. Adam was not only expecting to lose his lovely nighttime companion, but when the new baby arrived in his world, he feared he'd lose his mom altogether. Pretty heavy stuff. If I'd had such a worry, I would not only develop a facial twitch, I'd probably come down with shingles or phlebitis.

Adam was the same kid at age seven, who, when we asked if he would like a dog, answered, "No. A dog would take too much attention from me." So, back to his premonition. I told Adam, "Mom's in good hands. Her doctor brought you and hundreds of boys and girls into the world just fine. And besides, I'll be by her side every step of the way to make sure all goes well." I held Adam close as we walked further into the thick forest that soon obscured much of the day's remaining light. About ten minutes into the woods, both of us watched four newly hatched birds cross a path about ten yards in front of us.

Within seconds of our forward march, a mammoth owl opened her wings to what seemed her fullest extension. Her wingspan made her easily four feet wide. With her outstretched claws, this sight was far from anything I had ever encountered, except by way of National Geographic's cameras. The owl immediately dive-bombed us, claws seemingly pointed at my eyes.

At that very second, the owl and I were going on pure instinct. I tackled Adam and threw myself over him onto the ground. As the mother owl vengefully swooped toward us again to protect her babies from us Philadelphian brutes, we could feel her wings flapping. All I wanted at the moment was for this flying creature to understand just a little English. I thought, *Big Bird, relax. We come in peace. I was a Vietnam War protester and Adam's a peace-loving dove, too!*

Instead, I screamed, "Adam, shut your eyes tight!" Mine were already closed. Then I peeked to see where this creature was hovering, and with my arms extended, I madly searched for a loose stick, which, fortunately, I found nearby. Like a madman, I waved the stick at the mother as I straddled my own twitching chick and squirmed to turn the two of us in the opposite direction. Adam was directly under me and we inched ourselves forward as if we had been glued together. I whispered to him, "We must become GI Joe soldiers, and body-crawl, like they do in the army."

What I really wanted to say was, "Adam, we need to run for our lives!" But I had the good sense to keep that thought to myself. I don't remember a moment before this incident or after when I was so totally controlled by fear and instinct. For a time it felt as though I was going on pure adrenaline.

I whispered, "On the count of three, buddy, we will both get up and just like with a fast break, we'll run with all our might. See up there, to the bend in the path? Do you see the turn in the path, Adam?"

With tremendous seriousness he said, "Daddy, I see it. On the count of three, Daddy?"

"Three, Adam. I'll wave this big stick over our heads and I assure you, this owl will think it's a sword or a gun or a big, big antler. That way she will stay clear of us."

"When do we start, Dad?"

"On three, buddy." I whispered one last time, "Now give me your fastest of fastest breakaways."

Adam was 100 percent earnest.

"One, two, three!"

We both shot up as one and sprinted. With the resolve of Jesse Owens, Adam streaked along with me toward the finish line.

Then, quietly but self-assuredly, he leaned into me, "Daddy, shouldn't we run a little longer to be sure?"

I knew we were out of harm's way, but still waving the stick, I said, "Good idea, Adam. To the next bend." Which is where we zoomed.

Adam asked, "Do you think she's gone?"

"Yes, sir, we out-flew her. We ditched that mama. But you were right to keep us running. And, buddy, you were almost right about your dream. What you had in your head was a warning. But this is important—the characters turned out to be different. It was you and me, not Mommy and the new baby, who were in harm's way. You saw some troubles ahead and it turned out your dream was about us. Not about Mommy. Mommy and your new sister will be just fine."

"You really think so, Daddy?" he asked.

I said, "I know so. God just told us that."

Adam's face brightened as we cleared the trees to greet what was left of the sun that had dropped in the sky. In about two days' time Adam's twitching stopped. And to whom did we owe this breakthrough? Why, I'd have to say, this wise old owl.

The tenth day into our two-week vacation in Vermont, and three days after Mikey and his family settled in at their bigger house further up the mountain, I got a call from my brother. Usually, when he called at home or on trips, he'd find a way to get me to pass the phone to Amy. But in this instance he awkwardly and somewhat formally asked me to stay on the line, as I could picture him grimacing over something about me or our folks that he couldn't tolerate any longer to the point that he had to pitch a fit.

I deflected whatever was on his mind by asking, "Are you sure you're not trying to reach Moose Mountain concierge service to complain about some overhanging branch that might be obstructing your more perfect view of the mountains?"

He said, "I beg your pardon. What on earth are you talking about, Samuel?" He knew precisely what I was referring to. "I was just calling to ask my kid brother if he'd like to join me for a hike down the mountain for some coffee and breakfast tomorrow morning."

I asked, "To what do I owe the honor?" I knew it was coming coated with one favor or another. I just wasn't sure what he might be angling for this time up in the Green Mountains.

"Yes, Samuel, your poor brother is asking his mogul sibling out for breakfast and looking forward to it. Exactly what time does Prince Charming rise these days?"

Oh yes, the picture was forming. "I can be ready to go by eight."

As I stood in front of our house at the designated time, I spotted Mikey, ambling around the bend from further up the mountain. He was wearing a yellow glossy slicker. I looked at him with some amazement, having never seen anyone older than about eleven in one of those rain jackets. And when he got closer he looked like a tent walking toward me on stilts, which is when I said, "Mikey, have our plans changed? Are we off to play kick the can on the blacktop, or will a matching yellow bus be taking us to the playground?"

"Hardy-har-har, Samuel. It looks like it might rain and all this is… is being prepared. As your older brother, I'd advise you, no, actually demand that you to go back inside and put on your Patagonia parka, which I can't begin to afford on my reporter's salary."

"I think I'll just throw caution to the wind, big bro, and live life dangerously."

"Do as you wish. Just don't tell me I didn't warn you when you start screaming, 'I'm melting!'"

I continued. "So how are things faring for you back in the Big Bad Apple?"

"Well, you know the *Star-Ledger* has us on a salary freeze and this is three years running, Sam. And Sylvia, with a group of other teachers in White Plains, was furloughed to substitute teaching status for now, which isn't going to give her much of a salary this year. The coming months are going to be pretty damn rough for us."

"Well, I heard Mom and Dad made the decision to up their mortgage contribution on your house from half to all. And I'll tell you, Harry was near spitting blood for weeks on this issue until Mom and I tag-teamed him on your behalf, thank you. A little appreciation from time to time, Mikey, would go a long way."

"That's why I'm taking you out for breakfast. And if you must know, I've been salivating all night long over what will come out of the Café's kitchen this morning: those wonderful blueberry pancakes, those to-die-for hash browns so crisp at the bottom that each one makes that crackle sound in your mouth when you bite down. Not to mention the pork links slathered in Vermont syrup. That's what this is all about, Sammy. I'm treating you to a thank-you country breakfast. And I can see it already…you gearing up to make me feel like the Goodyear blimp, ordering a side of plain blueberries with poached eggs as a main course."

"Well, something like that. You know they make their own granola and their yogurt's from Jersey cows."

"In that case we might as well go back to Newark for breakfast."

"No, silly, their milk comes from Billings Farm and Billings imports these Jersey cows from the UK. The milk does taste better up here."

"Well, la-di-da, Sam!"

"But I'd be delighted to try a sliver of your blueberry stack slathered in butter and syrup, if you wouldn't mind a little sharing this morning." As I took my seat, Mikey was futzing to get his yellow slicker to stay on the hook by the side of the booth. Then it fell to the floor a second time. That's when Mikey decided to stuff it next to him as he rolled it into a big ball. Nix that. It looked more like a baseball infield tarp rolled up beside him. And that's when he started in on what this breakfast was really all about. "So I hear you're winning lots of new business, Sammy, and that it won't be long before you can sell Dad's place for the big bucks and retire."

"You always refer to it as Dad's place. I've been running it for almost a decade now. And Mikey, we're far from making a sale."

"Well, the day will come. I know you're angling for it. To be rich and famous."

"Actually, my goal is to do great work and just be comfortable."

"I'm asking you to think about releasing your part of Mom and Dad's estate to your poor brother-the-reporter and his out of work teacher wife, of course, only if such a day comes, which it will. And we both know there's one painting on Mom and Dad's wall that has appreciated and has the primary worth in their collection. Dad says the Mary Cassatt could fetch $200,000 in today's market."

"I think he's right. If you recall, I urged them to buy it."

"I don't remember it that way, but your poor brother could use the money from it down the road. You can have the rest of them."

"Thanks for having my back, Mikey. Looks like you're going for the entire enchilada plus the one painting worth anything over your kind breakfast treat that will cost you twenty dollars. How can I ever repay you?"

"Well, let's be real, Sam. You'll have the mansion, second homes, maybe even one of these Moose fixer-uppers in your portfolio. Mom and Dad are working with their lawyer on their wills, if you haven't heard. Think on it, Samuel. There is nothing wrong with us inputting at this stage. But whatever happens know this—I think I can get you in."

"In where?"

"Well, you know your niece's friend, Mica Walenstein, from the Dalton School? Her father, on numerous occasions, has assured me entrance, when the time comes, into Bernie Madoff's investment group. He has the inside track. They're personal friends. Maybe being in Philly you've never heard of Madoff, but he has a track record of doubling everyone's money within ten years while you keep living off the interest. I've told Dad about him, too. I know his fund might be too slow growth for a *Chacham* like you, Samuel, but I probably can get you in if you'd like me to try. I understand, with him, investors never have a losing year. He's why so many smart Jews have second homes in Palm Beach."

CHAPTER 21

Audrey, our newest Spiegel, finally arrived, and we bought a larger house in the Wynnewood neighborhood of Philadelphia. Borrowing money and trading up had become our pattern. And when Spiegel & Associates' name was in the *Inquirer* just about every other week for landing a new piece of business, and I was the Spiegel responsible for these wins, the perception this created brought me even greater borrowing clout.

Amy camped out with our two kids on the floor or in their beds for roughly seven years each. So these are what my generation referred to as the "Wonder Years," as in "Wonder-whatever-happened-to-having-sex-ever-again?" But well before Audrey's eighth birthday, she had had it with spooning with Mom, and it was Audrey who sent Amy an eviction notice to leave her bedroom…for good.

This was at the time when Audrey seemed to be feeling increasingly comfortable making her own life decisions, to the degree she was allowed. Another life decision around this time included remaining friends with her nursery school pal, Ralphie Kurtz, who would have made the greatest boy-doll model ever imaginable on this planet. He'd have sat in a cellophane box inside a '68 Maroon Metallic Mustang convertible. The commercials would have had him driving with his hair blowing in the wind, wearing the coolest pair of shades imaginable.

While most kids six or seven years old discontinued relationships with the opposite sex, that was not my Audrey's MO. She continued her friendship with "Ralphie-boy," as she called him, well into the years she should have tossed him. He had the most beautiful blonde hair with wonderfully straight bangs that covered his entire forehead and his eyes were Barbados ocean blue. It was no wonder Audrey wouldn't let him go.

They remained loyal allies and best of friends, at age seven, and still liked playing together with Audrey's collection of dolls. And by this point, I understood, yes, he might be a famous clothes designer or home decorator one day. But right then, Audrey had this idea for Ralphie to join her in giving chic hairdos to her dolls in a fashionable hair cuttery of her making, her own Elizabeth Arden Red Door Salon, in her room at the end of our upstairs hall. In their minds that day, the two were single-mindedly focused on scissoring away hair from the heads of twenty-four very cooperative dolls.

When the cut hair landed on the floor, they quickly whisked it into the corner of Audrey's room near the trashcan, but by no means were these tresses tossed in. They had a plan for the hair excess as well—building a "Leaning Tower of Locks" that boldly climbed up Audrey's bedroom wall like a well-fertilized wandering Jew.

Some floors of the Leaning Tower were adorned in shades of auburn. Others wore strawberry blonde. Then there were shades of brunette in between. On a few levels were multicolored streaks of skyscraper. But for the penthouse, this was my darling Audrey's idea and *pièce de résistance*, the crowning glory of her achievement that day, arguably of her entire childhood and marker, I feel sure, of my daughter's rites of passage.

This is when my sweet baby pulled from deep inside herself her most brazen command by far to date…when her father looked at her and asked the next day, "Who is this girl? And…where in the hell did she come from?" This is when Audrey convinced Ralph that his wonderful blonde bangs should grace the penthouse level of their new and very distinctive twenty-four story hair tower. And what did Audrey do next?

She cut every last bang off Ralph's broad forehead. Hours later, when Ralph's mother came to pick up her blonde from our house and realized that he was missing all his bangs, I saw Ralphie's mom make a face that will stay with me for the rest of my life and continue to haunt me in my nightmares.

Back to sex with Amy, or lack thereof. Wherever it was going or not, it basically wasn't imagined much any longer. When Spiegel won a big account like Humana, the AMA, Sears Craftsman Tools…these achievements got a little rise out of Amy. Small-to-midsize accounts never quite piqued her interest. Not even the sexy small ones like *The Economist* magazine or *The Audubon Society.* And spur of the moment trysts grew rare indeed.

Let me point out, though, that our small Spiegel family unit—despite the lack of parental sex—had exceptional karma. Things were going pretty much our way. Amy and I made each other laugh often and counted on our forward momentum, the abundant pleasures in raising our children, and the excitement derived from our work as meaningful blessings.

Although my libido was far from satisfied (most nights she went to bed wearing her sweats), my life was chock-full of other sorts of excitement that had a way of compensating—sometimes even too much, as often at work, I felt as if I was in the first seat of the roller coaster and would have been happy to be soothed by some quality time in the sack with an adoring wife from time to time. But that didn't seem to be in my cards.

Instead, I began to understand why my dad had worked so painstakingly to bring me into the company. There is some reassurance in having another pair of eyes you can trust watching the store with you. Let's face it—do employees really care about negotiating best possible deals with suppliers? Do they really care about curbing business travel and entertainment costs? In fact, they often drive costs up to whatever limit they can get away with.

Now, with my years of experience in running the business, I understood precisely what was behind my father's propaganda machine back at the Union League when he got me to return to Philly. By this point I clearly understood what drove him. And how interesting it was that history can't help but repeat itself, even when we all should know better.

I wanted to bring Amy into the family business for many of the same reasons. There's safety in numbers, or so I foolishly thought. More family members would mean greater fortification of our assets. More eyes, to protect us from the always encroaching poachers of what is *mine*, as in the extended family, *ours*. I brought this idea up to Amy with an offer of a higher salary than she was making at the time.

And with my invitation to join the firm, I thought I'd bring her a loftier purpose: to protect what we had been building, our nest egg, so to speak, and to help take the family business further. Noble enough, I thought. With her considerable talent in urban affairs and politics, it seemed as if she'd be a natural to start a political division at Spiegel and handle advertising for candidates running for office.

She bit, and we added Amy Spiegel to head up Spiegel Political Affairs. As for our workforce, by 1990 it tripled to more than forty associates and the agency expanded into a larger brownstone next door. This one sported new furniture, more Samson copiers, a hi-tech conference room, and a TV editing suite as we proudly were then well into the Television Age, thank you. We were zooming ahead with unabashed verve and more than a touch of competitor envy.

Four of the thirteen associates who had been at Spiegel when I entered the company in '79 were still standing (well, almost). Poor Harvey Lodenberg, due to a slipped disc and then an unsuccessful back operation, lost movement in his legs. These severe mobility limitations required a reduction in hours, and he worked primarily from his home.

Harlot was still making Dad his toast and cottage cheese, but now we had a new apparatus that, in addition to toasting, also baked and broiled. When Harry spoke about our upgrades, in particular the toaster oven, he'd say, "And...um...if you put it past broil...it will fly." Most importantly—it shut off when the rye was brown, which was not the case with its predecessor.

Sol Katz had become a one-word phrase by the "fall season" of his career. He was SolKatz; his two names glued to each other the way Goldman attaches to Sachs. He never let us forget the stranglehold he had on our Brookstone account even after the client was bought by Quaker Oats. He was our dog with his bone tightly clenched in his mouth and never allowed it to drop. I was convinced that even when he was having sex with his wife, Joanna, who carried two ample breasts where his bone might rest, as on a hollow between two mountains, he preferred to keep it in his mouth.

New ownership often means changing agencies. At first the sale of Brookstone to Quaker was a big worry for us. But we learned quickly, thank God, that Quaker respected the idea of keeping existing management teams in place to operate with their current choice of suppliers. The only real change for us with Quaker as owner was their deeper pockets and their interest in transforming SolKatz's regional electronics account into a national chain. So, realists that we were, most of the time, we tried to keep our "dog with his bone" pretty damned comfortable.

The growing attention by the press to Brookstone's expansion plans signaled the onslaught of many leave-behinds from all around the country to try to snatch our dearly beloved old client out from under us. Every week, national ad firms, including Lux, stepped up their overtures to Brookstone, which kept my father very much in the nervous zone. I used to think, *Simmer down, old man*. But his makeup just wouldn't allow it.

Despite the fact that I was now running Spiegel, my dad kept his spacious office with his partner's desk handed down to him by our founder, Louis T. Jacobs. Harry's horse racing trade association account had left us, but not for Lux, I'm delighted to report. Rather, it was due to a lack of funding when their largest dues payer, Magna Entertainment, a company out of Canada that was buying up tracks all around the country, became our client. Yes! Around the time of the win, I wanted to bump into Lux at the Union League and say, "Lawrence, my friend, we kept our humble thimble out there on that Monopoly board long enough to trade it in for the cannon. Last I heard, is it true? You've been walking around with that pathetic old shoe?"

CHAPTER 22

Within the next two years, to support our growth, the agency added twenty-five new members to our team. Our average age was now my own, which was thirty-seven. We were humming. Among the hot new associates that were knocking on our door, even taking pay cuts to join us, were two of my oldest and closest friends from the Party Circus days Ben Selborn, who left investment banking for advertising, and Billy Gottlieb (Billy G.), who bought me that cherished Hermès tie.

The coup de grace, though, was when I stole creative director Loren Rucker away from the hottest creative shop in our region, BRC. Loren was the young partner I had met when my father set me up with the BRC hotshots at Cuzzin's Restaurant some years back for our so-called merger discussion. Bringing Loren on board was a significant victory. It felt like a well-deserved congratulatory gift for a strong decade of building up my father's shop. And by this point, it had become, by all rights, my agency, with heavy lifters from all around to keep pace with our now rapid ascent.

Loren had the best creative reputation in Philadelphia, but more importantly, he and I clicked. Together, in this next phase, we built Spiegel from a respected regional shop to one that was becoming a national creative powerhouse. But that didn't come without lots of jolts, joy, and disappointments. Harry viewed Loren as my twin and both of us as a tag team. Although theoretically Dad might have understood the importance of Loren's entrance into Spiegel, personally, he saw Loren's involvement with me as not a good thing for him. And what exactly do I mean by this?

In the beginning, when a father and son work together in business, their exchanges in the workplace are respectful, at times, even deferential—sometimes both on the same day. Early on in my employment at Spiegel, with my heightened sense of responsibilities and early successes, I became more confident. And with early achievement came the desired payoff: greater wins for the agency.

When it got to the point where I had brought in much more business by far than what had existed before I arrived, and I had been a key driver in saving accounts that considered moving their business elsewhere…with this forward momentum, I had hoped my dad's pride in me would only deepen. And perhaps it did.

But what resulted instead was that he seemed left out. When this feeling intensified, it turned into what appeared to be significant paranoia on his part. He began to put a hold on me like a vice. Instead of allowing himself to let go, I found him constantly swooping in and trying to gather, on a regular basis, all the information he could abstract, account by account. There seemed to be no good reason for his meddling except to try to keep himself lodged in on things. But what he was causing was a time drain for me that became the catalyst for our developing schism.

I found myself using just about the same refrain each day when speaking to Harry, "If all I do is give you reports on accounts, soon we won't have anything to talk about because the work won't get done and the accounts will leave!" Then for a while, instead of applauding that I brought in such an able soul mate in Loren to help me run the place, Harry couldn't help but see him as overtaking his own role as my confidant. And he wasn't wrong about that. That's when the idea hit me to broker a system to alleviate some of our growing strife.

I said, "Harry, here's my deal: every night when I walk my dog Ruffy, I'll give you a check-in call from my cell phone." And for a while, this was a splendid solution. Better than he had hoped for. I had to end these calls by telling him, "I won't be able to report in on the accounts tomorrow because if this call goes on any longer, I'll have brain cancer." Fortunately, he always kept his sense of humor, and such a closing comment would leave him with a chuckle.

I could understand why Loren had affected him so. There is something extraordinary in this world when you find a business soul mate to share fears, celebrate victories, craft goals, and achieve as a team. On the occasions we were edged out by a competitor, there was no one I preferred licking wounds with more than Loren Rucker. Together in a bar, we'd share our dreams and disappointments. I'd sip my Dewar's and soda while Loren drank his Molson straight from the bottle—never from a glass.

As Spiegel grew, Loren and I counted on each other. In this tumultuous business, who you choose to count on can make the difference between success and failure. He could have gone to any agency in the country to fill an important creative slot. He was that good and had wonderful self-confidence that would never surface as smug.

Loren was Canadian-born. He was not Jewish, but was raised in a Jewish neighborhood near Montreal and was stunningly irreverent when he wished to be. Quite the diplomat when such behavior was protocol. Most of the time, Loren knew how to keep me focused on the right things. I loved his smart-ass side. But under everything, within this man was a huge amount of integrity.

He had one of the fairest minds I'd ever encountered, and his brain was always focused on the possibilities and on our potential. For a long stretch, nothing got in our way, because he had his priorities straight. He was always growing and perfecting his game and motivated associates. Loren was a take charge guy. His department was the largest in the agency—and he was respected by clients, comrades, and vendors.

My partner and I turned into an eight-legged horse that figured out, after a good bit of running, how to take the lead and hold it. Above all others in this business, in my mind Beinhauser had always been the sole bearer of the advertising platinum card—intuition, strategic strength, and creative ability—and he had it all. Aligned with Loren, I dared to believe we might emerge as some form of a Beinhauser Cerberus. Call us the two-headed version, what have you. I knew no one could fill Joseph's shoes alone, but with Loren, I imagined we could become highly respected leaders of the kind of national creative agency I had dreamed about and had a taste of while working at DDB.

The fact was that we were leaving behind, by lengths, some of the other horses we nurtured within our company. At first this made me wonder, "Don't we need to recruit more of us?" Then I understood this was as it should be. We couldn't run an agency with more chiefs. What we needed were stronger Indians, for which we were interviewing, daily. As we grew, we understood the need to upgrade talent to keep up with the demands of our largest and most challenging clients who, by this point in our history, were at a caliber that reflected our very healthy egos.

We had a few horses that had great difficulty wandering past the starting gate, including Ben Selborn, my closest friend, Party Circus partner, and best man at my wedding. He seemed mixed up about the advertising business, and often, just mixed up in general. Loren told me, "Ben's clients run him. It's supposed to be the other way around, Sam." Loren wasn't wrong. It was just hard for me to see Ben in such a light. Loren said, "He's giving my department fit after fit. As you and I were lassoing Sharp Copiers, what was Selborn bringing in? A local antiques dealer."

I told Loren, "I'll join Ben at his Left Bank Antiques meeting to pitch our print ideas and see what's what there." There was something strangely eerie about the time I spent alone with Ben in the car on the way to Left Bank. For the first time in my life I felt as if my oldest friend and I were coming to this meeting from two different planets. Loren was right...we had just slayed the dealer portion of the Sharp Copier business in Mahwah, New Jersey, one week prior, and here I was about to enter this overcrowded antique store on Pine Street, almost as if we were coming to them as door-to-door salesmen.

146

I told Ben as much when we walked in, with cowbells clanging as we opened the door. "I hope you have our whole line of dusters in your attaché case because this place is in desperate need of cleaning." For whatever reason, this moment with Ben felt as though we were lost in a time warp, as if we were back at the JCC pitching parties. Then I asked Ben, "Is it this appointment where we re-meet Dr. Loveless?"

I knew that my comments seemed a little demeaning. But holy cowbells, what were we doing there? Ben grinned nervously. He knew what I was conveying. *We're not teenagers any longer and the whole idea of sitting amid all this clutter on pretty much the same folding chairs we sat on when we were fourteen, selling parties at the JCC, seemed, at best, out of an absurdist play.*

We didn't meet up with Dr. Loveless, but instead I had the pleasure of meeting the husband and wife proprietors who both greeted me with limp handshakes. Then we were directed to our seats, and a puff of dust came up from both cushions when we sat down. The pair looked a lot like Morticia and Gomez Addams, straight from *The Addams Family* television series. I thought this encounter was only missing Lurch and Uncle Fester.

When Ben and I returned to the car after I had watched him fumble through selling them our least favorite ad of the three we brought, it was clear to me he was out of touch with where my company was going and the agency business in general. That day, I realized Ben was not cut out for the trade. In his eyes, he knew so too.

In the car back to the office, Ben said, "Thanks for coming along, Sam. I know this isn't exactly the plum account you were hoping for out of me," and trying desperately for some levity, he continued, "but I hope it can help at least pay for this month's electric bill."

I chuckled a little uncomfortably.

"It wouldn't offend me if you thought it best that we resign Left Bank."

"Well, I'm not sure it's exactly an account yet, Ben. Looks more like we just sold them an ad, and I think we should see it through to publication. Then see what happens from there."

147

STEVEN C. EISNER

That's when Ben said, "I can certainly do that. And about the time it gets released to *Antiques Magazine*, I'll be leaving Spiegel."

When I had recruited Ben, I naively thought he'd move into the role that Loren snatched up, building the agency with me. What happened was that, as Loren and I kept getting stronger, Ben was left in the dust, literally, or so it seemed at the Left Bank. The company and our community saw Loren and me as the powerful force.

We took our shots together on a court that, ironically, I had only experienced before with Ben when we were doing parties together. And now Ben couldn't return a serve. But with bittersweet luck, Ben's father died much too young, and Ben inherited some money. He was looking at several small companies to purchase and run and wanted to move on. I was so relieved to hear this news, as asking Ben to leave Spiegel was almost unthinkable to me.

Amy wasn't faring well either. Her attempts to build our political division, together with political creative consultant Merv Getten, who had earned acclaim in Democratic circles, were coming up short. As it turned out, Merv had a cocaine addiction. Whatever profits we had from this subsidiary seemed somehow to be going up Getten's nose. We made the decision to cut Merv loose and move Amy over to the mother ship to run the new Manor Care Senior Living account we had just landed. Changing Amy's responsibilities to oversee Manor Care was Loren's idea. He said, "Sam, I'm the only one who can say this to you. It's Manor Care for Amy or she should consider retiring there." He wasn't wrong. No one else had his nerve or his credibility to say whatever he had to say.

On the other hand, the buzz about Billy G. seemed quite positive. He built trust quickly. He loved starting in on things each morning. On business matters, I mainly connected with him during weekly status meetings. He had made fast contributions but sadly, he was determined to move on as well. "Let me leave your place on a high note, Sam, and bolt before I fail." I wore his Hermès tie from time to time. And when I did, I thought of it as my tie to Billy G.

Although my nightly phone conversations with Harry were helpful, by this point, we had reached a father and son impasse where our talks weren't running free. In fact, what I conveyed his way had become more guarded. To his country club friends, he acknowledged our growth with considerable pride, but never directly to me. Instead, he continued to display a fair amount of rivalry. When I looked at him as we passed in the hall, I'd often ask myself, "Aren't we supposed to be in this together?"

By this time I'd been back in Philadelphia for fifteen years building Spiegel. After Harry's second heart valve transplant, as he came out of anesthesia, he greeted my mother with tenderness. Even Mikey got a nice tap to his wrist. But when I leaned in to welcome Dad back from his fog, he said, "There's the brute!" I had only heard him use that term one other time—when describing Lawrence Lux stalking his accounts.

As Dad's convalescence from this operation shifted from home to more time at the office, we had a small parade of consultants who attempted to help us through the ambiguities, worries, and power struggles inherent in our transition to a much bigger company, and to place a price tag on the value of the business so that an ownership transition could take place. But when my own father called me (I was his baby after all) a brute, that was pretty hurtful, baffling and not exactly a relationship builder.

Things got worse. In December 1993, at a Christmas party hosted by our trade association, the 4As, a competitor approached my father. Or was it the other way around? I will never be fully sure. The competitor, ARC, was the largest New Jersey–based agency, also a father and son team.

The idea, as I understood it from Harry, was that the Caldwells, senior and junior, were pretty impressed with our track record and thought it would be a good idea to consider a merger. Axel Ryan Caldwell told my father that his son Jed, who owned their agency by then and was ten years my senior, would put forward a proposed merger plan for us to review. A preliminary meeting was set for early February.

Preparing for this meeting became my father's new obsession. I had a very bad feeling about what was evolving. My sense? Whatever the Caldwells and my dad were plotting behind my back was no merger, but instead a Caldwell takeover ploy, designed through pre-meeting negotiations until enough of the upfront work had been figured out by Harry and the Caldwells. Who was paranoid now? It was blatantly obvious to me these three men were in cahoots.

The stock transition from Axel to Jed had taken place some years back. Jed now had the majority ownership of ARC. Harry and I had hit some snags relating to the evaluation of our company. Most of the revenue that fueled us at that time was due to my work and the new Spiegel team I had built. This dynamic appeared to contradict all comparable family companies analyzed at this stage of transition, because normally the senior family member still controlled the majority of the revenue stream.

A takeover by people outside the family would put more money in my father's pocket faster. I was quite certain that this was what he was angling for. That's what I felt our corporate lawyer and accountant were reinforcing. Although Harry and Mikey had a very strained relationship, I had the clear sense that Dad had gotten Mikey's support as well as my mom's on this initiative. Mikey's occasional phone calls around this time quickly drifted to comments about ARC. "That ARC deal sounds pretty damn good to me and Mom, Samuel. What in the hell is your problem?" And I wasn't 100 percent sure where Amy was lining up here, either. In stark contrast, my mind wandered back to Beth, when in my run for president, she stared down my contender with the penetrating eyes of a believer in me— much as Bobby Kennedy believed in his brother, Jack. "Don't you dare fuck with my Sam, here!" Was Amy's support also there? I often wondered.

I nicknamed our attorney "Squint Willie" because his eyes could barely peek through his slits. He worked with "Neb Ted," my name for our accountant who specialized in stating the obvious, but always in the voice of authority. I could just hear him saying, "Third party transactions are richer, surer bets and cleaner deals, Harry." These two men were my dad's contemporaries and country club friends. Why should I ever have thought they'd be on my side? Why had I been born so trusting? Nothing could possibly be a bigger sinkhole for Spiegel & Associates or a richer goldmine for the lawyers and accountants, than a father and son at odds on transitioning their business. Our negotiations were starting to make Vietnam look like a short and inexpensive war.

My dad knew I really had no patience or time for this ARC distraction. But I realized this was now Harry's pet project, perhaps (in his eyes) the opportunity that his life had been building to. He asked me, "Sam, would you mind if I work with our accountant and lawyer to assemble all the paperwork we need to bring us where we need to be when we meet with ARC?"

"Harry, why in the hell do we need the Caldwells? I think we're doing a pretty damn good job building up our own shop. Why are you trying to muck things up for us?"

"It's the age of consolidation. From the day you started back here, you've told me you want to build us into a national player. This would be your chance. And what will you lose, having a meetin' with these guys? I'll get us ready. All you need to do is show up with an...um... open mind."

I told him, "It doesn't look like we're coming to the table with a point of view, or a voice or a direction of our own. It feels to me, Harry, that you're coming to the table with your tail between your legs waiting for marching orders. What is this meeting? What are you trying to do here? You lure me back to Philadelphia and when you get me here, I work like a hauling donkey to get Spiegel to a place where it's turning heads, and you want to sell it out from under me? Shame on you."

"Sam, I'm looking out for your best interest here and the interest of our entire family."

"The hell you are."

"Yes, your mother's and my security count, too. We're not...um... getting younger, you know. We don't want to go to our kids with hat in hand when we're older and grayer. You know I have a fragile heart. I could drop dead at any moment."

"Oh boy, bring on the violin section, Harry."

"Samuel, this is a very precarious business we're in. The stronger we become, the less risk we take on, the less can be lost. Look what the Saatchis are doing to the industry. Maurice Saatchi was the keynote speaker at the Christmas function when I talked to the Caldwells. Mr. Saatchi looked around to all the Mid-Atlantic Chapter members and said, 'One day, if you're lucky, gents, you can cash in your chips and be part of Saatchi & Saatchi Worldwide.' There's a movement afoot, Sam. Maybe with us combining forces with the Caldwells, we could...um...become a junior Saatchi. You and Jed can build your own network. I believe that junior Caldwell has some big plans in mind, Samuel."

Here I was, back in Philly in the bosom of my family, and I had never before felt so alienated or alone. How could this be? "Well, I'll see you at the Best Western in Ramsey, New Jersey on the fifth of February. You know, Harry, it's a day before my birthday. I couldn't think of a more magnificent gift a dad could give his son around the anniversary of when he came into this world...a nice stab in the back."

I slowly started backing out of his office, looking at his fireplace and racks of pipes and grandfather clock and partner's desk, as if I were staring back on the past. That's when I looked Harry in the eye and said, "Maybe it's time for you to clean out your desk and get it ready for Jed Caldwell. Better yet, get this beautiful desk and nice clock out of here before that son of a bitch snaps it up for his country house."

I slammed Dad's door as I left. The pipes rattled behind me.

CHAPTER 23

Christmas passed. New Year's came. The start of the year followed its normal patterns, but Harry and I stopped talking. Everyone in my family saw the two of us avoiding each other. And on February 5th, we traveled in separate cars to the Caldwells' Best Western joy fest. I had insisted on it. I wouldn't be a party to Harry's team of thieves—Neb Ted and Squint Willie—and the vivisection of my family. That morning I ran into my father as he was leaving the men's room with drops by his fly and he said, "You must be kidding about traveling in separate cars."

"No," I said, "I've never been more serious about anything in my life. You drive with your consultant friends. And I'll meet you at high noon."

The Caldwells had lunch set up in a private room without a view. Actually, there were no windows at all. I wanted to tell my dad, "We're in lockdown." It felt as cold and unwelcoming and as truly horrible as I had expected it to be. Maybe worse. But I have to admit that Father Caldwell had a great deal of natural charm as we all took some courtesy bites of the overdressed Caesar with wet croutons.

Then we moved to the turkey sandwiches. Mine looked pretty good until I tasted it. As my teeth sunk deeply into the honey mustard mayonnaise sauce, I realized there was no discernible taste of mustard. Chomping into it felt as I imagined quicksand might feel in one's mouth. I would have complained, if it weren't totally rude, and also so stereotypical that the Jews would send their mayonnaise-laden sandwiches back while our gentile counterparts happily sucked up the white slime as if it were pudding.

As I moved my unfinished sandwich to the same side of my plate where I had ditched the Caesar, Jed interrupted Axel's pleasantries. He immediately hijacked the meeting from his father, employing the same ten-minute rule I used when presenting to prospects over lunch: let your guests continue eating while you get on with things. Jed was a man who was well practiced at skirting foreplay to go straight to the fuck.

"We want to buy your company with the goal of completing this transaction by midsummer. That would mean we would send our auditors into your offices by June first. Yours is our first handpicked acquisition and there will be a dozen or so more prestigious regional agencies to follow under the ARC dome."

I thought, *vomit-vomit, piss-piss.*

My father thought, Nirvana! Harry cut in as he looked down at his yellow pad, "What other markets do you...um...envision as part of your expansion plan, Jed?" My dad's head seemed to be hopelessly caught up in Jed's tight ass. Where was his spine? I knew he'd escaped Buchenwald, but dear God, Jed wasn't his newfound Churchill. Why couldn't he see this?

"Harry, we're targeting Baltimore next, Miami third, and New York fourth. Then we'll take a break for two years to make sure the ARC is unifying well enough." He paused to survey our motel room without windows. "It's all part of our execution plan." Jed's cadence had a metronome effect. And his material seemed lifted from a Wharton textbook at around Lecture 32: *How to Tell the Assholes They're Getting Fucked.*

"We will buy your agency for 70 percent of your gross profit. We figure the gross stands at about a million five...give or take a hundred thousand. If we've got your numbers right, your stockholders will walk off with over a million, sir."

I took note of the practiced deference with which Jed concluded his pitch. And the stockholders he was referring to were Harry Spiegel, Harry Spiegel, and let me not forget, Harry Spiegel. At this point I looked at my dad licking his lips as dollar signs spun in his eyes.

Neb Ted then asked, "Jed, is this a cash deal upon signing?" He should have closed with "Mr. President, your Almighty or Supreme Court Justice, Sir."

"This is a cash deal with a sweetener for Samuel. At the point of signing the agreement, we will issue a check for around $350,000 to the stockholders."

Neb Ted continued, "So the initial exchange is roughly a third of the sale price? How is the rest to be paid?"

Ted had to travel all this way to Ramsey, New Jersey, to conclude that $350,000 was around 30 percent of the sale price? He should get back into Dad's car and be what he was born to be—a sniveling wimp.

My father nodded in delight.

"Theodore," Jed said. Everyone, including Neb Ted, looked around to find the Theodore in the room.

That was actually pretty funny. I wanted to shout, "Ted's his name, asshole, he's T-E-D and his name rhymes with J-E-D. Get it?"

"The balance will be paid over the next ten years with fixed interest at four or five points. Better for you to consummate the deal before midsummer and you'll lock in the higher rate for yourselves. The Feds have us believing it's coming down third quarter. If we choose to expedite payments, and say, shorten our installments to five years, clearly the interest goes away but the payments will be made sooner and that could mean the difference between the Kennebunkport house in short order, versus years down the road."

No real chuckles came from anyone at the table except for Jed.

Our lawyer, Squint Willie, chimed in so as not to be outdone by "Theodore" and also to show he was indeed still awake. "I have two questions for you, Jed. One, if you're paying a third down, you won't have control until the installments take you over the top, three years or so down the road. Is that correct? And tell us, Jed, about the corporate governance?"

"Well, on point one, let me say this: let's use the example of ARC buying a Jag. When we put our money down, William, at that point of sale, we own the title and possess the keys outright." All I had running through my head at that moment was the opening to *The Beverly Hillbillies* about that 'man name Jed', who couldn't keep his family fed. Until one day he was shooting at some food, when up came bubbling crude. I remember smiling broadly, as Jed rambled on.

"Harry will immediately become Chairman of the Philly office with a salary at his present level for one year, and he then will become Chairman Emeritus. Sam will immediately take the reins as President of the office with a 50 percent increase in salary."

And I said, "What's the sweetener you talked about for me in your opening monologue, Jethro?" And as the name Jethro tumbled from my mouth, I was so proud of this delivery—and without revealing a hint of it on my face. I just looked at him straight on, waiting for his answer.

He carried on as if he'd heard nothing strange at all, but my father shot me a look as if to say, "Jethro's not the formal name for Jed. That would be Jedidiah, I believe. And don't dare try to fuck up...um...my deal." I would wager a guess that Dad had never seen an episode of *The Beverly Hillbillies* in his life.

"Samuel, you'll become the second largest stockholder of ARC with a 7 percent interest in both agencies, and as we add offices, your interest in our growing concern will expand exponentially, for all of eternity." He laughed but no one else quite got behind this joke. To recover, he continued, "Since you're the first to join our network, part of the agreement is that no one else will own more stock than you, that is, besides me. We envision you as being most instrumental in growing the company with me." Axel shot him some kind of a look that suggested, "Good recovery, son." But in my eyes, Jed continued on as the rip-roaring ass he was from the start.

"So, Jed, if I decide not to join your company, what goes away, the sweetener and my salary?"

"No, Samuel, just the deal."

CHAPTER 24

My dad and I were now in our fourth month of barely talking, following that delightful meeting with the Caldwells in Ramsey. We would communicate mainly through Neb Ted and Squint Willie. The three were preparing some comeback to the Caldwells' Master Plan. Harry seemed to spend his days scurrying around with his consultants, burning up our money in fees faster than he could add one and two to make three. I was basically ignoring them while building Spiegel business and trying my best to ride steady.

Thank God for Loren Rucker. He was the coolest man I knew. He raced motorcycles and sailboats. And over the years when Amy and I visited with Loren and Lily, his wife, we'd see many a first-place skipper ing medal strewn throughout his house. Loren called me Red because of my strawberry blonde hair.

We would catch up with each other for lunch, dinner, or drinks at Kawasaki on Market Street, four blocks south of our offices. From time to time, Loren asked me if I'd mind walking slower through Independence National Historical Park so that he could savor a Marlboro before lunch. Loren sported a sleek chrome lighter. He held his cigarette squeezed between his left thumb and forefinger. He had disciplined himself to ten cigarettes a day. Never more. And he never smoked at home.

He told me, "I'm down to a diet of ten because I've got Franny now." Lily was the wife whom Loren loved, but Franny was the daughter he adored. "If I'm not here, Red, who will teach Franny how to smoke and drink beer?"

As we walked that day, Loren vowed, "Within six months, I'll be down to five cigarettes, and zero in a year. We'll mark it from this day." He looked at his watch, also sleek. "By June 1, 1994, I will be free of cigarettes. Watch me now and my Franny will never be the wiser."

And it would, indeed, be a year to the day that Loren and I would walk briskly to Kawasaki and he'd proclaim, "I quit for good, Red; just as I told you I would." Loren lived, breathed, and sweat Spiegel as if he were already a co-owner, and indeed, the future plan had been to make him a partner, until the Caldwells aimed their wrecking ball our way. It was now June 1, the day Jed had hoped to have his auditors in our offices reviewing our numbers so as to consummate their acquisition by midsummer. We were far from sealing this deal, but I continued walking the minefields I had to maneuver through, without blowing up. I felt signing away the company would end my dreams.

After Loren's smoke in the park, we arrived at Kawasaki, where he parked his favorite marble chopsticks. They were kept neatly next to the other special customized sticks, saved under glass, for those who knew better than I to break chopsticks apart as if they were stale Twizzlers. Loren's chopsticks were retrieved by the owner, Mr. Kim, and always with a broad bow. When he gave Loren his beauties, and handed me my pair of Twizzlers with his other hand, he said with a big laugh, "Yours, Mista Sch-pe-gal, make you look like a putz."

I leaned over to Loren and whispered, "Did he just say what I think he just said?"

Loren responded, "He's right! With those, you are a putz. You turned me into an honorary Jew and now Moses has rubbed off on Mr. Kim." About six months prior, Mr. Kim and a half-dozen other Asian restaurant proprietors up and down Market Street had been scooped up by Loren's production assistants to play parts in a series of commercials for Tokyo Shapiro, a Connecticut-based electronics retailer we handled. In these spots, Mr. Kim was cast as the lead negotiator for the Asian contingent. His role was to get himself worked into a dither as he got strong-armed by the God of negotiators, Mr. Shapiro, the northeast retail Titan. As a result of Mr. Shapiro's sharp cost-cutting maneuvers, he whipped the Japanese manufacturers into submission, saving Tokyo Shapiro customers big on every audio and video component in his stores. In these spots, Mr. Kim was so proud of his failure as a negotiator, it took him a while to come down from his celebrity pillar of commercial stardom.

What frustrated Mr. Kim was not being able to see these spots on his own television screen at home because they only aired in Connecticut. But he was more than okay with being Loren's favorite *putz* in these commercials. I can just hear Loren use the term when directing Mr. Kim. "Roll camera, and all you Asians make like little *putzes*." And then Loren would snicker and crack himself up, since these scenes were shot MOS, "mit out sound." Only Loren could get away with this kind of irreverence and still have Mr. Kim send us to "spe-cha" table.

Loren asked, "So, Red, how's it going with the Harry the Hipster? Still not talking?"

By then my dad and I had traveled from barely speaking to not at all. Through back-and-forth memos, our only form of communication at the time, we had both decided for the sake of the family and the business to seek counseling. Our separate discoveries brought us to the same man; Arnold Mandel. I thought there was hope. We planned to see Dr. Mandel that Friday, just in time to make my weekend.

I wasn't ready to discuss this with Loren. Instead I told him, "We're still not talking. I think the Hitler youth have chased us, or at least me, into Poland as they're working on their new angle. I'm hearing from Squint Willie that you'll be named the Corporate Creative Director and their existing one, Mickey Holden, will move into something Jed is positioning as grander: 'Brand Czar' or 'Honcho of Integration.'"

"Oh, you mean Holden is getting fucked along with the rest of us?"

"Jed's all about getting this deal done, whatever it takes. He could be stitching car leasing firms together, for all he cares."

"And the Hipster is Jed's deep throat. Nice fix you've gotten yourself into, Red."

"Loren, do you want that job? You'll become more of a *macher* than you already are."

"I just want to do what I signed up to do—build this agency with you. No distractions. This is just one big circle jerk, Red. It's time you pulled the plug."

"Loren, maybe you should ditch the insanity here."

"Right, so I can find it somewhere else? No thanks. I'll keep the *meshugas* I know."

CHAPTER 25

That Friday, Harry and I again drove separate cars and then took separate elevators up to the offices of Arnold M. Mandel. I walked into the small reception area. NPR's midmorning classical music station was playing. Harry had already arrived. He was drinking tea and grimacing, either because it was too hot or because, I suspected, it was Lipton's. I nodded his way.

To the right of the reception area was a kitchenette that displayed Taster's Choice and Sanka, Mandel's coffees of choice, and a small bowl of lemon-flavored Lipton tea bags. I badly needed brewed coffee. I really had never had instant before. Anticipating that it would be very weak, I improvised and adjusted the instructed "one level teaspoon" of freeze-dried bits into two heaping teaspoons. I figured that one teaspoon would just be swallowing weakened "horrid," so I opted to go all the way to "horrid."

At the center of the counter was a huge pale green gurgling tank of hot water. I added a spoonful of Cremora to my cup, and I pushed down on the plastic black lever to release the hot water. Then I stepped out of the kitchenette to have my "Taster's Choice moment" with Dad. We were two grown men sipping scalding hot drinks from Styrofoam cups, saying nothing as we stared at the closed office door. It was as if Harry and I were caught watching numbers change slowly in an elevator. How did I get to this place with my father?

Dr. Mandel opened his door and welcomed us in. We were his 10:00 doubleheader, so to speak, with back-to-back hours scheduled for opening day. Dr. Mandel looked like a man we could trust as we shook hands and entered his room. I couldn't help but notice that he definitely wore a toupee and his ears were disproportionately large for his face.

Arnold M. Mandel had a recliner chair that was in its "on duty" upright position. My dad and I each claimed our spaces on opposite sides of the off-white sofa across from Mandel, with our arms resting on the sofa's arms…my right, his left. With our hot drinks mostly gone, we coincidentally were both thumbing our Styrofoam cups as if they had turned into mandolins, our eyes fixed on Arnold M. Mandel.

I continued to scrutinize his toupee, but not to determine whether he had one, as that was clear. I was studying it in terms of whether he should be wearing one at all or go au naturel. As I sized it up in the context of his face, I concluded au naturel would be a huge mistake. The fact that I had already found something about which Mandel and I could agree gave me an odd sense of consolation.

"I'm glad you gentleman could make it. I'm Arnold Mandel; please feel free to call me Arnold. What you can't call me is Arnie. Only my mother has a claim to that name. Years ago she threatened that if I were to ever break this rule, as she put it, 'Arnie, you will never see another of my homemade matzo balls in my lifetime.'"

We laughed in unison and it wasn't just to be polite. Arnold was a good storyteller. And this story didn't sound like the hundredth time he had told it. He had Beinhauser's gift. And I wondered, do the gentiles get the same monologue?

"As you know, I've got you scheduled for a double session today. In my experience when two loved ones haven't been talking all that much for a bit, there is much stored up to say."

I immediately liked this man. As I spotted the two Kleenex boxes on the tables with companion lamps flanking the sofa, I wondered how often people cried in this room. Once in a while? Every other session? There were also two clocks within easy view. One on the wall that appeared to have come from a school gymnasium. A digital one on the table directly below the big one was running five minutes behind. I wanted to ask Arnold which one was the official clock.

I gave Harry a once-over from my side of the couch. He was dressed in a formal navy suit, darker tie than usual—appropriate attire for a funeral. Then I watched him pull his yellow lined sheet of paper from his left inside suit pocket. He promptly unfolded it. It appeared to be a list of numbered points prepared for this meeting. I could set my watch by his grab for his crib sheet. Always five minutes in. I could see the back of his painstakingly written scribbles, with the last point numbered thirty-six.

If he spent just four minutes on each point, the buzzer would sound well after our double session—and that would only be if Arnold and I didn't utter a word. I gestured with my left hand, "Please, be my guest, Harry. Kick us off, here."

He gestured back with his right hand opened, pointed it somewhere between Mandel and me, and said, "Arnold...um...is this kosher for me to...um...start in? I don't want to offend or disrupt protocol here or, heaven forbid, prevent you from your mother's fine matzo ball soup."

"Harry, it might look to both Sam and to me like what you brought with you is a treatise. What I'm hoping for here is a dialogue, an even exchange."

"Well...um...Arnold, I thought I could at least cover a few of the points that have brought us to this summit of sorts."

"Let me suggest that you pick the three most important to you. And I will ask Sam to do the same. So why don't you start, Harry?"

"Well, Arnold, I wish to thank you for seeing us on such short notice, on behalf of Samuel here and me."

"Thank you, Harry."

"And, Arnold, while we were...um...waiting to see you, I couldn't help noticing that you...um...have a middle name that starts with the same letter as your last?"

"Harry, the M stands for Mordechai."

163

"So you must be from Eastern Europe?"

"All the Mandels come from Poland."

"Please don't count my small banter here against my...um...three important issues you want me to bring up."

"Harry, I promise I won't."

I forgot to factor in all of his stammering and digressions that came with each point my dad made. He had run the big clock down by twenty minutes. The digital one cut him slack by five. Arnold added, "Harry, let's get to your first point. And then I'll give Sam a chance to respond to it. Perhaps I should have said this at the outset. Consider me to be an ambassador, someone like Henry Kissinger. Both sides need to leave room for rebuttal. Point one, Harry."

"I think what has brought us here is a business opportunity that I believe is important to seriously consider for a whole host of...um... reasons that I believe Sam is refusing to consider seriously." At which point Harry stroked the side of his hair, releasing a modicum of dandruff to the right shoulder of his funeral suit.

Arnold said, "What I hear you saying, Harry, is that you may be more tuned in to a business proposition than Sam is? Is that a fair analysis?"

"Fair enough but not nearly the complete story."

"So, Sam, what's your interest level in this deal? What do you see as the negatives? And what may you see as the positives?"

"Arnold, I'm mindful of the time and I really believe we need to make progress today. We're up against the clock here. I think Harry and I are hurting each other and frankly, by the hour, the distraction of this deal is weighing down the company."

"Weighing it down? In terms of time, money, or emotional strain?"

"All the above. I left New York at my father's urging more than fifteen years ago to help build this business and transition it to a third generation of leadership. Since I came on board, the company has tripled in size."

"Is that some sort of coincidence or could it be the fruits from your labor?"

"I think it's the latter. So why the hell would I want to screw up a good thing?" That's when I crushed my Styrofoam cup altogether and placed it in its newfangled form on the end table beside me.

Arnold cut in and asked Harry, "What do you have to say in re-sponse to Sam's question?"

"We are making progress due in part to Sam's many...um...achieve-ments and that's why we have this offer on the table."

I told him, "What does the offer do for me besides shut down my dreams?"

"It gives you security, Sam. It takes the risk away from us. It puts... um...money squarely into the family's pocket. And last I heard, you are still part of the family." Dad's hand stroked the side of his hair, prompt-ing more snowflakes to rain down on him.

Harry and I were dialing up the volume of our voices with every new sentence uttered. Arnold got in between us. "So let me point out, *fellers*, your feelings on this point are quite representative of the way you're sitting...at the farthest reaches of the couch."

I said, "So, Doctor, what does that mean?"

Arnold got back on track, "Because all of a sudden you two have decided not to love or respect each other?"

There was a long pause as Harry and I uncomfortably started look-ing around the room. That's when Harry started futzing more with his Styrofoam cup. Mine had been destroyed moments earlier.

"Actually, men, that's not this doctor's answer. So breathe easy. But here it is: Your debate, so far as I can see it, has nothing to do with lack of love or respect. So why then are you so polarized? I believe it has everything to do with where you are sitting in your lives, gentlemen. I'd argue there isn't a whole lot more to your predicament than that. As a pragmatist, I'd like to understand your up-to-the-moment dreams and aspirations."

I jumped in. "Dreams? When my father approached me about leav-ing New York and coming back to Spiegel, Amy, my wife, and I weren't ready, but we saw the opportunities here. At least I did. I knew it wasn't going to be easy. But I really believed in my heart I could take our little shop to the next level, frankly to rungs beyond. Time will tell us whether I'm right. That's what I thought I was getting myself into, Arnold. But it appears I got it wrong."

Arnold cocked his head forward as if to show us that his right ear was listening more intently. I could almost swear it had grown some more. Then, he added, "Nobody is wrong here. Wrong is off the table in this room. What we're talking about is vantage points, men...first and foremost, vantage points. Harry, what do your dreams consist of today?"

"Well...um...Samuel and I are in different stages of our lives. I guess if I'm going to be perfectly honest here..."

Arnold ducked in again, "Harry, sir, that's job one today."

"Then I'd have to say security is my most important dream. That is what's motivating me to proceed down this path."

"So let's try again to sum things up here. Sam, you want to have the opportunity to try to build and to fulfill your dreams at Spiegel. Harry, you would like to stop building wings on the house and sell what you've got, and maybe with some of that money, you and...your wife's name?"

"Elizabeth."

"You and Elizabeth can move to Brandywine or have a second home built in West Palm Beach."

"Arnold, we're not the Florida types."

"Okay then, the Vineyard."

"Closer."

Arnold shot Harry a thumbs–up, as if to say, "I'm getting you, aren't I?" And he was then operating like a symphony conductor. All he was missing were his baton, better teeth, and hair that would swing in time with the baton. "Men, do you agree with my restatement in both cases?"

I said, "I agree."

Harry said, "Agreement here."

"Now we're getting somewhere. Shall we move to experiences? The advantage you have, Harry, is that you've lived longer, so presumably you've had more experiences."

I inserted, "And always more to say. You got that right, Doc."

Dad added, "So that's supposed to be a good thing, Arnold?"

"Well, sorta. I know it comes with more aches and pains, Harry. But Sam over here is no *schlepper*. Clearly, he's been a doer and has packed into his early years much life. So, gentlemen, let's talk about where you are. Sam?"

"So you're trying to study the tree with the fewest rings around it first, eh?" I asked.

Arnold's rickety teeth showed through his lips as he said, "If there is nothing else you get out of this session, we'll have enough metaphors to fill an encyclopedia. But what I promise is that I'll make every effort to stick with the one at hand. I don't really much enjoy mixed metaphors in the same paragraphs during my sessions. So I'll answer you this way. It's not the rings on the tree, Sam. It's the quality of the tree. And then it's about how it's taken care of. I might point out...you'll grow yours better if you can find a way to keep it clear of chainsaws."

I liked his funny. "All right, here goes. Ever since I was a very little guy, I've been told that I have some leadership skills. Being an entrepreneur is in my blood. I started a business in my teens and continued running it for years. Then, while in college, I trained as an intern at the New York ad agency I most respected. After I graduated, they hired me. I was so excited to bring home what I learned to energize and build up my dad's shop."

"And you think you've done that?"

"You'll have to have Harry answer that one."

"Harry?"

"Yes, he has...um...in spades."

"Sam, please continue."

"My dad is a first-generation Jewish-American who has done well. And it has been my quiet goal for quite some time—I'm saying this out loud for the first time—to bring our family along even further." At which point I picked up my crushed Styrofoam cup, now in the shape of a ball, and tossed it to my other hand. "If what you're really trying to do, Arnold, is peek inside my head, you just saw a large swatch of what's motivating my drive."

Arnold summed up what I'd just said. "So, Sam, you're talking continuity, using your leadership, entrepreneurial skills, and learning from New York to take Spiegel & Associates to greater prominence in your immediate community, and perhaps far beyond that point. And by so doing, your family's roots in America will become more fortified. Does this sound correct enough to you?"

"On the mark, Arnold."

"Harry, is there any new news in anything you just heard from Sam?"

At which point Harry snuck a self-conscious look down to his right shoulder and then immediately swept his white debris onto the sofa, where he made it disappear. "Well, to tell you the truth, the whole further establishment tangent is rather new to me. The rest I know and I'm…um…very proud of Samuel's accomplishments."

"Harry, I don't think the further establishment 'tangent' is a tangent at all. Quite frankly, to me it's core to what Sam brought home."

Harry said, "I hear that."

"Now, Harry, where have your experiences taken you, right up to now?"

"Well, to tell you the truth, I'm…um…seventy-one years old with a tired ticker. This is one of the roughest businesses a person can enter. It's full of sudden turns in the road and steep hills. You can crash and recover. You can crash and recover somewhat. And you can crash and never recover. My father, after leaving Germany, crashed and never really recovered in the States. He was depressed and died a beaten man."

Arnold chimed in, "So I think I hear two big points you're making here. If possible, it would be your desire to protect yourself, Elizabeth, and your children from the disappointments of loss or misfortune. And Harry, you've got a 'nine lives' theory about business. Once the cat approaches his tenth, he tempts fate one too many times and will fall from the building. Have I gotten your drift right?"

"Arnold, I don't think we get near nine lives, actually. My experience tells me that there is always…um…darkness around the next bend that can wipe us out. My family lost everything when I was eighteen. Our livelihood was taken from us. Our…um…house was taken from us. Just about all our money…confiscated. Arnold, we came to this country with nothing." That's when Dad's thumb sliced right through the bottom of his Styrofoam cup to build a ditch.

"Nothing, Harry?"

"Nothing, Arnold."

"I don't know you well enough, sir, to say this, but I'll venture it anyway. Although I understand the severity of your pain, you didn't come here with nothing, Harry."

"How do you mean? What did we have? We were penniless."

"For starters, let me say, you had your life. You had your health. Harry, I would even wager," that's when he vigorously pointed a forefinger in Dad's direction, rocking it backward and forward, "you had your dreams, hopes, and desires, your independence, your chance to build for yourself and to build a family."

"Yes, I was one of the lucky ones."

"Harry, I know you and your family were stripped of all your worldly possessions. But what I also know is that you were stripped of more barbed wires, further inhuman guards, ferocious attack dogs, and, sir, of those awful gas chambers. There may never be a more apt time for me to say, 'But for the grace of God, go you, Harry Spiegel.'"

"Well, I've also experienced great pain, Arnold, and…um…worry that can't be easily erased."

"Harry, I need to correct you here, and I'm very sorry to report in here. That pain you have will never be erased."

"Escaping Germany with my life and the lives of my parents, my brother, my cousins, I don't take any of it for granted. But believe you me, there have been some aftershocks. I feel them every damn day, how precarious and unsure things are." That's when Harry gathered his two forefingers, both hands together, to make a steeple under his chin.

"You mean the world we live in, the business you're in, your family?"

"All of it. On one Halloween night, out of the blue in 1961, our other son Mikey Spiegel caught fire and almost died. Tell me I saw this coming. The hell I did, mister. My experiences suggest we take the money and run and….um…protect ourselves from all the worries we can't control." At which point the steeple he made came down from under his chin as he gently folded his hands palms up to rest them, peacefully, in his lap.

"And Harry, money stops worry? Everything will be safer? Do you feel that everything will be happier after the transaction?"

"I guess I believe money can buy us some peace, Arnold. Sam's on a reckless course. He's right—we're up three hundred percent. But we can be down by the same amount tomorrow. And then where are we? We're left with nothing."

Arnold interrupted, "Harry, what do you mean by Sam's reckless course? Do you mean he's a Vegas gambler?"

"He's a builder. He takes a lot of chances. Many more than…um… I'd dare take on. Many of them have worked out. Some have been less successful. There are prospects we invested in that we've won. Others have…um…not gone our way. But risks take money, Arnold, more than we have in our small vault. You can hit a dry spell and there can be a lot more money pouring out than coming in. And then where are we, Mr. Mordechai? Broke. *Mechuleh*! You hear me? *Mechuleh*!" That when Dad's right hand indignantly flipped over to drum the palm of his left.

"The nightmares you have of the past, the déjà vu will haunt you, Harry, I'm afraid, dear sir, for the rest of your born days. Edgar Allan Poe said, 'Nevermore,' but I don't think so for you, Harry. That is the one thing I'm sure of. For you it's more like forevermore. Those fears will follow you, I'm sorry to report, right to your grave. And you know what else, Harry Spiegel? You might be right. Doomsday may strike the Spiegels again. History would certainly attest to that notion. But there's nothing you can do about it. Except…" He brought his hands together and pointed toward heaven with his forefingers and eyes.

"So we came here today to learn to pray, Arnold?"

"Something like that, Harry. But I must ask you this, how many people do you know who can say, 'I've walked through fire and made it to the other side'?"

"I can count them on one hand."

"But you know what, Harry? Two are in your immediate family. I'm looking at one as I speak. Then, of course, there's your other son, Mikey."

"Sometimes only bad can come out of bad, Arnold."

"Sometimes? But Harry as I talk with you, who better understands that light can come out of darkness? The wisdom, Harry, you carry in your thumbnail on dealing with huge knocks in life…who knows this better? Can you imagine the inspiration you've already given to your own two sons, and Elizabeth, and now onto the grandkids? How do we Eastern Europeans like to say it? You, Harry Spiegel, understand l'chaim like the back of your hand."

"Yes, I know something on this topic."

"My dear sir, money helps, but I assure you it's no panacea. I maintain it doesn't buy you health, safety, dreams, love, or character. And it can't will away bad luck or misfortune. As the Beatles were famous for singing, '*I don't care too much for money. Money can't buy me love.*'"

I reached for some Kleenex to catch several tears sneaking out from my ducts.

What utterances I heard from Dad. True confessions, unlocked. Treacherous fears, unearthed! His ghosts were popping up all over Mandel's small office. Harry Spiegel seemed so frightened. And his urge to protect me from future harm seemed so naturally driven and earnest. I knew it tumbled out of him because of his unconditional love for me. Certainly not out of spite. That much became clear.

And all of it made me turn my head, almost as if my neck craned like a bird's, as far around as I could twist so as not to reveal my tears. I didn't want to allow myself to show Harry the streaks down my cheeks because I couldn't let these emotions blur what I was there for. I was fighting for my future.

"I think it would buy me some peace of mind so I could sleep better, Arnold."

"What will it do for Sam, Harry?"

My eyes cleared enough so I could turn to Dad, "Put an end to my dream."

Harry turned to me and said, "There can't be others, Samuel?"

"I guess that's easy for you to say. So why in the hell did you invite me in, with such passion, to grow our business, so you could turn it over to someone else's son?"

"I think of it as a way to get your mother's and my money out after a lifetime of work and still give you the chance to fulfill your hopes."

"The business will be gone. It will take the fight from me. Just send it off to the highest bidder. Is that what this is all about?"

"Well, to a bidder."

"Dad, I certainly expected to be in the hunt. I haven't asked for any free rides. You know that best of all. Each and every day, all I do is try my best to perform for our company. Whose war chest am I filling at the moment? It certainly doesn't belong to me. I expected for all I've done, you'd have wanted *me* to buy the keys!"

"I want you to go after your dreams, Sam, um, but..."

"Um, but what?"

"But your mother and I need to get our money out of the company. And this looks like the best way to do that."

"At the sacrifice of your son?"

"I don't want to hurt you."

"Then I'll tell you what..." I looked up. "The big clock here says we've just run the time down. The little clock says we've got five minutes to spare."

Arnold saw my hesitation and interrupted, "Please go by the small clock. The grandchildren were in this weekend *futzing* with the old-school clock. Please go on."

"As you may also remember, Harry, from the Caldwell son, your biological son must come with the deal for you to have a deal. If I walk, you have no deal, Dad. If I stay, I am not handing over our keys to Jed Caldwell. So," I paused and tried to calm down. I continued, biting for air. "Here's where I net out. Let's eliminate the Caldwells. I will match Jed's offer with no money down and a payout over seven years in equal installments, no interest accrued. I will immediately be named President. You will become Chairman. And I will need an answer before the end of the weekend."

As the last minutes counted down, Arnold summed up what he just heard, "What I'm led to understand then, is that we have a new deal on the table, Harry, that's time sensitive with an answer due by Sunday night. Is that right, Sam?"

Then Harry stood up. He folded his yellow legal sheet along the creases and placed it back inside his jacket pocket. Then he came over to me and said "Sam, I don't need the weekend to think this over. You've got a deal."

I stood up and shook his hand.

I said, "I hope it's the one that will make you the proudest."

Arnold stood up as well, a smile on his face, as he ushered us to a second door in his office, not the door to his waiting room, but to the public hallway so we could leave without encountering his next patient.

For Dad, this door to the hall was indeed his exit of sorts.

For me, it was an entirely new entryway.

As we shook hands with Arnold Mordechai Mandel, I said, "Thank you, Dr. Kissinger." Everyone got a little chuckle as tensions released. Harry and I walked down the corridor to the elevator.

As the elevator door opened, my father extended his right opened hand toward me, "Please, Mr. President."

And I answered, "Only, after you, Mr. Chairman."

As we continued to our individual cars parked on the same lot, I started to hear voices. *When you leave the shrink's office, isn't your head supposed to be released of all uninvited intruders?* But I learned differently that day as *The Beverly Hillbillies* theme song drifted back into my head. Now it's time to say goodbye to 'Jed and all his kin'. And we would like to thank you folks for dropping in…with your heaping helping of hospitality.

CHAPTER 26

Time was passing smoothly. Things seemed to be working for us at work and at home, as Amy and I watched our Audrey and Adam mature and their individual personalities take form. The day of Audrey's festive Bat Mitzvah, held under a tent in our backyard, had arrived. Our beautiful young lady stood tall with such poise and honor next to her Bat Mitzvah coach and Jewish studies teacher, Mr. Bernstein. He had been my fourth grade Sunday school teacher, the one who would only let me and my hooky-playing friends back into his classroom if, and only if, we each paid a toll of one Red Hot Dollar.

I wanted to share this man, with his wonderful stories and sense of humor, with my kids, especially when they had to learn Hebrew. So I brought Bernstein back into my life and the lives of our children. He benefited. They benefited. I benefited greatly. And as Tevye would say, "The Papa! Tradition!" I remember Audrey reading from the scrolls so confidently that late afternoon, then delivering a spellbinding speech to sum up the lessons of her Torah portion.

At the beginning of her talk, she recalled her earliest memory of her religious sojourn with Mr. Bernstein in the basement den of his house while eating chocolate chip cookies with milk. "And Mr. Bernstein, in my first lesson, asked me, So, Audrey, where does the Torah begin?' Innocent enough question. With a simple enough answer. He was asking me to convey the lessons of Genesis. Should have been a piece of cake. And had the question been 'What goes into gefilte fish?' or 'What are ingredients for the best *charoset?*' With my Jewish eating background and gourmet chef of a father, I'd have aced Bernstein's trial run and he would have said, 'Audrey, you're a genius!' But I grew up with nanny Elizabeth's strong influence on the family and her ideas about organized religion that just about align with Richard Dawkins.

"So instead, I had to give his question my best shot. Improvising, my nose crinkled up and my face cringed before I sputtered out, "Mr. Bernstein, 'I think it all started at the point Jesus died." And from our backyard-turned-synagogue, after Audrey hit with that line, the laughter decibels that were sent throughout Wynnewood that early evening in August could only suggest Jerry Seinfeld had been handed the mike. The joy of that evening continued from there, when Adam toasted his kid sister.

"Listen up, folks. If you don't know me, I'm Adam. Audrey's soccer idol, champion brother, and man about town for some years now. Let me explain how our home soccer games work. Our shoes, when we play, are always off. The field is on the first floor. One goal's the front door where our red oriental had been placed to mark 'inside the box.' And the other goal is the living room radiator cover.

"Now, it was right before I was taking off to become the soccer counselor at a sleep away camp in Vermont that I challenged my kid sister to a farewell game. Our soccer battles had become closer and closer, I'll admit that. And in this pivotal game before leaving town, I shouted for a time out because I was feeling the pressure of the moment like never before. The bugger! And this is when I proclaimed, 'There is only one Spiegel the Great, and lest you forget, it's not Audrey.'

"Then we resumed playing without Audrey quite realizing the game was back in full swing. I wasn't trying to pull anything over on her. Who me? [He winked.] And that's when I delivered a hard smack to the door, and with my loud gloating screams of sheer ecstasy echoing through the house, I said, 'I am Spiegel. The one and only Spiegel!' And frankly that's when I should have bolted for camp. But silly me!

"Instead, Audrey gives me this long stare. Now, come to think of it, it was more menacing than that. It was a very stern frown. Like one De Niro in *Taxi Driver* might have given out to the world. And with great concentration, resolve, and a mighty fake to the right to go left, she dribbled right past the one and only Spiegel. And this was with her left foot, mind you...which Spiegel the Great had never seen in her before, and she slammed that ball into the far right corner of the radiator. The impact of that smack caused the metal grating to unhinge and fall to the floor, and my sister took the lead and said, 'If you're Spiegel, that makes me Double Spiegel.'

"And the next morning...I slunk out of town in my Volvo. Don't even think I could bring myself to say goodbye to anyone. But here's what I say tonight: *L'chaim!* Double Spiegel! But you're still a bugger."

Amy and I exchanged glances that read, "We've done something right here."

Five days later when all the Bat Mitzvah bills needed to be paid, two of our largest accounts walked out the door, taking away 60 percent of our billings. Bally Fitness purchased Spa World, and their agency, J. Walter Thompson, took over. Quaker Oats sold Brookstone in a leveraged buyout deal. Their new management team broomed us for Lux.

All I could think about was how many people we'd have to let go and how horrible this round of layoffs would be. I had been through smaller "adjustment periods," as the accountants chose to call them, but this bloodbath felt as if I had already taken the first bullet to my own stomach, and it certainly didn't feel like a flesh wound.

I didn't feel like eating lunch but badly needed company, Loren's company. He had sworn off smoking some years back but as we walked toward Kawasaki, Loren produced a cigarette and proceeded to smoke three. On one prolonged inhale, he said, "Look here, Red, I'm giving us one long night, tonight, on me. We'll both get plastered, and I'll bring two packs of cigs as well. But tomorrow there will be none, as tonight we'll go through each blasted cigarette. At the end of the night, we'll find a bin to puke our guts into. Then, Red, sitting shiva is over for us. You hear me? Over! We're on our horses again, riding hard. No more cigs for Loren. No more wailing out of you. Besides, the fitness boom peaked years ago, and who wants to continue selling cheap gadgets that people tire of two hours after they buy them? It's irresponsible, Red."

You had to love Loren.

That night we got drunk at the Yacht Club, a downtown place about as far from a Yacht Club as it could be. But that was the idea. We settled into Loren's smoky bar and scooped up a bowl of unshelled peanuts as I watched my buddy smoke sloppily all night long; his schnoz had turned DuPont chimney. With all the drinking and smoking, I had a most sobering thought that evening—let's call it a "longer view" of the business and the accounts we win. Eventually they all go south. Staggered, of course, but for one reason or another, each one will leave us at some point. We never own a single one of them. That night, Loren and I put each other in cabs, with the realization that we boys were no longer punks in advertising. Darned pity.

We mounted our horses the next day and shook off our Lost Account Blues the best we knew how. With many prospects deep in our pipeline, we went to work to replace what we had lost. At such serious moments in the business cycle, focus is all business. I was up early. Returned home late. During this time, everything at home took a backseat. Loren and I had quite a task ahead, and ninety days to do it, before the fees and commissions from Brookstone and Spa World dried up.

No shortcuts for us as we worked harder than ever to cultivate a winning team. We let some people go, but we also added new accounts and showed the balanced realities of what is the ad business—glory along with defeat—sometimes in the same week. Leaders. That's what Loren and I had become. "Cerberus, the two-headed dog." We felt our mojo but weren't overly impressed by it.

I brought Spiegel a name change from Spiegel & Associates to Spiegel Communications. This move signified and celebrated the new services we had established beyond advertising: account planning, public relations, and event planning. Then came the interactive revolution that Loren Rucker embraced. He was searching for something new to turbo charge our craft and himself at the same time. This prompted us to become an early adopter of interactive services, and for the add-ons required. Loren was by far the most qualified person in our shop to ramp it up while retaining his Chief Creative Officer responsibilities. But this interactive business decision came with a stiff price to pay, a bigger one than either Loren or I ever imagined. And I'm not talking about the hardware costs—those actually paid for themselves.

Loren was smart, honest, and instinctual. He could be a street fighter, if pressed. Although strategic, Loren was not a born schemer, certainly not one with rancor or intent to be divisive. As we both gained a stronger handle on our industry—at the level at which we were playing—we realized that there were unicyclists, egomaniacs, and in some rare cases, bombers who wandered into agencies and tried to stay. A few such folks got past our doors.

These extremists weren't easy to identify. Once detected, though, it was critical to bullet them before they did harm. Loren unknowingly brought one such guy into Spiegel, Ace Willard, who sported a shiny dark ponytail. His trickery came well masked, but over a five-year stretch, call it a slow burn, his goal became clear: to push Loren further and further into the interactive world so that he could take over as Spiegel's creative leader.

Upon early inspection, Ace's mild manner disguised any early detection of his self-aggrandizement. Eventually, his maneuverings came out in the open, as my understanding of Ace's true character moved closer to the fore. I had learned, for instance, that too many nuns and priests paddled him in his formative years and his father, a police detective, never thought Ace was, well…ever ace enough. "When are you going to cut your god-damn hair? You look like a faggot," he told him.

Loren assigned Ace to oversee half of our business. And with this quick decision, Loren put half the creative control of the agency beyond his own reach and into the hands of a new co-creative director we barely knew. I don't think Loren understood the magnitude of what he had done. After all, as he saw it, he kept his title as Executive Creative Director, with the ultimate creative decision-making power still in his grasp. Everyone at our agency who was watching for clues, and that's everyone, saw what was coming.

It didn't look like trouble at the start, and for a long stretch. Over the following years, with a well-tuned new business discipline in place, we racked up a string of big wins that had competitors doing double takes as we really hit our stride. I was able to put our successes in perspective, and I merchandised current wins to help make rain for the next to come. I wasn't prepared for the extensive envy our successes evoked, and the resulting pettiness that surfaced from our competitors who attempted to undermine our triumphs.

Our wins gave us the income we needed to absorb investments in both stronger personnel and broader services. But the schematic that Loren put in place (and that I, unfortunately, sanctioned) by bringing Ace in, in the fashion he joined us, turned us into two agencies under one roof. Ace had his roster of accounts and Loren had his.

Years back, I thought Billy G.'s Hermès wedding tie might well become for me what Beinhauser's white socks became for him and the agency he served a lucky rabbit's foot. As our prospects became more formidable, I thought I needed something of my own that I could point to as our edge. Sounds silly, but the tie became, for all of us, one of the-percentage-gainers we believed might break ties. I began wearing it to all the big pitches over the next half-dozen or so years.

After the Clintons took a run at healthcare reform, which ultimately got defeated, the American Medical Association ramped up their image campaign, with us in charge and millions behind it. Chalk this win up to Ace. It was the strategic, creative team that we put together that brought it home. Not to forget Billy G.'s tie and its impact.

Next we snagged the Sears Craftsman Tools division, from Chicago's Leo Burnett. This was Loren's tour de force. In terms of how Joseph Beinhauser calculated his white sock wins, with that tie around my neck, Craftsman Tools represented the second leg of our first Triple

Crown. This was the one and only time I can recall Mikey calling me with congratulations. "Samuel, it never appeared to me that you were that well endowed to land such a big tool account." And he laughed and laughed and laughed some more before hanging up the phone.

Then we went on to win Hilton's DoubleTree chain, completing our first Triple Crown. This one landed in Ace's win column. I remember Amy's smart-ass comment the night of the win, "Had it only been the Ritz, we'd be having sex now, Sam." Lea & Perrins Worcestershire Sauce came next, which Loren shepherded in, as well as skippering the Go Boating account to our docks. *Ding, ding,* Loren.

Yes, we were cooking. Our mojo had magnified. And for some back-to-back years, this Loren/Ace competitive dynamic appeared to be nothing short of a masterstroke. When one creative leader was fatigued, the other came running off the bench, as strikers went in and out to freshen up World Cup competitions. It was something to behold.

By this point, Billy G.'s tie was fraying a bit at the knot, but I covered up the flaw by shortening one of the ends before I pulled it through its paces. We had reached six consecutive triumphs, or two back to back Triple Crowns, and there wasn't a runt in our big basket. The Volkswagen save for Beinhauser was his seventh straight victory. My tie as a lucky charm brought us to six and we were staring down at our seventh, the Pennsylvania Lottery. If we could lasso this one, it would mean a $100 million piece of business over a five-year contract period.

Following the "Go Boating" success, I assembled our entire team in the conference room for an internal "town hall meeting." I started by raising my champagne glass, prompting seventy other hands to do the same. "Here's to our extraordinary team as we take time to savor our big American Boating Association win. We learned about the boating lifestyle, the pioneering spirit that is innate to this product offering. We were also taught that the best family times for boating enthusiasts are when they're sea bound. So when it was our turn to make our pitch to their sixty-person board, we could confidently and enthusiastically describe what our homework taught us."

"When it came to the vote, after the four agencies had presented, including my alma mater, DDB, let me tell you how the levers went down. Ketchum got zero. DDB...the same. Fleishman Hilliard...also a goose egg. And where did that leave us? If I'm calculating right, we racked up all sixty votes. [I spotted Harry who had been retired for some years by then, but loved to come in on such celebrations.] Do I have my numbers right, Harry?"

He laughed and said, "Um, you aced 'em, sonny boy!"

"In the call I got from Carey E. Casey, the President of the Go Boating Coalition, he said, and I quote, 'It wasn't even close. You earned our business by an ocean of nautical miles.'"

"Now, friends, we've got our scopes fixed on the Pennsylvania Lottery. So who's our enemy on this offensive? I think only us. Overconfidence, smugness, resting on our laurels could lose this for us. Winners find ways to stay hungry. From the bottom of my heart, and on behalf of our growing Spiegel Communications brand, do me a favor and starve this week.

I raise my glass to our recent triumphs, future victories, and I send out my deepest appreciation to all of you for how far we've come as a team and how far there's still left to go. Onward and upward!" We clinked as we motored on and propelled ourselves forward.

CHAPTER 27

Add one more win for Billy G.'s lucky Hermès tie…as we announced our latest victory: the Pennsylvania Lottery. This triumph was a significant win for us. I put a moratorium on new business development for the next six months so that we could properly absorb this monster. With it, we totally outgrew our brownstone and extension space across the street. Due to our account gains, I initiated a citywide search to combine our two buildings into a refurbished warehouse overlooking an undeveloped, but soon to be *hip* part of downtown Philadelphia, at 12th and Spruce.

With this decision, our long-standing Philadelphia bank had become afraid of our move and we had to approach a new bank. Dad had gotten used to the pattern I had established of checking in with him while walking the dog. I had grown accustomed to our nightly ritual as well. Actually, it was comforting for me to review my days with him. Mainly because he enjoyed the tales of the business so much and would often say to me, "Sam, this call is the highlight of my day." And he meant it.

The evening of our existing bank's decision, Harry couldn't wait for my call. He had become too impatient. As Chairman Emeritus, this decision by the bank made him quite nervous. Although Dad's payout for the business had been completed a while back, he remained forever cautious, especially as a cosigner with Amy and me for our lines of credit, which helped make our dramatic growth possible. But his estate was as much at stake as Amy's and mine if all went haywire. "Um, Samuel, I suppose you've gotten the same word as I have that our bankers want no part of this big move you've envisioned for yourselves in that spacious loft."

"Yes, Harry, you've heard them right, we need a new bank. And with our recent successes, I would imagine we will have no problem finding one and securing lower interest rates for our lines. Matter of fact, I think it would be very helpful to me if you could be a part of our search and help make the decision."

He said, "I hope when we start talking to these other banks that I can gain your kind of confidence that they'll be fighting over us."

"I never said they will be fighting over us, Harry. We're an ad agency. No banks fight over ad agencies. But I feel strongly that, in short order, we'll have a new bank and a more competitive arrangement."

My father took an active role in our subsequent search and felt good about the bank we chose. We were making bold moves because we now had a track record of success and progress to bank on. "No denying that," Harry said, "but there's still plenty of risk here, Samuel."

This is when I pushed the company to develop a new schematic to build brand teams within our fresh, refigured space. Each group handled no more than three to five accounts. The total day-to-day staff for these pieces of business functioned in the same geographic area, which sounded like an obvious directive. But for our industry, this plan was radical, as agencies were normally configured around disciplines.

We created a room called America's Family Room where we conducted focus groups. We converted the turn-of-the-century boiler room into a two-story conference space, using its name, the Boiler Room. It was a build-out that ad agency Chiat/Day of Apple computer fame might dare create in LA, or Goodby in San Franciso (that coined "Got Milk") might have erected. But to think of an agency, in second tier Philadelphia in a space like this was nothing short of remarkable.

the bench. Day by day he became such a worry for me, especially when I lifted the new business moratorium and we resumed the pitching game.

Ace's final pitch came when we presented to our second large Mexican restaurant chain in one month, Chi-Chi's; the first had been Chili's. We were considered the odds-on favorite to win Chili's, following the scouting reports from inside our shop and what the trade journals were saying on the outside in handicapping us. Had we won Chili's, we would have no need to compete for Chi-Chi's.

But for the Chili's pitch, the underdog agency—and that was not us—who presented two hours before, simply out-energized Spiegel. They turned the auditorium into a discotheque. I remember thinking how outdated and inappropriate their design scheme seemed to be—especially at ten in the morning? Go figure. I guess that was the idea. "Go figure" was part of Spiegel-speak, the way "Heaven forbid!" had been used by everyone before pitches at DDB.

Go figure. How did we get beaten so badly? Go figure. How did we get so lucky? Go figure. What exactly happened here? More often there were no other words that followed "Go figure." It was like a Spiegel declarative, an amen that preceded a period. Loren had coined it, and I realized when I heard it that morning...it was all that remained of him at Spiegel, though it still echoed loudly in our heads. Or was he the wizard that day with a special hex cast on Ace? I so missed Loren.

For the Chili's pitch we batted second. I literally saw the tallest person on the first team unhinge a mirror ball from the ceiling. The changing up of pitching agencies—second presenting in, first tearing down—is one of the more awkward moments in our business. At such moments the first thing I insisted on checking is the AV system. Invariably, that's what gets screwed up or sabotaged. You stop reviewing your lines and become consumed with wondering if you can make the equipment work. But that was not our problem that day; our problem was Ace.

In comparison to the prior disco treatment, our setup seemed sedate. Ours was more in line with a sophisticated dinner party. This acknowledgment didn't bother me all that much, because the work we were presenting was fun and didn't need a whole lot of theatrics to bring it home, if only Ace Willard had been left off our guest list and Loren could have run in from the sidelines to save the day.

Ace's efforts to warm up the crowd over his version of gazpacho amounted to a lot of endless mutterings that spilled well into the time we should have been finishing the salad course. I kept thinking, as I watched him, and wanted so badly to say, *Speak into the mike, you asshole. We're dying up here.*

Finally I got up and moved the stand closer to his slow kill. By the time we served filet (and I must admit, chewy skirt steak would have been just fine if it hadn't been Ace serving it up), he went off script. Oh no! Improvising about his Uncle Jess, saying, "He's the man in our family who can't abide spicy food." *My god,* I thought. *What is he saying here, before all the drivers of the chain whose hallmark is putting "spice" into "quick serve"?*

How do you lose people over tenderloin? When we finally got to the dessert, no one wanted to stick around. Now tell me, who doesn't want crème brûlée or, for this gathering as we called it, a flan cake. But with Ace on the mike, our audience deserted en masse. "Got to go. It's time to relieve the baby-sitters."

Simply put, Ace served up ptomaine instead of a fine four-course meal and we got cooked at Chili's. Therefore, if there would be redemption, it would have to be two weeks later, at our pitch for Chi-Chi's, but only after anteing up another $40 thousand in out-of-pocket costs to have a second crack at another $10 million fast-serve Mexican restaurant chain account. I wondered how the Chi-Chi's pitch could possibly be any worse than our dry run at Chili's?

In a matter of weeks, I got my answer. One more without Loren to bring in off the bench. At the Chi-Chi's presentation, Ace managed to work in the prospect's brand name three times in the first three minutes, which usually is a wonderful thing to do. And each time he used their name, he did so with warmth and earnest admiration. But here's the catch. He called them "Chili's" not once, but three times in a row. Oops. Yes, we were presenting to Chi-Chi's. This was not a nightmare I could wake up from. We were soak-laden tacos, but still had another hour and twenty minutes to roll around in our refried beans.

At my sit-down with Ace following that fiasco, I delivered a kinder, gentler version of, "You burned-out fool! How could you do this to us? You're finished."

That same day, I announced that Sidney Reim would be our new creative director. He was a brilliant talent who hailed from Jolly Old England. Sidney was one of those odd fellows: wiry, kinky haired, most often acerbic, but with great amounts of talent. He was by no means cuddly, but never was he less than sharp and articulate when he talked one-on-one or addressed a crowd. His work for us over the prior three years had brought much positive recognition. We had talked for months about his possible promotion, as both he and I understood the end was near for Ace. I said, "With you at the helm, I think we could grab it."

"It" was the O'Toole Award, given annually to the finest breakout creative agency in the country. The winners are judged on their depth of work across accounts over the duration of one year.

Sidney said, "I think had you honored me in this role a few years back, we'd already have it on our mantle." Then he recovered from his brashness by adding, "I'm honored for the opportunity to try to take us there now." Spiegel had become a key breakout agency, one of the ones everyone was watching—the business community in the region at large, marketing directors nationally, and the advertising press. And we were quite good at maximizing our triumphs. Even our competitors were beginning to get used to hearing about us all the time. In retrospect, perhaps they were just patiently waiting for us to crash and burn.

CHAPTER 28

It was 9:22 in the morning. The Spiegel team was about forty-five minutes into its presentation of a new campaign for Canadian-based Magna Entertainment, the holding company for a whole host of horse racing tracks throughout the United States. Magna's marketing team flew in at 4:00 the previous afternoon to join us for some steamed crabs at Crabs Meet Dames on the Chesapeake Bay, about an hour-and-a-quarter drive from the airport. In the past, my father had made crab eating legendary before major pitches to the racehorse association Titans. The folks from Magna wanted to experience the treat. They were coming straight from the airport to the restaurant.

Amy was hosting the evening with me, and we were driving together to meet them there. Reminiscing about the first time she had crabs, she said, "We should turn back and pick up Commandant Spiegel to bark out her *Steamed Crabs Eating* lessons for our Canadians. 'And what is *das* knife for, you ask? To cut off *das* penis, *dummkopf*.'" We laughed hard. And Amy was right, as it turns out. Magna's junior marketing associate, Stanley Wintz, needed Elizabeth's lecture badly. Stanley, who grew up in Northeast Kingdom, Vermont, seemed befuddled by these Chesapeake

Bay critters and the how–to instructions on the placemat that sat on top of the brown paper table cover in front of him.

In the end, he got the inedible gills horribly confused with the back-fin meat as he chomped vigorously on the rubbery pieces. (There's a reason why regular crab eaters call it the "devil," as eating the devil can sometimes result in stomach distress.) I wondered whether Stanley would show up at all the next morning, which might have been a god-send, because, in this new relationship, Wintz was an early obstruction to imaginative work. At that moment I thought, *Let this devil be damned.*

The next morning, starting at 8:30 at the office, we reported on our coast-to-coast research findings gathered by our account planners, who had gotten racehorse enthusiasts to talk about themselves and racing. One participant said, "For me, racing sure beats inhaling speed, which is also fun on occasion. Seeing your horse nose out a 'shoulda won' makes me feel better about life in general: my wife, my boss, and my kids and holds at least until morning." This insight became the center-piece of our strategy, because we heard it expressed one way or another so many times.

Account Planning showed clips from across America, touting pretty much the same product attributes voiced by the guy we named "Speed Man." From our four-month study, we concluded: "Horse racing is a natural high." We were serving up nothing tricky or fancy. The best campaigns don't. "You just feel better about things when you win some races." And we were getting great buy-in even from Wintz, who did look a bit peaked.

That's when Amy came into the conference room and whispered into my ear. I'm certain I turned as pale as Wintz as I found my voice, and with a great sense of urgency and alarm, spoke to the assembled group. "Excuse me, Britney, for cutting in. Friends, I've got to interrupt our presentation with some very disturbing news. It appears that this morning, several terrorists hijacked some American planes and crashed them into the World Trade Center towers in Manhattan. There have been a lot of casualties and much destruction."

There were gasps.

"Another plane hit the Pentagon, with limited damage. This has become a state of emergency. All airplanes in the United States have been grounded. We're ending this meeting so that everyone can connect with their families." The Magna men worried that planes would be grounded for a week or so and had us secure tickets for them on the Montrealer train, which would be a long haul, but would get them home. Throughout the agency, our televisions were tuned into the latest news coverage.

By early afternoon, most associates with children had left to go home. But most others stayed cloistered around the television and waited on their pizza deliveries. From 9/11 forward I understood what the ultimate comfort food was: pizza. The carnage and imagery shown on the screens seemed surreal to me as I watched toppling buildings and people racing down streets to flee from the enveloping smoke and rubble.

The following day Spiegel was due to present as a finalist in pitching the DC Tourism business. We had planned to have our dress rehearsal right after the Magna meeting, but we got a call from the DC Tourism marketing director to say this meeting needed to be postponed a few days. She emphasized, "As a result of this attack, we need our new ad agency in place more than ever." I remember the word "attack" echoing in my mind. South Vietnam was attacked. Iraq was attacked. Israel was attacked. But America? Not in my lifetime.

A different kind of campaign was needed to deal with this totally upside-down moment in American history, especially within the nation's capital. At 2:00 p.m., instead of rehearsing the campaign that we had ready, we scrapped it entirely and sent a camera crew to DC to videotape interviews with Washingtonians to get their feelings on our nation's being under attack. Our plan was to rush this footage back to Philadelphia, edit late into the night, pick appropriate music, and put together spots that could run immediately. We'd portray the impact of 9/11 and how it felt in the hearts and guts of Americans, primarily in those areas that attract the most tourists to DC: New York, Philadelphia, Baltimore, Richmond, and the DC suburbs.

These vignettes would be incorporated into commercials but would also be used to make an electronic press kit for immediate distribution to all news outlets. Paid and earned media would be ready to go the day we got word we had won the business. While we adopted some of the patriotic themes created over the prior six weeks, primarily what we showed were images germane to September 11th. Our teams plugged away for thirty-six hours straight, as if we were preparing for a 60 Minutes exposé.

The fresh footage was quite gripping. As it turned out, we were the only agency to scrap the original presentation and develop a timely new campaign. Between reviewing edits, I talked to my daughter, Audrey, a number of times. Amy was home with her and she was very shaken, "Dad, don't send people to Washington. They're going to attack again." Her alarm rattled me for the rest of the day. Suppose she was right?

I called Adam, who was now in his second year at Wesleyan, and he, too, was jolted by this crisis. He had already begun questioning being in school when what he really wanted to do was create and perform his music. He was only nineteen, but his words resonated, "Dad, I've just got to get on with things. Time has gotten too damn precious."

When I checked in with my mom and dad, Elizabeth said, "It's much worse than a Pearl Harbor, Sam. They're bombing in our cities and the Liberty Bell could be next. Sam, you should go home and take cover."

Once we presented to DC Tourism, we became their unanimous choice; and we were not the most politic pick, since we were from Philadelphia instead of DC. We won the business the same day we pitched it. Our first ad appeared in the New York Times two days later urging people to come out of hiding to gather in our nation's capital to demonstrate solidarity, and connect to all the symbols of liberty that have made our country strong.

What we didn't see coming out of the DC Tourism ballyhoo, which was aplenty, was the attention it drew to us from Star Spangled Airlines based in Alexandria, Virginia. Unbeknownst to Spiegel and every other ad agency in America, including SSA's incumbent, McCann Erickson, the airline was conducting a private, closed agency review.

This meant they had preselected five finalists to compete for their business, and we were on the shortlist. McCann was the agency Beinhauser fretted over when DDB was trying to hold onto Volkswagen. McCann had been Star Spangled Air's agency of record for the past decade. We now had a shot at taking them out of the sky on this one and gain one of the most prestigious accounts in the United States. It was my "Oh, my God" moment.

When the request for a proposal reached my hands the week before Thanksgiving, I opened it and felt a rush that represented the culmination of two decades of hard work, building, worrying, and always believing in the possibilities. This fifty-page document and price proposal were due in Star Spangled's hands by noon the Monday following Thanksgiving. In their cover letter, they described the many challenges 9/11 had placed in their path and they promised a decision would be made before the New Year. I liked the tone of their inquiry, the urgency of their message, and the homage to a true partnership they seemed to want to establish. The month of January would be used to transition the business if the incumbent lost the account. February would begin the new contract period. "Holy mackerel, Andy!" That's what my dad used to say, especially when Norm Van Brocklin succeeded with a bomb to Tommy McDonald for an Eagles win.

By this point, Amy was Spiegel's writer of new business proposals. Like no one else, she had a wonderful feel for the company's voice. She, too, understood how momentous this account was as she dove in and went to work. Once she finished a section, she'd turn it over to me to review and edit. Then she'd go on to the next pages. We were a team. I understood over this big opportunity at the agency what had solidified in our marriage. We were partners at work as a way to compensate for what had not come together for us at home—an affectionate, loving marriage. *Why?* I wondered.

We headed to New York for Thanksgiving dinner at Mikey's house in White Plains, but except for the meal, we never strayed beyond our suite at the Drake Hotel on 56th and Park. Our kids went off with their cousins. They understood that this was the type of account we had dreamt about when we moved back to Philadelphia. When Mikey and I exchanged a few words before dinner, he said the same thing to me each year, "I've reserved the carving of the turkey for our family's *Chacham*." But on this occasion he added with great emphasis, "With Star Spangled on your mantle, I'll take the Cassatt and the rest of what we talked about years back over that planning breakfast in Vermont. What did I tell you, Samuel? I realized long ago, your ship was coming in. I just didn't know it would arrive on a big ass plane."

I just shook my head.

We kept polishing and polishing until we thought we had it right. I had never been more proud of Amy's work as we packed it up the following Monday morning. As I looked at Amy before handing the Star Spangled package to an ace junior account team that was making the drop in Alexandria, I said, "Not too shabby a piece of work from a pair of refugee dry cleaners, wouldn't you say?" (Often, and far too humbling for my sensibility if you must know, Amy would liken us to a neighborhood husband and wife team placing freshly pressed clothes on wire hangers to await the plastic wrap.) What we hand-delivered to SSA was not the long shot that, five years earlier, would have been dismissed by my enemies and friends alike as one of "Sam's mirages."

The waiting game began. Three days before Christmas, I was sitting in the Boiler Room with our client, Mal Walinski, the seventy-three-year-old chairman of the biggest home building company in Pennsylvania. Before his account came to Spiegel, this home-building executive had dominated his small retail ad agencies. He told me early on when we won his account, "Every so often I have to take the agency head honcho out to the woodshed for a good paddling when he gets out of hand."

What, exactly, was he trying to say? "Don't stand up to me?" Well I did. Spiegel would not be like one of those schlock houses he'd try to push around. His inference from the start was that I was too saintly to be subjected to such woodshed rituals, because, in the center of his mind, when we'd meet, he was overtaken by this overriding notion that I was a German Jew. And for that birthright, he always tried to be on his best behavior with his very own Mendelssohn in whose presence he always felt insecure.

I knew I made him nervous, and it ate at him a great deal. His son, Phil, the forty-eight-year-old president of their business, had orchestrated a leveraged buyout for his poppa that put more money in both their pockets than they ever dreamed possible. Their new owners wanted them to overhaul their rather "low-rent image" and build more upscale communities, and that's when Spiegel was called in. I figured I had starred in a fair number of Mal Walinski nightmares before he finally decided to hire us; but I think I appeared in even more after he brought us on board.

In his mind, I was one of the people he made crosses at with his two forefingers while he sipped Grey Goose with Phil. During these sloppy drinking bouts, Mal often amused his son with his latest rants. Frankly, I too was amused when I drank with them and I wasn't the subject of those rants.

I could just hear him all the way from the Capital Grille, "That Sam Spiegel is a schmuck, fancy-assed cuss of a German Jew boy. (Slurp.) That son of a bitch still thinks his shit don't stink. (Bigger sip yet.) Let me tell you something, Phillip, his smell's just as bad as every other Eastern European Jew sitting on the shitter." Then the swig he'd take would splash down onto his polka-dotted tie, always with a large knot. (I thought, when I saw his head caught up over that big knot, he must be compensating for something.) "And they think their shit don't smell? Shit! It smells plenty bad!" At which point another pour of Grey Goose covered new ice.

"They talk about Litvaks as if we're their Schvartzes. Let me tell you something, Phil, (biggest swig of the day) there's more money being made at White Manor Country Club than by those fucking Christmas tree worshiping members over there at Greenspring Valley. The difference here is we know exactly what's what with our shit. What do they think they're doing on their toilets, farting out Mozart?"

By then, Mal's rant would be winding down. He'd have Phil's head just about touching the leather of their special drinking booth, in uncontrollable laughter, while a waitress hovered nearby, delivering more pours, and waiting for those discreet moments when no one was quite looking to up her tip by lap-dancing them both.

My assistant, Jan, interrupted the meeting with Mal when the call came from the head of marketing at Star Spangled Air. I left the conference room and tried not to run to my office phone. My heart was pounding like a jackhammer. I picked up the phone to the sweetest announcement you can receive in the ad business: "You're on speakerphone, Sam…" Always, a wonderful sign! Jubilation comes with a crowd. Loser calls are always one-on-one…"So several of us can join in on this very happy occasion. Sam Spiegel, we wish to congratulate the proud new father of Star Spangled Air's United States account."

"Really? Yes? Yippee-hi-oh! Thank you guys." (Yes, I definitely said "Yippee-hi-oh" and my reaction—needless to say—was unrehearsed.)

The moment I hung up I found Amy, and we hugged and kissed over the news, and agreed to keep it under wraps until we could announce it to the troops later that day. As I left her office and passed Jan again, she was jumping up and down as she handed me a fax. "This just in."

> *Dear Sam,*
> *Here's to the conquering hero who just bested us on the biggest ac*
> *count we've pitched in quite a long time.*
> *Hail to the Chief!*
> *Best of luck,*
> *Lawrence Lux*

And then I said to Jan, "How about that? They called the losers first, so they could all gather to talk to me." My face never wore a wider smile than on that day. "Jan, could you get Harry on the phone?" She dialed him quickly and passed the phone to me.

I sang into it, "Harry, I'll be home for Christmas…with an airplane account."

"Um…are you shitting me, sonny boy?"

But after riding this incredible high, I had to drag myself back to Mal. When I peered at him through the window of the Boiler Room, he was giving his watch a crabby stare. Then his eyes shot up to the ceiling showing his impatience at me for leaving the room to take a call. As I reentered, he muttered to his "yes men" audibly enough for me to hear, "So the Big Cheese has finally returned?" Gesturing further to his cohorts, "Don't he know, I'm an important client?"

And he was. But he was also incredibly rude and unpleasant a lot of the time to a lot of my staff. Being with him at that moment was nowhere near where I wished to be. But there I was with "Jumbo Mortgage Man" and "Mr. 6% Down," and I couldn't hide my smile or hold back my news. I had to tell him what had just happened.

Very calmly, I said to Mal and to his henchmen, "We just got some very exciting news I'd like to share with you, because our achievement would not have been possible without the kind of retail success we've had with companies like yours. Spiegel Communications has just won the Star Spangled Air account."

Mal just about shit in his pants. Then he leaned forward in his seat and asked, in an almost bewildered voice, "You mean for Philadelphia International?"

I didn't miss a beat. "No, Mal, for the US of A."

He leaned back hard in his leather chair as the front wheels popped off the floor. "I'll be damned."

CHAPTER 29

Two years in, we had taken over just about all of Star Spangled Air's marketing and communications needs: advertising, interactive media, public relations, event planning, and direct mail. Most of our hires after this big acquisition were made to keep up with the growth of this account. And there we were in 2003, the year Southwest Airlines attacked SSA's biggest hub, the City of Brotherly Love. And, folks, Spiegel had a window seat.

Southwest had come into being decades after Star Spangled Air was established. And with their advent came labor rates that were about half of what SSA paid its pilots, attendants, and baggage carriers. Southwest figured it could use its cost advantages to stage a coup at Philadelphia International that would bring our airline, dubbed by them the "Star Spangled Dinosaur," to its knees.

In the aftermath of 9/11, many large carriers, SSA among them, were struggling to survive. Southwest, a relative newcomer far less impacted by the downturn than our airline, now had the verve and balance sheet to take on anyone in the sky. There was no stopping Southwest's charge on Philadelphia, as they prepared to eat us for lunch.

Speaking of lunches, Star Spangled Air had been one of the last airlines to cut out the free lunch. Only after 9/11, when the skies really thinned, did they abandon their midday meal in a cost-cutting measure. Free lunches morphed into $10 revenue-generating snack packs. And snack packs were now offered throughout the day.

Post 9/11, airline food had become a revenue driver, not a drain. And for snack packs, exact change was preferred. We helped our client with the pricing strategy, understanding that most travelers rely on ATMs and thus board the plane with plenty of twenties on hand. So with this $10 price point, parting with a twenty would neatly pay for two packs. However if someone produced a fifty, as I once witnessed and reported to our client, the passenger was just about maimed.

The ten didn't get you a generic box lunch, I'm happy to report. No, the snack pack was inspired by the esteemed kitchens of Wolfgang Puck. Our airline bought the rights to Wolfgang's name and his inspiration. I was excited by the concept, until my first encounter with a Puck Pack as an in-flight customer. To my disappointment, here's what I found when I opened my box: a ham and cheese on rye, a small lick of mayonnaise, a pickle, and bite-size Famous Amos Chocolate Chip cookies. Talk about hopes dashed! For starters, why weren't they calling their chocolate chip cookies Wolfgang Pucks?

Back to Southwest's battle plan: they'd come to the market with cheap fares and would force SSA to match them, further depleting our carrier's precious cash reserves. With the anticipated deep revenue losses that would follow made worse from old union deals, they'd force our dinosaur from the skies.

They reasoned that the combination of inflicted squashed sales along with higher fixed costs would keep SSA in the bankruptcy courts to never come out. Then they'd take over our temporarily dormant gates. In about how long? Just as long as it takes to say "Southwest Airlines." Back at the Spiegel ranch, we thought nothing was really at stake here. Well, except for everything.

Getting the right tone for our counterpunch became an all-encompassing enterprise. For a while we were at it around the clock. The simple truth was we had a far better understanding of the Philadelphia mindset than our competition did because it was our own. Here's what our vantage point suggested: If you're from Philly, you wake up each day knowing where you live…painfully in the shadows of New York—pretty much all the time in a rather permanent state of inferiority.

Yet Star Spangled Air was Philadelphia's airline and as close to a monopoly as monopolies get. Just as Rocky had become so imbedded in our city's identity so had SSA become a stranglehold! And year after year, we'd bitch about our airline and the high prices we paid, but coped nonetheless with our feelings of being gouged by our client. We thought, *This is what you get for living in Philadelphia!* The customer's only consolation for feeling so taken for an (air) ride, was the steady frequent flyer miles that continued to amass. Now, if the city switched to Southwest, our frequent flyer miles would stop altogether.

When Southwest Airlines decided to build a presence in Philly by buying into gates that became available, their plan was to fly to and from the most profitable and frequented routes controlled by SSA. But instead of having customers pay $423 for a round-trip to, say, Chicago on Star Spangled Air, Southwest would sell its seats for $58. And by coming in with these low rates, in short order SSA would be out for the count.

It didn't take SSA long to decide to go head-to-head and dollar-for-dollar to match these low-cost fares, every last one of them that mattered. But we knew that, with parity pricing, our customer base would want to stay with the devil they knew, and continue racking up frequent flyer miles. On Southwest they would have to abort collecting miles to get one free round-trip that would only come after booking five, which seemed so far down the road. *Nanny, Nanny, boo, boo. Stick your head in doo-doo.* Yes, we started name-calling right back at our cocky son-of-a-bitch upstart.

So here was our challenge. Why would it be believable for SSA to lower prices if it was perceived to have such a hold on the market? Nothing could fly in this cynical city, except for the truth. And that, folks, is exactly what our campaign served up: being honest. We opened with a television commercial featuring a palm reader telling a customer's fortune.

In our commercial, the palm reader told the gentleman sitting be-fore her, "I see a trip to an exotic beach and a beautiful woman. She has the face of an angel." Studying the man's hand further, "You're going to make a fortune [she spots a towel in the corner of her office] in ter-rycloth."

He replies, "Ah, the Cadillac of fabrics. So how am I going to get to this beach?"

The palm reader, groping for an answer, spots a Star Spangled Air newspaper ad on a table offering Caribbean flights for $29.00. "You're going to fly SSA for $29.00."

The man has bought into finding the beautiful woman and making a fortune in terrycloth, but when he hears $29.00 for a Star Spangled flight, that's when he turns skeptical and stands up exclaiming, "Oh, whatever!" And he storms out of the gypsy's office screaming, "Fraud!"

The spot ended with the line, "Go Fares from Star Spangled Air are unbelievably low, starting at $29.00."

Southwest was outspending us two to one in advertising, but that didn't seem to matter. Our self-deprecating spots and come-from-behind attitude appealed to Philadelphians as we were trumping our cocky "want a laugh a minute" low-fare rival. And right when they thought their campaign would chase our airline from the skies, we pulled off our death-defying victory. Although our success-in-the-sky energized me, all the turmoil, with its life-and-death implications for Spiegel, terrified my wife. Was Amy becoming the new Harry?

While dressing for a benefit dinner for the Pennsylvania Ballet and the Family Tree, a child abuse treatment center, Amy started in on me. "How exactly did you dodge that bullet, Sam? I mean, I guess 'we' dodged the bullet. But my God, all that combat was here in our own backyard. It doesn't get scarier than that, Sam. What a roller-coaster ride Southwest put us through."

"Do you remember the feelings when the Caldwells almost took us down?"

"Who can forget? You and your dad stopped talking for months. We haven't experienced anything remotely like that since. But, Sam, you were in control there. With our poor airline, we're so vulnerable. And if the Caldwells had won, would it have mattered that much?"

"It certainly would have to me. So you were with Harry, Mikey, and Elizabeth after all. I always wondered about that."

"Don't be ridiculous. But with SSA, if they go down, we go with them. Whether you're ready to admit it or not. You know it as well as I do. Everything we've got, will go away!"

"You're sounding an awful lot like the Harry of old. Actually, although it's taken him some decades, he's come around and is a believer. Amy, our campaign was smarter and harder hitting. Simply put, we chased them out of our skys."

"Sometimes I think we're so cooked, Sam. Maybe I'm getting too old for the business, or maybe I was never cut out for it to begin with. Where do you get your lucky pills? And the ones that keep you so calm? For Christ's sake, Samuel, please share!"

I smiled. "From Forrest Gump. He's both my inspiration and my dealer."

Amy smiled back at me. "Well, please fix me up with him, already. I'm having trouble sleeping!"

For the ballet gala, we bought a table for ten and invited my folks. Dad was home between long hospital stays but was always up for a night out, whether it was wise for him to go or not. Mikey and Sylvia came down from New York. And the team that produced the successful Family Tree commercial was also at the table.

The truth is that, at this point in my career, big-ticket galas were not my thing. But Spiegel had created the award-winning television spot for the Family Tree that dealt with the deep-rooted effects of verbal child abuse, which is often overlooked as simply causing temporary hurt when compared with the ravages of physical abuse. In reality, according to the Family Tree studies, the consequence of verbal abuse can be worse.

Our commercial illustrated this fact through abused children speaking to the camera, echoing what they'd heard pointed their way in their homes: "You'll never amount to anything." "You're as stupid as your father." "I wish you were dead." We had decided to attend this fundraiser because we were proud to be instrumental in educating people about this facet of the abuse issue and to be a part of this important public service campaign.

Spiegel owned the airwaves, and since Harry was still hopping around the dial with his remote control, watching all of our commercials, my mother kept saying, "Your damn commercials are so pervasive, your father and I can't watch a single show anymore."

The pro bono spot against child abuse had Philadelphia abuzz. Everyone we knew and saw that night seemed to make an extra effort to come over and register, "You two are on top of the world! You both make Philadelphia so proud!" We basked in these often repeated, and sometimes overly gooey, refrains all night long. At the cocktail reception before the ballet, we saw Daniel McAlister, our former landlord, from where we first lived when we moved back to Philly. He was there with his "manservant," Marvin. I wondered if Daniel still referred to Marvin in such a fashion, or if they'd finally come out of their closet. If they marked progress, Amy and I had come a long way since those days when we lived a floor below them in their Rittenhouse Square brownstone.

It made me sad to see the two men looking so worn out. When we first met Daniel, he had dashing James Mason good looks. That night his appearance was more like a retired mason hobbling from a Sunrise Retirement van. And Marvin, who once appeared to be lifted from the set of Amos 'n Andy, so shiny and new, that night seemed as if he'd fallen from the Sanford and Son truck.

I wondered if Amy and I seemed equally weathered? I greeted Daniel, who chimed, "Congratulations, chaps! [Daniel always referred to me as chap, but that night Amy was a chap, too.] on your special Delta Airlines win and such." I didn't correct him; I just graciously accepted his kind acknowledgment.

I spotted Mikey and Sylvia gathering up lots of hors d'oeuvres to take to our table. Elizabeth and Harry trailed us, trying to keep up, to share in our limelight. Harry had trouble steadying himself and should have brought his cane, as his heart had been in severe decline in recent months. By this point, he carried a defibrillator in addition to his pacemaker. He was on overdrive that night, bless his sweet ailing heart, as he hustled the best he could to keep up with all the naches that was coming his and Elizabeth's way.

At one point my mother leaned in to me to say, "It's like this airline is your phoenix and you know what happens to the phoenix? It's kind of getting nauseating, if you ask me. Our mayor isn't getting near the attention you have tonight. Don't let it all go to your head, Samuel." I just kept smiling and nodding.

After cocktails, we took our seats for the ballet. Our guests took theirs in pairs strewn throughout the auditorium. We'd reconvene for champagne and dessert after the ballet, when we got to meet the dancers. Amy and I were seated in the center orchestra of the Newsenhoff Symphony Hall. I couldn't help but smile, thinking about the praise old Newsenhoff might have had for me that night had he made it to this gala. "I gave your dad a break and look where the next generation has taken things. *Mazel tov*, young man."

I sat next to Patricia and Ted Baxley. Patricia was the chair of the Pennsylvania Ballet. On the other side of Amy was the Family Tree's board chairman and the president of the local cable company, along with his wife. We were talking politely and waiting for the Family Tree commercial to be shown, then the curtain would follow next. I complimented Patricia on her wizardry at pulling the charity into this event. Patricia whispered in my ear, "Sam, you created the TV spot that built the cause that filled this house that, how shall I say this, will allow Thad Tyler to see his way to another season."

I whispered with a grin, "Patricia, I don't know which I appreciate more, your flattery or your modesty." I glanced up toward the box that was positioned to the left of our row and did a double take. There was Beth Ehrenberg in a pretty red dress, scanning the room through a pair of sleek opera glasses. Thad Tyler was on one side of her, and Ailey's Barlow Gott, who Patricia had introduced to me at the cocktail hour, was on her other arm. There was no mistaking Beth. She seemed so animated as she talked with Thad, who was close to twenty years her senior.

I wondered what on earth she was doing there with him? I had heard that she'd gotten married to someone named Mark, but couldn't recall his last name. Where was her husband? Home watching a football game? Or was she no longer married to him, and at that very moment using her opera glasses to scan the concert hall to find me?

Last time I had seen her was a few years back at the French bakery in Wynnewood, when she leaned into me closely with a baguette clutched ever so perfectly between her arms and resting on her chest, so as to showcase that it was indeed popping its head out of its wrap (She knew precisely what she was doing.) and whispered, "Remember what you told me when you broke up with me?"

"What was that, Beth?"

"It will never get better than with us. And you know what, Sam? You were right." Knowing exactly whom I had spotted but not sharing this fact with Patricia, I leaned over to get her input, "So who's that between Thad and Barlow?"

"Rather cute, huh? That's Beth Ehrenberg. She's Thad's fag-hag or homo-honey. I really don't know what's politically correct these days."

"Pat, they both sound wrong."

"But she's one of them or both. They're always together in these situations. But if you ask me, Thad's here for Beth's husband, Mark Ferris. You'll see Mark in a moment when the curtain goes up and you'll understand why he won the 'Mr. Buff' contest."

"Mr. Buff?"

"Yes. Mark's Mr. Buff! Thad cooked up this contest idea to cast for guys to be part of the performance. Maybe that's how he got Barlow to do this event, so he could be in on the casting call."

I asked, "Is Mr. Buff a dancer?"

"No. He's more like a live prop. His job is to stand at the center of the set and hold up the sky, and when it turns cloudy, he moves his arms left to right, abs and pecs bulging, arms straining in the air to keep the sky from falling. It's Thad's innovation for the 2004 *Revelations Ballet.*"

"Are you sure we're not here to watch a burlesque show?" She laughed heartily. "*Touché!* Rather ridiculous if you ask me. But who am I to say what toys play for boy toys?"

Our spot was presented to the audience of two thousand. When it was over, Patricia lightly tapped my hand that was stretched out at the end of my armrest and leaned into my ear. "Boy, that spot packs a punch. Bravo, Sam!" Amy's hand on the other side of me rested, folded into her other in her lap.

The screen was drawn up to the fly space. The curtain started to open with Mr. Buff positioned center stage miming the motion of pulling the curtain apart. He was wearing nothing but a carefully positioned fig leaf. He extended his arms toward the sky, and for much of the rest of the performance Mr. Buff did exactly what he had been chosen to do: He kept the sky from falling.

After a beautiful ballet, Amy and I enjoyed another parade of congratulatory handshakes and kisses for our commercial. Although people might have thought I loved bathing in all the accolades, for me, it was rather embarrassing. As Amy and I walked back toward the tent, we should have been holding hands, but we clutched our programs instead.

We found Harry, Elizabeth, Mikey, and Sylvia huddled around an array of desserts. Mikey asked, "Something sweet for anyone?" Amy sat next to Harry and I to her right. Our creative associates had wisely scattered.

My mother spoke next. "Thank you, Amy and Sam, for including us in this marvelous Ailey performance. They haven't lost a step."

And Mikey continued with another toast to those assembled: "Although it's almost a miracle that your airline account is still in the air, we're glad it is because I'd dare say, you'd have to sell these fine tickets on eBay if they weren't. And... [he looked over toward Dad] 'Holy Mackerel, Andy!' we'd miss out on all these succulent desserts."

At this point, I thought he sounded sourer by the day and replied, "Always so kind of you to have such thoughtful words for me, Mikey." That's when I spotted Beth Ehrenberg in her red dress at the bar. She still had my heart. I stood up and said, "Would anyone like a glass of champagne?" A flute was parked in front of everyone except for Amy and me.

"I'd love one, Sam."

I patted my wife's shoulder and scooted to the bar slipping in line behind Beth. A flood of happy anticipation hit me. Her smell, being behind her curves in line, just all of her. I thought, *She's mine tonight! Mom, your "phoenix" has found his prize!*

With those thoughts came a very big and embarrassing woody. No mistaking what it was. And subtly...you say I didn't but I did, I pinched Beth ever so lightly on her right buttock. She turned around, probably thinking it was Thad, as it seemed Mr. Buff hadn't returned from changing out of his fig leaf.

"My, aren't we getting familiar and friendly tonight, Sam?"

It just came out. "You're the treat of my night."

"I'm honored! Because it seems you've had a lot of them this evening. I hadn't quite realized you were so much the man about town." As she brushed away the already poured champagnes in front of her to place an order for a Grey Goose martini, she leaned in to the bartender and added, "Please, with an olive I can chew on for a while." She then looked back at me, "Fancy meeting you here, Sam."

She took her martini. Shot me a big smile. And turned broadly as if on display in a big choreographed moment. She sashayed her way back to her seat, derrière swinging as if to the beat of a tuba over a throaty trombone. With my two flutes in hand I attempted to go left, while watching Beth go right, with an equally big smile. Some of the suds spilled over the top of the glasses. I returned to my table and handed one to Amy, who responded with her perfunctory, "Thanks." Immediately she drank it down, I might add with the poise of a truck-driver, while Mikey and Sylvia got themselves to their feet. "Thanks, you two. Could have stayed longer if the invite was complete with AMTRAK tickets home, oh well."

"And you two," my mother said, "got to get the *alter kocker* back in the sack before his defibrillator sounds its alarm."

CHAPTER 30

A week or so later, after visiting my father who was back in the hospital, Amy and I had dinner at our favorite Greek restaurant, Effies. I watched the owner/chef, Mr. Samos, as he oversaw each dish that left his totally exposed-to-the-patrons kitchen. How bold of him to bare his everything for the world to see. That night over dinner Amy and I talked seriously about what should come next in our lives. Adam had long withdrawn from college to focus on his music career, and Audrey would be attending college in just a few years.

We began to revisit a subject we hadn't discussed in months: our plans to sell Spiegel to a conglomerate before the end of the decade. To pull off such a feat, we needed outside help. I would need to hire an advertising financial sharpshooter first to build up our profits and set a sale price, and then negotiate a good deal from the highest bidder. This was not my strong suit. I was a good builder but not the bottom-line focused guy we needed at this stage.

Most years, when the agency had leftover funds, I chose to put the money earned back into the business to make the agency stronger. Call it an obsession, perfection, or just a disease, that's what I did.

After all, someone had to keep feeding Harry's mania—or was it now Amy's? So he/she could repeat, "Why so little on the bottom line?" And I'd answer, "So most of it won't go to Uncle Sam." That was my joke with Dad for years.

I built the Spiegel brand by making sure our product had impact. Cost never threw me. I always knew how to make more money to cover what we spent. I believed great work would always push us up and pull us through. Every so often, though, I remembered my father's words, "Samuel, you must work…um…on retained earnings." I wondered if my strategy might some day backfire. Still, in twenty-five years of consistently perfecting our product, which required significant money to grow, I rarely allowed myself to entertain such notions for very long.

That night, I told Amy, "If we want to sell the company in five years for top dollar, we need to make our balance sheet a hell of a lot better. We have too much money in work in progress and some of what's in that account needs to be written off." In the ad business the WIP accounts are the ones you always get around to next year, and then it turns into the following year.

"With all our large retainers, we should be able to clean everything up in about two years' time and just keep building our bottom line, but the selling game has changed. If we had sold Spiegel in the nineties, it would have been all topline related. It's all bottom line now and we need a son-of-a-bitch CFO. A guy like Bud Ashley, to push profits and sell us to the highest bidder. He helped bring about that stunning Godfried & Baklor deal." And that's when our first course, the calamari with lemon all over the plate, made it to our table.

Amy said, "I can really understand now where Harry was coming from when he was trying to sell the business."

"What? Right out from under me? How nice of you to say."

"No, Sam, it's just that it's all so nerve-racking as you get older."

I retorted, "Who says the kids won't want in?"

"Well, I know for a fact Adam doesn't want to go near our place. So we don't have to worry about disappointing our boy."

"You say it with such venom. The music industry isn't exactly a sure bet, sweetheart. What about Audrey, someday? She'd be a natural."

"Sam, don't start pushing another Spiegel woman into your goddamn business. Or you're toying with trouble."

"Why, thank you. It's been such a wretched ride. And by the way, Audrey is her own agent." And I went further. "Maybe I just picked the wrong gal for the job."

That comment was left unheard or simply unacknowledged by Amy. "Sam, we need a son-of-a-bitch. Someone we can rely on who won't be such a nice guy to everybody. No offense."

"You mean who won't give away all our money so we end up having to eat at restaurants where we can see ketchup squirt out from the kitchen?"

She chuckled.

Then I said, "You should have married your brother. You'd sleep better and you'd have three houses by now."

"I thought of marrying him but he can't cook worth a damn, and he and his wife starve their guests."

"That's certainly something upon which we can agree," I said. "I'm famished just thinking about Alan and Monica's so-called dinner parties."

"But you're right, Sam, I've settled for too much silver and not enough gold through the years. I think we could use Bud Ashley's handiwork. We're getting to a place where we could have quite a meaningful sale and second careers for ourselves, or second something or other."

The hummus with toasted pita came next, as did my wondering about "second something or other." I decided to let that one go for now, but it was the provocative statement of the night. Effies was a BYOB restaurant. That night I had brought a pair of 2000 Bordeaux from our home wine cellar. By the time we started in on bottle two, Amy and I had moved to another topic.

"Sam, we've had such clear sailing throughout our marriage."

"I beg your pardon, wasn't it only a week or so ago that you were squawking about the roller-coaster ride we're on?"

"Well, miraculously, our cars are still bolted to the track and the bank hasn't foreclosed on our house yet."

"Bite your tongue, Amy."

"When things got really bad for my mom, she sure knew how to make it through."

"Yeah, she certainly is a gold medalist. If you could bottle her sto-icism, she'd pour like a Rothschild and make herself some money. What made you think of that?"

Amy seemed unusually reflective that night. "I don't know, I was just thinking about my mom always skimping on everything and what little she had she's given away to her children. You know, Sam, nothing's really gone wrong for the two of us. We haven't been tested."

"I don't really agree. We're constantly being tested—in business, my brother's accident, your dad's business failures. I'm the son of a Ho-locaust survivor, and I think Harry's failing miserably and isn't long for this world. Your mother's sister died in a tragic car crash. My mother's dad died early from TB. I think our families have had plenty of shit to sift through, thank you."

"Death of a parent or grandparent, Sam, that's the order of things."

"Who says it's not? I'm saying our families have had great grief and tragedies."

"Well, we've certainly never had to weather one as a couple, Samu-el." Amy's favorite Seafood Santorini arrived from the kitchen.

"So you want to will a disaster our way over the Santorini? A nice catastrophe? Be quiet or God will hear you. Why are you looking for unhappiness?"

"I'm not."

Or so she said, but I think that deep inside Amy, she couldn't help herself. She had this perverse wish and also nagging fear that almost called out for trouble. The right kind of trouble would almost be a relief for her. I think she really believed something had to go very wrong for her or me in order to protect our children.

Then Amy could stand tall with her grandmother, grandfather, mother, and father, who actually had lost a child and sister, and Jack's

211

business, and set an example for shouldering an extreme loss. And although Amy's father, Jack, was mainly an enigma for her, she still loved him. I think that by feeling pain of her own, she figured that might make her a more empathetic daughter. Maybe she had something there.

Amy's respect for her mother's stoicism, I always thought, was a good quality. It was the closest thing she had to a personal aspiration or goal for herself. Over the years she had said as much. Her longing to survive an ordeal was so foreign to my dreaming big and working to reach my goals.

What did we have going here, yin bumping up against yang?

And if something unthinkable happened in our lives, what might come next for Amy? Would failure or tragedy trigger her greatest hour? Her chance to be a hero on her terms instead of mine? I had never embraced stoicism as a virtue. As a matter of fact, I had seen it mostly as a condition you acquire by necessity, like carrying around a bad back wherever you go because you have no other choice. I saw stoics as simply living a life of coping, and that wasn't really living for me.

That night at Effies I got some clues that Amy was scratching for something new in her life. I sensed some changes were afoot in her mind. I had the distinct feeling she was angling for something different. Maybe after we sold the business.

It may have looked as if I was distracted as I watched Chef Samos do his magic in the kitchen, but my attention was squarely on Amy, whether she knew it or not. Something in her had changed. She was stirred up, more than I had seen in a long time. There was something about the way she looked that night, the way she reacted to me—as if our paths were beginning to diverge.

CHAPTER 31

There was another separation in store for me—in this case, a consequence of humanity's plight. At this point in my father's life, he was
a veteran of multiple struggles, but now in his final act and above all
else, Harry had become a seasoned patient. For the prior two months,
when he wasn't home for a day here or there, he had been holed up in
hospitals.

Actually, that would be too harsh a term. Osama bin Laden and
Saddam Hussein holed up for a while. My dad had been confined, but
not at just any hospital. Initially, he had been a patient at Penn Medicine in what was referred to as "the Ritz Carlton," in the Pavilion wing.
There, when I had first entered his room, I felt as though I were standing
in a well-appointed hotel suite, complete with a spacious balcony where
my father often liked to be wheeled while eating grapes.

His friend and doctor, Artemis Klarens, had insisted on these first-
class accommodations when the latest round of hospitalizations started.
That was my clue that Dad's cardiologist had determined Harry was
clearly on his "ninth life." Klarens reasoned, "Why not let him go out in
style?" I assure you that on his own, Dad would never have made this decision. He was not one for paying a dime more than Medicare provided.

Simple pleasures…a baguette with Brie? That was fine. A fine Bordeaux, why not? A Royal Jamaican cigar? Of course. He really appreciated the better things in life. But Dad accepted being in the Pavilion, the first-class wing at Penn Medicine, only after Dr. Klarens told him he had booked the room and would carry him there on his back, personally, if he failed to register.

However, when such niceties came his way, he knew how to take gracious advantage. His personal Pavilion nurses were not only medically qualified, they were well versed in hospitality skills. These aides/concierges didn't feign affection for Dad; he earned their kindnesses each day. Harry was appreciative, funny, and warm-hearted. They were his when he said, "Honey…um…would you please…"

On the Pavilion dinner menu were items such as lobster tails, veal medallions, and filet mignon. Dad would painstakingly review his selections. Along with the food lineup was a large-print *New York Times* synopsis that he painstakingly tried to read, though his vision had seriously weakened. I watched him struggle, closing one eye and then the other in order to see what looked like a Dick-and-Jane primer. I realized we all eventually come full circle.

Penn Medicine had lavished the oil baron treatment on Harry, in and out for two months or so, before sending him prematurely to a local rehab center to convalesce. Within twenty-four hours of being admitted there, Harry's heart began to fail again. Rather than return him to Penn, the ambulance rushed him to the nearby emergency room at Mt. Zion Hospital.

There at Mt. Zion, the pampering Harry had received at the Pavilion became a dim memory. His brusque night nurse, getting ready to go off duty, bristled at every request. As I stood there looking on, she elbowed her way past me to roughly snatch the thermometer from his mouth. His eyes immediately shot open, which is when he first spotted me. Harry may have begun his hospital stay at Neiman Marcus, but he ended up in the checkout line at Kmart.

It was that Friday when I knocked off early and spent my last cherished time with Harry back at the rehab center. There he was in bed reading his big-print New Yorker, and right beneath him was a small dog sleeping contentedly. I realized that pets were on this floor as a way to help cheer up patients and transition them toward going home. I asked Harry, "Who's your little companion down there?" That was about the time his nurse walked in.

Harry looked at her and me, wagging his finger in front of his own puppy-dog eyes and wearing his characteristic endearing smile. Referring to my question and pointing at the dog, "Young lady, I thought I made it clear that I had paid for a private room." The nurse and I both chuckled. He was right there until the end as he then focused on me. "So what brings me the honor of your company so early in the day? Were you afraid I'd expire if you waited until rush hour?"

He—like Amy of yore—always made me smile. "No. I just couldn't keep myself away from checking out your new digs, complete with your own palace watchdog."

"Well, Sam, my days at the Gritti Palace are officially over. No more slumming it with the oil barons. I'll be okay in my modest dwelling, here. So, sonny boy, I'm damn proud of you pulling another rabbit out of that active hat of yours and drumming Southwest…um…right out of town."

"Yeah, call me Gary Cooper in High Noon. My darling wife said it another way, 'So, just how did you dodge that bullet, Sam? By all rights our airline and our company should be out for the count.'"

He leaned far forward in his bed, no longer relieved but looking worried, "That sounds more like a comment your father would make to you, not Amy."

We both laughed, a bit uncomfortably.

"So what did you tell her when she said, 'We should be out for the count.'"

I said, "It was simply the luck of the draw."

"And you're not sounding like me, too? What's going on here? But I know the truth, sonny boy. You outsmarted them."

"Well, we certainly put up a fight. We had to protect our client. Our city. What's ours, Harry. Our honor, your honor. So we rooted them out of town."

"I'm very proud of you, Sam. You've always made me proud."

I had some trouble holding back my tears. Dad was lucid but he looked awful. "So how does it go with my soldier here?" He had to have heard me choke on "soldier" as my wavering voice took over. Each sentence I got out pushed me closer to doing just that, choking up.

"I don't know. To tell you the truth, I guess I'll have to get used to this godawful walker." It hovered by the side of his bed within easy reach "Like I'm some sort of *alter kocker*."

"I think you can learn to work with it. Think of it as walking the dog."

"You mean the dog walking me."

I laughed. "Now that's the spirit, Dad." I hadn't referred to him as "Dad" in years.

"Well, if I can get my body to the kitchen every so often and get my hands on a crusty baguette with properly ripened Brie, it might all be worth it."

"There you go!"

For the past several weeks and certainly unbeknownst to him, I had been working on his obituary and eulogy. I wanted it to be ready because it needed to be right, and not jotted off a few hours before the funeral. There is an order to things in life, and so I learned, in death, too. And for me, sizing up his life, counted for a lot. I had almost completed it and found myself still crafting the ending, but had a question about the German expression *Auf Wiedersehen*. Who better to ask than my father? German was his native language, after all. But how could I ask him to help me finish his own eulogy? And then I just came out with it. Harry, *Auf Wiedersehen?* Does it simply mean 'goodbye'? Or more like 'I'll see you again'?"

He looked at me closely as if to size me up, one last time. "That all depends on who's doing the asking, and then of course who might be answering back."

I asked, "What if I'm talking to you, Dad?"

"Well, sonny boy, if it's about me...it's *Auf Wiedersehen*, I'll see you again."

And two days later he was right. In my command performance, I helped him end his life.

Auf Wiedersehen, sweet Harry. *Auf Wiedersehen*.

CHAPTER 32

What was most fortuitous about Dad's rather timely death was his complete miss of the coming months in my life, because had he experienced them, no doubt, they would have killed him. They almost killed me.

We hired that Australian financial sharpshooter, Bud Ashley, the one Amy and I had talked about at the Greek restaurant. And he turned out to be up to no good.

Bud was broad-shouldered, strong, and sported a big, blonde shaggy mane, that he flopped around pretty much all the time, reminiscent of the lion from *The Wizard of Oz*. Bud was headstrong and always in desperate need of a cigarette. When he'd light one up, it would hang on his lips like an overgrown mole. Outside our building, he had this terrible habit of flinging his cigarettes four or five feet from where he stood, to smolder on the curb.

Early in his tenure, he started approaching Amy, reminding her that she too, not just me, was an owner of Spiegel. And often when he passed her, he would swing around his right forefinger to grasp his thumb and form an "O" to signify "owner," and he'd rest this O in the middle of his forehead for Amy to imitate and brand on her own outside frontal lobe.

This signal had become their regular greeting. Initially, I thought what I was seeing was rather nurturing and endearing, but Bud's gesture seemed a bit abrupt and out of step for the office, like some sort of "Heil Hitler" thing. It was also somewhat hostile towards me.

One morning, I stopped by my wife's office as Bud's guttural sounds spilled out to the hallway. Nothing was subtle about this man. He pretty much gargled when he talked, like a bad character from a Dickens novel. Amy's door was closed, but there was no mistaking the two of them going at it. I hung outside for a listen.

"Darling,…" He called my wife *darling*. This was the extra sense of intimacy he invoked with her. (And he thought he deserved as much as we invited Bud to our inner circle so that he could try and make us more money so as to fetch the big payola later. What had we done?) "Darling, let me tell you something about your knight in shining armor—his company is upside down. You're an owner, too. And you don't want to be like your negligent mother." Bud actually howled this to Amy, and I could imagine fire blowing from his mouth with every word.

As he continued, I remained outside of her door. "You've told me about your innocent, trusting mother, how your father conned everybody and yet Jeannie stood right by his side. She's with him to this day, right? How dare she, after he robbed her and the family's money out from under all of you? And what happened? You and your siblings lost your million-dollar trust funds that were supposed to be inviolate. Your mother's jewels, all gone!"

To listen to him was to listen to the wolf in *Little Red Riding Hood*. It was clear, though, that Amy had been confiding in him and maybe lapping it up. He knew far too much about her past. Scary. Very scary.

Amy retorted, "But, Bud, Sam has been running this place for twenty-five years. We haven't missed a payroll or one lease payment. We stay current with our vendors. We'd hear it from our clients if we weren't."

"Well you can keep your blinders on if you must, darling, and be the naïve wife your mother taught you to be. But now you can't say I didn't warn you…Harry's gone. It's up to you to control your beast. Or take it in the ass like most of the other dumb-fuck American wives who have nothing better to do with their time, if you'll pardon my French."

How was Amy processing his diatribe? I wasn't quite sure. After all, I was out in the hall. Was she that impressionable? I realized Bud made it a practice to wander into her office to vent and make her worry about money, thin margins, losing accounts, and not filling the well fast enough to sustain what I had going. I knew what a balancing act it was to make the agency work. That's what I was so practiced at doing. Even my father stopped worrying because he knew I got it. But what was happening to my wife?

At home, I felt my relationship with Amy had become more distant and dislocated. And although Amy's expressions and comments were showing signs of souring on me, as my grandma used to think in Nazi Germany, *This, too, will pass.* For a while, I thought the same because I always looked at Amy as my rock, but then my rock began to crumble.

Bud's offensive barreled forward like a Nazi war tank through Poland. He operated with keen duplicity as he buttered me up to my face and tore me down behind my back. Was it, indeed, his plan to come to Spiegel to divide the Mr. and Mrs. and then essentially conquer and steal? Was this about to be one of the great con jobs in advertising history? At first it was too weird and Shakespearean to dare give it too much credence.

I had plenty of confidence, so initially it didn't bother me all that much that Bud was playing mind games with Amy, but gradually his seeds began to take root. I saw palpable changes in my life partner. My mind began to wander back to how Loren must have felt when Ace was shaking him down.

Bud's constant "You're an owner" reinforcements continued to come at Amy like rounds of pistol fire—the frequency was almost hypnotic. I began thinking he had brainwashed her, and when I got to this place, that's when I started to really worry. Lovely guy, that Bud.

Was Amy being carefully cultivated for Bud's terrorist assault? And that's when I began to get the notion of how thorough his infiltration into my company had been. There was a target on my back. But like I said, it took me a while to figure it out. Had I ingested too much Kafka? Was what I was feeling going through Franz's imaginative filter? I was

STEVEN C. EISNER

getting rattled. On some days, I thought I was losing my mind…becoming paranoid. Or was it that I had every reason to be concerned?

What made it all the harder for me to figure out was that although Bud was buddy-buddy with Amy, he was also exceedingly chummy-chummy with me. With me he'd say, "I've never met a 'Merlin' so up close and personal. You get a lead, Samuel, and what do you do? You end up turning the account into something three times bigger than their previous ad spend. How do you do it, old boy?"

Most haunting of all, if Bud could recruit Amy as his key terrorist, would it be unfair for me to believe she might have been a sleeper cell all along? Were there signs of this from our past? That's when I remembered her words from the car ride back to New York from Bethany Beach after that fateful crab feast when she asked, "When's it my turn to deal the next hand?" Had she been waiting for this all along? Her twin tower moment.

Bud badgered me for raises and first-class trips back and forth to Australia even though he had vowed to be so careful with every Spiegel penny. I began to understand. He was definitely careful all right when it came to having enough money to line his own pockets. We set him up in a posh rental apartment where he kept enhancing his add-ons, like better sound and video equipment.

To top it off, after Harry passed, I bought Dad's Mercedes from my mom so Bud could use it. No wonder he told anyone who cared to listen, "I've got the greatest gig going in the States."

After about a year of hanging around Spiegel, picking fights with anyone who might have my ear or, more aptly, who might have crossed him, I was beginning to see the devastation Bud was creating. While he trapped more profit here and there, as we had hoped, he was killing the spirit of my company I had worked so hard to cultivate.

But it got worse…. He was joined by his Aussie partner in crime, the more acutely deceptive of the two, the deadly devious, one and only Lance Winfrey.

We had been searching around for another senior creative director to work under Sid Reim. Bud produced Lance, a forty-one-year-old wonder whom he described as, "An international creative superstar whose name filled several pages of books written on the Australian ad revolution." It was true; Lance had won a slew of awards and was regarded as one of Australia's top creative talents. That much I read in the Australian trade publications online.

And, best of all, Lance was a Beinhauser protégée. He had worked directly under the "Vanilla Wonder," some years after I had. Lance was anointed by Beinhauser to return to Australia to run DDB's Sydney office, and Bud knew that when I learned of this connection, Lance Winfrey would be "signed, sealed, and delivered." Bud had found his "boy," as he called him, a home. And as old friends (and drinking buddies before Lance had to dry out), they reconnected to become partners in war games at Spiegel.

I was told by Bud, "I can deliver Lance for $300,000 when he's been getting two times that amount. Use him for only two weeks each month and pay him half. He can freelance the balance abroad. It doesn't much matter to Lance because agencies line up for his copy, and he has his trust fund to fall back on, but he won't be taken advantage of either."

When Lance arrived, he didn't look scary at all. I was relieved. He seemed rather mild mannered and pleasant enough. Lance often wore a black shirt. The type of shirt one would call a blouse if it weren't on a man. His repertoire included a lot of delightful "gee shucks" expressions and as many Aussie/British equivalents. We all wanted to hear more of this man's self-deprecating phrases.

Unlike Bud, whose accent was street and guttural and most unpleasant, Lance's turn of a phrase was quite a gift. Let's face it, even American colloquial sounds sensational when it comes out of the mouth of Hugh Jackman instead of Danny DeVito. When Lance got in a snit, even that sounded enchanting. As the women would say, "Can you give us one more 'that's bullocks' before leaving the room, Lance? Or pretty please, let us swoon over another 'sedual' (spelled schedule). What about hitting us with a 'sanar-i-o' (spelled scenario)? Or, please, master, let us sigh on one last 'lest it be known.'"

For a while there, his charm even snookered me, but for Amy—from the moment he walked in the door, she got shot in the heart. It was as if she knew Lance was about to become her Sir Lance-a-Lot.

CHAPTER 33

Several months after we hired Lance Winfrey, Amy and I had dinner with our friends, the Blues, at a very good offbeat restaurant in South Philly called the Chameleon Grill. We had had a nice time. The food was memorable, but not so the rosé the Blues chose. That didn't stop them from keeping it coming all night long. I've never found a rosé that I've actually liked but then, as you might recall, I hate the color pink.

By morning, I was experiencing horrible pain in my right side, just above my waist. I formed my two fingers into a cross the way Mal Walinski taught me to ward off curses. In my mind, it was aimed at those pink bottles of rosé. Writhing in a way I had never experienced before, I had no sooner walked down our steps to get the newspaper and turned on the coffee machine, when the ache in my side made me double over in the kitchen.

Amy was out getting her hair colored and styled before our trip to Bermuda on Tuesday for the annual meeting of the 4As—the Association of American Advertising Agencies. We had never attended this convention before, but were heading there that year because we, at last, had been nominated for the coveted O'Toole Award for creative excellence. If we actually won the thing, it would be huge for Spiegel.

I was alone as I doubled over to the kitchen floor. Audrey was spending the night at a friend's house. Adam was making music in Brooklyn. I was suffering while my dog Ruffy tried to lick the pain from my face. "That's not where it hurts, Ruffy-boy."

I finally got myself to my feet when I realized I needed to find my keys and drive myself to the emergency room. The closest ER was Mt. Zion Hospital. I thought of my father's final hours and wondered if I'd be checking out at Kmart, too. When I arrived, I signed in and told the receptionist I had a lot of pain concentrated on my right side. She asked me, "From one to ten, ten being the worst, what's your pain like, Mr. Spiegel?" I momentarily got lost in thinking about this for a little too long as she popped her second, "Sir, how are you feeling?"

I told her, "I think I'm an eight." And shit, it most certainly felt like it was a ten. Does anyone actually admit they've reached their threshold and blurt out, "I'm a ten!"? Don't you have to be shot in the gut with goop coming out to go clean with that number? And before I knew it, there was someone in a stretcher who was coming in for just that, a fresh gunshot wound.

To me, what he had was an eleven. He got waved through, but then again he might have been waved through because he was dead. The intensity of my pain was overwhelming. I couldn't sit. Standing was almost impossible. On the windowsill next to the one I was leaning on, a group of ants swarmed over a piece of a cheese sandwich in an open plastic baggie. The whole place looked thoroughly disgusting, just adding to my misery.

If the floor hadn't have been so dirty, I'd have curled up in the corner. Was this appendicitis? A gallstone? A hernia? I kept feeling as if I had to go to the bathroom. But after my first visit there, the ones following, every five minutes or so, only delivered spittle. And, my God, what would have happened if they called my name during my pit stops? Would I go back to the end of the line? And where was that precisely? By the ants' sandwich? Actually the bathroom break became my excuse to go to the receptionist to see if my name had been called. "No, Mr. Seigel, not yet."

"Perhaps you might have called Mr. Spiegel?"

"Not him neither."

This getting nowhere continued past 9:30 a.m. Still no doctor! By this time I figured Amy's hair had been fully restored to blonde and she had progressed to her cut. I thought it was time to interrupt her Sabbath service. I called her cell, and when she answered, I said, "I'm Madeline in one straight line at half past nine." With a sense of urgency, Amy left the beauty parlor and came to find me. Two or so hours later, I was pronounced "still alive" but had a kidney stone I needed to try to pass over the weekend.

It didn't budge.

Three days went by and the Codeine I was taking to ease my discomfort made me horribly constipated. What was worse? More aches? Or that horrible bloated feeling? I opted to tough it out and told Amy, "I need to pull out of the Bermuda trip."

"Sam, we have to go."

With that, I guessed Amy, knowing of my dilemma, had called ahead to get the inside information and that we had won the O'Toole. "So you're saying I need to prepare an acceptance speech?"

"Well, something like that."

So we headed to Bermuda. Not a locale one often associates with sheer agony. Within moments of arriving at the Fairmont Hotel, we had our bags taken to our room, and we walked toward the pool where lunch was being served. Bud Ashley, who had arrived on Saturday with our comptroller, Sheila, was having a margarita. Bud insisted Sheila needed to go down early with him for the financial seminars. I really liked Sheila. She was very able. Rewarding her with this Bermuda trip was probably a good idea. But as I was looking at Bud, all I could think of was, *How many other agencies has he hustled on my dime?*

Bud, Sheila, Sid, and Kirin Reim joined Amy and me at our table. Orders were taken and Sid welcomed us. "Sam, I'm so glad you could make it. Sorry about the stone. I've heard it's a pain worse than delivering a baby." If you were following his thought balloon at that moment, here's what you would've read: "Why couldn't you have stayed in the hospital a while longer so that I could get all the glory?"

I was beginning to understand how Loren felt when he had decided to check out of Spiegel to get away from the jockeying and advertising bullshit and concentrate on just interactive. I always thought he was just trading bullshit. That day I began to realize he knew exactly what he was talking about. There is something to be said for keeping one's sanity. Was I reaching my threshold, as well? Was my intense pain signaling something bigger going on inside me?

The O'Toole Awards were a "who's who" in our industry and I had my eye out for Beinhauser. Had we gotten to Bermuda a day earlier, Amy and I had planned to attend his commercial seminar that would include his picks of the best TV spots from around the globe. But what I really wanted to do was have a couple of drinks with him. I had stored up questions I'd long wanted to ask. It had been twenty-five years since I'd worked with him, and ten years since he left DDB to start his own production company, making commercials and feature-length films. But drinks would have to wait.

At 10:30 the following morning, Ron Berger, the Chairman of the 4As, delivered a speech on the state of the advertising business. The presentation of the O'Toole Awards came next—the main event. It was exciting to have industry muckety-mucks from all over the world see our print work displayed and our most recent television reel showcased. Bud leaned over to me and whispered, "All the takeover sharks are out in force. Pull this one off and Spiegel's stock will go through the goddamn roof, my boy. I'll be able to sell tickets at the door."

I remarked, "No pressure here."

"Just do me this favor," he said as he pointed at Richardson Valk, who was looking over at us. "Richardson, Valk the Hawk, has been circling me like a damn fool. He wants to buy us and concluded it will be his first purchase of strength. I thought, over my mate's dead body. Don't let him trap you, you hear?"

"Well, hold on, Bud. If the price is right!"

"He's a bottom-feeder, Sam. That's all he knows. We don't want any parts of this creep."

The pain in my side subsided some as I stood as straight as I could. It was six days and counting. Sid Reim and his wife, Kirin, were seated several rows in front of us. Bud and Sheila took their seats in the same row. I had jotted down a few remarks on an index card the night before and tucked it into my inside pocket. There were two other finalists in our category, the midsize agency group that makes up the largest sector of the association's membership—DDB/Chicago, and J. Walter Thompson/San Francisco. They were two of the heaviest hitters in our industry.

I flashed Amy a look that said, "Wouldn't this be something!" She shot the same back at me. Would it have been so inappropriate for us to have held hands at this moment? It struck me that she was more business partner than wife. It hit me right then in Bermuda that our relationship had fallen fallow for far too long.

Then the big moment came. There were even honest-to-god kettle-drum rolls and horns to build further suspense. Ron Berger, doing his best Monty Hall, said, "And the 2005 O'Toole Award goes to...Spiegel Communications of Philadelphia, PA."

Someone behind me said, "An agency from Philadelphia. How 'bout that?"

We got some vigorous handclaps. I went to the podium, accepted the statue, took out my index card, referred to it for a moment, and started in. "Thank you, Ron." I set the statue down. "Many of you in this audience understand this moment doesn't come easily. There are so many reasons why, year after year, we can't quite realize our creative dreams. Not enough horsepower. Not enough fieldwork to find the jewels to inspiration. Not enough fight to the finish. Settling too soon. And of course, there's the economy we're always bitching about. Not to forget timid clients. We give out any one or all of these excuses on any given year to justify losing."

I pointed my finger toward Sid and continued. "This year under the leadership of Sidney L. Reim—please stand, Sid—we were able to submerge all the 'coulda, woulda, shouldas' and just plain come through with a win. There are one hundred or so people back in Philly who have helped bring this statue home. Talent and desire have been percolating over a lot of years. Spiegel Communications has never stopped pushing to get to this place and we won't rest now." I lifted my hand out, palm toward the ceiling and winked at Amy. "That includes my very special wife and business partner, Amy R. Spiegel, and people like Sheila Winter, our comptroller, and our COO, Bud Ashley, who are also in attendance today."

"On behalf of all of us at Spiegel, we'd like to thank the Academy. This is an achievement and honor we're most proud of."

I walked down the center aisle toward Sid and shook his hand and gave him the statue, a simple design in the shape of an A. I gave his wife a kiss. I waved to Sheila and Bud who were further down the row, and I walked back to where Amy was standing and gave her a hug and said, "We did it."

"Out of a puff of smoke."

As she made this pronouncement I smelled the scent of vanilla in the air. Beinhauser caught up with me and slung his arm around my neck as we mugged for the paparazzi. Then he snapped into my ear "Sam-I-Am, the way I figure things, not everything I taught you amounted to a hill of horseshit."

He leaned over to Amy and shook her hand with a hearty, "Congratulations, young lady, I think I'd keep the bastard." Then Beinhauser turned back toward me. "Your business partner's rather striking. I came for the big moment, to see my boy win. I knew it would be you. I'm heading to the small bar off the lobby. I want to buy you a drink. See you in a few?" It was as if God had paid me a visit. As the awards show wound down, I told Amy that Joseph was buying me a drink. She left and caught up poolside with the rest of our team. I joined Beinhauser at his table in the dark-paneled bar, the only place in the resort that felt like Manhattan.

Beinhauser smiled as a happy father might. He was drinking a white wine spritzer. I had just celebrated my fiftieth birthday, which meant Beinhauser had pushed past seventy. "A Dewar's and soda, please, with a twist."

"You'll have to do better than that, Sam. Dom Perignon for my winner."

"Well, thank you, doc-torrrr."

"Sounds like you haven't forgotten your past."

"Certainly not. Nor your fragrance."

"But now I'm such an old curmudgeon. I must smell like mothballs. How are you, Sam? That's some goddamn good work you've cobbled together."

"Thank you. I owe it all to you."

"Yes, my seedling. I'm such a towering tree. Have you seen any of the old gang?"

"I bumped into Sandra at the Effie Awards a couple years back and we cracked each other up recalling the little mercy you had for AV Alvin, everybody's favorite chipmunk."

"Poor Alvin. He would have been best off working for the telephone company. Clocking in at eight. Out by four. And climbing poles with metal spikes. I guess that job went the route of the secretary. Sad how times have changed so...some of those secretaries we had at DDB were so luscious, Sam-I-Am."

"Speaking of cute, I haven't left the subject of Sandra."

"Whoever can?"

"She's still quite a fox, Joseph. Did you ever?"

"Bonk her? No, sorry to disappoint here. Her husband, Harley, kept a close watch out. He is no wimpy Jew. He was trained in the IDF."

I said, "And packed, I'm supposing, more than a stellar creative reel."

"Oh yes." He looked at me and tilted his head. "Did I seduce Sandra? In my mind...a million, trillion times. She's on more bunched-up wads of Kleenex than I'm willing to admit; I must have filled garbage cans with her. Occasionally, for old time's sake, I still fire one off, if you can call it that, with her in my mind. But now I'm too old to get up out of my bed and flush the evidence down the toilet. So I just fling her behind my headboard. Sadly, it's been years since I've stopped up the septic tank." I laughed. In his best Sinatra voice, he sang, "And what about you? You know she liked the young grips, so tell me now?"

"Moi? Sandra could have been my Mrs. Robinson? Coo, coo, cachoo!"

His nice laugh followed. "So tell me, my friend, how are you getting along with advertising? Still a believer?"

"What do you think? And aren't I still the kid who gets to ask the questions?"

"Carry on; you're Queen for a Day. Do as you wish."

"I was so clueless when you decided to throw all the projectors to the floor in VW's conference room. I thought all that hard work had just gone up in smoke. And then Günter delivered you a bouquet two days later. Go figure!"

"Oh, so you remember my little hissy fit?"

I laughed.

Then Beinhauser said, "On this day, when your creative excellence has been so broadly recognized, you don't really want to know what happened at VW."

"It's twenty-five-plus years later, Joseph. I've earned the right to know."

"Things aren't always what they seem, Sam. Why don't we leave it at that? You know this game, or you wouldn't be sitting across from me sipping champagne."

"Joseph, my favorite high school teacher, Kevin Groth, told me, 'It's really not about the answers you give. It's much more about the questions you ask.'"

"Okay, then, how well did you know Günter?"

"I met him for the first time at the pitch."

"So the wise old professor told you to ask me all the questions. Well, here's another for you: Why did Dustin Hoffman in *Kramer vs. Kramer* want that job so badly at Norman, Craig & Kummel?"

"He did it for his kid."

"Final answer?"

"Final answer."

"What we won't do for our kids, Sam. What did Kramer say in the movie, just a few days before Christmas, when he was negotiating his pay?"

"This is a one-day offer."

"Right again, kiddo. You sure know your ad movies." He studied me for a moment as if there was something he was debating. "Sam, this story you're so eager to hear? It goes nowhere outside this bar. Deal?"

"Deal. Well, I've never told a soul what you made Sandra do before big pitches."

"You didn't have to. Everyone saw with their own two eyes."

"And, Joseph, you led me to believe all the good luck came to us because of your socks."

"Well, it did…because it took the socks to bring about what ultimately did the trick. Remember what I say: Things are never quite as they seem. Take it from the man who smells too much like mothballs now."

I smiled. "So tell me about Günter."

"Günter. Hmm…we had worked together for over ten years before Project Trio. I was his go-to guy whether I created the winning spots or not. It didn't much matter. Our families were both from Berlin. Had we lived on the other side of the pond, we'd have grown up together and gone to the same *Gymnasium*. Maybe that's why Bernbach wanted me so badly on this account. I was Bernbach's smart German goy. Günter and I understood each other."

"Go on."

"We'd often have a working lunch at the Four Seasons, his favorite restaurant. There were only two of us, but we'd be seated at a table for four. I always used the extra room to display our latest storyboards. Always small boards, packed into my black portfolio pie case, easel-backed, so no one could see from afar."

"Didn't you worry about being overheard?"

"Günter would warn me before lunch meetings, 'Joseph, let's not make a display of ourselves. Pretend you're presenting to your Reverend.' But it wasn't only business, you see. These lunches would go on for hours. We talked about our kids, politics, movies, books, theater, and always advertising strategy. Günter knew good work."

"So?"

"So a month before VW was going public on Project Trio, we were at the Four Seasons and Günter told me of their plans. He said they were going to further test these three cars out in Europe. Toyota, Datsun, and Honda were scaring the bejesus out of them in America. Of course, I understood all this; we were detecting shrinkage before VW saw it clearly in their own numbers, and the latest work in my pie case that day pushed price points and fuel efficiency. I was taking a board out when Günter said, 'My friend, we need to talk first.'"

"'My friend' and those five words certainly send chills up the spine, don't they?"

"So you've had this lunch before, Sam?"

"More times than I wish to recount."

"And here was his soliloquy to the best of my memory. He told me that the company loved me and DDB."

"Oh, brother."

Joseph raised his hand to stop me as he continued on as Günter, "But with Project Trio we're going to be a different car company. And my CEO and the other members of our executive committee have urged me..." we spoke in harmony, "to open this project to a review."

"Ah! The blame-it-on-the-CEO trick."

"You probably can fill in some of the rest of this dialogue."

I whistled instead.

"'Now, Joseph,' he said, 'we go way back and I'm on your side. So here's what we're going to do. I'm going to bring in only one other agency, McCann Ericson. You don't have to worry about a pile-on. No Wells Rich, Scali McCabe, or Ali Gargano.' I said, 'Bless your sweet, tender heart, Günter,' to which he replied, 'Yes, they won't be necessary. And McCann has been sworn to secrecy about pitching us.'"

I said, "Nothing in advertising ever gets out. Everything's bottled up and top-secret."

"'Let me cut to the chase, Joseph. It'll look like a fair fight, for your own good and mine. But it'll be nicely tucked away in your pocket. You need to go to Nick Germaine.' You remember him, Sam? He was the God in the sky of DDB at the time. 'Tell him about Project Trio and the rules of engagement. They're really quite simple.' He was very well rehearsed. 'You know my three lovely children. Among the three, Josephine starts college in September. Thomas follows her a year later, and sweet, little Kimberly, the apple of my eye, in some years following. Of course, there are private school tuitions in between.'"

I was riveted and reminded of what a wonderful storyteller Beinhauser was.

"'I'd like you to carry out a small favor for me during this highly taxing period over the next five years. My request coincides with my recently signed, five-year contract. At our Christmas lunch here next month, and for four subsequent December lunches, you'll arrive as usual with your portfolio case, storyboards, and the usual fare.'"

"Oh, so Günter found another way to use the pie bag. Bless his heart."

"Precisely. 'And tucked behind the boards, neatly bound or not so, makes no real difference, but neat and stacked flat is better, danke, will be $75,000 in one-hundred-dollar bills. Yes, and, Joseph, when your bank cashes the original check, they'll think it's employee Christmas bonus cash.' I was stunned. Günter had planned this out with such fine German precision, right down to the bank teller."

"And as far as this quiet review?" I prompted Beinhauser.

"Günter said, 'Don't for a moment read me wrong, Joseph. I'm going to ride you hard in front of every last teammate around that room. I have no worries that what you will bring to us is what we will need. You have your reputation to uphold. And here's a heads-up—use every passion play you can think of. Wasn't it you who told me it must be theater?'"

"So when you threw the projectors onto the floor, you knew you were going to win the best actor award for passion in a boardroom?"

"It was Günter's idea. Tell me I didn't deserve an Oscar!"

"In spades."

"Günter went on to say, 'We'll get ourselves straight before the presentation.' So I knew his every move and he knew mine, right down to the projector toss."

"No *Second City* that day."

"Not at all. It was a well-rehearsed sting of the finest order, right down to me going out for air on the patio. No, actually, as I recall, that creative ditty was my only improvisation. So Günter continued, 'This will be the last time we speak about such distasteful things as money upfront. Do we have ourselves an understanding?'"

"And you said?"

"Without hesitation...'Which college will Josephine be attending?' He told me, 'I'm so happy you asked. Josie was accepted to Wellesley, early decision.'"

"I said, 'I speak for DDB when I say, splendid news, Günter, we like supporting first choices. Now let me buy you a late-lunch nightcap. Waiter, that'll be two Manhattans, please.' After we clinked, Sam, I could barely choke mine down."

"Awfully sweet of you, Joseph, to toast your seedling. Before we break up this lovely and enlightening gathering, I have one other question."

"Shoot."

"Are you still in touch with Lance Winfrey?"

Joseph gave me one of those long pauses he was famous for. "No. Why do you ask?"

"He now works for me. What do you think of him?"

The master of the expressive pause didn't seem to be in control of this galled expression. "Sam, what's the name of your wise old teacher?"

"Kevin Groth."

"Right. The one who says it's not about the answers you give, but the questions you ask. I have one for you... Is it possible Lance Winfrey is Charles Ponzi reincarnated?"

CHAPTER 34

I was in the tiny bathroom on the plane flying back to Philadelphia. For nearly a week now I had fought pain and constipation and murmured out loud, "I wish so for a bowel movement, please God. And also while you're being charitable, Almighty, would you consider letting me pass my stone and resume my life?" I towered over the steel toilet, accustomed only to a steady stream of number ones, and even these seemed only to sputter out of me of late. But at that moment, my pee seemed interminable, when out of nowhere, my pee stopped to drop this shooting pebble—I had given birth to my stone.

All the days of intense punishment ended as soon as my shot was put into the airline can and was washed away by that blue toilet spray. Is it ever any other color? Then I put the seat down and relieved myself with a whopping number two. "Yes, there is a God!"

I returned to my seat, and I never felt so relieved in my fifty years of living. It was a two-thumbs-up movement. But my respite from misery was ever so brief, lasting only as long as it took the pilot to land the plane, for Amy and me to retrieve our luggage, and for us to head to the long-term parking lot.

Amy carried our proud statuette to the car. I rolled our bags, freed from the weight of my stone. *Hallelujah!* I turned on the ignition, which brought on radio station WHYY, Philadelphia's NPR news station. I smiled both inwardly and outwardly. My wife and I were aglow until we heard the lead story on *Marketplace*. "Star Spangled Air and Southwest Airlines have just reached an agreement to merge. Southwest's executive team will run the combined fleet." I thought we had beaten them in Philly, but they had just won the war.

In that instant we knew Spiegel had lost its biggest account. If I could have willed my stone back, with the necessary constipation, to stop this merger from happening, I'd have done it in a heartbeat. I looked at Amy. "God gave me about twenty-five minutes free of pain and then said, 'Now it's time to go back to jerking Sam Spiegel around again.' Do you think God's getting back at me for all the practical jokes I played as a kid?" This was a comment that normally would have amused Amy.

But she wasn't amused that night. "You mean God wants to put us both on a bed of nails right about now." The very cold fact was this: SSA had become a huge part of our business and it would be gone in ninety days. Spiegel's recent Bermuda victory seemed so incredibly short-lived and in the scheme of things, almost irrelevant. How could this be? We had done so much right. Couldn't we have had a little time to bask in our glory? "This morning you giveth. This afternoon you taketh away." I knew what I had to do.

Within the following week, I made an appointment with Spirit Airlines. Their president had been a senior executive at Star Spangled Air and had become my friend and confidant. I drove to New York to catch a Spirit flight to their home office in Fort Lauderdale so that, over lunch, I could make my pitch for their account. "Alex, with you as our client, we saved the tiger in Philadelphia. It was one of my greatest triumphs."

"Mine, too, Sam."

"And, Alex, you were my client with all the necessary balls to buy our gutsiest campaign. I'll never forget your vision and that's why I'm here with you. We're yours if you want us back. And as old buddies, I'm asking for that chance." My pitch was lean because I knew he under-

235

stood the story, accepted my offer to come visit, and would hire us if he could. Beinhauser would have been proud of his Sam-I-Am. I thought when delivering my sound bites, 'The Vanilla Wonder' couldn't have done it better himself.

Alex was all prepared, like a true champ. "We love you and we love Spiegel. Sam, you must realize that, in comparison, we're a boil on the tail of Star Spangled Dinosaur." We both laughed at Alex's mimicking of Southwest's symbol of our old, ailing airline a few years back, which had become a part of our lore. "But, Sam, we're an aggressive online marketer with, at present, a subpar team helping us in this capacity. We know what you can do for us there. If we can reach agreeable terms, we're back in your saddle in a heartbeat." I spared him my "yippee-hi-oh," which we both laughed about for years after I delivered that line on the call when we won Star Spangled Air back in late 2001.

Within ninety days, I not only delivered Spirit but also, at the same time, took the lead in reeling in Citizens, a large regional bank. This was the Sam I knew how to be, filling the well after loss, and normally, Amy, would have been right there with the champagne to celebrate such victories. Sometimes I might even have gotten lucky. But a lot was different this go-round. Amy and her Bud-induced transformation were affecting my psyche. This once soft woman of mine had hardened fast. Her usual praise for me was gone; all I felt was her wrath.

Although these two nice wins in quick succession perked up agency morale, with the loss of SSA, we were still about 40 percent in the hole. Given our position, the only thing left to do was to downsize. After all my years in the game, I had never developed enough calluses to take agency slaughter in stride. I hated it. I gave Amy and Lance Winfrey, her newfound comrade, the task of looking at all departments and subsidiaries and making recommendations on how best to shrink our workforce.

In the past, this was something I'd do quietly with our COO after getting counsel from department heads, but this time I knew I needed to delegate. I withheld just one firing for myself—it would remain my solo pleasure to send our current COO, Bud Ashley, packing. He knew we could no longer afford his services and perks and that my confidence in him had sunk to the sewers.

His nastiness and the wielding of his baseball bat around the great talent in my shop had grown outrageous, as had his outbursts at our clients. I had gotten word that, behind my back, Bud was trying to fleece the international portion of our online gaming account to take home with him to Sydney. I derailed his covert plan, but he wrangled a severance package out of me in exchange for a more comprehensive noncompete and confidentiality agreement.

When Bud, our former devil in residence, understood he wouldn't be a part of saving Spiegel, he decided to destroy us instead. And his way to speed up my faltering mental state was unleashing Sir Lance-a-Lot on Amy. Bud understood that she already had taken a shine to Lance, and I was becoming convinced that "shine" was an understatement.

When Bud returned to Australia, he stepped up his plans to destroy Spiegel. I knew it. Lance knew it. Amy knew it, and worse—she was part of it.

We all know what happens to divided empires, they go down.

Although Amy and I were still sharing the same house and working in the same building, my wife of nearly thirty years abandoned her husband in spirit, belief, and support. When a queen turns on her king, there's no way to stop the strife that gets unleashed, unless, of course, the king orders, "Off with her head." And the sad truth is, while I thought of doing that, I was in too deep a depression to muster the energy to do it.

What had I triggered when I sacked Bud? I had ignited his complete rage, as if his incomplete rage wasn't potent enough. Daily, via text messages and emails to Lance, I imagined Bud methodically and deviously working to bring Spiegel closer and closer to the edge of disaster. Being a former financial officer, he understood all the trigger points.

The cutbacks needed to be made in a hurry. Before I had a full handle on Bud's plot, I had chosen Amy to lead this charge because of her intimate understanding of our history and what got us this far. And what topped my support of her deeper involvement was that we were in this together. Who better to watch out for our interests than the mother of our children? Although there were signs that things between us had swelled to disrepair, I had no concept that my life partner could fully turn on me. I just wasn't prepared yet to accept that change.

Who should I have trusted instead? Loren, had he still been around. And regarding Lance, I thought he, in the pure, might bring some fresh thinking into our fold to accomplish this difficult downsizing task, because of his varied experiences at other agencies around the world. And I also figured Amy and Lance got along well. Maybe too well. These were confusing times for me, to say the least.

Lance and Amy laughed at each other's jokes, championed each other's points of view. Suddenly, I noticed Amy texting Lance all the time. She had never texted before. What had come over her? After each text there was always laughter from Amy. They had become flirting teenagers.

I was overhearing all of her gaiety from the bedroom, where I had been napping much more often than usual with my pal, Ruffy, by my side. He knew something was up. And coming from our upstairs office, I could hear Amy on the phone with Lance, tearing our relationship to tatters. We rarely laughed together any longer, which had always been a good part of our unswerving identity. And trust was dissipating along with laughter.

Our dinners with Audrey, now a sophomore in high school, had usually been sacred and lively, but this once satisfying family ritual turned sour and sedate. Actually, I'd call our nightly family gatherings as brittle as peanut brittle, without the sweetness. Amy and I would break into fights on just about every topic, at which point Audrey excused herself and went to her room. Who could blame her? She'd crank up her music as we grew louder and more vitriolic.

"Sam, you're throwing your business away by failing to see reality and taking action. We have no cushion at work or at home. Mr. Big-Biggest-Best, who do you think you are?"

"I think I need to become Al Capone about now; he seemed to know how to get his hands on money when he needed to." No laughter.

Not even a smile. "You used to put a high value on my vision and leadership skills, my darling."

"Well, no more. The day we heard the report about the merger, that fucking day when you had your head so up your ass, we should have slaughtered half our workforce."

"Which insultant had your ear today? And which one of them has run an ad agency for twenty-five years, and over time, fed about a thousand families? We've been here multiple times. Why is this night different from all others? You know the drill—it's a blend of cutting costs and bringing in new business. It's the nature of the beast."

"You mean the beast's mouth you shoved me into! I wanted to do something different with my life."

"Oh, my God, Amy! The life I forced you to have? It's been such a horrible ride." I began to stammer, "My heart...really...bleeds...for... poor...you." Then my voice returned to my own. "Spiegel is a successful brand. For starters, who in the fuck just landed Spirit Airlines and Citizens Bank back-to-back? Where was my head when I lassoed these two new ones? Still up my ass? There was a time you'd be the first in line to toast me. Maybe you'd even give me the pleasure of a screw. I haven't heard you utter one congratulatory peep."

"*Mazel tov*, Merlin. You're such a genius. And on screwing? Our screwing days are over."

"I beg your pardon...which decade were they 'on'?"

"I don't get the air you breathe, Sam," Amy said, ignoring that one. "We have no cushion. We can't make it without a cash infusion."

"Says who? Bud Ashley? I see his tracks all over you. He went into your office every fucking day and riled you up, and made that smug face of his as he told you, 'Darling, you're an owner! Act like one! Take over this place before everything goes to hell in a hand basket.'"

"Well, I am an owner!"

"Of course, you are. Bud knew he was out of here. You're in this right here beside me. Only you've been guzzling Bud's Kool-Aid while you take your rage out on me. He's turned this place into a goddamn cesspool and he's dragged us headfirst through piles of shit. But not before he succeeded in having you mow me down. So tell me, dear heart, who else has the ear of our queen? Could it be, Sir Lance-a-Lot?"

"Some days I wish you'd just drop dead already."

I really didn't have a comeback for that.

"You pushed me to Philadelphia, Sam. You pushed me into this god-damn business of yours. And I wanted a third child. Why couldn't you deliver?"

By then we were upstairs in our bedroom and Amy had launched the first feather pillow at my head.

"So this is now about not having a third child? So he or she could be running around this nurturing insane asylum you've created?"

"It's about everything related to you, Samuel Jacob Spiegel! Your fucking brand, your fucking ego, your fucking exaggerations. When in the hell does what I have to say count?"

"Honey, let me tell you, s'il vous plaît...for how many years have you had your way and crashed in some distant corner of our house? Has it ever occurred to you, that isn't what I signed up for?"

"Jesus, Sam! Let it go! We're talking goddamn survival here. Not romps in the sack. You know it. I know it. And besides, Lance has promised he'd use some of his trust fund money to buy into our com-pany, but not unless we change our stripes. He won't step up unless he's got a real say."

"Oh, here it comes. You want me to turn over twenty-five years of building my family business to your wonder boy, whom Beinhauser calls Charles Ponzi reincarnated and who you are so desperate to seduce, if you haven't already."

"That's ridiculous. Fuck you. I hate you." Another pillow flew by my head.

"Come on, baby, put one on the kisser. Throw your husband of twenty-seven years a fucking strike, already."

"Riders on the Storm" blasted from Audrey's room. What an ap-propriate pick. And as far as the flying pillows, Amy's approach toward a face-off could have been harsher—she could have started throwing plates...or cleavers.

Top of her lungs now: "You schmuck!"

240

"Do ya think? It's all around Spiegel that you and Lance's schmuck have something going."

"For Christ's sake, Sam! Lance is my friend."

"Your friend, my ass! Darling, wait until he starts lighting matches throughout the building. Perhaps you'll be roasting his pole in your behind when the fires start surfacing around you both. I hope all that heat will at least awaken your clit. That would be a first."

Amy took her wedding rings off and heaved them to the middle of the bed. "Take your grandmother's *tinnif* back, Samuel. I want a divorce."

"Well if we're throwing things in the ring, I certainly want in on the fun." I opened my night table drawer and pulled out the watch that Jack so happily handed over to me on our wedding day. "You can tell your father, when you next talk, that it stopped working altogether at eleven-ten about two decades ago. Maybe Sir Lance-a-Lot can find a way to start it ticking again."

So there we were. The perfect couple, the caring parents, the successful husband-and-wife business team, strewn out on opposite sides of the room with the tokens of our union caught between us like a pile of rubble on our king-size unmade bed, minus two of my favorite feather pillows.

CHAPTER 35

During the days of Amy's due-diligence in finding ways to downsize the company, she became determined to build up her own stock and that of her friend, Sir Lance-a-Lot. She got it into her head that she was in and I was out. In so doing, Amy undermined me daily. Her mission was to push down the wounded king and orchestrate the ascent of her knight.

Bud Ashley, from his world away, remained in touch. A self-made Osama bin Laden in Spiegel's story of destruction. He gave Lance basic pointers like, "Let's sink the fucker, already." Many managers within the company were jockeying for Amy and Lance's attention to keep their jobs. My wife of almost three decades was initiating a *coup d'état* right in front of me.

When the trust that forms between life partners is destroyed, what's left? For me, there was really nothing more profound than her betrayal. My devastation didn't come from the business challenges and the tough decisions that needed to be made to turn my company around. I'd been there, figured these things out many times before. Her betrayal was what cut me down. It made me wonder whether the bond between us had ever been there. With this realization, I got Amy to agree to a session with Dr. Arnold M. Mandel.

In the good doctor's office, I asked her, "Amy, don't you think, for the kids' sake, we should try to salvage what's left here before imploding like all the other disposable marriages of our generation?" Then, I brought up the question of unconditional love, thinking we'd certainly have some common ground there. Boy, did I have it wrong!

"Sam, I have no unconditional love for you. You're not blood. The only unconditional love I carry is where blood's concerned."

You want blood curdling? I had never experienced that kind of chill and disappointment in all my life.

"What if you adopted a third child, Amy? No blood there either. Where would you drop this kid off when you tired of him?"

The many blistering blows and retorts Amy launched at me could well have been made into a Family Tree commercial, this one on spousal verbal abuse: "Sam, you're an idiot...Sam, I fucking hate you...Sam, you threw your company away...Sam, you've brought us shame...Sam, I wish you'd drop dead." And the worst: "There's no unconditional love for you."

Her comments and this new revelation became the centerpiece of my fully developed depression. But on that "no unconditional love for you" note, the little strength that was still left in my being was expressed like this: "We're through, Amy. The kids will have to just handle it. I'm out of here."

Although I continued on with Mandel solo, I never invited Amy back for another session. We were over.

It was Amy's newfound power, and then her resolve, that blasted her forward on such hurricane winds of her making. I was blown under in my shark's cage where I remained captive for about nine months. Eventually I began to understand, like so many lessons that come from adversity, why the sneak attack has such velocity: When the missiles get launched, you don't see them coming until you've been leveled.

With our marriage over, Amy and I began to consider what to say to our kids. Meanwhile, Amy continued hand-in-hand with Lance as Spiegel sank deeper and deeper into the abyss. Crippled by loss and drowning in depression, I was powerless to stop it.

STEVEN C. EISNER

I looked for someone who could save me. I thought of how much I longed for Loren's presence. I knew in the end there was no one I trusted more. He was pure. He was honest. He understood me, and he'd get in there and fight to the finish. But when I went to him, he needed me to be *his* rock.

When my life was falling apart, he had worse news. "Sam, I'm dying." He'd just been diagnosed with Mantle's cell lymphoma, a rare and deadly cancer. I didn't have the heart to lay my shit on him. How could I tell him that the beautiful company we had built together was dying, too?

Then I thought about my dad. If only he were still alive, because like no one else, he had had a lot at stake in my business and we grew to really love, respect, and understand each other deeply in the winter of his life. And boy, could I have used him. Harry knew how to pilot out of adversity.

As for my brother, Mikey, my precarious situation created conflict for him. In one sense, I was the family's pride, joy, and *naches* provider. But more to the point, for twenty-five years I had been growing Spiegel to heights no one really expected to reach, bringing reward, money, and status to everyone connected, directly or indirectly. Mikey had some understanding of what drove me, as the person taking my father's efforts in business a whole lot further. What he saw was discernible and undeniable in our family and community, and although Mikey never much acknowledged this directly to me, he must have taken great pride in the success, because of the way it made him feel. He believed that as long as Spiegel stayed successful, when Mom died, I wouldn't need any inheritance and he'd get it all.

On the other hand, Mikey also seemed to take pleasure in watching the scaffolding of my life tumble. It was as if he'd been waiting a lifetime to see the Golden Boy fall. I pictured him on both sides of his own tug-of-war between my success and failure, still wearing, in my mind, that large yellow schoolboy slicker.

The loss of the business would directly impact his inheritance, upon which he'd been banking all these years. But if Spiegel went down on his brother's watch, what would it signal to his one surviving parent and to all who understood our family dynamic? "See, Mom (and Dad if you're still tuning in up there), Samuel's not all you cracked him up to be. He's the one who brought everything down. We're *Mechuleh*, Dad! Your most dreaded fears have come to fruition and the blood's on the hands of your Golden Boy!"

So where did Mikey go with his feelings? He stopped talking to me. I was out as a brother. *This time*, I thought, *for good.*

Which brings me to my mother. It was as if she was listening to Amy and Lance and Mikey, and in her eyes, her Golden Boy suddenly looked more like the Tin Man. It's mind-numbing how money can change people's opinion of you. Even one's own mother.

CHAPTER 36

So how exactly did it all go down in the final months? Sir Lance-a-Lot exhibited the behavior of a managerial pyromaniac. After the first round of layoffs in November of 2005, he dropped his first lit match on Spiegel. This was a month after all the fees from Star Spangled Air had dried up. Amy and Lance delivered a memorandum to me, signed by Amy, containing a list of flattering comments about my entrepreneurial skills that, in short order, transitioned to something unflattering.

In the memo I was likened to Philadelphia's Sidney Kimmel, an en-trepreneur with great vision who built the Jones Apparel Group, Evan Picone, 9 West, and a movie production company, while at the same time, being an active philanthropist fighting cancer on a large scale. Amy knew I held great respect for Kimmel and lauded his vision, but she also outlined his shortcomings by paraphrasing our newly appointed real estate agent who had been given a shot at subleasing some of our unused office space.

I could hear Lance whisper to Amy, as if she were taking it all in as dictation. "Liken Sam to Kimmel. That'll go down well." Then they'd laugh. "Then tell him as good as Kimmel is as a builder, when it came to streamlining overhead, he delegated." I could hear Bud Ashley encouraging Lance from thousands of miles away, "Give Sam some honey, before you sting him hard in the ass." As I read their note, I said aloud, "How about letting me try to save my own company?"

The memo continued, "Sidney Kimmel had the foresight to add new leadership to shore up his companies in those areas that weren't necessarily his strong suit." Then Amy stated, "Lance is ready to invest in Spiegel and to build us back." (Didn't she mean take us over?) "If, and only if, he can, along with me, take hold of the reins. And a firm promise from you, Sam, of no end-runs or courting of other investors without his or my prior knowledge and agreement."

In other words, if I wanted the money from Lance to keep the business afloat, they were talking about surgically removing me from everything I had built. I felt fully violated. My depression worsened. Gone was my "come out swinging" nature that earlier had renewed Spiegel when we counted on it most. Amy threatened that Lance's promise for an infusion would go away if he didn't become CEO and if I didn't accept a figurehead position as Chairman. Amy's memo hadn't ended there. There was a clincher, which she knew would make me step aside: "Our bankers and corporate lawyers are very much in favor of this transition from you to Lance, as he has assured both that he would soon give the word to transfer $1.5 million from his trust fund to Spiegel as necessary fortification."

Remember that all of this had been planned behind my back. My depression overtook my fight and I let go. Amy assumed Bud Ashley's former position as Chief Operating Officer, and Lance became our new President and CEO. With this single stroke, Amy broke my mind and my heart, and then my spirit.

My "wife" had become an expert on our future. Before her ascent, she could hardly balance a checkbook, but now she was hell-bent on saving our agency by doing just about everything except the work that was at the core of our business...bringing in new accounts. Through my years running Spiegel, and my contact with the many consultants, lawyers, lenders, and turn-around bandits, I had learned one thing: They all keep their eyes on the money. And Amy and her 'insultants' had their eyes on Lance. Yes, it appeared Sir Lance-a-Lot was Iago to my Othello, perceived now as the spigot from which the money might flow as I walked against the wind clutching my collar. Beaten.

And I was. My mind cycled to the place I learned Mike Wallace's had gone to, when CBS was wrapped up in a $120 million libel suit lodged by General Westmoreland. The response to my predicament was not unlike Wallace's, who was told, in the throes of his depression, that what he was feeling was weakness due to circumstances.

I heard my fair share of "Snap out of it, Sam." "You're a strong man, Sam." "You can get through this, my boy." I faced these feelings myself until every day I felt worse and unable to sleep or to concentrate on making simple decisions. I was unable to read after a few sentences or stay with the simplest television shows. Joyful chores, like making dinner and walking my dog, became nearly impossible. I called Arnold Mandel for more help, which led me, in addition to therapy sessions, to take stronger doses of Ambien and the addition of Lexapro. As I hit bottom, I understood the power and value of those tiny pills.

And as I started to feel some changes in my depression, a bit of a lift, I thought seriously about removing Lance and Amy from my company and taking back the reins. I spent several emergency sessions with Arnold contemplating this move, but concluded more radical change within Spiegel, considering my questionable mental state, was not the wisest call to make at that hour.

Mikey hosted the Christmas brunch that year at his home in White Plains. His house was actually half my mother's, since she'd paid off his mortgage. I wasn't really up to going, but my mother loved this Christmas tradition that my father imported from his childhood memories in Germany. "Go figure!" When I was refusing to go, Mom insisted it was the least I could do for her, and then it came, "I helped you with that loan a month back to save your company that seems to be going to the dogs and we can't celebrate Christmas together?" So Amy and I obliged her and spent Christmas with Mikey's family.

Mikey was always trying to find a way to connect to my mother, and thus recreated every main dish and side course that my father and mother prepared when we were young. The "O Tannenbaum," Mikey picked out and decorated was stout, the way our Harry used to like a tree. Harry would have said something like, "It's nice and…um…bushy." But this evergreen had something most in the past didn't: a vibrant pine smell. I could hear my dad saying, "You must have dragged this one in…um… from the Alps."

As I returned from the bathroom, after my first soaked undershirt attack of the day (for more than a month, my depression had led to breaking out in cold sweats, for which I was now always prepared with fresh undershirts), I walked back to Mikey's lunch spread and learned the source of that special Christmas tree fragrance. While everyone was starting in on Mikey's first course of waffles and bratwurst, I caught my brother sneaking off and spraying the living room where the tree stood with an aerosol can. My mother kept sniffing and saying to anyone who wished to listen, "Mikey Spiegel, we've never had such a sweet-smelling tree." Mom wasn't wrong. Mikey's smile was huge. Would he stop at nothing to dethrone the Golden Boy?

Later that evening, my mother, Amy, Audrey, Adam, Lila (Adam's fiancée), and I returned to the Drake Hotel for the last time. This had been our hotel of choice for our entire marriage. (The following year the hotel closed forever and that irony has not been lost on me.) After handing my car keys to a parking attendant, I brought up the rear. As my mother saw me entering the lobby through the revolving door, she said, "Samuel, I can hardly recognize you. You look about fifteen years older, hunched over so. You always stood straight and had such a confident gait. You don't look like the Sam I know. For a moment there I thought it was your father."

And she wasn't wrong. I wasn't the Sam she knew or *I* knew.

CHAPTER 37

In January, Amy and her henchman emailed the staff with some wonderful news. (Don't get excited—they weren't announcing a new sizable account, although that would have been good news to people who wanted to continue receiving paychecks. When it came to new accounts, Spiegel went to bat ten times during the eleven months Amy and Lance ruled and came away without a single win.) Instead of a nice victory, which everyone was so desperate for, what was the good word for the troops?

Spiegel was opening its doors to associates' dogs!

I just shook my head in disbelief…Spiegel was literally going to the dogs.

Lance and Amy had decided we were now accepting hounds in our house. Heaven forbid we allow a few new clients in instead. Employees' dogs were now invited to roam freely throughout our hallways. I congratulated Amy and Lance on their "Canine Doctrine." Lance got a hearty laugh over my turn of phrase. Amy remained stonefaced. I was starting to regain my sense of humor, but now I primarily just amused myself.

A few weeks after Sir Lance-a-Lot's first major decree, I had to confer with Amy, who was locked away with Lance, working through other important business decisions such as, perhaps, what bulk food to procure for our newly established kennel. Would it be Purina Dog Chow or Kibbles 'n Bits? Would all bonus checks hereafter be earmarked for chew toys?

For some reason, there was a certain time of day when the pooches started barking and growling. Perhaps we needed to hire a dog-walking service as well. Amy was always tied up in important meetings and running very much behind "sedual," but I finally confronted her during one of these bow-wow hootenannies.

She was in the war room, the room we always had used to stage our next pitch. She now used it to help craft Lance's "end of the world speeches to the troops." I barged into their obit writing session. "Do you know what the fuck is going on around here? No wonder we can't win a goddamn piece of new business. Our prospects can't possibly hear what we're saying over the barking." I continued, "There must be a full moon out or these buggers badly need their potty break." I was getting very cheeky with my Aussie expressions.

"Oh, fuck off, Sam." And wearing her bent pair of bifocals, Amy continued to mouth the speech she was writing or editing for Sir Lance-a-Lot. It was at this moment I knew for sure my once serious contender of an agency had come crashing down forever. The dynamics of its demise, orchestrated by Amy and Lance, seemed impossible to reverse. I was imprisoned on my own ship, shackled and watching it sink. The only thing that was left to do for me was to try to save myself.

A tenant in our office building called the police at the height of one of the barking marathons. When the officer entered our reception area, I had just slipped out of my cage for a trip to the bathroom. I figured this guy had seen it all. But I was wrong. His expression, as he looked around our offices, said it all, "What dope-smoking, cocaine-snorting nutcase idiot is running this place?" His mouth was unable to close. Canines of all sizes and breeds were everywhere. It was our very own *101 Dalmatians*, starring my very own Cruella De Vil.

Some of the dogs carried toys in their mouths. Others were on the prowl for snacks: uneaten sandwiches, potato chips, Reese's Pieces, and plastic wraps were left shredded everywhere. Trash cans were overturned. One morning when I was leaving my office and passing by Amy's, I saw a dachshund lift his leg by her door. When he proceeded to go into her office to make number two on her rug, I couldn't help but praise, "Good boy," as I passed. Had my pharmacist mistakenly given me a hallucinogen instead of filling my antidepressant prescription?

By March, before the end of the first quarter, Sir Lance-a-Lot addressed the forces with what was traditionally a very upbeat speech, the one Amy had been working on so diligently when I rudely interrupted her. Since we moved to our new building, I always gave it in the Boiler Room in order to review our accomplishments. I would show our best new work and outline our opportunities and challenges ahead. I called these get-togethers "town hall meetings," and at the close of each we served wine and cheese so that people would stay and mingle.

Instead of assembling everyone in the boiler room, he found the most cavernous, impersonal spot in the building, the large conference room, and then for an hour, he rambled on to our shrunken workforce about slow vendor payments, salary freezes, cutting accounts that weren't profitable, and making sure to chase only sure bets.

Of course we had won no new business on his watch, so his credibility was minimal. Standing there, Lance waved his hands as if he were consulting a crystal ball. Perhaps it was the one shining in his head. He hung on a long pause, his eyes transfixed on this imagined crystal circumference as if he had his mouth on pause. Then he resumed with more of his malarkey. "There will probably be another round of layoffs." He said it as though he was offering anyone gathered at his circus, "If you don't like my hotdogs or the direction I'm taking the company, resign right here and now."

Amy kept nodding her head in agreement. Occasionally, she mouthed his lines right along with him as if she had become Lance's teleprompter. But most of all, she had her game face on and supported all that he was saying. I could barely hold back from vomiting onto our dog-stained carpets.

My once beautiful agency stunk. Lance closed his speech by telling everyone that he had a big surprise awaiting our team. Some clown (or genius, depending on your point of view) screamed, "What, Lance? You finally got around to bonus checks?"

Sir Lance-a-Lot said, "Afraid not this year, but here's my consolation prize. Behind the reception desk is a brand-new pool table that will grace our agency, and in just a few moments, it will be open for play. I bought it with my own money. A gift to spread some cheer around here."

Just imagine the expressions on our clients' and vendors' faces when they visited us in the coming weeks, as our talent, with average billable hours of $135, were out in plain view around a pool table with Coronas in hand...and we were now slow to pay vendors. I later learned that Amy had authorized Spiegel to front the cash for this purchase and Lance would never pay us back.

Although Sir Lance-a-Lot was busy making changes all over my once pride and joy, he also got rid of our loyal receptionist of nine years because, as he told me after the fact, "She had too much attitude." Client feedback about her was always positive, but Lance felt compelled to give her the boot. The real reason, I heard weeks later, was he thought she looked "just a little too Jewish." He replaced her with two women he called our "concierge service." He found a pair of attractive twins on one of his ten daily latté runs to Whole Foods. Were Lance's days of addictive behavior really far in his past?

Lance went on to tell our staff, "Our concierge service will now offer refreshments to clients upon their arrival." He solicited the remaining employees for feedback on the beverages. No one could believe it. While he and Amy were talking about more layoffs, they were serving up fancy drinks at the front door.

In the past, I always made sure that, on any given day, sample work in our reception area and main corridors would feature ads prepared for the clients coming in for their meetings. Gail, the receptionist Lance fired, kept her calendar current and made sure the right samples were always showcased. That seemed to be a simple, reasonable enough concept that sent a message of reinforcement and pride in our work to our visiting clients, who paid the bills and kept us employed.

When Lance and Amy took charge, they decided this gesture was a waste of time. Lance had a better idea: to project a DVD loop with our best work from all our clients on a screen (actually, a broad curtain) in our lobby...excuse me, our concierge station. He sent our production manager on a two-week search for just the right screen to match his specifications. In his mind it couldn't be white. It had to be of burlap material, and tan to match the concierge twins' complexions. I guess he was giving new meaning to the phrase "the devil is in the details."

For two weeks as Lance worked out the kinks of his newest innovation, the new curtain blocked the entryway to our concierge area. To get into the agency one needed to grab hold of the side of the curtain, fold it back, and duck around it with one's belongings in tow. Coming into Spiegel was like entering a cheesy Indian restaurant. The difference was, at a cheesy Indian restaurant, you can easily pull the beaded curtain to one side; Lance's creation was a burlap blockade. Whatever he had intended to project with it was lost on everyone who attempted to squeeze through it.

Amy kept insisting that Lance's $1.5 million wire transfer was just a couple weeks away and was being worked through with our bankers. She often said things like, "Learn to be a whore like I am, Sam."

Who *was* this woman?

If the fall of my business wouldn't have directly affected my entire family and I hadn't been contending with a paralyzing depression, the best way to infuse money into this agency would have been to turn this fuck show into a sitcom and cash in.

In the midst of all this, one day I saw a huge metal desk, too big to fit into our elevator, being hoisted up our wide stairway by four of our key creatives. Each of these guys was straining to get this unwieldy weight into their boss's corner office, the biggest office in the entire building. It had once been a moderately sized conference room before Sir Lance-a-Lot made it his kingdom.

Off in my cage, at first I had mistaken the desk for a silver mid-size Mercedes. Of the four people doing the hauling, one was our top creative talent, who had been responsible for a significant amount of the award-winning work that only ten months earlier helped snag the O'Toole Award. Now Lance had turned Rex into his head moving man. That prized O'Toole statue still stood at the concierge station as a re-minder of what we once were. I wondered if Lance had readied a place for it on his new desk next to the pair of brass balls that were once mine.

Apparently Spiegel had paid $18,000 for this desk, but Amy prom-ised that Lance would reimburse us for it, along with the pool table. And the coup de grâce…Amy wanted to treat her new CEO to a surprise bonus gift for all the new business he hadn't brought in so far, for his lack of promised paybacks for company gifts, and for his the-check-is-in-the-mail promises.

This gift must have been sanctioned by one of Amy's latest financial advisers who worked from New York. She went through six such advis-ers in eight months. The gift Amy presented to Lance with such enthu-siasm was one of the 1,000 minted BMW M5s made that year, leased for Lance by Spiegel for a cool $1,995 per month.

At this point I advanced from detached bewilderment to serious consideration of how I might end my life. Pills seemed like the best bet.

CHAPTER 38

Before I downed my final Ambien cocktail, I called Ben Selborn. He was my oldest friend. I always saw him as a brother. He was my last hope if I was going to maneuver through the minefields. Ben was rarely prompt, but he met me at Villa di Roma right on time. "Go figure" snuck from my mouth and out to him as he was taking his seat across from me. "Go figure," I repeated again as I wished Loren, who had coined this agency phrase, were the person by my side at this moment, sipping away at his Molson.

"Thanks for joining me, Ben."

"I'm happy to be with you, Sam." But he wasn't, really. He had never seen me as anything short of being in charge of all parts of my life. At first my vulnerability frightened him. Perhaps he thought he was seeing another pillar in his life fall. He was just twenty-six when he experienced the early death of his father from Lou Gehrig's disease. "So what's really up, Sam?"

"Things are pretty shitty, Ben. Actually, believe it or not, much of my life is coming apart." That night at Villa di Roma, I felt anything but comforted by my old friend. I was feeling enveloped by him in ways I had never experienced before. I was reaching out for some of his warmth as

I revealed what was going on. Instead of empathy, I received something very different.

"Maybe you needed to change your grip sooner, Sam."

"I don't understand what you mean by that."

He raised his voice. "Maybe, Sam, you were doing too much on too big a scale." He seemed overtaken by his savage sense of power, his first chance for dominance over me, and he appeared to relish it. Amy must have gotten to him before I did. That seemed to have become a pattern—so much of what she did during those months had been carried out on the sly.

I said, "Ben, this is the moment of truth." And if there was ever a moment like this one in my life, and an opportunity for Ben to show his support for our long friendship, here it was.

"Sam, what are you asking of me? To blindly reach into my pocket and hand over piles of money I don't have in order to save your company? I don't know what is going on at your place. But I'm not made of gold."

I learned as the meal progressed that Ben had read my comment only in terms of lending me money, which was not my primary intent. Had Amy intentionally polluted my message by suggesting otherwise? I had let Ben know I no longer trusted Amy. But as I stared across the table, I wondered if I could trust Ben? How Kafkaesque was my life becoming? Could I trust anyone?

Ben, my childhood friend, could have been my ballast, helping me to ride out the emotionally turbulent seas. But then I understood, like an alarm going off, there had been Beth who had loved me and not him. At Germantown Friends, it was I who became President. He coat-tailed me into the VP slot. It was his lack of success at Spiegel that resulted in Loren becoming my partner, not him. I had kids. He couldn't. My father survived to an older age. His didn't. My business was national in scope. His remained local. I was beginning to see something I hadn't seen before in all our history together—as with Mikey, my troubles were making Ben feel better about his life. As much as I wish I hadn't, that night I saw his delight in my fall. So instead of really trying to save me, he just mimed the actions. And for the most part not well.

My *tsuris* had become Ben's tonic. Had he always felt this way? I began to remember the little digs and daggers. When I told him a decade earlier that we were hired to handle the Sears Craftsman Tools account, his immediate reaction was, "So what are you doing for them, a few brochures?" I told him, "No, actually a few network television spots." He had showed me a Mal Walinski face of disbelief. "Oh, Sam, you've got to be exaggerating."

My teetering had turned three of my supposed allies—my wife, my oldest friend, and my brother—more alien to me than aliens, and worse, allies of each other. My fall was making them feel more empowered and maybe even happier about their own lives. And what did this say about me? What kind of man was I if I provoked such feelings?

As Ben ended our dinner encounter, he said, "Let me see what I can do for you." What I heard was, "Don't expect much of anything."

CHAPTER 39

Very much alone, I was now on a serious mission to try to save myself, so I called Dr. Mandel for an emergency visit. Mandel had far too original a mind to wash gimmicks over my situation unless he believed in their healing power. "Please, Sam, carry a picture around with you of Audrey, Adam, and your mom. Keep them in your wallet for easy reference, wherever you go. I suppose you could put them on your phone, but this luddite shrink wouldn't begin to know how to, except to call Kreskin for help."

Since I wasn't allowed to call him Arnie, when I wanted to be extra-endearing during these sessions, I'd call him by his middle name and he always seemed touched. "Mordochai, if I may…allow me, please, to contemporize your material a smidgen?"

"By all means."

"Reference David Copperfield, instead. He's a little closer to this decade."

"Why, thank you, Sam. Consider it entered into my cumbersome computer. And do me a favor: Look at those photos at least once a week." I cried when he gave me this order. This was serious business, as I reached for more Kleenex to the left of the couch where Harry used to sit when we visited Mandel together. It was my spot now. I knew Arnold Mandel worried that I was going to jump, overdose, or drive off some bridge. And there were a few days he'd have been right to worry.

I had asked him, "How do you think I'd do it, Arnold?"

He looked at me with his wonderful Mike Wallace eyes and unfortunate Mr. Spock ears, the same brittle teeth and unaltered hairpiece he wore a decade and a half earlier. He touched the bottom of his chin with the hand that had been resting on his lap. Then his hand traveled a distance further as he stroked his entire chin. And then I saw what was coming. He was actually going to show me how he thought I'd take my life. I remember wondering at the time: Is he actually daring me to do this? Don't you get your license revoked for such a presumption? Or is it the opposite?

His hand moved back toward his lap as if he had a bowl of M&Ms resting on his thighs. Then his hand started in as he scooped up a fistful of them. At that moment he rather reminded me of an elephant, his arm and hand now more like a long trunk sweeping up some peanuts. When his trunk reached his mouth, he threw his head back. He did it sloppily, swallowing what he had scooped. Something like a couple dozen pills stuffed into his mouth with some falling back into his lap as if to say, "Let's get this over with, already." Then his head fell to his left shoulder and his eyes shut tightly. At that moment in the middle of my agony, I intently tuned into Arnold Mandel's image of me.

He showed me his best guess. It would be pills.

And when I fully took his message in, I knew I was better than that. I think he knew it, too. Everything at the moment in my life was so tough, and I could feel it all getting worse, but when he showed me what he thought I might do, I knew I didn't want that. I wanted to be around for my children. I wanted to be around for a redo. And I thought Arnold deserved some applause for his performance, maybe even, matzo balls, or a big hug.

Instead, I leaned over for more Kleenex.

Ever so slowly, during my sessions with the good doctor, I began to believe in myself again. Ideas started forming. There was suddenly a fluttering that had been dead for far too long. It was as if my internal elevator became unstuck. There were flashes of sunlight I could glimpse through darkness ever so quickly between floors. I was feeling a sense of purpose again. Was hope, perhaps, around the corner? I was realistic enough to know my elevator had a greater distance to fall, but I realized one day as I left Mandel's office, I was no longer free-falling. He helped me restore hope.

And Sam, there's one more snapshot you need to carry with you."

"Which one is that?"

"A picture of Harry. He, in the end was the greatest of all your admirers. He's the one who knew what you're made of. I saw that with my own two eyes. There is no one who adored you more. He got so much from you, Sam. Do you remember his endearing 'sonny boy' expression? But let's never forget what he gave you in return. In this room. Even with me present. Sam, it's deep in your makeup and embedded in your gene pool."

"What is?"

"What he gave you above all else, Sam. Harry's teachings to you about advertising were tangential at best. Matter of fact, as your witness, you taught him more on that subject. But it's what he really taught you, through and through that will survive."

"What's that, Arnold?"

"Survival, Sam. He prepared you well for it. He was the best teacher. Show him what you've learned. You thought all your achievements would start and stop with advertising. Life works in funny ways, my friend, and you got it wrong. Now, Sam, there is a higher calling in your life. It's survival."

I cried myself out through his back door, then down the hall to the elevator with my wad of Kleenexes sopping up first my eyes then bunched up wet in my hands.

With pressure from the president of our bank, Burt Summerville, clearly I was on my own to bring in the necessary cash infusion to save Spiegel. As I'd suspected all along, Lance's money, which Amy truly believed in, was all blarney.

While Ben Selborn was doing pretty much nothing to help me make progress, he also could not quite stay away. I understand now something more about the personal nature of aphrodisiacs. I was quite sure the picture of my failure was better than a Viagra cocktail for Ben. And I felt sure he was taking his new and improved self home for some good Beatrice loving. "Benjamin, what in God's name has gotten into you, and now me, honey? You're performing like a teenager all over again!" And why not keep showing up for some daily catnip? It was free and helping things a whole lot at home.

I was desperate, so I contacted another old friend, Lester Gordon, who we hired back in the days of my Party Circus syndicate. It's funny how you drift back to beginnings when in trouble. He followed up with me immediately and was initially quite responsive and intensely curious as to what was going on behind Spiegel's new burlap curtains.

Obviously, he had talked to Ben. In turn, Ben connected him with Amy, purportedly the sane and functioning Spiegel. Ben and Lester even got their chances to meet privately with Sir Lance-a-Lot. It was all too juicy for Lester not to want in on. Matter of fact, he wanted his front row seat.

When both Ben and Lester sprang into action, so to speak, to pantomime help, they did so with the bravado of Batman and Robin. Ben would say, "Holy Toledo, Robin!" And two more accountants would surface at my front door to peruse our books. Then Ben would rush off a cell phone with a quick, "Got to go. I'm very, very busy today, Samuel." Knocking wood continuously those days and restating, "Happily at least one business is booming!" And down the pole Ben would fly to fetch his Batmobile. Ben always seemed to be zooming in, but just as fast, zooming away from me.

As for Lester, when he first heard my shout for help, he seemed to want to come through. But his fascination and excitement for saving the day was dwarfed by his desire to watch the heavyweight fall. That was clearly the main attraction at my place. Then there was an old family friend I contacted, an elder statesman of sorts named Armand Ribacoff. I guess I was on the prowl for a father. I just found the wrong one.

We connected because, as it turned out, he wanted to become my mother's self-appointed advocate, since Elizabeth was a cosigner on our bank loan. He understood that my tumble might make her tumble, too, so Armand wanted in to protect my mom, while expressing mild interest in helping prop up the Spiegel fortress. His terms were, "As long as it won't cost me any money, I'm in, Sam."

He, like many others I approached, offered up venture capitalist acquaintances. That was the convenient move—giving me their favorite schmuck to try to wangle money out of. They knew it wouldn't work. But it made them feel like they were doing something.

And although my mind wasn't totally back, it was a whole, whole lot better. I was able to create a low risk investment plan with my assembled circle of "friends," Ben, Lester, and Armand. They halfheartedly backed a scheme concocted by Burt, the banker, to make up for Lance's default on his initial promise of $1.5, later lowered to $1 million. And my three amigos would each sign unsecured notes for the balance to pacify the bank's board of directors.

In every respect it was a charade and we all knew it. That's why my buds signed on. Because if the business did crumble, these men would walk away unscathed, and Burt knew this best of all. He just needed a deal. My three investors would join Lance, each getting an appreciable amount of shares in Spiegel, forming our new governance, in exchange for their so-called commitments. If it all looked like fool's gold, understand that's precisely what it was.

Part of Lester's so-called help was in opening doors to some venture capitalist community members, what he called "the backup plan for my old friend Sam, in case all else fails." Most of these men were second- and third-generation investors of their father's or grandfather's largess with money to burn. Not a lick of which they ever made on their own. I decided to meet with a few and present my case and see where it went, but I knew it was mostly for the entertainment value I'd provide.

One such acquaintance was Ari Gil, a highly successful transplant from South Africa, whose family made their money in diamonds. Ari would say to anyone who ever cared to listen, "I came to America for one reason only—to make more moola!" He was the father of one of Adam's old school pals from Germantown Friends. He owned many sports cars, actually thirty-three in all. When I arrived at his estate in the Brandywine Country, I got a quick tour of his property, which I had never seen in its entirety.

He had even built a temperature-controlled indoor carport so his cars could be kept warm or cool all year round, just like his horses in their stables. He was known as Philadelphia's Michael Milken but hadn't served time yet and told me "the cars and the horses are kept at sixty-eight degrees year round."

"Very comfortable and thoughtful of you, Ari," I said.

That day in the barn there were three foals. He told me, "Each one has quite a pedigree, Sam. And each will try to compete for the Triple Crown in a few years. This here is still horse country, *yuppers!*"

I asked Ari, "Could one of your horses use my Hermès wedding tie? My days of sentimentality for it, I'd say, are over." Waiting for the laugh that didn't come, I added, "But let me tell you, Gil, this tie brought me to a lot of winner's circles."

He looked at me as if my partial madness had mushroomed to straightjacket status, but I knew my sense of humor was barnstorming back to me. I thought, *You jackass! I'm funny.*

I'm sure Lester, with much *Sturm und Drang*, had recounted in detail where things were for his wounded friend, the one who was paying Ari a visit purely for fun and games. How could I ever repay my buddies for all their acts of kindness?

As we next walked through the barn to see every last stable, I looked for Ari's trophy wife. Do you really want to know why I made this visit over the other overtures? I wanted to see Lola. My libido was very much back. And as I understood it in the community, Lola (*Was that the name this buxom dame was born with? Or did she change it for Ari?*) spent most of her hours caring for the horses.

We walked into Ari's office, also a distance away from the main house, which according to Adam, at last count, housed twenty-two flat screens—three were in the family room so there would never be a bad seat for Super Bowl night. Ari's office was in a farmhouse, one of four remaining buildings spread out over his forty–acre estate called "What Goes Around, Comes Around." The other three houses were kept for staff and overnight guests. Ten minutes into our conversation, Ari looked me straight in the eye and said, "Let's cut to the chase here, Samuel. For me to get involved with you, I'd have to be one of the three Fs."

I took the bait, "What are the three Fs, Ari? New term for me."

"Family, friends, or fools, and for you, I'm afraid I don't qualify for any one of those roles."

I wondered what one said or did at a moment like this? Run to his barn. Cower in a corner and wait for a pat on the head and a carrot stick? Instead, I rose and extended my hand in thanks for his time.

If Spiegel Communications went bust, Amy, my mother, and I were the only taxpayers on the hook. It would also indirectly affect Mikey, who expected not only his share of my parents' savings, but mine, and the Mary Cassatt as the cherry on top. In particular for Amy and me, the loss of our business would cost us our house, our savings, and by all rights, the default on our loan might well do the same for my cosigning mom. Collectively, we lived comfortably but never extravagantly. Our combined net worth did not exceed the worth of our loans.

The loss of the business had the potential of wiping the three of us out. At a minimum, it had the capacity of hurting us a fair amount. And our particular bank president didn't carry out the kind of pious games I saw in many of his counterparts. He understood the entrepreneurial spirit and knew he made his money from it. He was smart, nowhere near the crusty stereotypes that harken back to the days of Scrooge. In fact, Burt looked like a handsome croupier, and we were his largest corporate gamblers.

The passion that I always worked so hard to instill and maintain in my company, by this point, sadly, was gone. I hoped it was only temporary, but Bud, Amy, and Sir Lance-a-Lot had effectively knocked the stuffing out of me. Although I knew my nice gig was over, I was beginning to ready myself for new rounds ahead. New vistas. I had my head back. I was no longer living for my wife. She had abandoned me. My childhood friend, Ben? He was getting hard on me. And my brother, Mikey? He just pulled out of my life altogether.

And so it went. Lance reduced his financial risk in buying stock in Spiegel to the level of $1 million, down from the original $1.5 million offer. My friendly trio of investors showed up just enough for the deal that wouldn't hurt them, to squeak by the bank's board on March 31, 2006, appropriately on the eve of April Fool's Day. And Spiegel? We didn't go into default.

Amy and I were still living together, but in different bedrooms, and on the evening the deal went through, in one of those many in-between moments of our lives at that time, she and I decided to go through the motions of celebrating the saving of the family farm over dinner at Villa di Roma. Whoopee! For the moment, there would be no dust bowl. However, instead of toasting victory, Amy continued clawing my back; but her talons didn't faze me at all.

It was there that my lion reared up for the first time in months, but with a sense of calm and resolve. It felt good to be me again. "These meds are good," I uttered aloud. All the machinations over the prior weeks had worked out in our favor, certainly in our bank's mind; I brought the parties together, and for what it was worth, sealed this crummy deal. Amy demeaned my efforts throughout the meal as that of a "lucky magician" and another in a series of "rabbit tricks." Which is when I said, "To catch a new beau, sweetheart, someone needs to write you some new material. The 'lucky magic tricks' material is so old." And I got a smile out of her.

That night, it seemed to me, Amy knew she had been duped, but I had moved on, and during the course of this celebration I told her as much.

I felt liberated! I started in on my toast to Amy that night, "So Lance's money is finally on its way, bravo, mate, to… [I raised my glass and I tried to be serious, no discernable tongue in cheek.] …as my dad would have said, to clinch this *farkakt* deal with the bank."

She smiled at me again and said, "I guess it was worth all the effort." For a moment there I saw my adoring wife, the one I remembered.

Once I'd eaten enough of my dinner, I quietly asked for the check and for my half-eaten veal chop to be wrapped to go.

Amy flashed an astonished expression and then asked, "So you're tired of our date?"

I thought for a moment she might have amnesia. Was she confusing us with old times? Which is when I started to sing, "You're the top. You're the coliseum."

At which point she didn't know what to say except, "Sam, what are you trying to say to me?" Before I stood up to get my coat, I calmly unfolded my feelings. There was no rancor or hysteria in my voice. I was well past those feelings, as I had been working hard to heal myself.

My words were resigned, almost tender. "Amy, we're over. We've gotten to a place in our lives that I'd never thought would be possible. We were Sam-and-Amy Spiegel. We were something special. And then one day, you disappeared. No, really, that's too kind. You turned on me. And I was in disbelief for a while because, for the life of me, I never saw it coming. What happened to us? You're not the person I proposed to. Or perhaps you are and it took me all this time to understand my mistake."

"Oh, Sam! If you could have just kept it all together a while longer, it would have been as if nothing had changed."

"So we could continue to live a lie, Amy? More than half of our lives are gone. I don't want to go through any more fake orgasms and all the pretending that goes with them. You've made me angrier, sadder, more disappointed, and humiliated than I would have ever thought possible. But here's what I know tonight—as bad as all this is, and boy it stinks to high heaven, I'm better for it. I will do everything in my power to eliminate pretenders like you from my life, and I will dedicate my efforts to what I can find that's real. We did make two wonderful kids, whom we love. And that was real. And for me that will remain revered."

"That we did, Sam. But what are you saying here? Is this really it?"

"Remember that spring night when we first arrived in New York with such excitement, and you surprised me with that blow job? Then seized up midway with one sneeze following another? I knew it was too good to be true." I smiled. "If only we had understood that was an omen."

Amy blushed and said nothing more.

I signed the check, picked up the Styrofoam container carrying my half-eaten veal chop, spinach, and pasta, and kissed my once compatriot, Amy, goodbye.

CHAPTER 40

On April Fool's Day, Amy and I arrived at Ohev Shalom Synagogue at 10:40, right before the Bar Mitzvah boy, Lester Gordon's son, Eli, opened to his Torah portion. Since Lester had come through for us with the bank loan, Amy and I felt obligated to attend the event together. So who do you think I immediately saw on the pulpit, as if there was a higher authority calling my plays now?

Beth Ehrenberg.

It turned out that she was a board member of the synagogue, and represented the officers that morning on the bima. My eyes locked onto her while I listened to Eli. She laughed and was joined by a chorus of laughter from other congregants, as Eli's yarmulke fell to the ground multiple times while he tried in earnest to read from the ancient scrolls. Then the rabbi lifted a bobby pin from his own head and clamped down Eli's skullcap. Everyone seemed grateful except me, because Beth's wonderful laughter subsided.

Amy had never met Beth and was oblivious to where my attention had focused. Lester and Beth grew up together but hadn't remained friends as adults. I suspected Beth wasn't invited to the celebrations that followed, but I knew one thing that morning: I had a little time between leaving the sanctuary and joining the private Kiddush when I could connect with Beth. If I had to knock bodies to the floor to get to her before she ducked out, that's what I'd do.

My heart started to pound as I thought about reengaging with her. Was it possible? Was this a pipe dream? What about her marriage? All I knew was that suddenly this is what made complete sense to me. My instincts were working again and my vision felt telescopic, and nothing, I mean nothing would get in my way. I had to find her, and find out if there was a chance for us after all these years.

The ceremony ended, and Beth made a short and witty speech as she presented Eli with his Kiddush Cup. I jumped to my feet as I saw her walk out the sanctuary doors. I was focused on my destination as I passed Lester and congratulated him on his son's performance. Then Lester wrapped his arm around me and said, "We got it done yesterday, Sam. You should feel a whole lot better." It was a tight but meaningless squeeze he had around my neck that I so wanted to be over with.

"Oh, Lester. I do." But I didn't. The only thing that counted at that moment was getting to Beth. I gave him a half-hug and a handshake and a clipped "Thank you, Lester." And off I went.

"Sam, glad I could be there for you."

His words echoed in the distance. Beth's eyes were as ravishing as I remembered. She was in the lobby talking to Greg, her old neighbor—another guy from our Party Circus days who housed the equipment when Beth and I were an item. She saw me and we hugged each other tightly. She said, "You're as cute as ever, Sam, but you're getting gray." The fact of the matter was I had remained pretty much a strawberry blonde, more blonde than when she knew me well. Must have been the glare in the room.

I told her, "Well, you're still a striking brunette, and we've got about thirty years to cover. How about we get started over a few drinks and then we'll see if we get caught up?" I knew I had gotten to the point fast but I was thrilled with my "caught up" double entendre. I think she was, too. She was standing with her jacket slung over her arm, and what can I say? I did precisely what I set out to do. I pounced and placed the order.

"I'd love to catch up with you, Sam, if you'll make me an offer I can't refuse." I thought she had her practiced line, too, which she seemed to almost punctuate by the way she pressed down behind her on the push bar of the door, using her curvy derriere. It was as if to say, "I've completed what I set out to do. And so have you. Now let's get on with it."

I could hear my mother, "You spend one morning in temple and think you found God."

I waited a week to call Beth. She wasn't home, and I left a message with her daughter, Rebecca. When ten days passed and there was no return call, I worried Beth hadn't gotten my message. Then I got busy tracking down her email address. Once I found it, I went to work on crafting just the right note and just the right subject line. Why had every detail become so important? Because Beth had become my newest and most important campaign of all. I was absorbed in getting every nuance right. This could be our second chance.

"We're still much younger than most turtles." That was the all-important subject line I chose. Then I hit "send" and our exchanges started flying. We were like kids again. Happiness sprung loose from my toes to my head. Glimmers of hope that my wardens had so sucked from me for far too long, welled up again.

See my thumb? See my thumb now resting on my nose? Now Amy and Lance, watch how I'm moving my fingers your way.

From: sjspiegel@Spiegel-Communications.com
Sent: Monday, May 01, 2006 3:09
To: bethehrenberg@aol.com
Subject: We're still much younger than most turtles.

Dear Beth,

Philadelphia isn't exactly Tokyo. Why haven't we bumped into each other more? Could it be the gods were forbidding us for fear of too much combustion? I enjoyed seeing you at Eli's Bar Mitzvah...so much that I couldn't take my eyes off you.

I hear you're basically running that synagogue when you're not pushing people around to clean up our waterways. What else are you up to? I gather you have at least one daughter.

So let's make good on our promise and catch up. Now as you're another year wiser, I wish you a happy birthday. (I don't forget much.) We have a small gap of years to cover, three decades or so. But we're only as old as we feel. And we're certainly younger than most turtles. Let's plan a time and place to meet soon. I'll buy the drinks. It will be so good to see you.

Cheers,

Sam

From: bethehrenberg@aol.com

Sent: Monday, May 01, 2006, 4:12

To: sjspiegel@Spiegel-Communications.com

Subject: We're still much younger than most turtles.

Hi Sam,

I would love to catch up. There is quite a bit to catch up on. Rebecca told me you called, so please don't shoot the messenger. And your phone number is in my number-one space of what's left on my to-do list, after beach shades but before digging up the boxwood.

How did you remember my birthday? I wonder how much else you do or don't remember? I remember things, too, but selectively. It's funny, we're back to writing each other. There were so many beautiful letters that came before, which I so cherish.

Ta,

Beth

From: sjspiegel@Spiegel-Communications.com
Sent: Tuesday, May 02, 2006, 10:09
To: bethehrenberg@aol.com
Subject: We're still much younger than most turtles.

To be caught between the beach shades and boxwoods is rather disheartening. But I do understand the importance of digging things up that are dead and gone…then starting anew. How do you look for the 6th, 14th, 15th? I'm caught in Dallas in between.
Sam

From: bethehrenberg@aol.com
Sent: Friday, May 05, 2006, 9:03
To: sjspiegel@Spiegel-Communications.com
Subject: We're still much younger than most turtles.

Hi,
I can't make the 6th work. The 14th or 15th is OK…idea for a place?
Beth

From: sjspiegel@Spiegel-Communications.com
Sent: Friday, May 05, 2006, 9:33
To: bethehrenberg@aol.com
Subject: We're still much younger than most turtles.

Hey Beth,
Here's my thought on the place. The 10 Arts Lounge at the Ritz on the 14th. We can pretend to be two long lost friends who meet up, of all places, at a bar in Philadelphia. We'll reminisce about our love letters.

By the way, this romantic kept all of them. They're in my files after Taxes but before the Toro mower instructions. For some reason, your letters were filed under Tonto. Maybe you can help me remember why you were called Tonto.
Sam

From: bethehrenberg@aol.com
Sent: Friday, May 05, 2006, 3:26
To: sjspiegel@Spiegel-Communications.com
Subject: We're still much younger than most turtles.

Sam,
Lester called me Tonto because I was your loyal friend. So why did
the Lone Ranger leave me? I think I am going to see if I have any of your
letters in the closet somewhere. I'm impressed you seem to know the ins
and outs of the Philadelphia bar scene. Your Philadelphia bar idea might
make for a great movie.

From: sjspiegel@Spiegel-Communications.com
Sent: Friday May 05, 2006, 4:53
To: betheherenberg@aol.com
Subject: We're still much younger than most turtles.

I think that movie's been shot. It's called Lost In Translation. But
I'd be honored to costar with you in the sequel if we can create a happier
ending.

From: bethehrenberg@aol.com
Sent: Friday May 05, 2006, 4:58
To: sjspiegel@Spiegel-Communications.com
Subject: We're still much younger than most turtles.

Would you, now?

From: sjspiegel@Spiegel-Communications.com
Sent: Friday May 05, 2006, 5:01
To: bethehrenberg@aol.com
Subject: We're still much younger than most turtles.

It would be the thrill of my life.

I felt Billy G. was the only person I could confide in about how things were going with Beth. Billy and I had started to meet weekly for dinner. One night we were heading to Gnocchi on South Street as I started in. "You know everything about my life except this."

"What's this?"

I said, "*This* is about Beth."

Billy G. giggled. "So those emails flying back and forth are finally taking you somewhere?"

"I think to the Ritz Carlton bar on Thursday night if I don't gut out."

"Fucking A. That's my Sam!" Then he paused as if reviewing more closely what I had just said. "If I don't gut out," Billy G groaned, "Are you fucking kidding me? Who ever gets this kind of second chance!"

"You sound emphatic."

"And you sound more cuckoo than I thought you were alone in your loony bin all these months under the Titanic. You know, Sam, there is only one person who ever stood up to you."

"Maybe that's why I offed her back when."

"I'm trying to be serious here, skipper. No one could go toe-to-toe with you, no holds barred, no stuttering, stammering, or stumbling around except for Beth. There's only been one Beth Ehrenberg for one Sam Spiegel. And you know what? You blew it. And here you are getting ready to blow it again. Not on my watch. I've got to go. Have the pizza yourself."

"Sit down, buster. This is what you've always thought about Beth?"

"Never wavered…as sure about Beth as I am about my nutcase of a mother. And lord knows you wouldn't want to be around her these days. When you and Beth were together on any topic, I could never predict whose plan would win, yours or Beth's. That happened with no one else. Some days it would be you. But on as many others, Beth would come out on top.

"I think you might be recalling our former sex life…"

"Maybe that, too. And numbskull…don't just book a table for some drinks, book a room! And make it a damn nice one."

CHAPTER 41

We planned to meet at the Ritz at 6:00. I got there ten minutes early to get a prime spot. A small crowd had gathered at the bar, and it primarily looked to be staying at the hotel, as I had figured. I chose a table away from the center of the room by a window facing east. I could see my office building blurred in the distance. Beth had established in an email that she drank vodka martinis and had asked if I still ordered Dewar's and soda with a twist.

It was happy hour and that I was, happy! I assembled a plate of appetizers that included shrimp, Brie, crackers, and oversized strawberries. As planned, the drinks were brought out before Beth arrived. There were red tulips on all the tables. I traded with the table next to us for a pair that had opened more. One final prep detail… I slipped into the restaurant to make a reservation for 7:30 just in case we stayed on for dinner, which I hoped we would. I asked the maître d' to put aside two soft shell crab entrees since there was usually a run on them in high season, and I remembered how much Beth loved soft shells.

After fifteen minutes, Beth turned the corner. She walked with great purpose and wore a striking red dress. Her shoulder-length hair seemed recently blown dry. It was thick and sexy and she smiled as she brushed past the bar. I stood up, leaned forward, and we kissed on the lips without hesitation. Hers were as soft and moist as I remembered. Mine were a bit rough, chapped, and very much out of practice. I spoke first, "Is this not like in the movies?"

"It's better, Sam. It's real."

It was magical. I had missed Beth and was so ready to be with her again. In an email I told her I'd share photographs of my family if she'd do the same. We both surfaced with pictures. Beth took a sip of her martini and plucked one of the olives off her skewer with a very sexy tooth tug.

"This is Rebecca, the one who you weren't sure passed on your message. But she did, Sam."

"So you were just playing hard to get?"

Beth continued as if I hadn't said that. "Rebecca's my middle child, and I think the most like me."

"Uh-oh."

"Uh-oh is right! And this is my eldest, Laura."

"The one who's at Harvard? So exactly how big is her brain?"

"We supersized it with fries when she was younger. She's my activist, and I wouldn't at all be surprised if she became a senator one day."

"Then, of course, she'll need a seasoned ad man. Perhaps an introduction's in order?"

"I'll take that under advisement. And this is little Abraham. He's a bundle to contend with but born to litigate. Your go-to guy when you get your ass in a sling."

"Thanks, and I'll take *that* under advisement."

"Now it's my turn to explore your litter."

"Well, this is my baby, Audrey, at her Bat Mitzvah. She's now two years further along, so sweet and full of joy. Here she is playing soccer. I love watching her on the field."

"She's beautiful, Sam."

"Thanks. And here's Adam, also at Audrey's Bat Mitzvah. He's a songwriter, has a band. He's a visual artist as well. Lives in Brooklyn with his fiancé, Lila, who is from Norway."

"Every Jewish boy's dream, but I guess he's living it. They certainly look like they're headed for the cover of *Spin*."

"And here's my third born, Ruffy-boy at his Bar Mitzvah."

We both laughed.

"And this is Amy."

"How adorably sweet to have thought to bring your wife along with you, Sam. Just when you were doing so well…waiter, could we please have the check?"

I slid the picture behind the pile. "Oops."

Beth took another swig of her cocktail, second olive lovingly snatched off her toothpick with her teeth.

"A mistake, Beth, like my marriage evidently turned out to be."

We began to talk about the years in between, and the choices we'd made.

"Why did you leave me, Sam?" Beth asked, suddenly in the most serious of tones. "We were so in love."

"I think it was you who left me, Beth."

"*Au contraire*, my dear."

I paused, "I think we made the mistake of our lives."

"Is that perhaps what brought us here tonight? To correct our actions?"

"Perhaps. You certainly never wandered far from my mind."

"Nor you from mine. Why wasn't it us, Sam?"

"You tell me."

"Because you left me for Amy."

"I was a kid. I thought we were too much alike and one day I'd come home and you'd strangle me."

"Nice image you've got of your old girlfriend. Waiter, second request for the check, please!"

"So why didn't you fight for me?"

"Why didn't you for me, Sam?"

"Because we were both too stubborn."

"So, Mr. Heartbreaker, rumor has it that you and the Mrs. are fighting like cats and dogs. What's going on? Where are things with you?"

"Here with you at the Ritz Carlton."

"You were always such a smartass."

"Beth, I'm not a hundred percent sure what all is going wrong. But I can tell you this, life's not feeling very good right about now. And I don't want to have come all this way to find just a hill of unhappiness as I move toward the sunset. In a paragraph, that's where I am. I'll spare you a lot of the gory details for another night on the town. Or maybe we'll just leave it at that and make the next night all about fun. How's it for you?"

"Well, I love my kids and my job and have a lot of flexibility as an environmental lawyer for the Feds. My staff calls me 'Chief' now, with my big promotion."

"How exciting. I'm wooing a Chief."

"We've been working a lot on issues surrounding the Chesapeake Bay of late."

"So eating the softshells I've set aside for tonight is a safe bet?"

"Safe enough. How sweet! That's my old thoughtful, Sam. I've had the joy of watching all three children grow. Mark has his good days and bad, but I'm not in love with him. Haven't been for a long time. I have this close relationship with Thad Tyler, with whom I compensate."

"Ballet, Thad?"

"Is there another? Who in their right mind names a child Thad?"

"I saw him with you at the gala, and not on the arm of Mr. Buff."

"Oh, right, Mark had his coronation as Hercules the night you were there. Listen, Thad's the person I drink with, go to the ballet…Walnut Street Theater. We have opera tickets together. When he joins us at the beach, it's Thad I drive down with, not Mark."

"So you've had all this neatly configured and tucked so nicely away."

"Since I couldn't have you, I had to have two. Don't we boomers write the book on how to push things around on the plate so no one really knows for sure what we've eaten?"

"I guess with only one…that puts me at a huge disadvantage."

"And I'm imagining that's why you're here tonight, because you've got the wicked witch and I'm the good one you've been seeking all along. And what do you say about that?"

"Where the hell have you been hiding?"

CHAPTER 42

Hiding seemed like a good option, but with a grimace, I greeted the new day. I had business to do and fast. It was four months after the meeting with the bankers, and Spiegel Communications was still waiting for Sir Lance-a-Lot's check to wash up on our shores. By this point even Amy gave up hope. It wouldn't have helped to remind her of her sage advice months earlier, "Sam, be a whore like me. It's just a matter of time until Lance will come through with the money. He's assured me."

In one of our quick hallway meetings, I said to Amy, "Tell me if I'm wrong, my dear, but don't whores get paid?"

Finally, Lance's charades were revealed for what they were: just a bunch of bull crap and lost time. Many months of confinement, depression for me, and a lost marriage. For what? To watch this flaming idiot fuck up my good company and then torch my wife. Based upon my prior track record of leading us to victory in new business, we would have averaged two good-sized new accounts by then. And that would have increased revenues and cash flow dramatically. Under Lance's leadership, we landed zilch.

How could I make up all this lost time? I hadn't explored other cash-infusion options because Amy was adamant that such explorations would drive Lance's deal away. And like an idiot, I listened to her. My circle of friends who had signed for the $500,000 portion of the loan plus interest in the company, contingent on Lance's $1 million deposit in the bank, happily fled. The power of a wife's betrayal in business is lethal—take my word for it.

My mind was back, all the way. But Spiegel was now struggling to make obligations. By using good cash management, we met payroll; current media and production vendor terms were scrupulously managed, and portions of our rent were being paid. I was back in, running what was left of my nuthouse. We had seen our way clear through July. But by this time, I ignored all of Amy and Lance's mandates to "Stay out of our way, Sam." I was back in, trying to save us via a merger with OCV, a New York–based bottom-feeder agency. Wonder of wonders, miracles of miracles!

The head of OCV, Richardson Valk, came from the financial sector of our business—he was the guy Bud had assiduously steered me away from at the 4As. Valk was often referred to as "Valk the Hawk," as he stalked the wounded. He cobbled together weakened ad agencies that temporarily helped him offset his own roster's losses and had acquired eight agencies in this fashion over a pair of decades. The last he swept into his fold was an agency out of Schenectady. I learned how quickly life can change. He operated his company as an S corporation so that all agency profits went to him.

With his profits stowed outside the company and with the help of a rather vibrant stock market, if his company needed a transfusion, he'd transfer some of the funds he had protected, and for pennies on the dollar take over a struggling shop, usually in an obscure market. Then he'd lay off most of the incoming employees, except for those most crucial to client relationships (that much of a fool he wasn't). Then he'd absorb most of the work and cover it with his own staff. This was Valk at Valk's best.

A merger between OCV and Spiegel, although a very demeaning idea for me, could become a game changer for Valk if he had the capacity to understand what I'd bring to his party. This would also require me to finesse my attributes with my shaky financial picture, which I'd

281

come to learn was a near-impossible thing to do. Additionally, what was absent for the first time in my career was the vision for Spiegel's future that I had cherished for so many years. I had charted a new course. Thank you, Amy. In all those lonely months, I had felt no real sense of foresight, which most assuredly had always been a key factor in my success. My immediate community reduced me, by this point in my fall, to "Sam's delusions of grandeur are over."

Our negotiations started when Valk, after touring Spiegel, but joined me for lunch at Villa di Roma—my comfort zone of times past, but which had become my villa of lost dreams. I kept going there because I didn't want to jinx all my other favorite restaurants. Valk and I used the same New York law firm and the same managing partner, Mitch Meltzer, who brokered our lunch. Over the years, Valk and I had met here and there, but had never gotten beyond the perfunctory "good to see you again" at industry functions or in the lobbies of companies we were both pitching.

The fact of the matter was he liked being known as "The Hawk," and with his gray slicked-back Vitalis-laden hair he looked every bit the part of a hawk caught in an oil slick. Everything about Valk—from his tie and matching pocket hankie—appeared to be Car Sales Manager of the Year, circa 1975. He wasn't creative, affable, or particularly nice, but other than that, we'd make fine partners.

I studied Valk as he ate his lunch of veal and ziti. I noticed that Valk had lovely manners. He neatly cut and then chewed his meat and pasta with his mouth closed. And all I could think was, *When do you start chasing me around the restaurant like your new bunny to gnaw on?* A merger with us had the potential to be something new and exciting for the Hawk, a real creative breakout move if only he'd find a way to hatch it right. But I knew he wouldn't. He couldn't. He was who he was.

If I could go back to building an ad agency, and if Valk could be comfortable just overseeing the company finances, we actually might have had something here. But as I learned over a lot of years in business, as much as we might wish to change the paradigm, most people are too stuck in their ways to even understand what a change could mean.

I had no delusions. I knew I was about to get fucked. The only real question was, how badly? I just needed to put a deal together that would protect my mother's assets and then I could restart my life, perhaps with Beth. Considerably humbled at that moment, I knew exactly what I was doing there, buying a little time to figure out just how horrible a deal it would be for us, but the clock was ticking down.

I knew I had to move fast before we'd blow. Before the Hawk left Villa di Roma, he leaned back, rubbed his two hands through his slippery hair, got up, and walked around a little bit. Then reached out to shake my hand. All I could feel when we clutched was his hair lotion, "Sam, my man, we'll figure something out here." What I thought of when we unlinked, were the words Harry said to me before he died, "Sam, I'm drowning here. Get me opium or put a pillow over my head." That about summed it up.

After lunch, guess who paid me a visit? Sir Lance-a-Lot. It was one of those halting, sheepish knocks to the door. He asked me, "Sir, could we talk somewhere, where the walls don't have ears?"

To which I said, "Is there anyone left to hear us?" There was only one place in our building where I felt safe in such situations and that was the Boiler Room—and that's where we headed. I had disdain for this man, but when groping for survival, it's wise to hear out every last gasp.

If Amy, Lance, and Bud hadn't done such a number on my head…I would have shoved this asshole so down the toilet, he'd have arrived ass first back in the Outback. It is very hard to understand the debilitating power of depression until you experience it firsthand.

Interestingly, I was prepared now for the worst to happen. I felt the same way I did with Amy on April Fool's Eve months earlier at Villa di Roma, the day we struck our so-called deal with the bank… the night I told Amy that we were through. And over the subsequent months, I had only looked forward. A quiet calm came over me as Lance and I took our seats. We wheeled our leather chairs to face each other, and before Lance started in with further blabber, I overrode him to say, "My, it's nice to be free from my shark's cage." He laughed uncomfortably.

At first, his face seemed contemplative. Then it traveled to wounded. Only to progress to somewhat sorry, which is when his expression transformed itself to one that looked an awful lot like a crazy man. There was some foam forming over his lips. And for a second or two there, I wondered, was it rabies that made him do all this? But he ended up mostly with the face of someone who had spent the afternoon smashing flutes of Waterford against my bricks. My pearls! I knew I was making him feel awfully uneasy…seeing him this close, this way. Just shifting around, we two, on our leather chairs with our wheels on pause.

Then, Lance hit me with his opening, "Sam…um…" He gave me a Harry "…um…" I hadn't heard spoken from anyone since Harry died. Same cadence. I wondered if it was intentional and Lance was playing more head games with me? Harry's stammering was legendary at Spiegel, imitated all the time by lots of associates. I'm certain he picked up on it.

And then his words followed: "When I first met you in this room, having already toured your plant, I was in awe of what you had achieved, Sam. You started in that it all didn't come easy and you recounted the time in the shrink's office when…um…Harry was close to selling the company out from under you. And how sad it made you feel because it would put the end to all your dreams. And who in the end appears to have obliterated your hopes, your dreams, your desires altogether? That would be me. I bet you feel an awful lot like killing me."

"It's crossed my mind on several occasions. And I appreciate your honesty, Lance. But let's get something straight here, I'm not your priest. This is the Boiler Room, not a confessional, and I'm Jewish. I don't do penance, friend. Most importantly, if I did, I wouldn't believe a word you'd be telling me. Sorry to disappoint, but take it to your own Father wherever he resides. We're well past this moment, young man." (I never used "young man" before with any other associate, mainly because I never felt old enough to use it. But at that moment with Lance it felt right.)

I continued. "If I can dump this agency into Valk's lap and save my mother's paltry savings and get on with my life, that'll suit me just fine. In certain ways, I owe you a debt of gratitude for helping me get on with it. You've shown me what Amy is made of. I think you did a fine job teasing out her opaque insides…who she really is. Not an easy feat. At the Met they'd stand up, clap, and say bravo. Quite clever of you, mister. If Valk doesn't come to pass, I'll just have to take what's coming. I think our meeting's over."

"There is a little more I'd like to say, sir, if you'll just allow me."

He always added in the deferential "sir" just to gall me and make me feel like I was eighty-five.

"Lance, you don't know when to quit, do you?"

"I guess you could say I might have to live with that problem for a long time coming."

I just stared.

He continued, "We both trained at the knee of Beinhauser, and we probably made advertising our life's career because of him. I think what intrigued us about Joseph was his passion and ability to tell stories so well. The way he could be so entirely riveting. The way his tales made you feel when he came to the end of them, that you couldn't leave because you wanted more. And if he was selling…oh, my goodness, we were buying. Sam, can we at least agree on this point?"

"Yeah, I think we both have a fair amount of admiration for this man. But I've learned a thing or two about him recently that might cut him down a notch or two."

"To where? Human?"

"I wouldn't go that far. Let's just say somewhere at Christ's level."

"You mean human."

"I guess that depends on who's making the observation"

"So where might you place me, sir?"

"That's the kind of lob over the plate, and I'm partial to the Yankees these days, that'll get you clobbered, buddy boy. You know, I'm back to swinging away. If you're asking me where I think you should go? I'd suggest Danvers State Hospital in Massachusetts. Now, if the call is fully mine, I'd rather see you at Topeka State Hospital in Kansas. I understand they still castrate there."

Lance laughed, "I had the feeling you'd drift back to my penance."

"Unless you're even more insane than I think you are, just living with yourself should be punishment enough. What more can I say?"

"Well, I can wrap this visit up quickly, and I dare say, nicely...um... and deal directly with what it was I came to see you about today. I'm sorry for all that went wrong on my watch."

"Your watch? You'll fly away free as bird. I'll be the one left drowning in poop."

"You're probably right...I learned something here at Spiegel, though, about one of Beinhauser's finest protégées, Sam Jacob Spiegel. Beinhauser might have the lock on the God of Advertising award, and for a long while there, I thought he was also the finest storyteller alive, that is until I met the most memorable raconteur. I had to come all the way to Philadelphia to meet him. I stare at him as I speak."

"Aren't you kind."

"Everyone who knows you well, Sam, knows that advertising was just your warm-up act. What you got when you hired me, little did you know, was the advertising story of a lifetime, maybe of the millennium. Now go and write it like no one else can. Don't hurry it along. Give it a little perspective, of course. In time, I assure you, it will be a page-turner. Should be a best seller if you handle it right."

I said, "That no one will ever believe."

He stood up. "That's why you'll call it a novel. And one day you'll thank me for blowing up your joint!"

Sir Lance-a-Lot saluted me—much the way Beinhauser did many moons ago, as he left in the same black shirt he wore when he first came to Spiegel, and it still looked like it belonged on a woman. He was on a plane to Sydney the next day.

CHAPTER 43

Beth and I spent more and more time together, and she had become my greatest advocate, confidante, and my rock. Her marriage had been in the grave long before I reentered the picture, so I wouldn't get called out for releasing hand grenades and blowing up something that was already in the dumpster. And with a clear conscience, Beth was hopefully my new start, as was I hers. I was believing there would now be a new beginning for both of us, and this time I'd get it right.

Billy G. was in there swinging on my behalf. My children were rooting for me, but it was bittersweet, as they were trying not to take sides in the dissolution of their parents' marriage. Beth represented life, and if I wanted to survive, which was still a question on darker days, I feared the impact of what was to come…the big "pop goes the weasel." As Mandel had taught me, I had to focus on the basics.

He kept calling such moves, "Baby steps. Sam, think of Harry getting out of Germany to board a train to meet his pen pal in England. Then go no further in your mind. Just stay focused on getting out." He was a good man, that Mordechai.

By this point I knew approximately how the OCV deal was going to go down. There were some questionable ethical sirens going off in my head related to the coziness between Valk and Mitch, our mutual lawyer. But time was running out and I wasn't going to find a better deal. So I decided to take my shot.

And if it was all about to come tumbling down…I figured I was as ready as I'd ever be for the scorched earth that would surround me. But first I had to get through Amy's fiftieth birthday celebration in Vermont. I wanted to do it for our kids before I moved out of the family house for good, and this was, I suppose, sweet, sweet Harry…an *Auf Wiedersehen* of another sort.

Why were we going through these motions? What would Amy's fiftieth birthday vacation be like as we headed toward divorce and the collapse of our sixty-seven-year-old company? Perhaps it was my last goodbye to my family unit as it once was. This trip wasn't easy to imagine or plan. For starters, where would Amy and I sleep? We had been living in separate bedrooms for the better part of ten months by then. How would we pull this off, in particular the birthday night?

Amy only wanted to stay for the first week, so she could return to be with her siblings who were coming to our house in Philadelphia for some more 50th birthday bonding without me. This was all planned. Audrey would return with Amy for varsity soccer practice. To be honest, I think Amy was in deep mourning for the loss of her Sir Lance-a-Lot. By this point, Amy knew as well as I did that our business was either going to the Hawk or the dogs. Pick your legacy, sweetheart!

For the second week, my angels were flying up. I had asked both Beth and Billy G. to join me in Vermont. Billy had been a great friend and supported me throughout all my recent troubles, and I knew he would welcome a break from Philadelphia—about eight months earlier Billy G. had closed his small advertising firm and was having difficulty coming back from his loss. Beth and I were getting very close, but our times together for the months leading up to this vacation were in short snippets and we both wanted to experience some sustained days together. With Billy in our midst, the getaway was positioned as a *Big Chill* moment. Not a *Roman Holiday*.

As Beth's plans firmed, she seemed to have started a war at home. By this time, Mr. Buff and her three kids knew I was Beth's teenage sweetheart and surmised that this trip was perhaps, an affair and not exactly a reunion. This getaway would have the potential of changing all of our lives forever.

Audrey understood the unhappiness in her own parents' marriage and recognized the time I'd have with Billy and Beth might turn out to be something quite uplifting for me. I knew she was watching my back, like a kid penguin who might worry that her dad, one day, may just not come home from hunting. By this point in August, Audrey had gotten to know Beth rather well, and as difficult as this may have been for her, she took to her dad's new friend in stride.

Audrey had the good sense to bring one of her friends, Vickie Blue, so Amy, Audrey, Vickie, and I drove to Vermont from Philadelphia. During the trip, we listened to three *Seinfeld in Concert* CDs and then Jackie Mason's one-man Broadway show, *The World According to Me!* It got us through a peaceful eight hours of what ended up being a nine-hour trip to Moose Mountain.

We all laughed, and with bathroom breaks, there was no time left for anyone in the car to argue. By anyone, I mean Amy and me. When I wasn't driving, I stared at the passing scenery, so green and bucolic, and reflected on how this trip marked the end of an era. I felt confident that a new beginning was being ushered in. I was glad Audrey had someone with her, to go off with in case things went south with Amy and me, though we both vowed to be civil with each other during this last hurrah as an "intact" family.

I really liked Audrey's friend, Vickie Blue, despite the fact that it was her parents who kept pushing that rosé at the Chameleon Grill on the eve of my kidney stone attack, which was the first day, I had figured, of the tortured pink period of my life. When I would occasionally think about the start of everything going bad, I'd also had in mind Billy G.'s lucky wedding tie. Did it have to fray? Had it stayed intact, would I have been spared all these troubles?

Adam and Lila arrived at the start of our first week, driving his Volvo up to the mountains. As the songwriter and lead guitarist of his group, Adam worked with Lila, who was the drummer in his band. And what do they say about history? It certainly is capable of repeating itself. They usually traveled with a small trailer in tow behind their car to carry Lila's drums, their amps, speakers, and guitars. But on this getaway to Vermont, the Volvo came unhitched with only two acoustic guitars, a stack of drum pads, and portable CD cases strewn across the backseat.

In the days in Vermont leading up to Amy's actual birthday celebration, we kept very active. We took long biking and hiking trips in the Green Mountains. We went tubing for hours down the White River. We played volleyball on the grounds of Silver Lake in Barnard. Amy would watch us play. Most days we'd swim and while the sun was setting, we'd canoe and fish until we were ready to eat.

For Amy's birthday, Adam and I set the table on the high hanging long porch of our Moose Mountain rental house, overlooking lush scenery. We grilled lobster and a medley of farm fresh vegetables and sweet white corn picked directly from the stalks that morning. We drank champagne, and with fresh blueberries, I made my famous Betty with a dollop of vanilla Ben & Jerry's on top.

We spent the birthday dinner reminiscing, staving off the cold truth—that in less than two year's time Amy and I would be officially divorced. We knew it was more than likely that we would lose our business and our entire life savings, while the house Adam and Audrey grew up in and loved would be sold at auction with the proceeds going directly to our bankers. Champagne and lobsters would need to be savored now, because I'd be forced to liquidate my entire 401(k) fund to pay lawyers to help deal with the shutting down of the business and to prepare for our bankruptcy proceedings.

Ironically, November 10th, the anniversary of Kristallnacht, would be the day our family business, Spiegel Communications, would close forever. All those wonderful memories of building a hotshot company while connecting at home would haunt me for the rest of my life. Like a film director in his viewing room when the celluloid just rips, I'd be left alone with the flickering light of the projector. Everything that once ran so smoothly over the sprocket holes would come to an abrupt halt. No more familiar images. No more vivid colors of my past illuminating the screen. Just emptiness, and need for a transition.

That night in Vermont we didn't talk about the future, but we quietly recognized that Amy Spiegel's birthday dinner would be the last time our family, as we knew it, would assemble in this manner. To this end and to the good times that were, we were happy to raise a glass. After dinner, Adam and I insisted on clearing the table, to complete the meal we had jointly taken on. When we were rinsing the purple stains from the dessert bowls, Adam leaned in to me and asked, "Do you mind if Lila and I stay another week?"

I said, "You and I should take a walk and talk."

It was about ten o'clock when the two of us ventured out with our flashlights beaming into the darkness. First, we shared a joint that Adam had freshly rolled as we descended the mountain toward the river where we had been tubing the day before. I said, "Adam, this has really been a nice week. It was wonderful of you and Lila to have come. I know you're in the middle of recording your album."

"Are you kidding? For us this is like coming to heaven and maybe we'll get lucky and stay another week. That is, if it doesn't detract from your adventure with your chums."

"We'd love you and Lila to be a part of it, but there's a matter that might make you feel uncomfortable. In addition to Billy G., my old friend Beth will be joining us."

"Oh, so you're saying I'll get a chance to meet the other woman?"

"How weird will that be?"

"How weird will it be for you, Dad?"

"I'm not sure. I've never been here before."

"Nor have I. I've told you I'm all for your happiness and it looks like you and Mom aren't making it anymore. I want you to feel good again, Dad. We'll be fine."

We reached the bottom of the mountain, and Adam put his flash-light down and shined it toward the river in front of both of us. He said, "Why don't you hold your thought for a moment?"

He took off his shirt, jeans, and underwear and looked at me. "Now, come on, I'm not facing the leeches myself!"

I mimicked his actions like a dutiful kid and that's when we both ran hard into the water, making sounds like warriors. Before the river got up to our groins, we dove in, surfaced, and shook the water out of our bushy manes. Adam brushed a handful more of the river toward my face. I splashed some back at him. Side by side, we silently treaded water and swam together under an almost full moon, bearing an indentation that suggested that at any minute, with a little more pressure applied, it might pop!

CHAPTER 44

The next day I dropped Amy, Audrey, and Vickie at the Albany Airport to catch a 7:00 p.m. flight back to Philadelphia. Right after their send-off, I would be picking up Beth and Billy G. on an incoming Southwest flight. I wound my way with the outgoing group toward the airport without Seinfeld in the CD player. Instead, we were all quiet, in our own thoughts.

I reflected on the previous day when the six of us were tubing down the river. The girls chatted up a storm. Adam and Lila had tied their floats together as they took in the beauty at every turn. And there we were, Amy and me, like a lost unmatched pair of shapes quite literally on opposite sides of the river.

When Amy's tube got stuck on some rocks, instead of helping her get unhinged, I just watched her struggle with her feet and hands. She seemed oblivious to the fact that we were actually sharing the same river. Simultaneously, the only place my mind kept going to was a picture of Beth with me floating slowly but inexorably with the current, reviewing our lives and perhaps making plans for our future. I was aching for it.

The Albany airport is small with one onsite parking lot. I helped Amy, Audrey, and Vickie with their larger suitcases and they pulled their wheeled bags themselves. When we got inside the terminal, there was a pair of escalators, one leading up to security and onto the gates, the other leading down to the baggage area, which is where we entered from the parking lot. I walked the three ladies to the escalator. Amy took one of the strapped bags from my shoulder, and Audrey took the one that most resembled a tote. I kissed the three goodbye…Amy and Vickie once on the cheek, and Audrey once on each cheek.

As sweet Audrey stepped onto the escalator and turned to look back at me, our eyes welled up. I blew my sweetheart a kiss. She blew one back at me. We both knew from this point on, things would be very different. I remember the exact feeling I sent up to her as I backed away from the escalator. "Be brave, my dear, dear, brave heart. Be brave."

Shortly thereafter, as Amy, Vickie, and Audrey moved through se-curity, Beth and Billy G. descended. It was an amazing moment: this departure of Amy and Audrey parallel to the arrival of Beth and Billy… my old life going up the escalator as my new one was coming down. I instinctively shifted where I stood, waving from the far right to moving to the far left, now completely out of view of the departing three and into sight of the arriving two. I moved closer to the escalator. Beth and I embraced tightly and then kissed. Billy G. hugged me, too, gave me a bop on my behind, and leaned into my ear and told me, "I smuggled in a trio of Cuban stogies," as if he were now a member of a cartel.

I said in a Bogie-sounding way, "That'll make us happy."

Billy G. said, "Beth told me that Adam and Lila are going to stay with our motley crew. So Adam can have one with the boys. I'm sure I'll get better stuff from him in return, hee-hee."

I gave a big wink toward Beth, whose eyes were sparkling.

We drove out on all the roads I had come in on. Beth was comfort-ably situated in the front seat. Billy G. rested in the back, his legs up on the leather. Beth's hand was in my lap as I reached down to hold it. It felt so good.

"Daddy, I'm hungry," Billy G. said.

I told him, "I have some barbeque chicken that I marinated all day yesterday and put on the grill last night after the lobsters came off."

Beth chimed in, "I like a man who's so well-prepared." Was she talking about the bird on the grill or the one in my lap? I figured it was both.

When we arrived at the house among oohs and aahs, Billy G. asked, "So Adam's going to have his dope already rolled for me and the Coronas have been chilling in the fridge, right?"

"He's always ready for you, Billy." We grabbed the bags from the trunk and walked down the path to the house. Lila and Adam had already started in on the beer. Several empties stood lined up on the dining room table. I knew there would be enough empties to fill a bowling alley before sunup, maybe two alleys' worth.

Beth and I had a glass of Chardonnay. Billy G. immediately followed Adam to the treat table as he opened his first beer and took a piece of lime that he carefully stuck into the neck of his bottle. Adam and Billy G. had always gotten along well and loved each other. Adam was actualizing what Billy G. wished he had done over his career—making music for pay.

Of my friends, there was no one who had a greater understanding of blues, jazz, or rock than Billy, and he had great talent on the drums. Adam and Billy embraced as if they had resurfaced as brothers. Billy was also crazy about Lila and gave her a big hug. Adam then took a long look at my other woman and said, "So you're Beth. I've heard a lot about you. I'm Adam. This is Lila." Adam and Beth shook hands.

Beth said, "Pleased to meet you both."

Lila came up to Beth and hugged her and said, "Welcome to Vermont." To me this felt like a functional and animated family gathering. I smiled and slipped into the kitchen to start heating the leftover Blueberry Betty.

I moved the party out to the porch where we all turned our chairs to face the mountains. The moon seemed to have grown to a full-blown glow, but tonight it didn't look like it was about to pop. There was a chill in the air and we had our sweaters on as we swigged beer and wine, then dug into the chicken. Beth and Adam started to check each other out. They were both skilled in provocation, and Adam started in.

"So, Beth, I hear you're an environmental lawyer, the kind of lawyer who is trying to save the planet?"

"I suppose so, at least a small part of it." Beth tore her wing apart and moved in on the drumstick.

"Do you win your cases or mainly settle them all?" Adam asked as he pointed his Corona at her as if it had become his forefinger. Adam must have been thinking about Beth for a while, and his clever questions might just have entered the hostile zone.

"I guess that depends on the case, Adam. I would say if your implication is that a settlement is a cop-out in trying to save the planet, then I'd tell you, in many instances, you'd be wrong."

"How's that, Your Honor?" His lime left the neck and took a belly flop into the beer, and immediately started to tread water.

"Sometimes it's better to save the bay with a warning shot over the bow, instead of just racking up fines and wins. After paying the fines, sometimes abusers go back to abusing. Our job is to change the offenders' habits for good. That's when you change things up, Adam." If this was their first round, I'd say Beth took it handily.

Beth initiated the second round. "So, Adam, I understand that you're both a musical artist and a visual artist. How do you balance the two?"

Good question. I was quite interested to hear the answer. The skimpiest part of Beth's wing got placed in her napkin like a smashed bug.

"Oh, I can see you've been hanging around my dad a fair bit because I think that's his tune, too." I detected some defensiveness in Adam's response as he sent a dagger my way. "Dad often talks on about me balancing the two. I don't really juggle much these days, because you can only excel at one art at a time."

Was this the end of their face-off or would there be more? If it was the end, I'd call it a draw. Clear question—clear answer. Only Beth wasn't finished. She continued, "I know an opera singer...[*Oh boy*, I thought, *here it comes!*] ...who is also a rock star." Oh my God! I called this one too soon. Adam's eyes opened up wide as Beth had something further to deliver. "And he manages both art forms very well. A year or so ago, he sang the Met and then Madison Square Garden, both in the same week."

Adam nodded his head up and down a few times as if Beth were making perfect sense. He retorted, "I think I know this guy that you're talking about and I think we'll agree, he's an able musician." He threw in a nice pause, the way Beinhauser might have, or Loren for that matter, by taking a big swig of his Corona to punctuate his point.

Beth nodded as if to say, "We're copasetic here. I'm connecting, Sam." She seemed to think she was scoring, but I knew she was so wrong.

Adam went on to say, "We've got to be talking about the same man."

Another quick pause and acknowledgment from Beth, that they found a like wavelength. "Dino, you know, the incomparable and versatile Dean Martin? He does have that incredible range you speak of."

When Billy G. heard this, his laugh was that of sounding an alarm to the mountaintops. It fired off him like a rocket. He was so giddy he almost fell off his chair, and I worried he was about to fall off the porch. Round three, knockout punch, Adam. Beth laughed, too, and shortly thereafter we turned in.

As I walked upstairs behind her, I lingered between floors, backing my way up while gazing at the three I was leaving for the night. One slow step at a time I took, watching over each one, as if looking for signals for how it was going. First Adam, then Lila, then over to Billy G., who was hogging a reefer before reluctantly handing it back to Adam. And that's when my son shot me a wink.

Then he hit me with his smile that broke through, which allowed me to turn around with a sense of contentment and climb the remainder of the steps in a forward direction. It was about midnight. Beth and I fell asleep spooned in each other's arms, windows open and bathed by moonlight.

CHAPTER 45

The following morning, Billy G., Adam, and Lila slept in after a very late night. For Beth and me, I made blueberry pancakes, Vermont cured bacon, and a large pot of coffee. After breakfast we decided to hike down the mountain and then continue on to the nearby general store where we'd rent tubes and hitch a ride to a designated spot some miles upstream. This would give us about two-and-a-half uninterrupted hours, without distractions, a nice stretch of time.

A small rope had been attached to each of the inner tubes. I placed the tubes side by side in the water and tied them together. Wearing my Speedo river shoes, I helped Beth into her tube and walked our tied contraption deeper into the water at about the level of my bathing suit, which is where we caught the current and found liftoff. There were the occasional soft rapids, but primarily, we meandered serenely down the river hand-in-hand, just as I'd imagined.

We passed beautiful tree-laden knolls covered with wildflowers of every color imaginable, the lush Green Mountains in the distance. We were together in paradise, far away from our troubles, with whole days lined up for nothing more than each other. I had almost forgotten what happiness felt like.

"How did we pull this off, Beth?"

"You asked, Sam. I just accepted. Maybe a loftier voice beyond ours has intervened."

"Perhaps."

"Sam, my kids had an interesting reaction to my coming here. They seemed jealous that I'd take a trip without them...heaven forbid I should try to have a little fun with some friends. It's as if they caught me breaking out of jail."

"Perhaps that's because you did. That would mean I'm up here with a fugitive. Yeah, a fugitive—you're getting more exciting by the moment! Don't you realize we're not supposed to have lives for ourselves? Don't you get it? We owe everything we've got to our children and our jobs. After you had kids, did you and Mark ever sneak out for romantic getaways? Amy and I never did."

"Yeah, right! Well, I do remember one time around one of Mark's birthdays. We were at a Food Bank Gala and in the silent auction I saw a daytrip to a ballgame in New York. On a lark, I put down a bid. They called it 'Phillies for the Mets.'"

"So you made Shea Stadium your tropical paradise, eh? You must have put away a few Grey Gooses before putting your money down."

"Well, not exactly. You see, right next to the Mets' display, was the longest line of bidders for Yankees tickets, but no one was in line for the Mets. I felt sorry for them. What did I know? Until my smart-aleck son told me the next day, 'No one wants to see the Mets.' It didn't make any difference to me where I was. The whole time Mark watched the game, I had my earphones on and listened to *Aida*. Story of our marriage...each of us content, but in separate zones. I think the Mets won that day."

I laughed and squeezed Beth's hand. She continued, "It really didn't much matter what all was going on around me, by the seventh inning stretch, I started in on Carmen. And for much of the bus ride home, I listened to *Tosca*. For all he or I knew, I had spent the entire day at the opera."

"So you went to the Met after all."

Beth laughed. "Sam, you're funnier up here. Throughout my marriage, I just couldn't really bear being alone with Mark. The kids were always my buffer. And just look at me now. Please, please, pinch me, Sam, so I know this is real. I'm in this most beautiful part of the world sailing down a river with the great love of my life. This can't be earth."

"It's heaven."

"I love you, Sam."

We kissed.

"You know how radiant you are? I've never forgotten all the life that's in your being. Hey, look over at the trout popping out of the water!"

"This is too perfect. That's trout? I think you're seeing frogs, Sam."

"No, ma'am. I know my freshwater trout, and I've always wanted a pair of those high rubber brown boots that I'd stand in to cast off with that ridiculously long rod."

"Who's stopping you?" As she whispered, "But don't wear anything but the boots when you cast off."

I smiled a wow. "Beth, what did you think of Adam?"

"He's a trip. In many ways he reminds me of you. His comebacks are sharp, expressive, and borderline over-the-top."

"But I dare say, you know how to keep up with him."

"I think I need to get out of this dingy and hail myself a cab."

"Why, because I acknowledged that you're sharp and expressive?"

"Goddamn it, Spiegel, you're the most expert person I know at wiggling off any hook."

"It's a refined skill of mine."

"That you refined about thirty years ago on my watch."

"Jesus Christ, what must Adam be thinking? That Ward Cleaver's lost his mind up here with Sandra Bullock?"

"I thought you told me I was more the Gwyneth Paltrow type."

"I think you're a blend."

"I see. When will all this pleasant flirting come to an end?"

"When we get married," I said.

Beth squeezed my hand, smiled toward the mountains but ignored my remark. "Sam, Adam's on a serious mission. He's throwing himself out there. You should be proud of him. He's courageous and vulnerable, like someone else I know."

"Do you think he and Lila can make it?"

"It's too soon for me to call that one."

"But early returns?"

"They seem to have a lot between them. Maybe it's what we've talked about that's been missing in our own marriages. They respect each other and seem to have the same mission and chemistry, but you never really know unless you peek into their bedroom. If my early impression is correct, I think they could have a run."

Beth became quiet and looked around, as I did. "You know, Sam, every sight from where our floats spin us, is more beautiful than from where we just came. To think of all these trips we missed out on…"

I laughed. "Billy G. seemed so happy last night, talking music with the kids, being up here and out of the city. It's like he's been liberated and is back at summer camp. You know, Billy really appreciates life when he can find some of it to hold onto."

"You mean in what Adam rolls for him?"

"No, what I mean is I think he's lived the wrong life."

"Can't you say that about all of us?"

"The sad thing is he's resigned to it."

"Maybe that's the only way Billy can get through, Sam. We're all tethered one way or another."

"I suppose. Hey, look at that jet in the sky, cutting a thin river above us."

"Sam, if that's supposed to be the river we're on, it's fading fast and I've been down it with you before."

"Hm."

"Hm?"

"Here I am with the princess of my dreams, the one I could never forget. And all I can think of is, can you believe my timing? You should have known me when." I looked away to hide the fact that my eyes were beginning to fill.

"I did know you and I do now. Don't you understand you're still the guy? And it's not the image of this man that I'm in love with, or even the memory of the boy; it's just the man. Sorry to disappoint you. I really wasn't paying close attention to all your glory days that seemed to culminate at the Ailey Ballet. I just know I love the way you think, the way you look, the way you look at me. You're the most fascinating person I've ever set my eyes on."

"But what bad timing, Beth. I think about what's coming my way and it's going to be horrendous, nothing short of that. I've got the picture in my head and it's bloody awful. And as much as I love you, I just can't see putting you through that kind of hell."

"So tell me, Sam, if I've got this right? You invited me all the way to Vermont so you can tell me you're going to leave me again? Excuse me?"

"No, not to leave you. I'm just trying to save you...from me."

"Sam, call this whatever you wish to diminish it to. You've always been an expert on what's what. Thirty years ago you made such a call and it was Amy. And you know what you did? You blew it. Big-time. So you want to repeat history? Step right up and blow it again?"

"Beth, I just can't put you through what's coming."

"So what do you think is going on here, Sam? You think this is some sort of midlife crisis boondoggle where you can wind me up like a play doll? Give me a break! You're right; they're all right about you. What am I doing hanging around with a falling star? Sam, we're both separated but not divorced yet. We can go right back to what we know, to what we're used to. We're both expert at making it all work. Maybe you've lost your grip a bit on that score, though I sure haven't. But understand this, Sam, the life I have is not the life I want anymore. As much as I'm sure my family is praying that all this will go away...I've made up my mind and I'm not turning back."

"What makes you so sure, Beth?"

"Because...I want a life, Sam. I like the way I feel around you. I like your food. I like your ideas. I like your stories. I like your wisdom. I like your heart. I love your body. Believe it or not, I even like that you're an asshole sometimes, and I'm ready to take you on in whatever shape you bring yourself to my doorstep. Because I know this about you, Sam: You won't lose in the end if there is something in your life to live for. You'll come back. Have you forgotten? You're Sam Jacob Spiegel. Anyone who really knows you knows that. As for us, we're soul mates, we deserve some happiness. I want to live with us. I'm as serious and certain as I get. But if you want me to go, I'll pack my things."

"That's the last thing I want. I just need to feel that we can make this work. Pointedly, can you love a man who's fallen so, who has been privately and publicly humiliated and taken apart piece by piece? Can you love a man who's lost his money? That's what you're getting yourself into. If your answer is yes, my answer is you're crazy. But in the same breath, I'll tell you this...I'm yours. Beth, I don't know this world I'm heading into. It's such foreign territory. I'll say it: I'm a novice at failure. What will your parents think? And your kids for saddling up with a man in my condition? I'll tell you what they'll think. That you need your head examined. Beth, I'm struggling just to hold myself together and worry every day that I'll never begin to be me again. And you want in? For what?"

I steered us to the left bank and docked our floats. I pulled out the white plastic bag I had tied to the side, which Beth thought only carried our shoes. In addition to shoes, I had brought a small bottle of Piper-Heidsieck and two plastic champagne flutes.

"Sam, what a nice surprise! But the champagne won't help you change the subject."

"Well, it might help everything go down a bit easier."

I popped the cork and poured. We both sat quietly sipping for a while under a tree, listening to the natural music around us, hands still locked together. We watched a small group of fluttering hummingbirds. They looked more like they were scurrying in the air, like large bees around wildflowers. I had never seen these creatures close-up before. They didn't seem real—certainly not birdlike. More like something out of a Disney movie. "In all these years, Beth, if I'm really being honest with myself, I've never had a partner. When I come to think of it, from the time Amy and I returned to Philadelphia, I never thought she was by my side. She'd never wanted to move from New York. Maybe it was a payback when she turned on me."

"I've never had a partner either, Sam."

I continued, "I mean someone I can trust implicitly, who can knock sense into my head. Someone I can look at and listen to and say, 'Now that's an idea.' Someone who really gets me. Who might even have my best interests at heart. Honestly, I don't think I've ever had that some-body."

"Nor have I, Sam, and yet I've craved it. I've wanted it all my life."

"Beth, every time I'm with you I'm reminded of what Billy knew all along. There is nothing quite like the two of us when we're together. And what did I do? I got it wrong. We were too much alike, I thought, and I blew it." We took the final sips of our champagne. Over the years I had become familiar with the river's twists and turns, and knew that we were about to hit a pocket where we could pick up speed. I put the empty bottle and flutes into the bag, tightly pulled the cord, and tied it back onto my float. I helped Beth into her tube. I climbed into mine and launched us out there in tandem.

"All right, Sam, go ahead and tell me what's going to happen next in your life."

"I think I owe you as much."

"You don't."

"No, I really do."

She continued, "When I knew you way back when, you were al-ways such a strong young man who never shirked responsibilities, but let me spare you this one tale because I think I get what's coming down, and I can save you some of the humiliation by reciting just the high-lights for you."

"All right, smarty-pants, shoot."

"Okay, Sam, here goes. You're going to lose your business and for whatever reasons…your marriage partner betrayed you. Her work's been done and you're finished with her and you're going to have to reckon with both of these failures. With the business gone, I think it's going to be very tough for you. It will feel like you've lost a child. That bad! With

Amy, the anger you have now will turn into deep disappointment and greater loss. At times it will almost drive you crazy. Eventually, some of the anger, hurt, and rage will subside. But you'll never be fully over it."

"How could I be?"

"That's what I'm saying. And from time to time, unfortunately, I'm going to get your misplaced wrath, which I'm not at all looking forward to. And frankly, I do worry about that."

"Nice forecast, Cassandra. And you still want in?"

"I don't think I have a choice, Sam. I think I'm here with you now. Want me to stop? I can stop."

"No."

"You'll have no choice but to own up to all this or do what a lot of cowards do; they end it all—pow! It's certainly simpler, might even be cleaner. And if you do it right, there will be insurance money for the kids and your mom. And I predict this, too. You'll have a great big funeral. There will be people showing up who don't even know you."

"Who want to dance on my grave?"

"Well, I won't go that far. Others might."

My mouth hung open as I studied Beth. Then I closed it again. "Shit."

"There'll be plenty of that too, Sam. There will be days you're so knee deep in it, you'll wonder if you'll ever stand without it around. Now, if you pull off that merger business and the Hawk takes over... whatever you might get will go to the bank or to save your mother from total devastation. That's another thing you might have to live with, bringing your old lady down."

I smiled, "Now tell me, whoever gets this lucky to have such a witch to foresee their upcoming woes so clearly? Perhaps there are some quick-serve water hemlock or strychnine trees around the bend for me to graze on."

"Maybe. But there's more. You want it?"

"I think I get the picture. But how are you processing all this, Beth?"

"You're going to lose your house, so it might be a good idea for you to get used to my gardens. I'll train you on how best to prune roses. But

I'll warn you, you'll get scratched, Sam. You're going to be a mess for a while. And this is all absent of what's around the corner for me."

"Well, the picture can't get worse." I watched her eyes closely as they sparkled even more than before, picking up flashes of sunlight that reflected off the river.

"Trust me, it does. But that can wait for another joyride down the river. Just do me this favor, Samuel Jacob Spiegel, just understand we will get through this. I will be by your side every inch of the way. We're going to have a shitty year, maybe a string of them, but we will heal, Sam. We will heal. You must believe that."

"Will we?"

"And we'll have each other. We're a team. We just took a long detour before we got together again. Maybe it had to wait for this river ride. So, Sam, here's the deal," Beth said. "We continue with our nice getaway and you check all your ideas of separating from me under that rock over there. Or stop the float and take me to the airport."

I thought of my father and how he had come back from adversity. Yes, I thought about Mitch and Richardson Valk, and how Arnold M. Mandel would say that the deal I'd have no choice but to accept when I returned to Philadelphia would ultimately free me. My father had started over, and so would I. All I needed was to be me again, with Beth by my side.

"See my hands, Beth? I'm paddling over to that rock as if my life depends on it."

I had my muse back. The one who never stopped believing in me. I stood up on the sides of my float as if I were about to go waterskiing. Then I jumped in the river and made like a dolphin. I dove under Beth's tube, pushed her up from the bottom as she flipped headfirst into the water. I grabbed her around the waist and pulled her into me. We stood in the middle of the river in the tightest of embraces as our life rafts meandered over the soft current and out of sight.

EPILOGUE

Dear Sam,

I was sorry to read of your recent setbacks in your otherwise successful business career. But you've always been so imaginative, from the Party Circus period to so many creative schemes in advertising.

I am confident that you will emerge from these temporary troubles you've encountered. Joe DiMaggio had an off season in 1946 (.290, I think), but came back to win M.V.P. in 1947. Johnny U. got demolished in a game against the Bears. Still bloodied, he returned to throw a winning TD. And look at Napoleon & Nixon? No, forget them! I'll bet you will be sufficiently resilient and be a major force in whatever endeavor you choose next. Maybe you should take Billy G. and Beth E. along for the ride.

Best,
Kevin Groth
(Proud to have been one of your teachers)

ACKNOWLEDGMENTS

In the words of Hillary Clinton, it took "a village" to move THE MINEFIELDS to the finish line. Without the generous dedication and skills of the following readers and collaborators there'd be no novel: John Ottenheimer, Don Volatile, Kim Houser, Pat Preller, Leslie Ries, Geri Langan, George Bacharach, Jon Reisfeld, Bart Walker, Joan Gordon, Rex Gordon, Avon Bellamy, Barbara Blair, Gerry Blair, Kristin Kight, Joel Ottenheimer, Ed Feingold, Jackie Smelkinson, Bob Smelkinson, Steve Baklor, Keith Shapiro, and Peter Gladstone. Then came the publishing dream team: Susan Leon, Lisa Davis, Alice Peck, Alan Kaufman, Asha Hossain, Sue Collier, Kathleen Schmidt, and M. J. Rose.

THE MINEFIELDS would not have taken form without the belief and support of my beloved muse and wife Neile Friedman Eisner and the heart, talent, and literary deftness of Kenneth Greif. Finally, to my children Jane Eisner and Tommy Eisner, I thank you for your love, understanding, and unswerving encouragement.

ABOUT THE AUTHOR

Before writing his novel and after learning the ropes at Doyle Dane Bernbach, New York, **STEVEN C. EISNER** created and led Eisner Communications,a Baltimore-based advertising agency, for more than two decades, creating hundreds of effective ad and PR campaigns for leading corporations and associations including Black & Decker, Marriot, McCormick Spices, PhRMA, US Airways, Lenox China, the Maryland Lottery, the Nature Conservancy, and the United Way. Eisner Communications won numerous industry awards including CLIOs, ADDYs, and EFFIEs, and the O'Toole for creative excellence across its entire client roster. THE MINEFIELDS is Steven C. Eisner's first novel. Visit the author's website at: StevenCEisner.com